FORCED PROXIMITY

Jaymin Eve & Tate James

WSJ AND USAT BESTSELLING AUTHOR

USAT AND INTERNATIONAL BESTSELLING AUTHOR

Tate James

Jaymin Eve

Forced Proximity: Bluebell House Duet #1
Copyright © Tate James, Jaymin Eve 2024
All rights reserved
First published in 2025
James, Tate
Eve, Jaymin
Forced Proximity: Bluebell House Duet #1

Cover design: Steph at Vicious Desires Design
Editing: Kiezha Ferrell – Librum Artis

CONTENT WARNING

Your mental health is important to us! If you need any specific information about what might be included, please contact one of us at
jaymineve@gmail.com or contact@tatejamesauthor.com

Triggers include:

- Flashbacks to school shooting
- Gun violence
- General violence
- Panic attacks
- Student-teacher relationship (college level)
- Car accident
- Parental abandonment

For those who love the one-bed trope.

Only it's one house. One girl. Five broken, rich boys.

And delicious forced proximity.

For months.

1

EVELYN

Breathe. In and out, Evelyn. In and out.

The last month of therapy had given me a greater understanding of the importance of breathing through pain and panic, but today, no matter how many times I told myself to *fucking breathe*, the terror of what awaited me on the other side of those fancy gates was all I could focus on.

Being back at college might be what broke the final hold on my sanity.

Running my hands up and down my denim skirt, I used the rough material as an anchor to keep myself calm.

"Almost there, Ms. Lewis. I'll get your bags while you head in and speak to the dean."

The driver was employed by the college and had given me a little introduction speech on the way from the airport. He kept calling me by my new last name—changed since the attack for my own safety—which was going to take some getting used to.

Once Evelyn Marie Cromwell, I was now Evelyn Marie Lewis, foster child of Karolyn and Mitchell Lewis and brand-new student at Meadowridge College. Nothing like switching colleges in your junior year of a four-year economics degree. But here I was, *living the dream.*

Thankfully my guardians had made sure I got credit for most of my completed classes, and there were only a few prerequisite courses specific to this college that I'd have to catch up on. Better than a bullet in the brain, though. So I'd take it.

"Tha-thank you," I managed to get out, the panic barely at bay as I continued to suck in breaths like a pug with a sinus infection. Dr. Graystone had warned me I was far from ready to give up therapy. My trauma remained a driving force in my life, and until I could go days without nightmares or face new situations without panic attacks, I needed *all* the trauma-coping skills from regular therapy sessions.

Too bad he was now over a thousand miles away from me back in Tennessee—I could have used his particular brand of tough love to get me through the next twenty minutes of hell.

The driver stopped before the gates, opening his window to chat with the security guard who emerged from a hut off to the side of the black, wrought-iron gates. I studied the entrance, taking in the impressive gold filagree and large "MC" etched in the center. "I need your identification, Ms. Lewis," my driver said, drawing my attention.

The process of ensuring I was a student took longer than I'd expected, as they checked my identification, ran a quick background check—I had no idea how Mitchell managed it, but I had an entire online history as Evelyn Lewis now—examined every inch of the car to ensure there were no unauthorized tagalongs, and finally declared we were free to enter.

"This college is reputed to be harder than Fort Knox to break into," my driver said, picking up the conversation as he drove through the gates and up the long driveway to a Victorian-style building with creeping ivy along the red and black brick walls. "I don't know what your parents did to get you in here, but you'll be taking classes with royalty, politicians, and the richest of the rich in our country. Security is paramount, so you have nothing to worry about."

He didn't know about the attack. No one knew I was the sole survivor of that dark day at Tennessee Hallows College. My face and name had never appeared publicly, and I'd been swept out of there by my concerned guardians so fast there was no chance to even say goodbye to the friends I'd made in my first two years. "That's good to know," I said, pressing my face closer to the window of his Chevy Suburban. "Hopefully I won't have to move again before my degree is finished." Or dodge bullets raining across a room.

When he pulled up, a welcome committee was waiting for me. Classes officially started tomorrow; I was late and had missed orientation, but I still earned a personal greeting and tour by the dean himself—a dean who knew my story—and I half wondered if that was what got me in here in the first place.

"Ms. Lewis," the distinguished older gentleman said as he opened my door. "I'm Dean Henry Attworth. Welcome to Meadowridge College. We're delighted to have you joining us this year."

The Lewis family were solidly middle class. They hadn't exactly struggled since my dad dumped me on their doorstep "for a week" when I was ten—and then proceeded to disappear for a good ten years after—but we'd also never had any excess. I hadn't been in the headspace to ask how they'd managed to get me into such a prestigious college after the attack, but now, standing here and staring up at the imposing building behind the arched entrance, I found myself curious.

How *had* they managed this?

"I'm excited to be part of your college." I was proud of myself for not sounding as freaked out as I felt. "I know graduating from here will open many career opportunities for me."

In and out. In and out.

Breathing was an autonomic reflex, for fuck's sake. Newborn babies breathed when they were two seconds old. I could do this.

"All the opportunities, Ms. Lewis. Now, if you'll follow me? You can leave your bags; our staff will bring them to your dorm."

Pulling my gaze from the brick building, I gave Dean Attworth my full attention. He was a few inches taller than my five-feet-seven, with a head full of silver hair, piercing gray eyes, and a sharp navy suit with a blue-and-gray checkered tie. There wasn't a wrinkle to be found on his clothing, every line ironed to within an inch of itself, and even his face was strangely smooth in spite of clearly being well past his youth.

The rich probably weren't allowed to look old. Nothing like mortality to remind you money can't buy everything.

The first building we entered was unusually quiet, the dean pointing out the main office, guidance counselor, registrars, and where we sign up for clubs and sports. A few students emerged from the offices while we stood there but didn't even bother to look my way, much more interested in their phones than the new student.

The rest of the tour took a few hours, as we visited the many different buildings that made up the massive grounds. A grounds that was fenced on all sides, with that same high, black, wrought-iron structure as the front gate.

"It's electrified," Dean Attworth told me, his final to-do item being an overview of the safety of the grounds. "Please don't accidentally stumble into any of our security measures. The guards patrol twenty-four-seven, and we have satellite imagery of the grounds beaming to a secondary company. If you have any visitors, they will need to go through the same checks you did upon entry this morning. Your safety is of utmost importance to us here, and my door is always open if you ever feel threatened or unsafe."

For the first time since we approached the gates, a semblance of calm replaced the abject terror that had been holding me in its grip. "Thank you. Safety is the first priority for my family. This will go a long way to alleviating their worries." *And mine.*

The dean beamed like I'd just told him he'd won the lottery and could retire to his favorite beach and drink cocktails for the rest of his life. In perfectly pressed three-piece suits.

"This is where I leave you," he said when we arrived back in the main entrance. "You can grab your welcome information from the registrar's office before heading to your dorm. I believe you're in Marigold Hall. Your bags should already have been delivered."

He was gone in a waft of expensive cologne, and I was left to hope that for the rest of the day, I'd just get to hide in my room. Stepping out into a new state and school for the first real time since the attack was already a lot for today. Tomorrow I'd attempt to make it to classes and get my life on track.

But first, I needed my schedule and welcome information. The office was right there. Sure, I had to pass a few groups of students who had gathered, but it wasn't a huge deal. None of them were going to whip out a gun and start shooting into a crowd.

We'd been all but strip-searched on the way in, and I was safe here.

Safe.

In and out.

In. And. Out.

As I approached the entrance to the office buildings, there was a loud crash and one of the girls let out a screeching laugh. This was followed by a second crash, and at the sound of glass shattering on the paved entrance, terror gripped me and my mind flashed back to that day.

The day my world almost ended.

The day I hid behind a desk silently sobbing while a maniac called my name.

The day bodies were scattered around me as I prayed he wouldn't find me. Prayed as I ran and screamed, until my back exploded in pain, and then there was blessed darkness.

I'd lived when others hadn't, and this was my second chance.

I was just too fucked-up to enjoy it.

Most of the time, panic locked me in place, my lungs screaming for air until I all but passed out. Today, with all those students staring at the crazy chick in their vicinity, I found myself running. Running with no destination in mind and just an incessant need to escape.

I ended up in front of a building that was familiar, but I couldn't remember what the dean had said was inside. When I burst through the doors, I found myself in the library. *Thank God.* Libraries had been sanctuaries for me in the past, and desperate for a moment of peace and to escape how utterly broken and fucked-up I was, I pushed deeper into the shelves.

I found myself in a dark corner near the last rows of shelves, my mind fuzzy and frantic. I hadn't encountered anyone until the very last row, where I found a student already in the stacks. He was dressed casually, in faded denim jeans and a black fitted shirt, leaned back against the shelves, his eyes closed and expression calm.

I had just enough mental capacity left to wonder if he had been searching for a moment of peace as well, but not enough to quiet my breathing as those tendrils of panic still rode me. His eyes popped open, and I was greeted by the darkest green irises I'd ever seen, framed by inky black lashes.

He straightened from his relaxed pose, towering over me as I tilted my head back to keep his face in view, like it was somehow my new anchor in this storm of panic. A face built of perfect masculine lines, a straight nose, and sinfully full lips.

He was one of the hottest guys I'd ever seen, and I was about to embarrass myself beyond repair.

Our gazes clashed, and he didn't say a word as he examined me with a furrowed brow. I had no idea what I looked like, but no doubt my purple-black hair was in complete disarray while panic drained the color from my normally golden skin.

When he took two steps toward me, I couldn't find the strength to move away. "Are you okay?" he asked, the deep timbre of his voice strangely soothing.

Unlike me, he was the epitome of health, with natural blond highlighting strands of his brown hair, perfect bronze skin, and those spectacular eyes. "No." The truth escaped in a harsh whisper, my ability to lie gone in my moment of vulnerability. "I'm broken beyond repair."

A shadow crossed over his features, but he didn't run screaming from the morose chick cornering him in the library stacks. "How can I help?" he asked, moving even closer, until I picked up hints of a spicy aftershave mixed with his natural masculine scent.

Help. Fuck, I needed so much help.

Before I could think through the consequences of my actions—no doubt a man this gorgeous had a girlfriend—I pushed up on my tiptoes and slammed my lips against his. Desperation had initiated my action; I had to escape the torment in my mind. But I never expected him to kiss me back.

I never expected a damn thing these days.

He stilled at the initial contact, and I let out a breathy groan when mint and spice caressed my senses. Clarity returned with the kiss, and that was when the embarrassment hit like a freight train; I was so fucking far out of line. Lifting my hands from his chest, I was about to jerk away when his firm hand snaked around the back of my shirt and yanked me into his huge, hard body.

Heat exploded between us everywhere our skin touched,

and there was a brief second between my sloppy attempt at a kiss and when he took control. His tongue demanded entrance as he devoured my mouth, and whatever panic had lingered in my system was swept away by his lips moving against mine.

Our tongues danced, two strangers sharing a second of grief and attraction.

Then it was all over.

2

EVELYN

I ran.

I *bolted*, like my damn heels were on fire, knocking over stacks of books and tripping over my own shoes in a desperate attempt to flee. The gorgeous guy said nothing, but I also hadn't waited around to give him a chance.

How embarrassing. What the hell was I thinking? I mean, aside from the obvious—how insanely attracted I was to the library stranger—but that was no excuse. Christ, knowing my luck his girlfriend would be an absolute smoke show, too, just to make me feel like more of an idiot.

He'd definitely kissed me back, but maybe it was a reflex thing?

By some stroke of luck, I found my way back to the office building without any trouble and forced myself to calm the fuck down long enough to collect my schedule, room assignment, and key.

"Stupid, stupid, stupid," I scolded myself under my breath as I located the Marigold dorm, which was right next door to Hibiscus Hall, both following Meadowridge's lovely flower theme. "What the fuck were you thinking? You can't just kiss random guys without speaking to them!"

I managed to keep my volume to little more than a whisper, not wanting the entire floor to hear me talking to myself, but damn near choked on my next words when I looked up and found a girl sitting on my bed with a curious look on her face.

"Um...hi?" she greeted me, tilting her head to the side. "Are you lost?"

I frowned, glancing around. No one mentioned that I'd be sharing a room and..."Where's the other bed?"

The girl wrinkled her button nose. "What other bed? Are you okay? You were just talking to yourself."

I shook my head, thoroughly confused. "I'm...yeah, I'm fine. Is this room 338?" I took a step back to check the door and verify this was indeed the right room. "I think you're in my room."

The girl snorted a laugh, her delicate features crinkling. "Doubtful. This has been my room since sophomore year. Should I call the college medical wing?"

Why would she...Oh. *Oh.* "You think I'm crazy. Okay, sure, fair assumption given the evidence, but there must just be a mix-up. I picked up my key and welcome packet just five minutes ago, see?" I held up the key ring and showed her my booklet with maps and important information like how to connect to school Wi-Fi and what my room number was.

She hopped off the bed and took the booklet from me, then snickered. "Room 833, dummy. Not 338."

I blinked at her like an idiot, then peered at the booklet myself. Yep, sure enough... room 833. My cheeks flushed with heat. "Shit, I'm so sorry. I accidentally kissed a stranger, and it got me all flustered—"

Now it was her turn to blink at me, before it turned into a massive smile. "Well, kissing random strangers has that effect, or so I hear. I'm Nina, by the way. Nina Liu."

"I'm Eve," I replied on reflex.

"Cool. I'll walk with you up to your room so you don't bust in on anyone else. Not everyone in this dorm building would be so nice about it." She rolled her eyes dramatically but led the way back along the corridor to the small elevator at the end. "So who was the guy?"

I followed her into the elevator, raking my fingers through my messy hair. "What guy?"

Nina gave a short laugh. "The one you were berating yourself for kissing. Wait, didn't you literally just arrive? That's... quick."

More embarrassment, and I groaned. I had to try to offer *something,* though, because otherwise she'd think... I didn't even know what. "I was in the middle of a panic attack, and I ran into the library, and then there was this *gorgeous* guy and he asked if I was okay and then I kissed him because apparently I was having a stroke or an aneurysm or something that makes people do totally out of character dumb shit and—"

"Whoa, girl, take a breath." Nina laughed, but it wasn't unkind. "Longest run-on sentence I've ever freaking heard. How hot are we talking here? One to ten?"

"Fifteen," I responded quickly. "At least. Tall, dark, chocolate-brown hair with kind of natural blond highlights, and the most intense, breathtaking green eyes with these long, dark lashes and—"

"Oooh, sounds like Connor," she said thoughtfully. "Although the library isn't his usual hunting ground."

"Connor?" I repeated, testing the name against the image in my head.

Nina nodded with a shrug. "Sounds like him, but maybe not. Anyway, here we are. Room 833."

I hadn't even registered the fact that we'd reached the eighth floor, let alone that we'd arrived at the *correct* dorm room, which was, logically, locked. "Oh, cool. Thanks, Nina. And I'm sorry about the mix-up downstairs."

"No problem, Eve. If you want directions to class in the morning or whatever, you know where to find me!" She gave me a little salute, then sauntered back toward the elevator at the end of the hall, leaving me to unlock my room.

Sure enough, there were my bags waiting inside, next the neatly made bed. The school had its own housekeeping staff, so the linen was all provided, which was kind of nice. My room held a queen size bed, and a quick look around unveiled an attached bathroom and walk-in closet. A huge upgrade on my last college dorm, that was for sure.

I busied myself unpacking and setting up my room, venturing out only later in the evening when my stomach demanded food. I kept my head down the whole time, terrified I'd run into the sexy guy from the library. Connor, apparently.

The last thing I needed was another encounter, when my cheeks were still pink from the first.

THE NEXT MORNING I woke well in advance of my alarm, a ball of sheer anxiety bouncing around my stomach over what the day would bring. Thankfully, I only had one class for day one, and it was a leisurely midmorning timeslot.

Because I had a crapload of extra time, I headed over to the campus coffee shop before class and ordered myself coffee and a breakfast sandwich. It was crowded, being the first day of classes, so I busied myself scrolling social media while I waited for my name to be called.

A few minutes later I was utterly engrossed in an old article about a sex scandal involving an Olympic figure skater, her coach, *and* her skating partner.

"Venti cold brew for Connor!" the barista yelled, and I startled so hard I dropped my phone.

"Shit!" I exclaimed, praying I hadn't broken the screen. I definitely couldn't afford to buy a new one right now. Not until I found a part-time job.

A man's hand grabbed my phone off the floor before I could reach for it, and I sucked in a gasp as I met his piercing green eyes. Except this guy, with a cold and calculating stare, brow dipped with a frown like he was judging me for having dropped my phone, was definitely not library guy.

"Connor?" the barista called out again.

He handed my phone to me as he muttered, "Clumsy," and turned away to collect his coffee.

My breath wheezed slightly as I took another look at him from the side profile. No question he was gorgeous, with very similar green eyes to library guy, but his hair was darker and longer, and his body language screamed *perpetually irritated*. If I'd run into Connor during a panic attack, I'd have been more likely to faint from fear, not kiss him.

"Brown sugar oat milk shaken espresso for Eve?" the barista called out, and I snapped myself out of the weird little trance I'd fallen into, watching Connor leave the shop.

With a small sigh, I collected my coffee and sandwich, then wandered across the grounds in the direction of my class while I ate. Once I was done with my food, I headed into the lecture hall early to pick a seat.

A couple of other students seemed to have had the same idea, but I was able to decide on a spot in roughly the middle of the room. Not so far back that I couldn't hear well, but also not right at the front where I might be called on for answers. Middle of the road, that was me.

Five minutes before the class was due to begin, the hall began to fill up steadily, and it was no surprise when someone soon loomed over me to ask if the seat beside me was taken.

"No, you're welcome to it," I replied, distracted as I continued reading through the course syllabus to refresh my head on what the class would be covering.

"Thanks," the guy replied, dropping down into the chair and instantly manspreading so hard his knee bumped mine. *That* got my attention, and I shot him a scowl.

"Uh..." I started to protest his trespassing on my personal space but lost my tongue when he met my gaze. There was something vaguely familiar about his hazel eyes and impeccably neat golden-brown hair. "Have we met?"

It was a stupid question. I hadn't met *anyone* at this college... except Nina and library boy. And Connor the moody prick.

His lips curved in a confident smile, flashing perfect teeth. "We have now. I'm Andrew."

He offered a handshake, and I took it cautiously, thrown off by the nagging sense of familiarity. "Eve," I offered in return.

"Nice to meet you, Eve. How are you finding Meadowridge so far?" He made no effort to get his laptop out in preparation to take notes, instead seeming genuinely interested in... me. Weird.

I wet my lips, my heart racing for some reason. Were all the students at this school so breathtakingly good-looking?

"Uh, it's that obvious I'm new here, is it?" I winced slightly, hating that I clearly didn't fit in. Then again, the driver had mentioned that a lot of students were celebrities or heirs to massive fortunes. I was neither, and the lack of designer labels on me was only the first tip-off.

Andrew offered a sympathetic smile. "Everyone sort of knows everyone here at Meadowridge. Bennington isn't that big of a town, and we're the only college." He shrugged. "You're an enigma, so don't judge me too harshly if I'm curious."

I found myself drawn to how incredibly articulate he was, as he spoke so clear and concisely, without the slightest sign of mumbling, like most guys. If I had to guess, Andrew had been on the debate team his whole life and wanted to be a lawyer. Or go into politics.

Before I could reply, the hum of chatter around us died down suddenly. "Good morning, students!" a man's voice projected through the room, and I dragged my eyes away from my handsome new friend. "Welcome to ECOS3026, Economics of Crime. I'm Professor Sullivan, but you can call me Ethan."

Oh *fuck*.

The blood drained out of my face so fast I could *feel* its descent, and I stopped breathing entirely. Somehow, despite my middle-of-the-room placement, the teacher's unforgettably green eyes locked on mine.

I hadn't kissed a hot classmate in the library—I'd kissed my *teacher*!

3

EVELYN

I swore that the world just stopped spinning for the few seconds our gazes clashed. In that time, I debated if I was going to panic or vomit, and in the end, when he finally removed his intense stare from my burning face to give the rest of the class his attention, I did neither.

"You okay?" Andrew whispered as he gently nudged me, and it took me forever to find my brain to answer.

"I—Yeah. Fuck." Okay, so maybe I didn't exactly find my brain.

The slightest of smiles tilted up his lips. "You've really painted a picture for me, Eve. I feel like I was there."

For some unknown reason, that snapped me out of my state of shock, and I pulled what was left of myself together. My therapist might have given me a laundry list for what I was going through, but he'd never once said I was a complete basket case —no matter how fucked-up I acted.

The last two days *really* had me second-guessing his qualifications.

Ethan moved toward a screen and started to set up the first

slide, so I leaned closer and murmured, "Sorry, it's just been a lot. First day at a new college and all that."

Andrew patted my hand, and I was surprised to find that the heated sweep of his fingers felt comforting, rather than weirdly invasive, even though we'd only just met. I couldn't shake the familiarity he exuded, and I tried to place its origins.

In truth, it was nice to feel anything that wasn't anxiety or terror. Between the kiss last night and meeting *two* new possible friends, I'd stepped way out of my comfort zone. Qualified or not, Dr. Graystone would be proud of me.

Realizing that I'd kind of checked out of the class already, I focused on the professor. Or at least on a spot just over the top of his head, so I wasn't sucked into the depths of his eyes.

"—not going to be an easy course. If you don't absolutely need this for your degree and you joined for an easy pass, you should walk out now and change to Professor Simmons. He's here for the laughs."

Economics of Crime was essential for my degree, but even so, there was a part of me tempted to walk out anyway. It'd save him failing me after my unintentional sexual assault in the library.

Was it still classified as assault when they kissed you back? Maybe more of an uninvited attack via the lips... which actually didn't sound any better.

I doubted he'd tell anyone; he'd returned that kiss and surely he knew I was a student. We were both adults and legal, of course, but every college had rules about students and teachers fraternizing. Rules he didn't appear to give a fuck about as he continued to let that enigmatic gaze of his rest on my face. If he didn't stop soon, everyone in the class would be wondering what was going on.

Squirming in my seat, I sank behind my laptop to block his view, relieved when he spent the next forty minutes going over everything we'd cover in this course, without letting his attention rest on me. He outlined the four major assignments due throughout the year, along with a ton of reading that I already planned to get ahead on this weekend.

I was a straight-A student, which I got by working my ass off. This class, I'd be giving two hundred percent. No fucking way would I let Professor Ethan Sullivan screw my future because I made one terrible mistake.

Even if it meant I needed to apologize first and explain my breakdown, so he'd hopefully dismiss it.

When the hourlong class was over, I was impressed by Ethan's intelligence. No matter what questions students asked, he had a detailed explanation *that actually made sense*. This could have been one of my favorite college classes of all time, but instead, it'd be spent in panic and silence.

After packing up quickly, I joined the mass exodus of students with the intention of avoiding a confrontation. I knew I had to apologize, but I wasn't in the headspace for it today. I needed at least two or three weeks of sleepless nights and anxiety to run over every possible scenario in my head. Only then would I be ready.

Andrew called my name as I hurried down the stairs, but I didn't look back. No time for friendships when one had embarrassment to outrun. There was another deep, familiar rumble of my name as I closed in on the exit, and I knew exactly who wanted my attention.

Acting as if I didn't hear the professor, I made my way outside and breathed in the fresh air, sunshine warming my face. *That was too fucking close.* Pulling my bag to my chest, I decided to head for the dining hall and grab some food, all the while wondering how I kept getting myself into these sorts of messes.

I'd thought my greatest worry after my kiss-attack had been the possible wrath of an absolute ten of a girlfriend. Now, that didn't even feel like a concern. Unless she was a professor of another one of my classes, leaving me at risk of two failures. Eeep.

"Girl, why do you look like you're about to shit yourself?" I swung around to find Nina with a concerned look on her face as she took in my panting, sweating, panicking self. Her brows drew slowly together. "Did you confuse numbers again?"

I opened my mouth and then slammed it close. I couldn't tell her about Ethan, not if I wanted to ensure my enrollment here remained valid. Forcing a laugh, I said, "Oh, no. I met this guy named Andrew, and he was... intense."

Poor Andrew didn't deserve to cop the blame, but I'd blanked on any other excuse.

Nina's expression cleared, like the sun peeking out of a stormy sky. Apparently, boy drama made perfect sense to her. "There are only three Andrews here worthy of that reaction." She linked our arms together and leading me toward the counter to order food. "What does he look like?"

"He's hot in a preppy, I-iron-my-boxer-briefs kind of way."

She smirked. "Okay, that rules out one of them. What else did you notice?"

"Brown hair. Gorgeous hazel eyes with more brown than green. He was tall, with a sporty, muscular frame. Broad shoulders. Maybe a swimmer."

I was surprised by how much I had noticed about him, especially while distracted by the hot professor I'd kissed.

Nina stared at me like I'd just spoken another language. "Are you fucking with me right now?"

We'd reached the cashier, and I pulled out my student ID. "I'm not sure what you mean."

"Andrew Knightsbridge," she rasped. "You sat next to Andrew freaking Knightsbridge."

The moment I heard his last name, I gripped her arm tighter. "The president's son? The president's actual, real-life son was in my economics class?"

Had that been why he looked so familiar? But if so, why did he also *feel* familiar? As if that hadn't been the first time I'd sat at his side and listened to his cultured voice.

"The one and only," Nina confirmed. "He's the eldest son of President Geraldine Knightsbridge, and she loves him more than life itself. You should see when she visits and brings the whole Secret Service. Andrew is the light of her life."

"I had no idea," I whispered, jolting when a student behind us yelled that we needed to move our asses. We were still standing at the cashier, and flustered, I ordered a chicken salad sandwich and grabbed a bottle of water. After swiping my student ID, I waited for Nina to follow me over to an unoccupied table.

"I shouldn't be so surprised," she said as she opened her fruit and poured in a tub of yogurt. "I forget that most people don't know their faces. All of our zillionaire parents are out there ensuring no one knows of our existence, either because we're annoying gnats in their world or because they don't want to keep paying ransoms while we lose our pinky fingers as proof the kidnappers are serious."

I blanched and returned my sandwich to the plate. "Does that really happen?"

She shrugged. "Twice last year to people I know, but never from the school grounds. No one gets to us here."

Excellent news.

She dug into her food like we hadn't just been discussing severed body parts, and I picked at the edges of my sandwich and glanced around the dining hall. It was much fancier than my last school, with proper tables and chairs, white tablecloths, and real silverware. Even my sandwich was nicely presented on a plate with a side garnish.

As Nina finished chewing a bite of her sandwich, I asked, "Are your parents important out in the real world?"

While we'd been sitting here, she'd waved to a few other

girls that passed by, but so far no one else had joined us. Maybe she was a loner like me. Or maybe her friends were unsure because I was here. Either way, I was curious.

"In comparison to everyone else in this school, not remotely. My grandparents were shrewd enough to buy into shares and property back when it wasn't nearly impossible to make a return on your investments, and when they died, they left their fortune to Mom." She laughed humorlessly. "That was the day my parents retired and decided that it wasn't much fun having a kid around the house. I've been at some form of boarding school ever since, so it just seemed natural to continue into tertiary education in the same boarding school format. This one at least has more coed fun and alcohol."

My backstory was screwed up too, and while I assumed my father had legit reasons for dropping me off for "a week" at the Lewis home, the fact that he hadn't bothered to even contact me since left me with more than a few daddy issues. I was just lucky that Karolyn and Mitchell hadn't kicked my freeloading ass out of their house.

They were good people. Really good.

Deciding I needed a subject change, since it wasn't in my best mental-health interest to dwell on the past, I said, "Okay, give me the breakdown of the hierarchy here. Who should I watch out for? Who should I avoid? Who hates who?"

Her feet hit the ground as she straightened. "You flashed the Batman signal, and I am just the woman to answer the call."

A snort of laughter escaped me. "You're a true superhero, my friend."

She beamed in response. "You've actually met two of the heavy hitters already. Connor Sullivan and Andrew Knights-bridge are absolute powerhouses at Meadowridge. The crème de la crème of men here. They're huge rivals in both academics and popularity and hate each other with a passion."

I didn't correct her about meeting Connor, because I could

not let her start trying to figure out who else it might have been that I kissed. Especially now that I had another piece of the puzzle. "Connor *Sullivan*," I murmured.

That explained how two devastatingly handsome men could share the same unusual, piercing eyes.

"Oh, yeah, Connor is sexy as hell, but he's also scary as hell." Nina dragged her tray closer, as if needing a shield. "I don't know what his family does, but I would bet Gran's fortune that they dabble in the darker side of life. Most of the school is scared of him, but Andrew never flinches. His clout is solid thanks to his mom running *the whole damn country.*"

Releasing the tray, she leaned closer again. "If I were you, I would not mess around between those two. It's not worth getting caught in the middle of their fuckery since they're practically sworn enemies at this stage."

"I have no intention of going anywhere near either of them," I said, because I couldn't be about the drama here. "My priority is graduating early and getting out of college once and for all."

Nina's gaze remained shrewd. "Let's hope both of them feel the same way. They're used to getting what they want, so if I were you, new girl, I'd stay as far off their radars as possible."

Annoyance whipped through me at her unsolicited advice, but I didn't snap back. Just because it was unsolicited, didn't mean it wasn't valid. It was not in my best interest to get too close to either of them. Or the *other* one. If Connor was bad news, then Ethan *Sullivan* was even worse.

Whatever it took, I needed to avoid all three men for the next two years.

Which would be no fucking problem when I already shared a class with two of them.

No problem at all.

4

EVELYN

By some stroke of luck, I managed to avoid running into Ethan for the rest of the week. Connor and I literally didn't cross paths after that café incident, so that was a relief, but Andrew seemed unusually persistent.

By the following Monday, it was starting to draw attention in a bad way...mostly from his girlfriend, Laura Sandiconte, who'd taken an instant dislike to me when Andrew insisted I join them for coffee—even though I'd declined and taken my order to go.

Which was why I had seriously considered faking a stomach flu when he sat down beside me in my most dreaded class: Economics of Crime.

"You don't mind if I sit here, do you?" Andrew murmured, keeping his voice low as Ethan—*Professor Sullivan*—started the lecture in his strong, commanding voice, not even bothering to use a microphone to be heard. Hot.

I wet my lips, tearing my eyes from the thirst-trap teacher and refocusing on Andrew. Gorgeous, up-tight Andrew, son of the president, and inexplicably determined to be my friend despite how irate his stuck-up girlfriend was about it. "I...um... no, it's fine. Sorry."

He quirked a brow, seeming like he wanted to ask something more but the bang on the lecture hall door opening and closing distracted us both.

"Brodie, how nice of you to join us," Ethan drawled, pausing the presentation he'd just started on the huge screen. "And almost on time, too. You've only missed four days of the semester so far."

The dashing blond who'd just sauntered into the class flashed a toothy grin. "Don't get used to it, Eth, it'll only get worse from here."

My jaw dropped as he started up the stairs and I got a good look at him. *This* guy I definitely recognized. "Holy shit," I whispered. "Is that—?"

Andrew gave a small groan, shifting in his seat. "I take it you're a superhero fan, then?"

I gaped at the late arrival who continued casually strolling up the stairs, looking for an available seat, then glanced back at Andrew. "You're *not*? That's...*that's Brodie Keller*," I squeaked in a hushed whisper. "He's the *Bloodstone Sentinel*—"

"Trust me, I'm well aware of his fictional alter ego," Andrew muttered. "He doesn't let us forget."

My breath caught in my chest as Brodie Keller—superhero heartthrob and drop-dead-gorgeous icon—looked my way. For a second our gazes locked and he ground to an immediate halt. Color drained from his golden skin like he'd just seen a ghost, and then he shook it off, a smile breaking through whatever had shocked him as he approached and took the vacant seat on my other side.

That was super weird. Maybe I had something on my face? Or maybe my crazy obsession with his superhero character was written all over me, and he was scared of a crazy fan girl? Nah. He wouldn't sit beside me if that was the case.

"'Sup, new girl," he drawled, propping his designer sneakers up on the seat in front. "I like your hair."

Blink, dammit! Blink and breathe, Evelyn, stop gaping like a starstruck fool!

Forcing myself to look away, I glanced to the locks of purple-washed brunette draped over my shoulders. *He likes my hair? Holy shit, I could die happy right now.*

"Why are you sitting here, Keller?" Andrew asked in a low growl, his eyes narrowed. "This isn't—"

"Because the new girl is sitting here, and I wanted to say hi. Hello. I'm Brodie."

Almost choking on my own breath, I nodded like a bobble head. "I know. You're—"

"Brodie!" Ethan's voice barked from the front of the room, making me physically jump in my seat. "If your only purpose in attending class is to distract Miss Lewis, then you can leave. Some students actually attend this school to *learn* something."

Brodie Keller—the fucking *star*—didn't even seem the slightest bit humbled by our teacher, seemingly totally relaxed in his seat beside me. "Cool story, Eth."

The green-eyed wet dream lecturing our class just scowled, then shifted his gaze to me in a way that made me squirm in my seat. Focusing on my notes seemed like a *much* better option, so I tucked my head and tapped out a few nonsense words on my laptop to act like I'd been paying attention all along.

Thankfully, both Brodie and Andrew seemed to take the hint that I was trying to concentrate and stayed mostly quiet for the rest of class. My notes on Ethan's lecture were a goddamn tragedy, though, thanks to how scattered my mind was for the whole hour. The only small mercy was that I didn't get called on to answer any deeply thought-provoking questions, as I would have one hundred percent embarrassed myself.

When the class finished, I packed up my stuff at lightning

speed, intending to escape the class before I could do or say anything stupid.

"Miss Lewis," Ethan said as I impatiently waited for Brodie to get out of my way so I could flee. "Can you stay behind for a moment?"

Oh *God*. I knew I'd avoided this confrontation for far too long, and it was bound to happen sooner or later. But fuck, couldn't we just pretend it'd never happened and move on with our lives?

Probably not, considering how I kept thinking about it. Damn him for being so hot and *such* a great kisser. It's like I'd formed an addiction in just the brief time our lips had locked, and now I was forcing myself through a cold-turkey withdrawal. Ugh.

"Um." I wet my lips, unable to just ignore him entirely as he waited by the door while students filed out. "No."

His brows hitched as I descended the stairs toward where he stood. "No?"

I shook my head, searching for a plausible excuse. "No. Sorry. I have... a thing. I can't be late. Sorry."

"A... thing?" he repeated, seeming equally confused and amused.

I nodded, sticking with my lame excuse. "Yeah." Sometimes the best lies had the least details. Less to pick apart.

Ethan's jaw tightened like he wanted to call bullshit and maybe flex his authority to force me to stay. But then his lips twitched in a ghost of a smile and he sighed. "All right, then. Have a good day, Miss Lewis. I'm sure we can speak another time...in the library perhaps?"

Fuck a goddamn duck, is he flirting?

Panicked, I just nodded. "I do like libraries."

Ethan's smile spread wider and became somewhat wicked. "As do I."

"Ahem." Andrew fake coughed beside me. "Eve, didn't you have a thing to get to?"

I jerked a little, realizing I was getting a little lost in Ethan's gaze, and glanced around. The class had almost entirely emptied in those few moments, and I was very close to having that private chat with the teacher after all.

"Yep!" I squeaked, hugging my bag to my chest. "See ya next week, Professor Sullivan." Academic distance. That's what we needed.

"Or in the library," Ethan murmured as I hurried past, and it took a lot of concentration not to trip over my own feet.

Andrew kept pace with me as I hauled ass out of the building; Brodie had disappeared already. At least that was one less thing to worry over. I never thought I'd be the fan-girling type, but I also never thought I'd be meeting *Brodie freaking Keller* in real life.

"So where's the thing you need to get to?" Andrew asked when we started down the cobblestone path.

The imaginary thing that I absolutely did not have on my schedule? I only had one other class on Mondays, and it wasn't until later in the afternoon, so my only plan was to meet Nina and her friends for lunch.

Thankfully I was saved making up a lie when Andrew's girlfriend called out from across the immaculate lawn. "Andrew! Over here!" She waved at him, her expression pinched even at a distance, and I bit back a smile. She *really* didn't like me.

"You better go," I said, gesturing. "Bye."

Andrew frowned but murmured a farewell and started across the grass to where his friends all sat under an old oak tree.

As pretty as he was, I wasn't interested in breaking up the future of American politics. No fucking thank you. The Sandiconte family was likely to put a hit out on me if I threatened their little girl's perfect relationship, and I'd already survived one near-death experience. Which was more than enough.

A shiver ran through me as my mind skipped back six months to the attack...to the utter terror I'd experienced while hiding from a gun-wielding psychopath. The pain that had ripped through me when his bullet found my back as I tried to run...

"Stop it," I hissed to myself, pinching the bridge of my nose in an attempt to keep the waking nightmares at bay. Beneath my shirt, my scar itched. "You're alive. You're safe."

That was the whole point of transferring to Meadowridge, after all. For safety. Because although I'd survived the attack, the gunman wasn't caught, and his motives remained a myster—

Boom!

The sound came just a split-second before the impact, which knocked the air from my lungs and my feet from the ground. A forceful blast tossed me through the air moments before my tense body smacked into the grass so hard it rattled my brain inside my skull.

What the fuck?

"Ow," I moaned, blinking against the stars dancing in front of my eyes.

"Evelyn!" someone shouted, but it was dim through the ringing in my ears.

Holy shit, had something exploded? My vision swam, but it soon became clear that I was on the grass, surrounded by what seemed like chunks of brick. That explained the all-over body-bruise sensation.

Someone skidded to their knees in front of where I lay, their huge hands cupping my face ever so gently, and it took a moment to recognize who it was.

"Ethan," I groaned. "What happened?"

"You're conscious," he said, sounding out of breath. "That's good. Can you move your legs?"

I frowned, my ears still ringing. "I'm not paralyzed." At least, I didn't think I was. My left leg was hurting a whole lot, and I doubted I'd be able to feel that if I were. To prove my point, I pulled away from his gentle touch and sat up.

"Evelyn, *fuck*, you shouldn't—" Ethan protested, his handsome face pinched with worry.

"I'm fine," I growled, angry at the intense waves of fear rolling through me, at the way my skin was covered in a cold sweat. In the back of my mind, I could hear echoes of the taunts of my attacker from six months ago. "What happened? Was it... Did someone...?" I couldn't even form the sentence out loud.

Did someone just try to kill me?

Because if yes, then I needed to get the fuck out of here ASAP.

"Explosion in the chemistry lab," Ethan replied with a flick of his hand toward the smoking rubble of a classroom. "We need to get you to the medical center. Can you stand?"

I was pretty sure yes, but when I pushed to my feet, the whole world tilted dramatically. Before I could eat grass, though, Ethan caught me in his strong grip, sweeping me up into his arms.

"That's a no to standing," he murmured, seemingly to himself. "I think you might be concussed."

He started walking with me cradled in his arms, and for a moment I panicked about what people would think. Surely this was setting off alarm bells about inappropriate student-teacher conduct? But then I glanced around to find the entire campus in chaos. Security guards in dark suits swarmed the students, guns at the ready as they assessed any potential threats.

"Holy shit," I whispered. "That's different."

Ethan just grunted and shook his head. "Protecting the VIP students first, regardless of who was in actual danger."

It made sense, though. An explosion goes off in the general vicinity of the president's son, of course they'll think it's a targeted attack on literally anyone *except* a nobody like me. In this case, I hoped Ethan was right and that it was just an accident.

"Don't worry, Evelyn," Ethan murmured. "I've got you."

God damn it straight to hell, why was he making it *so hard* not to like him?

"Eve," I mumbled, the pounding in my head so intense I needed to close my eyes. "Call me Eve."

He gave a small, husky laugh. "More like Lilith than Eve, with lips like that."

Shock rendered me speechless so I just kept my eyes shut and pretended I hadn't fucking heard that because *holy hell.* What was this man doing to me?

5

ANDREW

It was turning into an obsession, keeping an eye on Evelyn Cromwell...well, Lewis now. I couldn't fucking forget that.

Not that she made it easy on me, and not like I had a choice, since her father was all but blackmailing me into the arrangement, which meant I would be the new girl's shadow for the foreseeable future.

When Laura dropped her hand on my arm, I was momentarily distracted from my task of watching Eve wander across the courtyard. "Baby, we haven't had a proper date in ages," she whined. "You're always so busy with family events and extra study. Can't you take me to Finnegan's this weekend?"

As she batted her eyelashes at me, a few of their fake lengths scattered in different directions, and I fought the urge to reach out and fix them. I didn't like when life was out of order, and generally she kept her appearance smooth and refined, but today Laura had an unkempt feel about her. The urge to shake off her touch was strong, but since we were bound through family ties, and she *occasionally* graced me with half-decent blowjobs, I resisted.

"Can't this weekend. I've got prior engagements. But I'll get my assistant to check my schedule and figure out when we're due for a publicity photo." Afterall, what was the use of this political arrangement if not the publicity?

Her father was the vice president, and the rest of her family powerful players in mom's world, and Madam President was one of the few people on this planet I gave a damn about.

Laura pouted but knew better than to push me. I controlled the direction we took in our arrangement, and right now, she was not a priority.

I returned my gaze to the other side of the courtyard to search for Eve once more, catching sight of her purple-tinted hair just when a blast echoed through the air, the explosion rocking the ground. The force knocked me down, and by the time I gathered my wits, security had descended.

Laura and I ended up under a pile of trained soldiers, all using their bodies to shield us from further attack. "Get the fuck off me," I growled, pushing at the muscled back blocking me. "I need to check out the damage."

Not to mention they were in my personal space, and I was barely resisting the urge to start punching them to get free.

"Sir, stay down. You're being moved to Secure Location Alpha until we can assess the threat level."

Dammit. Eve had been close to that explosion, and I had to check on her, but these men were too well trained to let me anywhere near the explosion. They took their orders from Mom, and they wouldn't back down from the normal protocol —which was to get me and other politically important students into the bunker.

Sure enough, Laura and I were yanked to our feet and dragged between the agents until we started to move on our own. Guns appeared in their hands as more security stepped around us. I tried to ignore Laura bawling and yanking on my arm as I peered through the guards toward where it looked like one of the walls had been blown out of the science building.

Right where Eve had been standing when I saw her last.

Fuck.

I ducked my head and attempted to dodge my way through our human barrier, but before I made it three steps, two burly men grasped my arms and yanked me forward. Their comms chirped with orders as they moved us into the storage room that hid the door and stairs leading down into the bunker.

There was no chance for me to do anything but bark orders, which most of them ignored, more focused on locking us away. "Just make sure she's fucking okay!"

Benji, the security guard I knew the best on these grounds, nodded. "I'll see if I can find her, sir. And as soon as we've established the threat level, I'll be back to release the lock."

My back teeth gritted together as they closed us into the ten-by-ten room. It wasn't a huge space, but it had enough essentials to get us through a week of isolation. Not that I'd last that long, of course. Not when I was stuck in here with Laura, her two best friends, and the other three dickheads my mom insisted I be friends with for political gain. The only one I gave a single shit about was Prince Oliver Thorningale of Denmark, who I actually considered a friend.

Even so, eight adults in a small space had my skin crawling, and I'd be clawing it off within a few hours.

"You okay?" Oliver said, sidling in next to me and running a hand through his dark curls. "Need me to distract Ms. Can't-take-a-hint?"

Too tense to joke, I nodded my head, and he accepted that, wandering off to occupy Laura.

There was a very good reason I considered him a real friend.

I started to pace in front of the door like a caged beast. Thankfully, Benji was back within ten minutes, giving us the all-clear. "Explosion in the science lab," he said shortly, waving his hand to let us know we were free to leave. "Try to avoid that area if possible. They're in the midst of a cleanup."

"And the girl?" I asked, lowering my voice as Laura glared at me.

Benji nodded. "Yes. I found out that she's been taken to the medical center. She has injuries but apparently nothing too severe."

Relief almost sent me off the step and back into the bunker. "Thank you."

Breaking away from security, I pulled out my phone and sent a text to the person I trusted most in this world. If anyone would know how to help me keep my promise, it was him, because it was growing abundantly clear I couldn't do this on my own.

He hit me back in less than a minute, and I broke away from the group, ignoring Laura's calls as I headed across campus toward a small grove where all the shady deals went down. It wasn't in my best interest to meet publicly with my best friend, not when our worlds were so far apart, but no one who cared about politics would be caught dead in the grove.

Choosing one of the few trees not designed to drop shit all over me, I waited in the shadows for Connor. He appeared without a sound, stealthy despite his massive frame. "Hitting the roids again," I said with a tsk, eyeing the way his biceps strained at his shirt.

Connor flashed a smirk my way and flexed his arms. "Don't be jealous that I'm naturally more jacked than you. Your prissy ass just needs to lift heavier."

At home I was in the gym every morning. Here, though, I'd rather eat rusty nails than step foot in that germ-ridden cesspit that smelled like month-old ass. It was on my list to figure out if I could commandeer a space for a private gym.

Once I got through everything else that was pending.

"So, not that I don't love our clandestine meetings," Connor said as he dropped back to rest against the tree, uncaring that his shirt was now covered in bark and moss, "but I'm assuming there's a reason you've called me today right after that explosion."

"I need your help."

The smartass expression he'd been wearing dried up, replaced by a lethal intensity that reminded me why he was not only one of my best friends but my first call in a crisis. "You never ask for help. You're Mr. Independent."

It was how I survived, but this wasn't about me. "Every aspect of my life has been controlled since I was born, with the aim of building the perfect political family for Mom to achieve her goals. You know that. I know that. I don't have to ask for help because it's either done for me, or I'm forbidden from doing it. But this... it has nothing to do with that side of my life."

"Tell me what it is, and I'll make it happen. Or I'll make it go away." He slapped his hand onto my shoulder before smoothing down the crease he made and releasing me. Connor and my other old friends got me in a way very few did, not even Oliver. I'd learned how to keep my idiosyncrasies under control, but with my core group, I didn't even need to try.

Taking a breath, I admitted my darkest secret. "I'm sure you remember when I was sixteen and my dad was caught fucking his secretary." The whole world remembered it, and that was the turning point for Mom in having the support of her country. "I went off the rails for a few months—I honestly can't even remember those days. One night I got super fucked-up and took out Mom's Bentley and by the time I sobered up, I was wrapped around a pole." Connor started to pace, and I could tell that he was not going to take this next part well. "Daisy was in the car with me."

Connor cursed so loudly that there was a chirp of birds nearby taking flight.

"Daisy. I wondered what the hell happened to her. She just vanished from your life after you spent weeks fucking her on every available surface."

"I was a piece of shit during that time. And I got one hell of a wake-up call after the crash. Daisy was dead by the time I came back to consciousness. Her throat was slit by the broken glass, filling the entire floor of my car with blood. I fucking killed her, and when I realized, I panicked and called Abraham Cromwell."

Connor stopped pacing. "Who the fuck is that?" His shoulders were tense in a way that suggested he wanted to punch shit.

"Evelyn 'formerly Cromwell' Lewis's father."

It took him a beat to realize who I was even talking about. "New girl? Why would you call her father? What's her connection to you?" Connor detested not understanding a situation—his instincts had saved his life more times than I could count, and they made sure he never walked into a situation blind.

The fact that he hadn't known one of my secrets was no doubt throwing him for a loop, but this was one I'd expected to take with me to hell, where I belonged.

"Abraham was friends with my mom in high school. Like old, *old* friends, and he was around for years, even when my parents were married. Not that Eve remembers it, but we used to hang out all the time when we were younger. She went to live with relatives for some reason and we lost contact, but her dad remained in our lives. Mom always called him Mr. Fix-It. As in, if you had a problem, he was the one who could fix it. I don't know why the fuck I called him that night, but in my panic, all I could hear was Mom's voice telling me to *fucking fix it.*"

"He covered it up for you." Connor knew how the seedier

side of our world worked. "Are you sure Eve doesn't remember you?"

I nodded with a huff. "Yeah, she shows no recognition at all; she was pretty young the last time we hung out. But I remember her." Even back then she'd been all wild hair and stormy-gray eyes, always following me around.

Connor stared out across the covered path for a few minutes, mulling over the story. "So what do you need my help with, then? What's new girl and new girl's dad got to do with the trouble you're in?"

This was the part he'd be most pissed about. "He called me a few months ago and told me Eve was in danger. He asked if I could get her into this school and keep an eye on her while he cleaned up whatever mess almost got her killed at her last school."

A realization dawned on Connor's face. "That's why you've been all over her. I couldn't quite figure it out. I mean, sure, she's hot, but nothing like the straitlaced bitches you usually enjoy."

Evelyn was gorgeous, with her thick, purple-black hair, long tanned legs, and intense blue-gray eyes that shifted color with her emotions. I wasn't immune to her charms, that was for sure, but Connor was right: she was quirky and messy, which was far from my type.

Not to mention I had a politically advantageous girlfriend, which meant Evelyn was solidly off-limits.

"This explosion today almost took her out, and I'm not sure if it was intentional or not, but I'm not taking a risk with her again. Abraham knows a secret that could destroy not only my life but Mom's. I need to ensure that I don't fuck this up."

Connor growled, his chest rumbling, which was the signal he was about to lose his shit. "Fucker is blackmailing you. Maybe we should just take him out and wash our hands of the entire situation."

I shook my head. "Nah, I don't think he'd actually reveal it, but it's still a debt I owe him. A huge one."

Connor nodded as if he understood; in his family's line of work, he was rather familiar with debts. Blood, money, life—they dealt in it all. "While I don't think this is a good idea, bro, especially since we don't have enough information to know what we're protecting her from, I get why you've got to do this. You know that your debts are mine. I've got your back in whatever way you need. Do you have a plan?"

Thinking about how the last plan ended, I was ready to try out the new one. "I had a plan, but today showed me that, in an emergency, I'll be too far away to keep her safe. I think we need to bring in the other guys. I have a feeling that keeping one Evelyn *Lewis* safe is going to require a team."

Speaking of, I needed to get to the medical center and make sure she was still doing okay.

"Okay, what do you need from me?"

Leaning in, I lowered my voice. "You have to go to Dean Attworth and get him to agree to move us, the guys, and Eve into a co-ed dorm. Right now she's in the female dorms, outside of our protection and far too vulnerable. I need her under the same roof as me, and I need all of you assholes there too. It wouldn't hurt to get one of us into each of her classes as well."

Connor rubbed his hand across the scruff he hadn't bothered to shave this morning. I had no idea how the feel of it on his skin didn't bother him, but very little bothered my best friend except his brother. With that in mind, I added, "And we need Ethan."

His fists clenched, and he almost looked like he was about to throw punches. "Fuck, no. We don't need that bastard."

"The dean will never agree to this without a teacher chaperone, no matter what you threaten him with. It wouldn't look good to the school committee and parents' union."

Connor fumed for a few minutes, pacing up and down,

before he released a cursed snarl. "Fucking fine. I have so much shit over the dean, I'll have the request approved by the end of the day. Start packing your shit, Drew. We're about to be roomies."

He left as silently as he arrived, and I smoothed my shirt down, making sure everything was in place. Stepping from the grove, I glanced around to make sure there was no one else lurking. No doubt most of the students would be in their dorms while the aftermath of the explosion was dealt with.

I was about to do the same. First thing was figuring out if that was a deliberate attack, and, if so, what I needed to do to end whoever tried to hurt her. Second was locking Eve to my side until I completed my end of the deal with her father.

Then I'd finally be free.

6

EVELYN

The campus medical staff concluded that I *probably* just had some nasty bruising, but as a precaution they'd sent me to the local hospital to check for internal bleeding and concussion monitoring. Ethan had tried to accompany me, but the college nurse had waved his concerns off as unnecessary.

It was a relief, but at the same time I spent the whole eight hours of observation at the hospital thinking about how easily he'd carried me, like some kind of medieval knight protecting his damsel.

Damn it. I had a *massive* crush on my Economics of Crime professor.

It was way past dinner by the time college security picked me up and dropped me back to campus, and my stomach growled angrily. The hospital staff had offered me food while I'd been there, but it was unappealing at best, and I'd only picked at a cheese sandwich to appease them.

Checking the time on my phone, I groaned. The dining hall had *just* closed for the night, and I had no snacks at all in my room. There were a couple of vending machines over near the administration building, though, so I headed in that direction with plans to at least grab a protein bar and some soda.

"...fucking idiot!" a man's gruff voice echoed through the night as I passed a building en route to the vending machines. "...do that one more time, I will slit your throat. Dickhead."

I stopped in my tracks, shocked.

"As if you could," a familiar voice replied with a scoff. Was that Andrew? "My guys would fill you with so much lead, you'd be a human pencil before you could get close enough."

"Try me," the other guy snarled. Then the voices dipped low enough I couldn't make out the rest.

Holy crap. Did someone seriously just threaten to slit Andrew Knightsbridge's throat? That was treason or something, wasn't it?

Before I could fully process the thought, a door burst open a dozen or so feet ahead of where I stood, and a tall guy with broad shoulders stalked out into the night, muttering something under his breath about *neat-freak, mommy's boy prick.*

As tempted as I was to spy through the window and check if it was, indeed, Andrew whom he'd been arguing with, I shook off the curiosity and hurried past the building. I had enough drama and excitement for one day—I was staying firmly out of Andrew's shit.

My leg was aching—I had an *enormous* bruise on the side on my knee—so I limped a little as I reached the vending machines. To my surprise, I wasn't the only one with the late-night snackies.

"Oh," I said when I realized the man at the machines wasn't grabbing snacks at all. "Is that one broken?"

The guy looked over his shoulder from the open control panel he was tinkering with, dark eyes peering at me in the dim light. His hair was buzzed so close to the scalp it was barely more than a shadow against his deeply tanned complexion.

"Not broken," he replied with a hint of an accent. He spoke

softly, with a voice deeper than the ocean. "Did you want something?"

I blinked a couple of times, confused, then took a few steps closer to see what the options were. Maybe he was doing maintenance? He seemed too young, though. More like a student than staff. Then again, I'd have said the same for Ethan and look how that turned out.

"Um, yeah. I can wait, though. If you're fixing something?" The control panel seemed totally dead, and he had a couple of screwdrivers on the ground along with a bunch of wires hanging out the side of the machine.

He just stared at me a moment, then gave a little frown. "What did you want?"

British. He was British.

"Just the giant cookie, and the Doritos," I replied, pointing out the two snacks I wanted from that machine. "But I really don't mind waiting."

He didn't reply, instead turning his attention back to the inside of the control panel. A moment later the machine whirred to life and dispensed the two items I'd requested without requiring payment.

"Thanks," I murmured when he indicated for me to take the snacks. "Are you like maintenance or something?"

"Or something," he mumbled back, activating the machine again to dispense one of every candy bar. Then he closed up the control panel again with his little screwdrivers before collecting his loot.

When he straightened up to his full height, I sucked in a gasp. He was huge. Maybe a full foot taller than me? Basketball tall, but built solidly.

"Are you okay?" he asked with a frown as I stared, wide-eyed and stunned. "You have a bruise." He gestured to my forehead, where my skin had turned an ugly shade of purple.

I wet my lips, trying not to stare. "Um, yeah, I got caught in that chemistry lab explosion today."

He grimaced. "Sorry." Then he stuffed the dozen or so candy bars in his hoodie pockets and walked away into the night. Weird guy, but also oddly intriguing. Like I wanted to call him back and ask if we could hang out.

It was nice of him to give me free snacks, though. I grabbed a can of soda from the other vending machine then headed back to my dorm to have my little late-night feast...and take some painkillers. That all-over body bruise was really setting in.

It was going to be a long night.

THE NEXT MORNING WAS A STRUGGLE. Thanks to my private bathroom, I was able to sit under the hot shower for the better part of an hour to loosen up my stiff, sore muscles. The blotchy bruising was a sight, but it could have been worse. A lot worse. The angry, six-month-old scar on my back was evidence of that.

Nina knocked at my door not long after I dressed for the day, and her grimace at my appearance told me I hadn't put enough makeup on.

"That bad?" I asked with a groan. "I used concealer."

She shrugged. "It's fine. Seriously. It just looks like you've put concealer on a huge-ass bruise, that's all. Wanna come get coffee with Ursa and Sven?" I'd met these friends of Nina's once; they were a brother-sister duo from Norway whom I'd have sworn were twins had they not informed me otherwise.

"Sure," I agreed, grabbing my bag. "I've got an hour before Applied Microeconomics, and caffeine sounds heavenly."

Nina peppered me with questions as we walked over to the coffee shop, and when we passed the vending machines, I remembered to ask her about the argument I'd heard.

"Sounds like Connor," she said without even a hint of surprise. "He and Andrew have basically been sworn enemies as long as I can remember—which is ages, we've been at a lot of the same schools—and he's the only one insane enough to threaten someone like Andrew with shit like that. Honestly, I wouldn't be surprised if that explosion was one of them trying to murder the other."

My jaw dropped. "You're kidding, right? And the school's just okay with this? Andrew's...like..."

"Oh, I'm fully aware," Nina laughed. "They sling a lot of insults and butt heads constantly, but they both know they can't *actually* hurt one another. No one here can. Didn't you read the handbook?"

I had but just assumed it was flowery wording for the stock standard "no violence" policy at all schools. The way Nina said it, though, sort of sounded like the punishment was worse than academic suspension.

Sven and Ursa were already at the coffee shop, waving us over when we entered and gushing over how awful I looked, in a nice way, but still...sometimes a white lie was nice.

I gently extracted myself, telling Nina I'd order for both of us. There was a short wait at the counter, then I rattled off our go-to drinks before fishing around in my bag for my wallet.

"I'll get those," a guy said, smoothly tapping his phone to pay.

My brows shot up and I tipped my head back to say thanks. Then I stiffened. "Um...thanks. That wasn't necessary, though." My face heated at the idea he thought I couldn't afford the coffees somehow.

His deep green eyes studied me with curiosity. "I never said it was. You're Evelyn, right?"

I wet my lips, wondering how in the hell he knew my name. Or why he was even talking to me. "Eve," I corrected, moving out of the way for the next customer as I waited for my drinks.

"You're Connor, right?" I was parroting him deliberately, but it didn't have the intended effect.

"Have we already met?" he asked, tilting his head to the side and seeming genuinely confused.

Of course he didn't remember picking up my phone last week. "I know your"—*brother's*—"reputation."

That seemed like a totally reasonable explanation to Connor, who just nodded his understanding, then collected his coffee when it was called a moment later.

"See you around, Evelyn," he said with an ominous edge, then sauntered his sexy ass on out of the coffee shop without another glance. He oozed confidence in a way I couldn't even begin to imagine and paid no attention to the looks he got as he passed. All I could think of was how he'd threatened to slit Andrew's throat. Which then made me picture it.

I shivered, shoving the bloody thought aside. It was just an empty threat, surely.

"Um...did we just see you chatting with Connor Sullivan?" Nina asked with a sly grin as I returned with our drinks. Then I remembered how I'd never corrected her on who I'd kissed that first day in the library.

Fuck.

"Yeah, he paid for our coffees," I admitted with an awkward smile.

Sven pursed his lips and exchanged a long look with Ursa. "Everyone wants to check out the pretty new girl, hmm?"

"Everyone, indeed." Ursa nodded. "I heard Brodie Keller sat with you in Economics of Crime yesterday, too."

Nina's jaw dropped. "You didn't tell me that! Eve, what the hell? How am I going to give you all the relevant goss when I don't know what you need to know?"

Sven let out a low whistle. "Popular girly, right here. And unlike both Connor and Andrew, Brodie is single."

Ursa scoffed. "Is that what you call what he is? Single?"

It didn't take a genius to guess. "Brodie's a bit of a manwhore? Shocker. I know this will sound really weak, but I'm not here to meet guys, and I have zero desire to sleep with *anyone* I've met so far."

Except maybe Ethan. Definitely Ethan. Shit, if he kissed like that when he was surprised, what could he do when he was putting in effort?

Nina's grin was smug, but she didn't bring up my *incident* in front of her friends. Thank fuck for that. Sooner or later, I needed to set the record straight...without admitting I'd kissed a teacher. Shit. It'd be easier to just kiss Connor.

7

EVELYN

Over the rest of my second week, I settled into classes, finding that while the course load was intense here, it wasn't much harder than what I'd experienced at my old college. The students, on the other hand, were so vastly different that at times I felt like I'd stumbled into a foreign world.

Despite that, I noticed how a new tension held the campus in its thrall. There was something brewing between the various very-important factions here, I was sure of it.

"What the hell is going on?" I murmured to Nina as we waited in the dining hall line. Thursday's lunch was fresh wood-fired pizzas, which was both slow and popular. There were more students in the dining hall than I'd ever seen, and the daggers being glared around were forceful.

Nina arched a brow as she grabbed a side salad. "Rumor has it, Connor made a pass at Laura."

I blinked a couple of times. "Andrew's girlfriend? Why would he do that?"

"Probably just to piss Andrew off." Nina shrugged. "Connor doesn't really need a reason to go after other guys' girlfriends.

He could have been bored. Or maybe it was too cloudy. I don't know. But Laura apparently tried to make Andrew jealous, and it's turned into a thing."

Huh. Okay, yeah, I could see how that would create tension. Most of the college seemed to be either Team Andrew or Team Connor. The only people I'd encountered who didn't show a clear bias were Brodie Keller...and the maintenance guy. Even Nina had made her allegiance known—she was Team Andrew purely because Connor scared her a little.

I peered over my shoulder to where Andrew's group of friends sat, having already received their pizzas. Laura was positively glowing under all the attention, but Andrew scowled. His fucked-off expression directed right *at me*. What the hell?

"Uh...are you sure that's all that's going on?" I asked nervously, my gaze tracking around the room until I found Connor. Thankfully, he was engaged in a broody conversation with his heavily tattooed friend, Hawk.

Nina shrugged. "Nope, not sure. But that's all I've heard about, and I have really sharp ears, you know?"

I chuckled, turning back to the pizza line. "Yeah, I know. Queen of Meadowridge gossip. Did you ever hear who caused the chemistry lab explosion?"

She nodded. "Yup, it was Haze. Totally un-shocking, and apparently Dean Attworth can't decide on a suitable punishment because nothing like this has ever happened before, and he can't send Haze off campus. Like at all. It's a safety thing."

This was *all* news to me. "Okay, hold up. Who is Haze, and why can't he leave campus?"

"Um, something to do with him being wanted by a couple of European countries on espionage allegations or some crap? I dunno, it's probably just hearsay and rumor, but he's super mysterious so it's plausible." Nina dropped that information so casually, then got to the front of the line and placed her pizza order.

I waited my turn, then right as I started to order, all hell broke loose.

The tension that had been holding the school hostage all week exploded into a mass of students inside the cafeteria. Nina and I were five tables away from the initial chaos, so I couldn't immediately see who was involved, but I already had my suspicion, which was confirmed when she dragged me closer to the action.

"Shouldn't we be running the other way?" I gasped as Connor slammed his fist into Andrew's face, the pair at the center of the ruckus, between the tables.

But they weren't the only ones.

At least half a dozen other guys were shouting and shoving, fists flying so fast that I couldn't keep up with who was smacking who in the face. The noise grew louder and louder as more students circled the group, laying bets.

To my surprise, it was fairly even odds for Connor versus Andrew.

"Where the hell is security?"

Nina took the briefest look around before returning her gaze to the fight. "Someone would have paid them off to stay away." She squeaked as Andrew tackled Connor to the ground, slamming his knee into the big guy's gut.

A shudder raced through me; violence was a trigger, but I was keeping it mostly under control from where I stood. Except Nina kept edging us closer, until I could feel the breeze from swinging fists, which was far too close.

"What are you doing?" I shouted at her, and she just shot me a brilliant smile. Crazy bitch was enjoying this.

I mean, not to say that there wasn't a certain poetry in watching these perfect specimens of the male species getting down to their base instincts. There was so much testosterone, I was surprised we couldn't smell it, but all I got was fresh sweat and expensive cologne.

I blinked as I noticed the guy who'd been tinkering with the vending machines in the mix, standing out as the tallest out of an already tall bunch of guys. He moved like a ninja, though, ducking and diving, all the while annihilating anyone who gets in his way. And was that—

"Is that Brodie fucking Keller?" Nina choked out. "Oh, bro, his agent is going to wring his neck if he damages his pretty face."

Sure enough, the blond actor was in the midst of the chaos, cackling loudly as he threw punches left and right. I had no idea he could fight so well, and it didn't look as if anyone had landed a blow on him yet.

"How's he moving so fast?"

Nina shot me a salacious side-eye. "Girl, have you not seen how powerful his thighs are? They need their own fucking movie. I'd watch ten hours of him just flexing them."

I was about to ask her when she thought I would have had a chance to *see his thighs* when she let out a muttered curse and, to my utter shock, raced into the midst of the fight.

"Nina!" I screamed after her, worried she was about to get herself killed. None of these guys were in their right minds to know who they were swinging at.

Cursing impulsive friends, I raced around the outside, my heart slamming in my chest as I dodged a few of the tables to keep her in my line of sight. Somehow, she didn't encounter any of those swinging fists, and I had no idea what set her in motion until I saw Laura sitting at a table right near the edge, frantically waving and calling to Andrew.

At that stage, a lot of the other guys had cleared out, leaving just Andrew, Connor, Brodie, and the big janitor. Oh, and Laura.

Nina snuck up behind her and, when she was close, fisted a handful of Laura's hair and slammed her face straight down into the cafeteria table.

The bang was so loud that everyone turned in that direction, seeing Laura with her hand over her busted nose as blood trailed between her fingers…and no sign of Nina.

Somehow, she'd vanished, and as I bounced up on my toes, I thought I caught a glimpse of her down on the floor, sneaking away.

When Laura's shock wore off and she finally looked around for her attacker, I was the only one close by, and she screamed and pointed my way. "I'll have your head for this, new girl! You're fucking done here at Meadowridge!"

I held both hands up, silently professing my innocence, but it was too late. A few seconds later security *finally* made its way into the room, and I was still frozen in place, unsure if I should run or just face the music and explain I wasn't remotely close enough to her to have carried out that attack. Fuck, I'd been twenty feet away. How fast did she think I could move?

In the end, I didn't get to make the decision, as the four main instigators of the fight, Laura, and I were dragged off to the dean's office. He was already waiting for us, and when security ushered us inside, they took up sentry at the door, ensuring no one was escaping their fate.

Dean Attworth stood behind his desk, expression thunderous as he glared at each of us. For the most part, there weren't that many signs of the fight. Connor and Andrew were a little worse for wear, with bruises already forming, and Connor had a small cut above his right eyebrow that occasionally dripped blood onto his cheek. Brodie and Janitor boy sported busted knuckles and a few torn shirt buttons, but otherwise their faces remained completely untouched.

Oh, and then there was Laura. Who had two black eyes forming and what looked like a broken nose, which was a fucking excellent look on her.

"Can someone please explain to me what the hell just happened in my college?"

The dean didn't shout. Nope. His voice was calm and reasonable, but there was an undertone that told me he was two seconds from losing his shit.

"That bitch slammed my head onto the cafeteria table," Laura said, pointing a red-tipped finger at me. "I want her expelled and charged with assault."

"What!" I gasped. "I wasn't anywhere near you, Psycho Barbie. Not even I could move twenty feet in a few seconds. I think that blow to your head might have rattled your few brain cells out of your broken nose."

Laura lurched for me, but Andrew stepped into the way. "Laura had nothing to do with this," he said shortly to the dean. "She shouldn't even be here."

To my surprise, the dean didn't question that statement, waving toward Laura as if to say *you're dismissed.* Laura looked like she was about to start raving again, until Andrew leaned down and whispered near her ear. She calmed almost instantly, and with a final dirty look shot my way, she flounced out the door.

No doubt she was off to regale her sycophants with the harrowing tale of her attack.

Good for her.

But also—why the fuck was I still in here?

"I had nothing to do with the fight either," I said as I hold both hands out in front of me to do a spin. "See, not a drop of blood, sweat stain, or wrinkle in my clothes."

Outside of the normal wrinkles, because only lunatics ironed their clothes.

"If Laura said you attacked her, we're believing it," Andrew said shortly, blatantly lying about what happened. Which proved my point about ironing. That lying, perfectly pressed asshole had all but agreed with his insane girlfriend.

"I wasn't anywhere near her. And I wouldn't attack her

anyway. I have absolutely no reason to dislike Laura, and I've never hit anyone just for the fucking fun of it."

"Language, Ms. Lewis," the dean admonished. "If Andrew isn't verifying your story, then that leads me to believe that Ms. Sandiconte, who is an exemplary student from an even more exemplary family, is telling the truth."

I had barely opened my mouth to express how utterly unfair this was when he pointed a finger and said, "You're in just as much trouble as these four, so it's in your best interests to remain quiet and accept your punishment."

Punishment. Was he for fucking real?

If he punished me worse than these rich douchebags, who actually started the fight, I would lose my shit and start smashing up his fancy office—starting with the shelf of awards sitting in a brown cabinet right behind his desk.

Meadowridge was so prestigious, it had dozens of glass plaques dedicated to its greatness.

They'd look great in pieces.

My revenge plans were put on hold when I realized I'd missed some of the dean's next words. "...feud between two of our best and brightest students has to come to an end. We've tried mediation, we've tried to bring your families in"—he glared particularly hard at Connor—"which was an even worse disaster than the initial fight. It seems I have to try a new tack now."

Connor remained silent, his face stoic, but every now and then, he leveled a glare on me. Which made absolutely no sense. How was any of this my fault?

Andrew, on the other hand, spoke up. "You could just expel Connor. I can dig up a dozen or more rules he's broken just this year alone."

Connor's lips twitched, but weirdly, he didn't bite back at his enemy.

The dean, on the other hand, paled a touch and cleared his

throat as he said, "That is not an option, and you well know it, Mr. Knightsbridge. But I have devised a different plan, and it's not going to please any of you. But drastic situations require drastic measures."

I had no idea what sort of punishment he was about to dish out, but I already knew that I was going to hate it. "You five will be moving into Bluebell House. You will live there for the rest of this semester, and even longer if I feel you haven't learned your lessons. You will work together to make it habitable, to the standard you enjoy living; otherwise, you will live in a hovel and not one contractor in this state is going to help you get those repairs done. This will require the sort of teamwork that builds bonds and friendships. You all have more in common than you realize."

There was a stunned silence in the room, and I was fairly sure I was the only one not familiar with this Bluebell House. Judging by their expressions, it was not a nice place to live.

I waited for the guys to object. Three of them hadn't said a single word since we entered the office, and it appeared that Janitor Boy was napping. His eyes were closed as he perched against the wall. Wait...why was the janitor even here, getting this sort of punishment? Shouldn't he just be straight-up fired? Maybe I'd misread the entire situation when I'd found him "fixing" the vending machine. He was just another rich-ass punk who thought he was above the law.

I decided to speak up, not that it had done me any good the last time. "I'm sorry, but I didn't think you allowed coed dorms here? Maybe there's another punishment for me? I'm happy to clean the kitchens or write an essay on the dangers of violence in college."

See, I could be the voice of reason in a room filled with stupid men.

The dean acted as if he only heard the first part I said. "Right, to ensure the school board remains happy with these mixed living arrangements, I'm going to add a teacher to the mix. To keep an eye on everything."

He tapped his finger against his chin briefly, and before he said it, I already knew what was going to come out of his mouth. "Professor Ethan Sullivan is the only one who doesn't appear to be afraid of you four and, therefore, won't let you get away with murder."

For the first time, a scowl formed across Connor's handsome features.

Not that I had a chance to worry about that, since I was about to find myself sharing what sounded like a shithole of a house, with five men.

One of whom was the professor I was crushing on and had already crossed far too many lines with. Fuck.

8

EVELYN

Walking back to my dorm after the dean dished out his punishment, I convinced myself it was all a misunderstanding. Or a bluff. Or a test? Yeah, that had to be it. The dean was testing whether I could stand up for myself. Or something.

Whatever the reason, I convinced myself there was just no way he would *actually* make me move into a house with five strange men. It was beyond absurd. So I made no effort to pack my room up when I got back, instead opting to call Mitchell. He didn't answer, but I left a voicemail, then settled at my desk to work on my Economics of Crime assignment.

Living with Ethan or not, I was still determined to be the best and brightest student in his class.

An hour later, my phone vibrated, and I gusted out a sigh of relief to see Mitchell's number on the screen.

"Hey, Uncle Mitch," I greeted him when I'd accepted the call. "I hope I didn't interrupt your work?"

Mitchell and Karolyn both worked at an auction house. Mitch was an auctioneer and could talk faster than anyone I'd ever met, and Karolyn handled customer service.

"No, you're fine. What's up? How's Meadowridge? Is everything... Are you *safe*?" The edge of worry in his voice answered the question I'd been calling to ask.

I swallowed back the bitter disappointment. "I'm safe," I confirmed. "I'm guessing they haven't made any progress?" He knew what I was asking. The cops had an open case to search for the man who'd opened fire in my previous school —the man who'd shot me in the back as I ran in terror. They had no leads, though. After I was shot, it was all a blur. I had no clue how I'd survived or how I'd ended up being dropped off at the Emergency Department before I could drown in my own blood, but the gunman had disappeared without a trace.

Since waking up in ICU, I'd been perpetually scared he'd come back and finish the job, but at Meadowridge...it was different. I wasn't looking over my shoulder constantly.

"I'm sorry, duckling," Mitch replied with a sigh. "They've gotten no further in finding the guy. Not even a name."

I nodded silently, even though he couldn't see me. "Okay," I murmured. "I guess I'm safe here."

"Nowhere safer in the whole country, kid. I'd better go, but Karo sends her love." He ended the call before I could even reply, and I slowly blinked at the blank screen of my phone. So much for that idea, whatever that idea had even been. Running...escaping. My usual MO.

A sharp knock at my door made me snap out of my melancholy, and I stood from my desk to respond. I assumed it was Nina, come to explain what the hell she'd been thinking with slamming Laura's face into the table, but then again, she never could have guessed I'd take the blame.

It wasn't Nina at my door, though.

"Brodie," I said with a frown. "What are you doing here?"

The gorgeous blond actor just grinned with all those perfect, movie-star teeth. "Came to help you move, Evie babe.

Seemed like the decent thing to do, since you're copping heat for a fight you had nothing to do with."

My lips parted in shock. "You believe me? I didn't touch Laura!" Not that she hadn't been asking for it, with all her snide comments and dirty looks my way.

Brodie shrugged. "Yeah, I believe you. You don't seem like the kinda chick to hit from behind."

"So why didn't you say anything?" I demanded, planting my hands on my hips.

Another grin. "I'm in enough shit with the dean already. The last thing I needed was to draw more attention. Besides, as far as punishments go, this one is not the worst. Sure, Bluebell House is crappy and busted, but it also means we don't have a curfew and literally get a million times more privacy than these dorm buildings, where the walls are paper thin and everyone knows your business."

Across the hall, a door slammed shut awfully quickly, and Brodie rolled his eyes. "Case in point. Are you letting me come in or what?"

Largely because he still had me starstruck, I moved aside and let him enter my room before shutting the door behind him. I guess when he framed it like that, I wouldn't hate the privacy, especially if—something occurred to me.

"Why do you think there's no curfew? We'd literally have a teacher living in the house with us."

Brodie snickered. "Ethan totally doesn't count. You don't really look packed. Dean expects us all to move in this afternoon, you know?"

"I...um...I didn't really think he was going to force us to move. Is he? I figured..." I trailed off, seeing his bemused expression.

"Evie babe...Dean Attworth doesn't bluff. And he *really* doesn't like having his orders ignored. Come on, I'll help." He crossed to my wardrobe and pulled out my empty suitcases, making himself right at home as he laid them out on the floor.

Speechless and still embarrassingly starstruck, I just did as I was told.

An hour later, Brodie carried my suitcases up the weathered wooden steps of a house that had a pretty name but the rest of it could only ever be described one way: haunted. If it wasn't for the trailing bluebell flowers that filled the two gardens on either side of the entrance, there'd have been nothing appealing at all about this ramshackle house.

"This is where we have to live?" I squeaked, my palms already sweating as I cautiously followed him through the front door. "It seems...um..."

"Like there's skeletons plastered up in the walls? I know, right?" Brodie agreed with an unhinged laugh. "I'm literally never going to fall asleep here. Acting in *The Phantoms* as a kid totally fucked me up, and now I see ghosts everywhere."

I loved that movie.

Brodie had only been six or seven when he starred as the lead character, who could speak with the dead, and the CGI effects had been *intense*. Some of the best jump scares I'd ever experienced. So yeah, I could see how that might fuck up a kid's imagination for sure.

"Evie's here!" Brodie yelled out into the house, his own voice bouncing back at him ominously. No one responded, though, so he shrugged and set my bags beside the staircase. "I think there's an empty room upstairs. Come on, I'll show you."

If I squinted, I could imagine Bluebell House used to be a regal home. The wooden banister was finished with decorative flourishes, and the well-worn steps were of solid construction. Graffiti decorated the walls as we ascended, though, and I wrinkled my nose at the musty, cat urine sort of smell.

"Dean Attworth said he'd send the cleaning crew over this

evening," Brodie called over his shoulder, reading my mind. "It's been empty for a while."

"No shit," I murmured. "What about furniture?" Because he'd just opened the door to a huge but *entirely empty* room. In fairness, it was more than double the size of my dorm room and had the most amazing bay window looking out into the woods behind the college, but...nowhere to sleep.

"Also being delivered this evening," Brodie assured me. "Do you like this room? Or I can show you some of the other available spaces if this—"

"No, this is fine," I quickly assured him. "We won't be here for long, right? Just until Connor and Andrew make nice?"

Brodie rubbed a hand over the back of his neck, avoiding eye contact. "Yeah. Right. Anyway, I'll show you where the bathroom is."

He spent some time showing me around, and by the time he was done, the furniture had started arriving. I breathed a small sigh of relief to see the truck unloading bedframes and mattresses first.

I thanked him for the tour, then grabbed an armful of cleaning supplies I'd seen in the kitchen. The cleaning crew had a big enough job as it was; I could handle doing my own room.

An hour later my room was as clean as I could make it, and I was hard at work on the shared bathroom down the hall when I heard the telltale sounds of more people arriving. I considered going downstairs and making nice, but anger and resentment stopped me. It was *their* fault I had been dragged into this strange and unusual punishment.

"You know we have a whole cleaning crew here, right?" Andrew asked, startling me as I scrubbed the base of the shower on my hands and knees.

Biting back my urge to curse him out—because he was still

President Kingsbridge's son—I settled on a frosty glare over my shoulder. "I'm aware. But they'll be here until morning if we don't pitch in and help. Or were you unaware how disgusting this place was?"

His pursed lips and pinched brow as he looked around said he'd definitely noticed. "You're strange, Evelyn."

"And you're a spineless prick, but you don't see me pointing out facts," I muttered under my breath, turning back to the scrubbing and hoping he hadn't heard me.

The shocked laugh he let out said otherwise, and I winced. "Fair call, Evelyn. Do you have any allergies? I'm having my people pick up dinner for everyone in town. Maybe Thai food?"

That was...nice of him. I thought these guys all hated each other?

"I eat anything," I replied, confused by the kind offer after I just insulted him. "Not fussy."

Andrew didn't respond immediately, and I found myself glancing over my shoulder to see if he was still there. He was, and he was staring at my ass.

Wait. No, maybe he was staring at the mold on the shower curtain, which was destined for the trash. That made more sense.

"Okay, I'll order a selection to share in that case," he finally murmured, his brow furrowing as he shifted his gaze around the bathroom. "We just can't order anything with shellfish because Connor is allergic."

"That's fine. Like I said, I'll eat anything." I meant it, too. I was yet to find a food I strongly disliked, which made it easy for me at restaurants.

Andrew nodded, then left me to my cleaning. It wasn't until after he was gone that I paused my scrubbing and frowned. Why the fuck would Andrew know Connor's allergies?

More to the point, why would he *care*?

This day was officially weird as shit. Maybe the cleaning fumes were messing with my head or something. Yeah. That must be it.

9

EVELYN

By the time I finished cleaning, I was a sweaty mess. I ducked into my room and grabbed new underwear and shorts, deciding to change before dinner. Not like I was in any great rush to hang out with the assholes who got me sent here in the first place.

Spoiled-rotten rich boys, who were clearly used to getting whatever they wanted and gave zero fucks about the consequences for anyone else. Especially innocent bystanders.

Andrew had dropped me in the shit to save his girlfriend, and therefore he was number one in my ranking of housemates —asshole rankings, as it were.

It would no doubt be a rotating list, but he could take the crown today.

After a quick shower, I examined my bruises in the mirror, relieved that most of the swelling was gone. Now I just had a nice colorful remembrance of almost dying in a science lab explosion. The rest of the green and yellow bruises should be completely faded over the next few days, unlike Laura's. I smirked. It was almost worth the punishment to know that she was heading for her plastic surgeon to get a nose job over the weekend.

Bitch.

When I couldn't delay any longer, I threw on my clothes and headed downstairs with wet and stringy hair, no makeup, and a scowl that hopefully indicated I was in no mood to be fucked with.

The four guys were already seated around a table, which was clearly new, its surface smooth and shiny, a great contrast to the old timber boards under our feet. I'd had to put my slides back on, as I was worried about splinters and tetanus.

"Evie babe!" Brodie crowed. "I missed you."

"It's been two hours," I replied drolly. "But hey, funny how you disappeared right when all the cleaning happened."

He slammed a hand against his muscled pec, a perfect look of heartbreak on his face. His acting skills were not in question at all, and I already felt myself softening, despite knowing it was all fake. "You wound me. Had I known you required my assistance, I would have been there without complaint. Your mess is my mess."

I had to shake my head hard to clear the haze he created with his perfect existence. Pointing my finger at him, I said, "No! Stop whatever you're doing. It won't work."

Before I thought it through, I jabbed my finger at each of them in turn. "All of you are in my fucking bad books, and I won't be playing nice just because we're roommates."

While Brodie remained visibly heartbroken, Andrew stared at me impassively, and the big "janitor" was buried in his phone, not even bothering to acknowledge my existence. Connor was the only one who reacted, his expression tightening.

Deciding I needed to stop calling him Janitor Boy, I turned and said, "Hi, sorry, I didn't get your name the other night when you were vandalizing the school. I'm Eve." I put my hand out to shake, pulling his attention away from his phone. "I'm assuming you're *not* maintenance staff?" Otherwise, he'd have simply been fired, not made to move in with a bunch of college kids.

"This is Haze," Brodie said, introducing the silent guy as I awkwardly withdrew my hand. "Um, what happened the other night?"

My eyes widened with recognition of his name. "Haze," I repeated, mood souring. "You're the one who exploded the science lab on Monday and nearly killed me."

His unblinking stare was becoming unnerving. "I said *sorry*."

That was it. I blinked a couple of times, remembering his vague *sorry* right before he'd disappeared into the darkness with pockets full of candy. Hardly an apology fitting of nearly killing someone, but that was just my opinion.

A chair screeched as Connor pushed it back, getting to his feet slowly, as if he really couldn't be bothered with my female hysterics. "I have an NDA for you to sign, and I won't accept a refusal."

I gaped at him, wondering if my ears had malfunctioned. "What did you fucking say?"

The smile that crossed his face was not nice. "You heard me, Cinderella. Before you get back to your fucking chores, you need to sign an NDA, so that nothing that goes on in this house is revealed to the world."

Crossing my arms over my chest, I shake my head. "Yeah, not happening."

Before I could blink, there was a gun pointed at my head, and I had no idea where he'd pulled it from or how he moved so fast. "If you don't sign the NDA, I have no choice but to take you out."

I opened my mouth, but my throat was too tight to even make a sound. We remained in a standoff as seconds ticked by, and with it, the pounding of my heart increased. *Thump, thump, thump, thump.* It slammed so brutally in my chest that the cavity around it started to ache, like I was experiencing the early symptoms of a heart attack.

"Eve."

Whoever called my name sounded as if they were miles away, and there was an echoing in my head that slammed as hard as my heartbeat. For a moment in time, as ragged breaths heaved in and out of me, all that existed were panic and memories.

The screams. That cold voice calling my name, getting closer and closer as he took out students, searching for me. A shooter that no one could find a motive for. The burning rip of pain as bullets pierced my flesh, and I felt my life fading on a cold ground, in the middle of my college. Alone.

I'd almost bled to death without a single person I cared about even knowing I was in trouble.

"What's happening? She's hyperventilating. Get her down on the floor before she passes out."

Their voices briefly broke through as gentle hands touched me, and then all I could hear was screaming. A high-pitched wail that took me forever to realize was coming from me. "What the fuck did you do, Connor? I'm going to kill you!"

For the first time, there was a sliver of clarity through my panic. A slight relief from the pressure crushing my body. Maybe because he'd eased my last attack, or maybe it was that he'd gotten to me after the explosion making sure I was safe. Either way, as soon as I heard Ethan's voice, I lurched desperately toward him.

His woodsy scent and expensive cologne filled my nose, and instinct controlled my actions as I dropped my head against his firm chest, desperately hoping I wouldn't pass out or vomit on him.

"Breathe with me, sweetheart," he whispered, his husky

voice close to my ear. "In and out, regulate your breathing. No one will hurt you. I promise. I will destroy anyone who tries."

In and out. In and out. I tried to do as he said and regulate my breaths, but they were still too fast and shallow as the fuzziness on the edge of my brain indicated I was about to pass out. As darkness filtered through the last of my consciousness, I heard, "Fuck!" And then Ethan was fisting the back of my head, fingers tangling in my hair as he pulled my head back and crushed his lips against mine.

As I tasted him, our breaths mingled until his breathing slowed mine. The dark spots retreated from my mind, and those fuzzy tendrils faded away. I would have fallen into a heap on the floor, but there was a professor wrapped around me, keeping me standing.

No—more than that, he kept me grounded.

The triggering event seeped from my essence, and Ethan absorbed it into his own, taking away the painful memories. I'd never found anything in all my time after the attack, not through therapy or drugs or desperation, that could bring me out of a full-blown attack the way Ethan just had.

Take that, Dr. Graystone. Counting to five and grounding myself in what I could see had nothing on Ethan Sullivan's pillowy lips.

"What the *fuck*?"

Connor's exclamation was like a bucket of ice water dumped directly on my head, and I leapt out of Ethan's arms as though he was electrified.

"Eth...dude..." Brodie said with wide eyes. "I don't think—"

Holy shit. *Holy shit.* I'd just kissed my *professor* in the middle of the kitchen with all four guys front row and center. Or had he kissed me? Sort of irrelevant, I supposed.

"Put the fucking gun away, Connor," Ethan snapped, making me jump a little.

The gun. That was what'd sent me into a panic attack. Connor pulled a fucking *gun* on me.

"Not until she signs the NDA," Connor snapped, stubbornness radiating from his every pore. The gun in question was no longer pointed at me but held loosely at his side. It was all I could focus on. Now that I'd been reminded, I couldn't look away, couldn't even blink as, over and over in my head, I heard the deafening sound of shots.

Brodie stepped between Connor and me, breaking my line of sight with the weapon as he snatched the document from the table. "She'll sign it, bro. Put the gun away. Can't you see what it's doing to her?"

My tunnel vision blurred out everything except Brodie and the paperwork in his hands. Connor muttered something about *sensitive snowflakes* and the surge of rage nearly eclipsed my panic. Nearly, but not completely.

Andrew cleared his throat, rising from the table and moving to Connor's side. I dimly paid attention as he murmured something to the dark-haired asshole, his voice low and his lips close to Connor's ear. Then Connor spat a curse and stuffed the gun out of sight in the back of his pants.

"That would have been relevant information a little sooner, Drew," he hissed then abruptly stormed out of the room. At least Haze had said sorry for the explosion, and that hadn't even been deliberate. At least I assumed not.

"Sit down, Evie babe," Brodie coaxed, giving me a very gentle push toward an empty chair.

I did as I was told, because I was in shock. What the fuck was wrong with Connor? Who pulled a gun on someone without provocation?

A warm hand stroked my spine, and I leaned back into the touch. Ethan. The magnetism between us was damn near supernatural.

"Evelyn, this was a disastrous idea. I'll speak to Dean Attworth and—" Ethan began.

"You can't," Andrew snapped.

Ethan's soothing hand on my back stilled. "Why the fuck not? Evelyn isn't safe here so—"

"Oh, but she's safe under your watchful eye, *Professor*? Do I need to report what we all just witnessed as irrefutable inappropriate conduct with a student?" Andrew's voice was like fucking ice, and his glare was even harder. My jaw dropped as I looked from him, to Ethan, and back again, wondering if they'd come to physical blows if I didn't intervene.

Quickly grabbing the pen from Brodie, I scribbled my signature on the paperwork without even skimming it first. "There. Done. Signed. Everyone happy?"

Andrew relaxed ever so slightly, and his expression thawed as he shifted his gaze to me. Then he nodded tightly and took the paper from my outstretched hand. "Thank you, Evelyn. I'll speak with Connor and ensure this unpleasantness won't happen again."

Ethan's hand dropped from my back. "No, I'll speak with him. I trust you'll provide Evelyn with a copy of that NDA so she understands what she's just agreed to?"

"Obviously," Andrew drawled, and Haze slid a duplicate contract across the table to me.

Ethan gave a small grunt. "You could have handled this without involving Connor."

"No shit," Brodie agreed, running a hand through his messy blond hair. It did nothing to detract from how handsome and alluring he was.

"Are you okay now?" Ethan asked me quietly, crouching beside my chair to meet my eyes with his own concerned gaze. "That's the second panic attack I've seen since you arrived."

My lips twitched with amusement, the adrenaline of shock

fading into loopy lightheadedness. "Good thing you knew how to snap me out of it, then."

Andrew cleared his throat, reminding me *again* that we weren't alone. "We are going to need to discuss that situation. It's not—"

The doorbell ringing cut off whatever high-horse judgmental shit he was about to pop off with but didn't stop me rolling my eyes.

"That'll be my guys with our food," Andrew muttered. "Eth, go deal with Connor. Brodie, get Evelyn some orange juice or something. Maybe her blood sugar is low."

With those orders, he and Ethan both disappeared, and I found myself locking eyes with Haze. True to what little I knew of him, he said nothing. He didn't need to. The slight raise of one eyebrow said plenty.

Shit. Maybe living under the same roof with Ethan was asking for trouble.

10

EVELYN

ndrew's people had delivered what seemed like an entire restaurant worth of Thai food, but for some *mysterious, inexplicable reason*, cough-cough, I'd totally lost my appetite. I said as much, then folded the contract copy into my pocket and went back to my room, ignoring Brodie's call to me.

Ethan and Connor were still absent—presumably talking about me—and I was glad for it. I didn't think I could handle another panic attack or meltdown right now.

To my intense relief, I discovered my room was equipped with a door lock. It was ancient and ornate, but it had a key. After some effort and jiggling, I even got the key to turn, and the lock bolt slid home in the frame.

"Small mercies, I guess," I muttered to myself, crossing over to my freshly made bed and pulling the contract out of my pocket. "Let's see what I just agreed to."

Blowing out a breath, I sat down and started scanning the document. Part of me was terrified I'd just signed off on becoming some kind of shared house sex slave with a list of required services for each of the guys, so I was surprised to find it was a very simple and standard nondisclosure agreement.

Whatever I witnessed or heard within the walls of Bluebell House, I was legally bound to keep it confidential. That was it.

What the fuck did they plan to discuss here that warranted an official nondisclosure agreement? God knew I couldn't afford to break it, even if I thought I could prove it was signed under duress—which I doubted.

Maybe it had something to do with how *friendly* they all seemed with each other? Certainly, a far cry from the thick tension and animosity that'd sparked an all-out brawl in the dining hall just six hours ago.

A knock at my door tugged my focus away from the contract, and I put it down on the little bedside table. "Yes?"

"Evelyn, could we talk?" Ethan called back, and I groaned.

"No!" It was the only honest answer I could give. My face was already flaming with embarrassment, and I needed to process the fact that I'd now kissed my teacher *twice*. This time was totally worse because I *knew* he was my teacher. And everyone saw it happen.

There was a significant pause before Ethan replied, "Okay. Well, when you're ready, just come downstairs. Connor will behave himself. I promise."

I snort laughed at that, because I seriously doubted Connor *behaving* would be a huge improvement from his usual surly attitude. "Okay," I called back, offering nothing further to continue the conversation. Sure, yes, eventually we'd have to address the huge kissing elephant in the room, but that day was not today. Not while my hands still trembled from the shock of having a gun shoved in my face.

Muffled footsteps faded, so I figured Ethan had given up and gone back down to join the guys for dinner in the dining room. *Our* dining room. Shit, this was my new home, whether I liked it or not. Maybe I should have jumped on Ethan's offer to speak with the dean again, but Andrew had cut him off before he'd even finished his thought.

Why?

Surely if they all required such intense privacy, they'd do whatever it took to get rid of me?

My skin itched with the uncomfortable feeling of being trapped, so I unlocked my door—quietly relieved it unlocked without much effort—then headed downstairs as silently as possible. I made it as far as the foyer before a floorboard creaked.

"Going somewhere?" Andrew asked, popping out of nowhere like a creepy fuck.

Gritting my teeth, I turned to face him. "Yeah. Is that allowed, or are you going to pull a gun on me as well?"

He had the grace to wince slightly at that and shake his head. "I wouldn't do that to you, Evelyn."

There was an odd inflection in his statement. Almost like the *to you* shouldn't have been a necessary qualifier but was. Would Andrew pull a gun on someone else, given the right motivation? The thought made me shiver.

"Am I allowed to leave the house, Andrew?" I asked carefully, my hand already on the door handle at my back.

His brow dipped in a slight frown, and his jaw tightened noticeably. "Of course. You're not a prisoner, Evelyn."

A small breath of relief rushed out of my lungs, and I turned the door handle to open it.

"But since it's after dark and the path back to the main grounds winds through the trees, it would be safer if you didn't go alone."

Irritation made my teeth clench, and I gave him a sarcastic smile. "Thanks, but no thanks. I've taken self-defense classes. I'm sure I can handle any rabid racoons that might harass me on the five-minute walk."

Not waiting for his reply—because like he said, I wasn't a prisoner—I exited the house and pulled the door firmly shut behind myself. I could not make my point clearer if

I'd written it into a legally annotated document for *him* to sign.

So why in the fuck did Brodie come jogging after me before I'd made it fifty yards down the path?

"Are you serious?" I exclaimed when he caught up. "I'm an adult. I've been walking independently since I was eleven months old."

He quirked a brow like he didn't understand my animosity. "I'm sure you can, Evie babe. I'm heading to Aster Hall to, uh, visit a friend." His sexy grin said exactly what kind of *friend* he was going to meet with. "Seemed creepy if I was just following fifty feet behind instead of walking with you, since we're living together and all."

"All of it is creepy," I deadpanned. "Don't get confused about how this situation reads."

Brodie just grinned good-naturedly, and I wondered how this famous, gorgeous, rich-as-fuck guy could appear so down-to-earth. If anyone ever questioned his acting skill in my presence, I would be setting them straight without hesitation. Because he was good.

By the time I made it to the main campus grounds, I found an empty cafeteria, and most of the students were either in their dorms or studying. I hadn't really thought through my intentions in marching out. Mostly it was to prove that I was in fact *not* a prisoner, and there might have been a secondary thought of catching up with Nina.

What could I tell her, though? I guess I could let her know I wasn't in the my dorm room any longer, but everything that went on in the house was firmly covered under the NDA, so if she asked me any questions, I probably couldn't answer them.

It'd be better to not mention anything until there was no other choice. She could just assume I was gone from the dorm every time she stopped by. I looked around the nearly-empty grounds around the cafeteria and sighed.

"Everything okay?"

I jumped about a foot in the air because I'd completely forgotten my stalker. "Shit, Brode," I said, slamming my hand against my chest to hopefully calm my heart's frantic beat. "I forgot you were even there. We need to get you a bell or something."

His lips twitched. "I have to say, you're hell on a guy's ego, Evie babe. I'm not sure I've ever had a chick *forget I was there* before. Though I do like the new nickname. Pretty sure that makes us besties now." He bopped me on the nose. "And besties don't forget besties are standing there."

"Please stop saying bestie. You're making it creepy *and* weird now."

Brodie just shrugged, like he was okay with that assessment. "Did you change your mind about coming to campus?"

Needing to conceal that I had nowhere to go and no one I trusted enough to talk to, I deflected. "Weren't you off to blow some woman's mind?"

He was suddenly a lot closer to me, his expression serious as he brushed back a strand of my hair, tucking it behind my ear. He let his fingers linger along my cheek for seconds longer than was required in the circumstances, and I felt that gentle touch all the way to my core. "I don't believe I said anything about blowing a woman's mind, but if you'd like to volunteer, I'm happy to change your entire existence. All you have to do is say yes."

Half of me was being seduced, while the other half was trying not to laugh, because there was no way he didn't use those lines all the time. The trail of women behind this guy would be longer than the distance to the moon.

Deciding he needed a little fucking with, I leaned in closer. He stilled, and I was glad to see that move take him by surprise. Letting my lips graze near the corner of his mouth, I whispered, "There's not a fucking chance I'll ever be another notch on your well-used bedposts, Brodie Keller. But nice try."

A desperate rumble escaped him, but I was already gone, heading back for the house. A few seconds later, a pounding of steps sounded behind me, and this time when Brodie strolled beside me, he remained quiet, but I caught him glancing my way a few times with an intrigued expression.

I'd wanted to deter him, but I got the sense that I'd just challenged the movie star, and he was about to show me the full force of his efforts. Efforts I wasn't sure I'd be able to resist.

To my relief, once I was back inside the house, Brodie left me with a kiss on the cheek, wandering into the living area where I could hear a few of the guys setting up the television. Or possibly a gaming system. I heard some shouts about *Call of Duty* and *how can we be expected to fucking shoot someone on a screen that size* as I headed for the kitchen.

I wanted a glass of water before I headed up to hide in my room for the rest of the evening.

When I stepped into the brightly lit room, I was surprised to find Haze, aka not a janitor, already standing at the sink, staring out into the darkness beyond the window. Trying my best to ignore the giant of a man, I focused on the kitchen itself. It was a large room but as run-down as the rest of the house. What was once a beautiful home had been left to fall into a ruin, and the thought of having to live here with these men was too much to deal with tonight.

There were a lot of cabinets, so I decided to ask. "Do you know if there are any glasses?"

He didn't show a lick of surprise by my presence, as if he'd known I was there all along. "High shelf next to fridge."

I'd forgotten how low and rumbly his voice was, and how few words he used to get his point across. As scary as he was, Haze still intrigued me, and I found myself searching for a reason to pry more words from him. "I'm surprised that you're part of this punishment."

That caught his attention as he turned away from whatever he'd been staring at in the darkened grounds beyond the window. Leaning back against the old silver sink, he crossed his arms over his chest and raised an eyebrow at me.

Okay then.

"I just meant, that you don't really seem like the *group activities* kind of guy. Unless of course the only ones you do jump in on are fights?"

There was no change in his expression as he observed me. His unwavering attention was disconcerting, and I found myself wondering if I'd ever get used to his intensity. "I protect my friends."

That was it. The only explanation. I didn't have a clue which of the douchebags out there were his friends, although I had a sneaking suspicion that there was a lot more to the relationship between *all* five men than anyone else knew. Even in my short time amongst them, I'd noticed a familiarity. Not to mention, why else would they need an NDA?

The intensity of Haze's gaze was different from Brodie's. He quietly assessed, and I had no doubts that if asked, he'd be able to identify every part of my clothes and features if he had to describe me to the police.

"Guess I better get to bed," I said with a shrug, having no idea what else to say.

"It's not even nine."

Did that mean he didn't want me to go to bed, or was it a simple noting of the time?

I decided to try and lighten the mood. "Yep, but some of us had a very stressful day and need our beauty sleep to recover."

No response, but his expression remained assessing as he continued to unwaveringly stare at me. Deciding it was now or never, I headed for the cabinet with the glasses and grabbed one, noting it was dusty. He was still in front of the sink, so I slowed my steps when I got closer, giving him a chance to get out of the way. He took a massive step to the side, leaving a large gap between us, as if he was afraid I'd throw myself at him.

Yeah, right, buddy. He was well over a foot taller than me and built like a freakin' linebacker. Sure, he was gorgeous, as was every other man in this house, and all of them were more approachable than Haze, even Connor, the gun-toting psycho.

Lowering my cup under the faucet, I reached out to get the water going. It took two hands for me to turn the stiff tap, and with an ear-piercing whine, the faucet finally started to drip water. Turning the tap harder, I screeched when the water sputtered, spraying me in the face.

Jumping back on instinct, I threw my arms out to the side and accidentally brushed my hand against Haze's arm. A guttural snarl filled the kitchen, and choking on my panic, I spun from the spurting sink to find Haze with his fists raised, looking like he was about to start throwing punches. The threat of violence hung heavy in the air as I lifted my shaking hands above my head and crouched to make myself smaller.

Not even a second later, Brodie sprinted into the kitchen and threw himself between me and the big man.

"Haze! Hey, buddy. You're okay. No one is touching you. It's okay."

He started to talk him down, in this low, soothing tone, and it weirdly worked on me as well, as I felt myself relaxing. Maybe that was part of the intrigue I felt around Haze—we both dealt with invisible demons.

When Haze lowered his hands, I caught sight of the minute tremble in them. The rage in his face faded until he wore that mask of indifference, though his eyes were screaming chasms of darkness. "Fuck. Sorry."

That was the second mumbled apology I'd gotten from him,

and then he was out of the room so fast it was hard to believe anyone his size could move like that.

Before I fully processed what had happened, Brodie had spun around to wrap his arms around me. His hands were frantic as they ran over my shoulders and down my arms. "Are you okay, Evie? I'm so sorry. We should have told you to never touch Haze, no matter what the circumstances are. He didn't hurt you, right?" He pulled back to look me over, and even in my dazed state, I managed to answer.

"No. He didn't lay a hand on me."

Brodie wrapped one arm around me and, with his free hand, turned off the tap. "Come on, sweetheart. I'll drop you in your room and make sure nothing else happens."

The fact that I needed an escort in the house I had to live in, and I'd signed an NDA to not reveal anything these guys did here, didn't bode well for my future.

My family had sent me here to be safe, but I might have wandered from one gunfight into an entirely different but equally deadly situation.

EVELYN

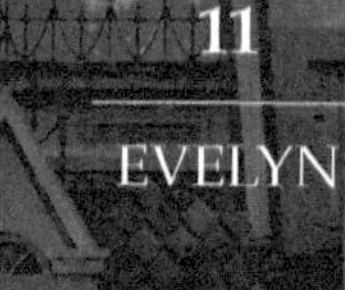

I t was no shock to me whatsoever that I didn't sleep that first night. Not a single moment. Every time I closed my eyes, I saw the gun in Connor's hand and then it morphed into the gunman who'd attacked my last college. How many innocent bystanders had been shot and killed as he stalked through campus, calling out my name? Taunting me?

Evelyn Cromwell...come out, come out, wherever you are...

Sleep was overrated anyway. Around two in the morning, I got up and distracted myself with studying. At least I could stay on top of my academic work even if my mental health had gone to shit.

My Friday schedule was light, with just one class in the late afternoon and—if memory served me correctly—none of the guys were in that class. Then again, I hadn't been paying a huge amount of attention to Haze or Connor. Andrew was the only one who'd made a noticeable effort to befriend me, for some fucking reason, and Brodie was, well, Brodie Keller.

I was more than ready for a break by the time the sun was up. The whole house was silent when I unlocked my room and headed downstairs. None of the guys really struck me as early risers, except maybe Ethan. But maybe he'd already have left for work? He must have other classes to teach.

Shit. Just thinking about Ethan had me touching my lips and remembering that kiss. And then remembering the fact that four guys who owe me no loyalty all saw it happen. Would they turn us in to the dean? There seemed to be no love between Ethan and Connor, despite the fact they were brothers.

Then again…would the NDA cover me as much as it covered all of them?

I made a mental note to check the contract, then headed out of the house in search of coffee. We really needed to tackle the grocery situation, because it was a hike to get to the dining hall for every meal. Trouble was, we'd need to leave the security of campus to get those groceries.

As early as it was, the coffee shop was quieter than I usually found it. Nina's friend Sven was seated near the window, reading a theory of relativity textbook and sipping his usual matcha chai latte. He waved to me with a smile as I entered, so after I ordered my coffee, I went to join him.

"We heard you moved out of Marigold dorm yesterday," he said by way of greeting, and I groaned. So much for keeping that quiet.

"Does everyone know everything around here?" Holy hell, what if people already knew that I'd kissed Ethan in the library? Did they know that the guys living with me in Bluebell House were all secretly friends of some sort? Surely not, or why did I sign that fucking contract?

Sven grinned. "You've met Nina, what do you think? She feels awful, by the way. She even tried to go to Dean Attworth and explain it was her who had attacked Laura, but he wasn't buying it. Apparently, Laura was adamant it'd been you, and someone else confirmed her story with an eyewitness account?"

I glowered, folding my arms. "Probably Andrew, the fucking

traitor. Totally took Laura's side even though I was nowhere near the bitch."

Sven shrugged. "He's pretty whipped by her, it makes sense. So is it true they made you all move into Bluebell House? That place is one hundred percent haunted."

"Brodie thinks so too," I agreed with a laugh. "It's just a house. A really rundown, old house, but it's got good bones."

A sly smile crept over Sven's face. "Brodie thinks that, does he? Are you guys friends now?"

I groaned again, remembering his infectious energy last night, how he'd insisted on calling me *bestie* and then how he'd kissed my cheek and nearly made me faint. Fuck, he was as gorgeous as on screen, but I'd really thought he'd be a total arrogant twat in person. His celebrity status was so huge, surely he would have an ego to match? But no...he was just as likeable in person as he was onscreen. Infuriating.

"Just watch yourself, Eve. He's a *huge* playboy. You're alluring, mysterious fresh meat right now, and he, among others, probably just wants to score." He was warning me with the best of intentions, I was sure, but that comment stung nonetheless.

I gave a hollow laugh. "Or maybe I have a great personality, and he wants to be friends without wanting to fuck me. Maybe." I shrugged, trying to cover my hurt feelings at being reduced to little more than fresh meat. No, I didn't seriously think Brodie and I could fall in love, but was it really *so* preposterous to consider tolerable as friend material?

"Eve, I didn't mean—" Sven started to backtrack, but the barista called out my name and I stood up.

"It's cool, Sven. I get it. I'm heading to the library, but I'll see you around." I hurried over to the counter and collected my huge drink, then exited the shop before Sven could apologize further. I was embarrassed, more than anything, because it wasn't until he said it that I realized I'd been getting a bit stupid about my friendship with Brodie. My therapist told me I already had attachment issues due to my daddy issues, which were compounded after the attack. I clung to anything that made me feel good, even if it wasn't actually good for me.

Brodie's attention made me feel good, but that didn't mean he actually liked me.

He wanted something, whether it be information or sex, but he wasn't being nice for the sake of being nice. Was he?

With a heavy sigh and a sour mood, I headed to the library. I had my laptop in my room and plenty of high-speed internet, but there was just something about the *smell* of a library. The quiet simply couldn't be replicated, and it gave a certain sense of calm that helped me sort my head out.

Like trying to figure out why Connor pulled a gun on me simply to make me sign a contract.

There was something seriously suspicious going on in that house, with those guys, and while part of me wanted to figure it all out, another part was sure I should have nothing to do with their drama. It wasn't my business. I'd just been in the wrong place, wrong time.

"I hoped I would find you here, Eve. Or is it Lilith today?"

I startled so sharply, I nearly spilled my drink. Nearly. That would have been an infraction worse than breaking Laura's nose—if I had actually been responsible for that.

"Ethan," I gasped, breathless in my shock. "What...um... what are you doing here?"

His brows hitched, and a small smile curved his lips. He was leaning against a huge shelf, a book in hand like he'd been looking for something when I arrived. I glanced around with a small frown. This area seemed...vaguely familiar.

"You didn't come here looking for me?" he asked, bemused.

Ignoring the twist in my gut at being near him, I realized exactly why this area looked familiar. This was where I'd run that first day in my panic attack, and I'd subconsciously walked right to it again, searching for the calm I'd felt in those few seconds Ethan had kissed the thoughts away.

As I met his stare, I waited for embarrassment, but instead there was just this weird sense of right*ness*. "Are you saying this is our spot, Professor Sullivan?"

Fuck me. Was I flirting, or was I trying to remind him that he was my professor?

Or was I doing both?

Was Ethan another attachment issue for me to deal with? And did I even care when his mere presence silenced the panic and anxiety I'd lived with for months?

He moved closer, until we were only a few feet apart. "What if I said that it was? Would you meet me here again?"

He was so relaxed and casual in his approach, and I had no idea how to handle it. He was the authority figure and would lose his job instantly if we were caught, but he showed absolutely no concern in pushing *whatever it was we were doing* in public.

"This isn't a good idea." That statement would have had more strength if my voice hadn't been so breathless. I really just wanted to kiss him again—to lose myself in one of the hottest men I'd ever seen in my life, who didn't hide in the shadows, who showed me what he wanted.

Ethan stepped even closer, and if anyone came across us now, there'd be some explaining to do. "I've got to get to class," he said softly. "But I need you to meet me here tomorrow, sweetheart. Just make it thirty minutes earlier."

He pressed his lips to the corner of my mouth, his tongue sweeping across my lip as if he needed to taste me, and then he was gone.

By the time I opened my eyes and caught my breath, it felt like the world had tilted. Everything spun, and I debated if I should race after him and demand he finish that kiss or race home and finish myself in the shower.

Because fuck. There was only so much teasing a girl could take before she combusted.

Stumbling over myself, I manage to get it together in time to collapse into one of the study desks. When I pulled out the assignment I'd been working on since two that morning, I got to work, only stopping when my skin suddenly prickled.

I wasn't sure who I expected it to be, but when Haze's dark eyes met mine, I found myself blinking like an idiot. His huge frame was crammed into a small study desk, and I was tempted to laugh. Or I would have been if every single part of him wasn't intimidating as heck.

He had his computer in front of him, but he wasn't bothering to even look at the screen, keeping that intense stare locked on my face. Was this about last night? Should I say something so he knows I'm not mad at him? I mean, he scared the fuck out of me, and I would like to know if there was a possibility that he'd actually physically hurt me if I accidentally touched him again, but other than that, I understood trauma.

He had trauma in spades.

It was almost comforting to know I wasn't the only one super fucked-up.

Deciding I didn't mind his gaze on me—it almost felt protective—I got back to my assignment, and by the time I packed up for lunch, my stomach screaming at me, Haze was gone, and I felt more at peace.

In the dining hall, I didn't see Nina or anyone else I knew, so I just headed over to order. By the time I'd decided on the pasta special and grabbed a salad to go with it, there were more students piling in.

"Evie babe!"

Half the room turned as Brodie's shouted, and I wondered if I'd be able to slip out the door and pretend I didn't see him standing in the middle of the room. Fuck. He looked good, hands on his hips, giving Xander Stone from *Bloodstone Sentinel* vibes. Brodie had been in the industry from a young age, one of those nepo babies whose father starred in daytime soaps. But his biggest claim to fame was when he was cast as the newest superhero in the largest franchise in the world.

Bloodstone Sentinel was powered from a rare stone found on an alternate Earth and cast into Xander's chest during a blood supermoon. Brodie Keller filled the role like he'd been born to play it, and here in Meadowridge College, wearing jeans and a faded band T-shirt, all I could see was Xander Stone.

This could not be my life.

When I didn't move, he called again. "Bestie, I *know* you're not ignoring me. Baby girl, you're breaking my heart."

He pressed his hand against his chest, and when his lower lip wobbled, a chick sitting at a table nearby all but sobbed as she yelled at me, "Get your ass over there, new girl! If you hurt Brodie Keller, we're going to hurt you."

With that, the faked sadness on Brodie's face dried up. He nailed her with a glare, and there was no mistaking him when he growled, "Don't ever threaten Eve. That's my last warning."

Shaking my head, I hurried across to him before another cafeteria fight broke out. There was no reason to avoid Brodie —at least not while I needed him as an ally in the house from hell—as long as I never forgot I was nothing more than a conquest to him. He didn't care about a deluded weirdo who formed inappropriate attachments to fill the gaping voids in her soul.

Thanks, Dr. Graystone, for that enlightenment.

If I could remember that, there was no reason not to enjoy the benefits of a hot superstar flirting with me.

EVELYN

Sleep was only marginally easier to achieve that night, and only because I was exhausted from not sleeping the night before. Even so, I woke myself up at least five times with nightmares. By morning I was almost *more* tired from fighting with my sheets and running from invisible bad guys than if I hadn't slept at all.

It was a worry. My nightmares had been awful right after the attack, when I woke up in hospital and came to terms with what had happened. When the doctors explained how close I'd come to dying, I was haunted by the most disturbing dreams and eventually prescribed medication to help me sleep dreamlessly. I hadn't needed to take those pills for a few months, though, and no longer had them.

Stupid me. I wasn't *healed*; I'd just repressed the , and Connor's gun in my face ripped it all right back to the surface.

"Good morning, sunshine!" Brodie greeted me when I dragged my feet into the kitchen not long after sunrise.

I paused, squinting at him, and then checked the time on my phone. Yep, the sun had just come up and it was the weekend. What the fuck was he doing awake so early? Andrew sat beside him at the kitchen table, sipping something hot from a mug. Did we get a coffee machine?

"Give her a minute to wake up," Andrew scolded, putting his mug down, then smacking the back of Brodie's head with a rolled-up newspaper. "She's not used to your level of permanent energy, bro. Fuck it, neither am I. I forgot how exhausting you can be."

Brodie just laughed, a warm, easy sound. "Don't lie. You missed me, Drew."

"What—" I started to say, then yawned. "What the fuck is going on?" I tried again.

Andrew gave Brodie a pointed look, and the Bloodstone Sentinel himself jumped up to grab a premade iced coffee from the huge refrigerator.

"Brown sugar oat milk shaken espresso, right?" he asked, presenting me with the coffee and grinning like a goofball.

I accepted it and moved to sit at the table when he gestured for me to join them. "Thanks," I murmured, taking a sip. "That was thoughtful of you."

"We figured you'd need it," Andrew said absentmindedly as he read his newspaper like a sixty-year-old man. "After the night you had."

I winced. That told me all I needed to know about how thin the walls were. "Sorry. It's not usually so bad, but—"

"Connor made things worse." Andrew cut me off with a nod and had me wondering if he somehow knew what had happened to me at Tennessee Hallows College. "Understandable."

I cleared my throat, searching for a change of subject. "How come you guys are awake so early? Do you have a weekend class?" Some people did, but it wasn't super common from what I'd seen last weekend.

"Nope, I've got an audition to go to," Brodie replied with an excited smile. "My agent is picking me up in an hour or so. It's a really exciting new role, and I'm up against some huge names. Wanna help me run lines to prep? Andrew fucking sucks at this."

Confused, I blinked between them both, then took a huge gulp of coffee. Maybe I was still half-asleep.

"A new role?" I asked, unable to help myself. "Not Bloodstone?"

Brodie shook his head. "Nope, it's totally different. Female-focused romantic drama adapted from a novel. I'm auditioning for one of the main love interests, a snowboarder." He slid a thick wad of paper across the table to me. "Have a look, tell me what you think."

My jaw dropped as I read the title and all the *Confidential* stamps littering the first page. "Um, Brode, I can't read this! It's—"

"Protected under that NDA you signed," he replied with a smirk. "You're fine. Go ahead. My role would be Drex Slater."

Shocked, I looked back at the script he'd given me to read. Funnily enough, I was familiar with the source material, as the romance novel was on my e-reader, but had no idea it was being made into a movie. This was huge. And perfect for Brodie to break away from superhero typecasting, too.

"Do you have any plans today, Evelyn?" Andrew asked, pulling my attention from the script I'd just started leafing through. "After you help Brodie run lines, of course."

I shook my head. "Not really. I'd kind of like to do some work to tidy this place up but need to get supplies. Is there a hardware store nearby?"

He gave a small nod, putting his newspaper down. "Yes, there's one in town. You can't go alone, though, and I have a polo match."

Brodie scoffed a laugh. "Because you were ever an option to head into town, Knightsbridge. Ethan can take her in when he wakes up."

I frowned, rubbing at my temples. "Why can't I go alone?" Aside from the fact I wouldn't *want* to, no one knew I was even in Vermont, let alone attending Meadowridge. I was safe...at least I was pretty sure I was. Unless Andrew really did know about the crazy fuck who'd shot up my last college in his attempt to kill me...

He met my gaze across the table, his expression unreadable. Then his jaw tightened slightly. "Because how will you get there, for starters? And then how will you carry all your supplies? Not to go sounding antifeminist, but surely it'd help to bring some muscle along to do the heavy lifting?"

Okay, he had valid points. And I didn't hate the idea of going into town with Ethan, since I had spent far too long thinking about that latest kiss in the library *again*. Maybe we needed to finally talk things out. Or fuck.

I knew which one had my vote.

"Fine. I'll wait for Ethan, if he has a car. We can pick up some groceries, too. Do you guys have any allergies or whatever?"

"Just Connor—no shellfish, remember? But I can write you a list," Andrew offered, pulling out his phone. "What's your phone number?"

I recited it out loud and noticed Brodie saved it to his phone as well. When I gave him a look, he just shrugged as if to say, *we're besties now.*

Andrew muttered something about putting together a shopping and supply list, then washed his mug and left the kitchen.

"So will you help me prepare for my audition?" Brodie asked once we were alone. "The excerpt is highlighted on page forty-seven."

I flipped through to the highlighted scene, then snorted a laugh. "You had Andrew reading lines with you? Did he use a girl voice or...?" Because the piece in question was Brodie's character interacting with the female main character. Flirting, to be precise.

Brodie pouted. "I asked him to, but he wouldn't do it. No wonder I couldn't feel the scene."

Chuckling, I took another sip of my coffee and sighed. "I guess I can help, seeing as you did buy me coffee. I should warn you, though, I'm a crappy actress."

"You couldn't possibly be worse than Andrew," Brodie replied enthusiastically, tapping the page. "Start here when you're ready."

For the next hour, I ran lines with Brodie and tried really fucking hard to remember that we were *acting* and Brodie wasn't flirting with *me*. I had fun with it, but I was quietly relieved when his agent arrived to drive him to the audition.

My phone chimed five minutes later, and I pulled it out to see that Andrew had started a group text thread.

> Andrew Knightsbridge: Here's the list of food
> for the house. The school has a running tab
> with both the hardware store and the grocery
> store. They will be covering the expenses.

Below there was a very long list of what looked like mostly health foods, including five different protein powders. Holy fuck. I was definitely going to have to sneak some junk food in there, or the weeks of my period would be a bloodbath. And I wasn't even talking about literal blood.

Another message popped up a second later.

> Connor: Was it really necessary to use your full
> name, asshole? I'm fairly certain even
> Cinderella could have figured out who the
> message was from with just "Drew."

Even Cinderella—*that motherfucker*. I was really starting to hate Connor Sullivan.

> Eve: Oh, you forgot the oysters, Andrew
> Knightsbridge. But don't worry, I won't forget.
> Shellfish is my favorite.

You pulled a gun on me; I poison your food. It was called balance.

Or karma.

> Brodie: LMFAOOOOO I leave you all alone for
> five minutes and all hell breaks loose. I've
> never been so excited to finish up an audition
> and get back home. Might want to stock up on
> EpiPens, Con.

And sleep with one eye open.

> Ethan: Meet you out the front in five minutes,
> Eve. The rest of you, sort your shit out. You
> don't want me to sort it for you.

Well, fuck. When Ethan took charge like that, it had me imagining him in charge in other ways, and if I didn't get laid soon, my lack of sleep was going to be the least of my worries.

Racing to my room, I grabbed my shoes and bag before checking my reflection in the bathroom and deciding that would have to do. There was no hiding the lack of sleep reflected in dark circles under my eyes or how pale my normally tanned skin looked. Ethan hadn't appeared turned off by my haggard appearance yet, and I was too exhausted for more than the minimal effort.

Okay, maybe lip gloss, because I wasn't a complete troll.

There was no one downstairs when I walked through, and I headed out front to find Ethan already parked and waiting. I eyed his ride, a black Suburban with heavily tinted windows, looking like a I-travel-with-bodyguards style of celebrity car.

"Nice ride," I said as Ethan moved around to open my door

for me. "Is this yours?" I hadn't known many teachers who could afford a car this fancy.

"Nope. It's mine."

I closed my eyes at the familiar, annoying voice behind me. Connor had followed me out of the house and was apparently pushing to be murdered today. Not that he was worth a lifetime in jail.

Ethan looked apologetic as he took my hand and led me to the passenger side. "Sorry, it's bulletproof, and we wouldn't fit much in my Porsche. More importantly, I want you to be safe."

I eyed him closely, wondering why they'd think I needed a bulletproof car to be safe. Did they know about the shooting at my last school? Was my cover blown already?

No. They'd have said something if they knew.

Most probably it was how I'd reacted to the gun being pulled in my face, and they assumed this would keep me from another panic attack. Actually...knowing it was bulletproof did ease a small sliver of tension I'd been carrying about leaving the school.

"Thanks, that does make me feel safer."

Ethan smiled, and after ensuring I was buckled in, strolled around to the driver's side.

The back door opened as he got in, and I spun to see Connor sliding onto the seat. "What the hell are you doing?" I asked, annoyed that he was here. It might be his car, but dangerous or not, I'd rather take a fucking bicycle than drive with this asshole.

"I need some shit from the store," he said simply, relaxing against the leather. "You'll barely even notice that I'm here."

Right. Because it was easy to forget six and half feet of asshole, who looked like a Greek god, with the personality of a garden gnome.

Ethan looked equally unimpressed. "Act right when you're out with us, Connor."

Connor held both hands up in front of him as he shrugged. "I'll be a perfect angel as long as Evelyn is one."

Deciding that my best bet of both of us surviving was for me to ignore him, I focused on Ethan. "What classes other than Economics of Crime do you teach here?"

There was a snort from the back. "Finally remembered that he's a teacher, did you?"

Ethan took a cue from me, ignoring Connor as he proceeded to explain all the courses he was involved in at the college. He was awfully young to be such a highly regarded professor at an even higher-regarded college, but apparently, he'd graduated high school two years early and was somewhat of a genius.

He never said it in so many words, but I could read between the lines.

It was relaxed and easy to converse with Ethan, made even more enjoyable by how frustrated Connor got every time he made a comment and we continued to pretend he wasn't there.

With his good looks, money, and power, it was clear that he'd rarely—if ever—had his presence ignored. But none of that shit would fly with me. You had to bring more to the table than superficial status symbols for me to give you my time or energy.

Sure, it might be a bit petty, but he'd been asking for it. If he wanted to be treated with respect, then he needed to return the favor. And soon.

Otherwise, the next six months of us all living in Bluebell House were going to feel like ten years.

EVELYN

We managed to make it through the hardware and grocery store without incident. Connor was on his best behavior, without a single snarky comment crossing his lips. He even lent his muscles to help get the sander, scraper, tools, and many gallons of paint into the back of his SUV.

He helped me get through Andrew's list and even joined in when I added my own array of junk food, much to Ethan's amusement. "Weird to see you not acting like an asshole. I'm starting to get concerned."

Connor shrugged. "Don't get used to it. I'm just trying to keep the peace for a few minutes."

Something told me Ethan was absolutely not getting used to it. He'd been so great during our outing, as well, and for a brief moment, as we argued about how to tell if the watermelon was ripe, it was almost as if we were a couple, doing our weekly shopping.

No attachments. Despite how familiar and safe they felt, these guys were strangers, and I couldn't forget it.

No one had to show their identification when we reentered

the college grounds, and when I asked about it, Ethan said, "Connor has special privileges that wouldn't be afforded to most."

Shocker.

I was surprised when Connor didn't make a comment about how much better he was than me, choosing to just sit in the back surrounded by grocery bags. When Ethan pulled up in front of the house, Andrew and Haze were already waiting, and I was left to twiddle my thumbs as the four men carted everything into the house. Oh, wait, they did let me carry the smallest grocery bag that only held extra cleaning supplies.

"That's what we're here for," Haze said shortly, carrying so many bags I couldn't see his damn arms. He was determined to get half of everything in one trip, and he did it with style.

Deciding my time was best spent putting it all away, I took out the cleaning supplies first and wiped down all the shelves in the pantry, fridge, and freezer. Thankfully, the appliances were fairly new, and after I got all of the cold and frozen items away, I moved on to organizing the pantry.

Andrew stopped in to supervise for a few seconds, and I tried not to smirk as his brow furrowed when I tossed a second bag of chips on the lower shelves—along with cookies, popcorn, and bags of candy. "For movie nights," I said innocently, looking over my shoulder.

I almost laughed at how adorably confused he looked that his order hadn't been carried out without a single deviation. Poor guy, he'd be used to it by the time he finished living with me.

"Where did you want to start with getting the house into shape?" Ethan asked as he strolled in, paint tins in hand.

"Eve's room," Andrew said, and I was shocked enough to stumble as I attempted to navigate all the empty grocery bags on the floor.

"Wait, no," I said as I caught my footing and straightened.

"There's no need for me to go first. Maybe we should focus on shared spaces?"

Ethan shook his head. "Andrew is right. You're the only one of these assholes who doesn't deserve to be here. Your room is first."

He headed out then, and a few seconds later I could hear him hauling shit up the stairs. All of the food was away now, so I went to help the guys tackle my room.

First we got all the furniture out or covered up, and it was Connor—to my surprise—who showed the most skill as he sanded my floors, before sealing the wide boards with a dark stain. "Try not to walk on them for a few hours," he said. "We can finish your walls tomorrow."

While I'd been cleaning up the dust and other debris from the floors, Haze and Ethan had been prepping my walls, scraping off the old paint and wallpaper, before getting everything undercoated. Andrew had been mostly supervising and helping me clean. His anal-retentive ways meant he cleaned like he was the boy in the bubble and a speck of dust would kill him.

"Hopefully the smell will be completely gone by night," Ethan said, looking around with a worried expression. "We got all the low-VOC and environmentally friendly products, so it really should." Plus, they'd left all the windows open and the fan on to give everything a chance to dry before I had to sleep in there tonight.

Connor, standing there covered in dust and giving blue-collar vibes for the first time, scoffed. "I'm sure she can share your bed, Eth, if hers is out of service."

I guess now was when nice Connor fucked right off to make way for the asshole again. It had been a nice reprieve.

I expected Ethan to snap back, but he just leveled the hottest fucking look I'd ever seen on me. "Excellent plan. Thanks, bro."

Connor shook his head. "You're the worst fucking professor. You know that, right?"

Turning away to hide my pink cheeks, I half-hoped that the stain and paint scents lingered for a few days, because it was growing abundantly clear that at some point Ethan and I would be fucking. Neither of us was trying to fight our attraction, and as far as I knew, there was only one way to get this level of attraction out of our systems. Just as long as I *did not get attached.*

"Like I give a fuck what you think," Ethan replied with a shrug.

"I think you all need a shower," Andrew announced, casting a disgusted look my way. "Might I suggest a cold one, Eth? Things are getting a bit heated."

Ethan just smirked, looking a whole lot like Connor in that moment. "Great idea. You wanna join me, Lilith?"

"What the fuck did you call her?" Connor snarled, and at the same time, Haze knocked over the ladder propped against the hallway wall. It went down with a crash and startled me enough to realize how out of hand things had gotten.

As quick as possible, I grabbed some clean clothes from the chest of drawers we'd moved into the hall and ducked into the shared bathroom. After just a short hesitation, I locked the door.

What was going on with me and Ethan? He wasn't even remotely trying to hide his attraction, and neither of us had addressed the age gap or taboo nature of our roles within Meadowridge. I really, really needed to have a serious chat with him before I slipped and fell onto his dick.

To my relief—and slight disappointment—no one knocked on the door to interrupt my shower, but I kept it brief anyway. The house had three bathrooms, but one was in desperate need of a gut-out renovation and wasn't currently usable. Which meant I needed to be mindful of others waiting on this bathroom.

After I dressed, I checked my phone and found a message from Nina asking if I wanted to meet her and Ursa for dinner. I debated declining, but then glanced at my room, which wouldn't be habitable again for hours. Downstairs, the raised voices of an argument echoed up to me, and I grimaced. Somehow, I had a feeling that was about me, so I replied to Nina and said I'd be there shortly.

Not wanting to be saddled with another escort, I slipped quietly out the back door while the guys continued arguing in the living room. None of them saw me, and by the time I reached the main campus, I found I could breathe a little easier. It had gotten more intense than I'd expected in the house with all the guys.

"Yay, you made it!" Nina exclaimed when I approached her little picnic set up on the lawn. "I wasn't sure if you had like a curfew or something..." She trailed off with a grimace, and I shook my head.

"Nah, nothing like that."

She'd already cornered me yesterday to apologize for breaking Laura's nose, so we'd moved past that. But I *knew* she'd want gossip from the house, and I was legally bound to hold my tongue.

"So...tell us everything," Nina urged with a grin. "What's it like? Are they being nice or total assholes? Has anyone punched anyone? Give us the juicy details, girl."

"Yes!" Ursa enthused. "Tell us!"

I bit the inside of my cheek, already regretting coming out when I couldn't *actually* talk about what was going on in Bluebell House. Then again...the NDA said I couldn't disclose anything *true*. It said nothing about spinning absolute bullshit. The guys all seemed determined to cultivate the idea they were arch enemies—Connor and Andrew in particular—so why not play along with that idea?

"It's *awful*." I groaned dramatically. "They're constantly at each other's throats. I seriously wouldn't be surprised if someone gets smothered with a pillow before long. And to be fair, it might be me doing the smothering."

Nina winced. "That bad? Shit, girl, I am so freaking sorry. I'll go to Dean Attworth again and see if there's anything I can do."

I shrugged. "It's fine. Seriously. Connor just has a really awful singing voice, and he insists on putting on a full-length Eras Tour performance every time he showers. Also, Andrew keeps using my razor and not rinsing the hair off." I gave a dramatic shudder, giggling internally at my fabricated gossip.

Nina and Ursa were one hundred percent lapping it up, too. "You're kidding! For his face?" I shook my head ominously, and Nina gagged. "Ew. Come on. Ewww. Maybe it's his legs? He seems like the kind of guy who might shave his legs, sort of?"

"He's the kind of guy who shaves his balls, too," Ursa added with a giggle.

For the love of all hell, now she had me thinking about Andrew's balls, and whether shaving them made his dick look bigger. Did he need those kinds of optical illusions? I really didn't want to find out, did I? No. Definitely not. Okay, maybe a little bit...

Pushing the mental image—entirely made up—of Andrew's dick out of my head, I focused on making up more harmless but ridiculous lies about the guys I lived with. Mostly about Connor and Andrew, to be fair. Brodie was too fucking likeable, and Haze genuinely scared me, so I wasn't keen to get on his bad side. And then there was Ethan. I was worried Nina would see right through me if I so much as said his name, so I danced all the way around the teacher supervision subject.

The girls convinced me to join them for a dorm party at Sven's building, and it was *fun*. More fun than I'd had in a long time, despite my refusal to drink anything.

Sven was kind enough to walk me home, which I was quietly relieved about since it was after midnight and the path through the woods was creepy at the best of times. I could have taken the road, but it was nearly three times the distance, as it circled around the outskirts of the campus.

The floorboards creaked as I let myself into the house as quietly as possible, and I wrinkled my nose. The last thing I needed was a lecture about ignoring my phone...which I'd done plenty of over the last few hours.

Fortunately, no one popped out of the closet to scold me. In fact, the whole house was silent. Were the guys asleep already? Tiptoeing my way upstairs, I noted that their bedroom doors were closed so it was possible. Or maybe they'd all gone out? It was Saturday night, after all.

Stepping into my room, I gagged at the strong smell of floor stain. The windows I'd left open had blown shut, and the fumes were lingering like a bitch. Someone had thoughtfully moved my bed back into the room so I could sleep, but just the few minutes I spent in there changing my clothes gave me a headache. There was no way I could spend a whole night inhaling that smell.

With a sigh, I gathered my pillow and blankets up in my arms and quietly padded back downstairs. The house itself had plenty of empty bedrooms but none were furnished, and I really wasn't in the mood to go hauling beds around in the middle of the night.

The couch would be just fine.

I made myself a cozy nest, then snuggled into it and closed my eyes, only to immediately open them again when the house creaked ominously.

"Stop it," I hissed. "You're not haunted, no matter what Brode thinks."

That was what I kept telling myself, over and over, until I eventually fell asleep.

14

EVELYN

My breathing was too loud. Way too loud. He was going to hear me, find me, and kill me. I needed to hold my breath, but it was so hard, with panic throttling my chest. Sprinting through the halls had left me winded and gasping, so all I could do was cover my mouth and attempt to breathe as quietly as I could through flaring nostrils.

"Evelyn Cromwell…I know you're in here somewhere…" The man's voice echoed through the classroom I hid in. Had he seen me dash in here? Or was it just a guess? Shit.

"Come on, Evelyn, no one else has to die. I didn't come here for them; I came for you." His voice wasn't familiar in the least. He was no one I knew, at least not well enough to recognize. Why the fuck was he trying to kill me, though?

Cold sweat dripped down my brow, stinging my eyes, but I didn't move. Couldn't move. He'd already shot at least a dozen people as I ran for my life, and now that he'd informed me he was here to kill me, those deaths were on me. But why? I was no one. Basically an orphan. What had I done to make someone want me dead?

"Evelyn Cromwell…come out, come out, wherever you are…" He sang it in an unhinged kind of way that made me question whether *the shooter was sane at all. Surely not. You didn't just open fire in the middle of a university if you were perfectly balanced in the head.*

Footsteps drew closer and my whole body trembled where I crouched inside a short cabinet. If I were taller, I'd never have fit, but for once my stature had been on my side.

He was going to pass by; he was going to decide the class was empty, and then I'd make a run for it. I'd run as fast as humanly possible and then—

"I've got you, Evelyn," he announced, yanking the door open and grabbing my hair. He dragged me out of the cabinet, and I screamed with all my pent-up terror.

This wasn't how it went. This never happened. He didn't find me in the cabinet; he heard me running and shot me in the back as I fled. That was how it happened, not this.

"Be quiet, Evelyn," he growled. "I've got you now."

Be quiet? Was he insane? I screamed even louder, fighting for my life. Fists flew and legs kicked and my attacker let go.

He. Let. Go.

What the fuck?

From my periphery, I saw a flash of red and gasped when a big man jumped between us—all I could see clearly was his red baseball cap. A cap that shadowed his face as he kept the gunman from touching me again. When strong hands wrapped around my biceps, I wanted to sink into the comfort...until I was shaken.

"Evelyn. You're dreaming. Wake up." He snapped the words at me from arm's length, and his voice seemed...different. Familiar.

I blinked once. Then twice.

"Andrew?" I croaked his name, my throat tight and raw from screaming. *Oh shit.*

"Yeah, it's me. Are you awake now? You were having a nightmare and—" I cut off his explanation by launching myself at him. Not to punch him again, like apparently I'd just done, but to hug him.

I wasn't fully in control of my actions, and I sure as *fuck* wasn't thinking things through. I was just so fucking scared and at the same time so fucking relieved that it was only a dream. Except it wasn't just a dream—part of it was a memory. Most of that had happened...except it'd ended with me being shot and left for dead.

"Uh, there, there," Andrew said, awkwardly patting my back as I sobbed into his shirt. All the adrenaline my body had created in response to my dream imploded, and I couldn't hold back my tears. I couldn't even get words out as my throat seized up, making the most pathetic whine as I cried.

Andrew was awful at comforting, but I'd take it. He was physically here, and I was alive. That was what mattered. I was alive, and I was safe, and I *really* needed a tissue because my nose was streaming just as badly as my eyes.

I sniffed hard to try to rein it in, but Andrew shifted away at the same time and somehow I ended up wiping my snotty nose all down the front of his T-shirt. Whoops.

"Is that—?" he started to ask, withdrawing until he fell backward off the couch. He tumbled to the ground, then sat there staring in abject horror at the mess I'd made of his shirt.

Sniffing and wiping my eyes with my blanket, I tried to get a grip on myself. "S-sorry," I said in a shaking voice. "I d-didn't mean to... I j-just..."

His gaze jerked up from his shirt to my face, and his disgust quickly shifted to cool concern. "It's fine, Evelyn. Really. I just wasn't anticipating...*this*. Uh, I might just go and change, if you're all right now?"

His discomfort was so extreme, I imagined he was physically shrinking away from the wet fabric of his T-shirt. "Yes, sorry, I'm fine. It was just a nightmare. Sorry I screamed." Then I realized his left eye was a little puffy and red. "And sorry for hitting you."

He stood up carefully, brushing a shaking hand over his

pants, then adjusting his somewhat disheveled hair. "No apology necessary, Evelyn. If you're sure you're okay…"

I mustered up a smile and nodded, since he was already backing away from the couch. The moment he saw me nod, he all but ran from the room and a moment later I heard the downstairs shower turn on.

Holy shit. It was just a little snot on his shirt. I didn't vomit in his lap or anything. Talk about an overreaction.

But still, my face burned with embarrassment nonetheless. How mortifying. I bet he'd tell the rest of the house all about it in the morning, as well. Maybe I was better off trying to sleep in my fume-y room after all.

Though, there was very little chance of any actual sleep again tonight, so with that in mind, I grabbed the TV remote and lowered the volume all the way, putting the subtitles on so I could watch without disturbing anyone else. Not that I imagined they'd all slept through my screams.

After aimlessly flicking through dozens of channels, while letting my pulse and heart rate calm, I finally settled on a true crime docuseries. Maybe not the best idea after living my own true crime story, but hey, all the better to see if someone else's misery could trump my own.

Snuggling under the blankets, I focused on the screen, hoping that my thoughts wouldn't slip back to that day. My therapist had said that I kept going back there with such clarity not just because of the trauma but because I had unanswered questions. My mind wouldn't rest or move past what happened when there was still so much unknown.

Who was the man who targeted me? Why was I targeted? What had I done to make that crazy asshole follow me for at least a week before the event? CCTV footage from around the school had picked him up tailing me between classes, among other creepy shit—he'd gone through my trash and been in my dorm room at least once before the day he tried to take me and half the college out.

The police and FBI had surmised that I must have unknowingly rejected him at some point through my two years at the school, giving him a hyperfixation on me that escalated until he cracked.I had no recollection of the shooter but it was plausible. It wasn't that I never went out, and there'd been a few occasions I even drank enough that my night was a touch hazy. So, yes, it was possible I brushed him off unintentionally, and in his unbalanced mind, he'd obsessed over my supposed rejection.

I couldn't believe they'd never found him; it had been a long and intense statewide manhunt.

Until he was behind bars, I'd probably never sleep soundly again.

I'd missed a lot of the docuseries in my musing and was about to turn the TV off and just sit in the darkness when a shadowy figure entered the room. Haze moved with grace and stealth, and if I hadn't been staring directly at the doorway as he walked through, I wouldn't have heard or noticed him at all.

He didn't say a word, taking a seat at the other end of the couch, his gaze on the TV. The reporter was talking about how the two girls had been well-known in the neighborhood and their disappearances had stunned their area.

We sat in silence, and I expected it to feel uncomfortable, but it was actually the opposite.

Haze's presence gave me a sense of peace and calm, shooing away the darker thoughts of my past, and I found myself getting right into the show, trying to guess what the ending was going to be. They had four suspects they'd been tailing across multiple states, all of whom had contact with the sisters before they were abducted.

"Oh, it's the postman for sure," I murmured, not realizing I'd said it out loud until Haze made a disparaging sound.

Turning my gaze toward him, I saw he remained in the exact same position, though he was a little more relaxed.

"You think it was one of the others?" I asked.

His lips twitched, and when he turned to meet my gaze, I wondered why my chest tightened as I stared into his eyes. His expression remained neutral, but I always saw so much in the dark depths of his gaze. "It's the cop."

Swinging back to the show, I gave it all my attention as they started to wrap up the final days when they uncovered the girls buried in shallow graves at the back of the old log cabin in a national park an hour from where they had last been seen. Sure enough, by the time it was finished, it was revealed that the cop who'd been first on the scene to investigate was the serial rapist and killer they'd been searching for all along.

He'd never left his state but had accomplices in other states, making it seem as if the killer was a transient drifter.

"Holy shit. How'd you know?" I whispered to Haze, staring at the small smile tipping up the corner of his mouth. "Have you seen this before?"

He shook his head. "Nah. But it was enough to guess after those first interviews. He gave himself away more than once, showing more of an interest than just that of a cop passionate about his job—he was into it. He was getting off on it."

The series had shown old recorded footage of interviews done by all manner of law enforcement as they hunted for the girls. Apparently if Haze had been partaking in the interviews back then, it wouldn't have taken them six months to figure it all out.

"What did you say your family did?" I asked him suddenly, trying to figure out this enigmatic man. Was there any truth to what Nina had said about him being wanted for espionage in other countries?

His low chuckle took me by surprise; Haze wasn't really the

chuckling type. "If I told you, I'd have to kill you." When his laughter died off, I couldn't figure out if he was serious or not.

He turned back to the TV, where the next crime show had started, and I wondered if he was about to disappear into his room again. Despite how downright scary he was, it was comforting having him close, and to my relief, he didn't move.

"I'm going to guess this one right," I said, mostly to myself but also as a small challenge to the giant scary guy on the couch.

I could feel his gaze on me and wondered if he was smiling again. Even though I was too chicken to find out, I'd pretend he was and that for tonight we were friends.

I felt like Haze Michaels could be a useful friend to have in more than one situation.

Even if I wasn't sure trusting him was good for my overall health.

But hey, I should have died six months ago, so I was already on borrowed time.

Might as well enjoy whatever extra was gifted my way.

15

EVELYN

I drifted off during our third true-crime story, and when I woke up, I was instantly reminded of my nightmares and how awkwardly Andrew had been trying to comfort me. More than that, I wondered how long this would go on before one of the guys demanded to know why I was a bit messed up in the head.

Unless they already knew, which would explain why none of them pushed me for more information. At least, if they knew, we were all on the same page of not talking about it.

Not keen to chat about the night, I ducked out of the house before anyone else was up, and when Ethan asked where I was in the group chat, I made up a lame excuse about working on my assignments.

Not that I was about to head for the library, which was *our* place, so I decided to camp out in Nina's room for the day. She was heading off-campus to go shopping with some of her friends but was more than happy to lend me her desk.

In the morning, I worked on my assignments and even read ahead in several classes. I grabbed an early lunch at the dining hall and took it back to Nina's room, then spent the next few hours reading a book on my e-reader, with my phone turned off.

Nina came back in the early evening with pizza and sodas, and we ate on her floor while she told me all about her day, then showed me her stacks and stacks of new purchases. The girl had a closet to rival the *Vogue* magazine wardrobe, I was sure of it.

"What time is it?" I asked when I was so full of pizza I could barely move.

Nina grabbed my phone off her desk, then frowned. "Why's your phone off? Did you need to charge it?"

"No, I just...didn't want to be bothered while I was reading." I shrugged, like it was a totally normal thing and absolutely not because I was embarrassed to face my hot housemates.

"That explains why you didn't reply about your favorite pizza toppings," she replied, passing my phone to me.

I powered it up, then groaned a little at how many messages popped up on the group chat notification.

> Andrew Knightsbridge: What time do you plan on returning, Evelyn?

> Bloodstone Sentinel: Bro, chill. Leave my bestie alone.

> Connor: Did you seriously change your name to Bloodstone Sentinel? Loser.

> Bloodstone Sentinel: Don't be a hater because you're not a superhero like me, Connie.

> Andrew Knightsbridge: Shut up. Both of you. Evelyn, answer me.

Five-minute gap.

> Andrew Knightsbridge: Evelyn?

Another five minutes.

> Andrew Knightsbridge: Evelyn. Answer my
> question. What time will you be home?

> Haze: Her phone is off. Texting multiple times
> won't make it turn on.

An hour time gap.

> Andrew Knightsbridge: Evelyn. Dinner is at
> seven, we expect you here. Sunday night
> dinner is nonnegotiable.

That message was sent at five-thirty and it was now nine forty-five. Whoops.

At seven thirty, there was another message received but it wasn't in the group chat.

> Brodie: You're in so much trouble, Evie babe.
> Don't worry, I've got your back ;)

Groaning, I rubbed my eyes. These guys were a lot.

"What's up?" Nina asked, tidying up our pizza boxes.

I sighed, remembering my NDA. "Nothing. Just...house drama."

She chuckled, rolling her eyes. "Someone left hair in the drain and Andrew Knightsbridge had an aneurysm?"

I grinned, picturing that scenario. "Something like that. Anyway, I should go. Thanks for letting me steal your room all day. It was nice to be alone."

"Anytime," she replied. "It's the least I can do. Hold up, let me text Sven to walk you home through those creepy woods."

Those creepy woods were supposed to be totally safe, considering they were within the campus grounds and therefore also within the security bubble. But I wouldn't object to having someone to walk with, especially after the nightmare I'd had last night.

My phone dinged as I packed up my stuff, and I glanced at the new message.

> Haze: I'm leaving the chemistry lab in five if
> you want an escort home.

I stared at the message a moment, shocked, then smiled as a warm, fuzzy feeling swirled inside and I replied to accept his offer.

"No need to bother Sven," I told Nina. "Haze is heading that way now. I can walk with him."

Nina's brows shot right the fuck up. "Okay..."

> Haze: Cool. Andrew's in a fucking mood, FYI.

Great. Just great.

I gave Nina a quick hug, then made my way downstairs to find Haze already waiting outside the building.

"Did you skip dinner at the house too?" I asked him by way of greeting.

His eyes traced over me briefly, as if checking I was in one piece, before he said, "No one misses family dinner."

Ah, fuck. I really was going to be in trouble when we got back, but it wasn't my fault Andrew didn't lay out the rules of the house beforehand. I couldn't possibly be expected to know about their Sunday dinners.

"Wait. How long have you all been having Sunday dinners together?"

Their personas at college weren't lining up with what I saw in the house. Behind closed doors, they acted like men who had a long history with each other and were more brothers than friends.

So what was with all the fighting on campus, and why did we all end up in that house together?

"You ask a lot of questions," Haze said.

"It was exactly one question," I said with an eye roll. "Are you going to answer it?"

"Nope." Haze started to walk, and I had to hurry a little to keep up with his long legs, even though he wasn't particularly hurrying.

"At least you don't lie," I muttered.

He stopped suddenly, and I almost crashed into him, which would have been a disaster. I hadn't even realized I'd been walking in his shadow, not leaving enough space between us. "I'll never lie to you, Eve," he said seriously, as I sidled around to stand beside him. "But that doesn't mean you will always want to hear the truth."

"There have been a lot of liars in my life, Haze." My father, for one, was very good at leaving me in the dark, oftentimes literally, as he shoved me wherever he needed me at the time. "So I appreciate the truth. I respect your decision not to tell me about your relationship with the other guys. But be aware, I know that all of you are not enemies. I'm not stupid."

There was the faintest flicker of a smirk at the corners of his mouth. "Never thought you were. Now, let's get you home so Andrew can lose his shit and get over it."

Forcing myself not to groan out loud, I said, "I already have two father figures. I absolutely don't need a third."

This time there was no mistaking Haze's smile. "Knightsbridge might be the worst of the lot."

At this point I really hoped he was joking, but I got the sense that he was dead fucking serious.

We made it back to the house without incident, and I shuddered at how creepy the place looked in the dark. We were slowly working on improving and updating the interior, but the exterior was still the epitome of a haunted mansion.

Haze reached the door and held it open for me, and I took extra care not to touch him as we passed. Weirdly, there was a pull between us when we got closer, and it took more effort than I'd expected to maintain the distance. Whatever had passed between us in our shared time last night had created a connection my body wanted to explore.

Another freaking connection.

It was hard because my trauma and hormones didn't understand a person's preference not to be touched, but thankfully, my brain remained in charge.

At least for now.

Inside, the whole house was lit up, and I was no longer thinking about Haze. Nope. I was mentally preparing myself for the wrath of Andrew Knightsbridge.

"Think I can make a break for my room before he finds me?" I muttered, and the big guy's eyes softened in what I hoped was amusement. He was a tough egg to crack, that was for sure.

"You can certainly try," he said right as I heard a yell.

"Not a fucking chance, Evelyn Lewis. Get your ass into the living room. Now!"

Jesus Christ. Who the hell did Andrew think he was? My voice rose as I yelled back, "I've already explained to Haze, but here it is again. You're not my father, and I'm not part of your family, so there's no obligation on my part to be at any arranged dinner."

He appeared in the doorway, and I wondered how he got those perfectly pressed creases in his striped and monogrammed PJs. Did he have a secret butler hiding in the walls or something? A house elf, maybe?

"Good evening, Evelyn," he said formally, looking me over, and I could have sworn there was a flash of worry in his expression before he smoothed it over. "Can we please have a quick word in the living area?"

He'd somehow calmed himself after his first shouted sentence and was now ultra-polite and intimidating. It would have been more impressive had it not been directed my way.

"Absolutely, Andrew Knightsbridge. It'd be my honor."

He grimaced as he waved a hand for me to proceed first. A quick glance over my shoulder found that Haze still stood in the same spot, watching our exchange. There was the sense that he debated if he should come along and save me.

Had that been what last night was about too? Haze saving me from my nightmares?

I'd assumed he just couldn't sleep either, but as I spent more time with him, I found that Haze was popping up a lot right when I needed him.

In the end, no one followed me as I marched behind Andrew into the living area. We stood close enough for me to see the flare of green in his hazel eyes, and there was a simmering sort of fury tangled up in his expression now. "It's common courtesy," he stated formally, "to let your housemates know when you're dropping off the radar for a full day. For all we knew, you'd been kidnapped and murdered, and we didn't have a clue where to even start looking for your body."

Morbid, but not out of the realm of possibility, considering I still bore the scars of a bullet through my back.

"Okay," I said, keeping my argumentative desires under wraps. "I promise not to do it again."

Andrew scowled. "Okay?"

I nodded. "Okay. Is that all?"

Confusion creased his perfectly handsome face, and amusement bubbled in my chest. He'd totally come at me full-throttle, expecting a blow-out argument, and I'd given him nothing. Diddly squat. No ammunition.

"Um..." He blinked a couple of times, squinting at me like I'd grown a second head. "Yeah. That's all, I guess. Just don't miss Sunday dinner again."

"You mean *family* dinner," I corrected, unable to help myself. That's what he'd called it, even though they were all "enemies."

Andrew's confused gaze shot from me to Haze somewhere behind me, then back again. "Yes. Family dinner."

I shrugged. "Got it. Can I go to bed now, or did you want to bend me over your knee and spank my ass for ignoring your messages?" *Whoops, there went my plan to not poke the bear.*

Whatever I thought Andrew's response was going to be, it sure as fuck wasn't the heated flush in his cheeks. I definitely hadn't anticipated the way his pupils dilated, and his gaze flicked down my body like he was considering how that scene might play out.

Shocked, I took a step back, which snapped him out of... whatever that was.

"Funny," he muttered with a brittle smile. "You can go."

Dismissed. Literally. I was more than fine with it, though, scurrying up the stairs like my ass was on fire. To my surprise, my room was all put back together. The floors looked amazing, and instead of painting the walls, they'd hung wallpaper. Way less fumes, and it meant I could safely close *and lock* my door.

Thank fuck for that stiff, old passage lock.

EVELYN

For once, I didn't get to class early. I dithered outside, drinking my iced coffee, until the very last minute before class and finding a random seat at the back of the room. I didn't give Andrew and Brodie the opportunity to sit with me, and I sure as fuck wasn't leaving myself open to chatting with *Professor Sullivan* before class.

As it turned out, my effort was for nothing. Brodie spotted me, packed up his shit, and moved to where I sat. Except there weren't any spare seats.

"Jessica, right?" he asked the girl I'd chosen to sit beside.

She looked up at him in awe, her mouth open and eyes wide as she nodded.

Brodie flashed his literal million-dollar smile. "Can I sit there, Jessica?"

Poor girl nearly tripped over her feet she stood up so fast, and I stifled a sigh as Brodie slid into her place instead. Ethan had started the class and didn't say anything about the commotion which was...odd. Wasn't it? He didn't usually tolerate shit from *anyone*, but the last few days had proven he and Brodie had known each other a long-ass time.

"Hey, bestie," he whispered as he got out his things once more.

Warmth infused in my chest, and I was finding it harder and harder to remember that Brodie was a world-famous, rich, gorgeous playboy who would most definitely break my heart when his fascination with me had run its course.

"Hey, bestie," I whispered back, because I wasn't ready to stop playing his games yet.

The lonely, broken parts of me that had started with the death of my mom and were made worse by my father's abandonment craved love and the deeper bonds of a true family. "I missed you this morning," he added, his deep blue eyes shining as he propped his head on his hand and stared my way. "Why are you always running out of the house at the crack of dawn? We're starting to think you're avoiding us."

And they'd be correct. "I can't fall behind on schoolwork, and I find it easier to study in the library."

Brodie's lips twitched. "Eth said you weren't there, babe. I'll give you some time to try again."

Fuck. I had to press my lips together to prevent laughter from spilling free. I was busted, but Brodie, thankfully, didn't give me too much shit about it as he nudged me gently and got back to his notes.

For the rest of class, we actually paid attention to Ethan, and I was struck once again by how clever and patient he was. I'd never had a professor explain complex terms in such an easy-to-understand way, and while I was attracted to his looks, of course, it was his personality that really sealed the deal on my interest for the professor.

He'd shown real care toward me on more than one occasion, calming me when no one else in the world would have been able to. He'd taken away my pain and fear and hurt.

Maybe for once, this wasn't about me attaching when I shouldn't. Or at least it wasn't *still* about my attachment issues.

It could build to something real. It was just super frustrating that the one guy who was able to offer me both attraction and peace was also forbidden.

He'd asked me to meet him at the library, but I'd decided it was too risky; I couldn't live with myself if I got him fired.

Not that I'd ever admit it to Brodie, no matter how long he gave me to come up with another story, but a large part of my reason for avoiding the house was avoiding Ethan. It was either avoid him or jump him in the halls and demand he ease the ache he'd created that first day in the library.

When everyone started to pack up around me, I realized class was over and I'd missed the last third of the lecture. Not that it was a huge deal, since I'd already read ahead and had a solid grasp of the concepts we were working on. Brodie stayed with me as we walked down the aisle to exit, only for Ethan to call my name. "Evelyn, would you stay back for a few minutes? I've got a question about your last online quiz submission."

Every week Ethan got us to fill in a short quiz and questionnaire, in the hopes of catching issues early on. I had found it easy enough this week, so I suspected this wasn't about the quiz at all.

"We should wait and talk at the house this afternoon," I said to Ethan, offering him a warm smile.

He remained by his desk, expression neutral as he crossed his arms over his chest. "Evidence suggests that's not going to happen. I'd prefer to speak with you now, since this is your only class for the day, and you've got nowhere else to go."

Brodie wrapped his arm around my shoulders and gave a quick squeeze. "Get it over with, Evie babe," he said, pressing a kiss to my cheek.

His lips were warm, and as his breath fanned across my face, I barely resisted the urge to turn my head slightly and bring our mouths closer together. Brodie Keller was potent, and when he left the room, I was both frazzled and flustered.

A deadly combination, now that I was alone with Ethan.

"Are you doing okay?" he asked quietly, remaining against his desk. "Andrew mentioned you had a pretty bad nightmare the other night, and we all know that's not been the only one."

My throat grew tighter as I recalled the reasons why I was having nightmares. Maybe it was time to try and find another therapist, but the thought of having to spill my entire history again had my skin itching and the urge to run strengthening—not to mention there was some risk involved with it.

The shooter was still out there, and a simple changing of my last name and a purple sheen in my hair didn't mean he wouldn't recognize me if my location was spilled. Equally as bad, in my last school, I'd been looked at with pity, hate, and even fear.

I didn't want that to happen here.

But there was an NDA. That protected me as well as the others, right?

"You're bound by the NDA, too, correct?"

Ethan's eyes narrowed. "I am. But you wouldn't need it to trust me with your secrets."

Weirdly, I believed him. "At my last college, I was involved in a school shooting. When Connor pulled that gun on me, it triggered me badly enough that I've gone back to the horrendous nightmares and insomnia I experienced just after the attack."

Intense therapy had helped me move to a place where I could sleep without drugs and only the occasional nightmare, and it was so frustrating that I'd stumbled so far back.

Ethan's arms twitched, as if he wanted to reach out for me, but he maintained his current position. "Eve. Fuck. I'm so sorry."

He closed his eyes briefly, as if fighting against himself, and I ended up being the one to step closer; Ethan constantly drew me into his orbit. Even with my issues, I'd never felt such an instant bond as I did with this man.

"I'm really okay," I lied, wanting to ease his distress. Not to mention, I still worked on the theory that if I said it enough, it'd eventually be true. "This regression was absolutely to be expected with all the changes in my life. New situations bring on the panic attacks, which is what you saw that first day in the library."

And then again with Connor, the fucking psychopath.

As if he couldn't help himself, Ethan reached for me, his thumb gentle as it brushed across my cheek. "I'm so fucking sorry that happened to you. Were you hurt?"

I silently nod, my throat working as I tried to explain just how badly. "I—I almost died." I sucked in a breath to try and calm my frantically beating heart. "He shot me in the back." My hand moved toward my side, where I'd felt the first piercing pain. "It took months of rehab to get to where I'm at now, and I probably won't ever be able to play sports again like I used to."

I'd been on the soccer and track teams at my old college. Fuck. I'd lost so much, and pushing it all aside in the hopes that I'd eventually move on wasn't cutting it any longer.

"Who was it that hurt you?"

I felt his rasp all the way to my center, and this time I couldn't speak for other reasons. Ethan Sullivan was a fucking nice distraction from the worst day of my life, especially when he wore a murderous stare like he wanted a few minutes alone with my shooter.

"They never caught him. By now they assume he's changed his name and identity. Possibly even left the country. They don't believe he's still a threat to me."

He straightened, and the darkness wreathing his features called to me on a primal level. I'd been subconsciously seeking out *safe but dangerous* men ever since the attack, and Ethan was no different. "He won't ever hurt you again, okay? Not while you're here. That includes the nightmares. It doesn't matter what time of the day or night you need distraction or to talk, I want you to find me."

Before I thought through my actions, I was throwing myself into his arms. There was a moment of shocked hesitation before Ethan wrapped me up so tightly, holding all of me together.

I wasn't fixed. Not even close. But Ethan did what he had done best since the first time I ran into him: he eased my pain.

"Don't run from me," he whispered against my hair. "I won't ask for anything you're not ready to give, and I'll always be your friend, sweetheart. I'll be the best friend you've ever had. Just stop running. It's stressful when I don't know where you are or if you're safe."

A sobbed laugh escaped me. "You'll have to fight Brodie for the best friend title."

Against my hair, I felt Ethan smile. "I'll kick that spoiled punk's ass."

I loosened my grip on him, intending to step away, but somehow, as I tipped my head back to look up at him, our lips brushed. I froze, holding my breath, but then Ethan released the smallest of groans, and my control shattered.

The last two times we'd kissed had been in the height of a panic attack. They'd served to shock me out of the dark corner of my mind and redirect my focus to something a whole lot more enjoyable. But this time, it was entirely different. My fingers threaded into the back of his short hair, and I pulled him down to me, crushing our lips together and eliminating any question of whether I was still attracted to him.

Fuck the rules. He wasn't *that* much older than me anyway. Maybe four or five years? That was my guess, and that hardly constituted it as an "age gap" by romance book standards.

He moaned again as our tongues met, and the sound did incredible things to my insides. Why was that *such* a turn-on?

"Eve..." he groaned between kisses. "*Lilith...*"

I grinned, loving how he'd coined my sexy, sultry alter-ego name. One of his hands was tangled in my hair and the other gripped my ass so tight, I mentally cursed myself for not wearing a skirt. If not for the pesky jeans, he could just—

"Yo. Ethan, dude. *So* not okay." Brodie's voice cut through our make-out session like nails on a chalkboard. "For one thing, you're in the middle of an unlocked classroom where literally anyone could walk in. For another, *you're her teacher!* Do I need to remind you about abusing your power?"

"Brodie...just *fuck off*," Ethan growled, not letting me go. In fact, he dipped back in and kissed my throat while I stared in panic at Brodie. Crap, now my imagination was playing out a fantasy where Brodie came over and joined us...

But no, he just scowled and shook his head, arms folded across his broad chest. "I'll say it again: literally *anyone* could walk in. Or did you want to get fired and removed from campus for indecent conduct?"

Shit. That was the wake-up call I needed, and I peeled myself out of Ethan's embrace.

"I should go," I muttered, not meeting his gaze. "I have a study session this afternoon."

Ethan gusted out a long sigh. "We can talk later. You'll be home for dinner, right? I'm cooking chicken parmesan."

Something about the way he'd asked those questions struck a chord in my chest, and I nodded. "Yep. See you then."

It wasn't until I brushed past Brodie and all but *ran* from that class that I realized why I had such intense butterflies. *Home.* He'd asked if I'd be *home* for dinner...like we really were a family.

For the first time since I was six, when mom died, there was a real sense of belonging in this world. Belonging in Bluebell House. And even though Andrew and Connor kept their distance, the other three were becoming both familiar and important to me.

That was another part of what I'd been running from, these feelings of belonging.

Belonging meant having people and places too important to lose, and I wasn't sure I'd survive it again.

17

EVELYN

The rest of the day was a total blur. All I could think about was kissing Ethan...and then maybe also what it'd be like to kiss Brodie. Ah, hell, I was thinking about a lot more than just kissing, but in my defense, it'd been a long dry spell for me since well before the shooting.

All it took was a little tongue action and my whole libido was revved up and raring to go. Why fantasize about one hot guy when I could imagine two? Or three, as Haze flashed into my head.

By the time I made my way to the cafeteria for a late lunch, I was a horny, flustered mess. Sure that my cheeks were flushed and my lips probably still bearing the evidence of our classroom makeout session, I detoured into the bathroom on my way.

Then stopped dead in the bathroom entryway when I realized the bathroom was currently occupied—by Laura Sandiconte, tits out and on her knees, with Andrew's cock halfway down her throat.

I should have immediately backed out and left—it would have been the polite thing to do regardless of how I felt about

Laura. But my feet wouldn't move. Not even an inch. I stood there frozen, staring, as Andrew tipped his head back into the sunlight streaming from the frosted bathroom window, like some sort of Renaissance painting.

Laura moaned around her mouthful, and Andrew's hands tightened in her hair, his hips thrusting forward savagely.

"Shut. The. Fuck. Up." He punctuated the words with thrusts, basically choking her half to death with his cock. His eyes remained closed, and the muscles of his forearms — below his rolled-up shirtsleeves—were tightly flexed, like he was barely holding on by a thread.

Laura whimpered, gagging, as tears streamed from her eyes, and still...I stood there watching. Like a fucking pervert.

Andrew must have heard that noise and realized he was being too rough, or maybe he was just turned off because he abruptly released her hair and pushed her away.

"Forget it," he snapped. "I'm not in the mood."

She immediately grabbed his hips, rising up on her knees to plead with him and *thankfully* blocking my view of Andrew's rapidly wilting erection. "No, baby, don't be like that. I can be quiet! I swear. No noises. Let me try again, Andrew...please, baby..."

Andrew smacked her hands away from his hips, his eyes snapping open as he glared down at her in disgust. "Do *not* touch my clothing, Laura. I said I'm not in the—" He cut off abruptly, locking eyes with me.

Crap.

My mouth went dry and my palms instantly turned sweaty and yet I just *fucking stood there*, unable to move as his eyes widened in surprise but stayed locked on mine.

"See..." Laura purred, fisting his shaft once more. "You *are* in the mood after all."

Oh fuck. Yep, that was what I needed to snap out of it.

Blinking rapidly, I beat a quick retreat, the door slamming

behind me as Andrew let out the most obscenely sexy moan I think I'd ever heard from a man.

Holy fuck. What in the hell was that?

Cheeks burning, I decided to skip dining hall lunch and head straight back to the house. My grocery store visit with Ethan and Connor on the weekend meant we had more than enough food in the kitchen.

As I hurried back to the house, I wondered how the hell I'd be able to look Andrew in the eye again after that. I had no idea. But at the same time, I couldn't stop thinking about it. How he'd reacted when Laura put her hands on his hips, no doubt smearing spit and precum on his expensive trousers.

Andrew Knightsbridge, I was coming to realize, was *more* than just a run-of-the-mill control freak. There was as deeper desire for control that had to come from somewhere.

"What are you doing here?"

The grumpy question shocked me out of my downright voyeuristic train of thought, and I shook my head to clear it.

"Uh..." I glanced around at the kitchen of the house that I definitely lived in. "Am I not supposed to be here? You guys made a pretty big deal of the fact that I—"

Connor glared actual daggers my way, tossing his dirty sponge back into the bucket of water and peeling off the yellow dish gloves he'd been wearing. "I meant, why are you here *now*? No one is usually home during the day on Monday."

I peered at the extensive deep cleaning that he was in the middle of and nodded slowly. "So...you wanted everyone to think that the magical cleaning elves had come while no one was home? I guess your secret is safe with me."

He said nothing, just glowered and reached for the can of energy drink sitting on the table.

In an attempt to sidestep the awkward, I opened the fridge and pulled out some supplies to make a sandwich. "Didn't the school cleaners do all this when we moved in the other day?"

"Not properly," Connor muttered, pulling his gloves back on. "Look at that water." He pointed to the soapy bucket, and sure enough, the water was far from clean.

I cringed but then continued with making my sandwich. "Fair, but I don't know many twentysomething-year-old guys who'd notice."

"Twenty-one," he offered. "And it's not me who notices."

He seemed to realize he'd given up too much information then because his lips tightened and he turned back to what he was doing: scrubbing the inside of the oven.

"Andrew really hates dirt and mess, huh?" I mused out loud. Based on the way Connor's back muscles tensed beneath his tight shirt, I'd guessed accurately.

"He has his reasons."

That was all he said, confirming my previous thoughts about a deeper reason for Andrew's frankly desperate need to control everything, and I got the sense that he wasn't about to go into any further details, even if pressed. "Why did you guys pretend to fight?" Because you had to give a pretty large fuck about someone to care this much for their neurosis. This was epic brothers-from-another-mother shit.

It was making less and less sense to me why they persisted with their enemies facade, and frankly, I was wondering if that cafeteria fight hadn't all been a ploy to live together in this house without anyone knowing they were actually besties. But it wasn't as if they didn't have any pull in the school. Surely they could have roomed together and pretended it was under orders from the dean.

They certainly didn't need to involve me to make it happen.

Connor's full lips curled, and the look he shot me was downright furious. "You should mind your fucking business, new girl. You've already caused enough issues, and just because my gun is retired for the time being, doesn't mean it's gone completely."

Dropping my knife, sandwich only half-finished, I must have lost my fucking mind because I took a step right into his chest. Slamming my finger against hard muscles, I barely stopped from wincing at how much that freaking hurt. "Are you threatening me, asshole? I could go to the police, you know. No NDA stops you from doing illegal shit, and pulling a weapon on a person is fucking illegal."

It surprised me when his anger was replaced with a mocking laugh. "Oh, you poor, delusional idiot. My family owns the police in this town. Fuck, in this entire state. Report me. See what happens."

We were so close that I could smell the faintest sweat from his cleaning, mixed with expensive and spicy cologne. It was a potent combination, reminding me how attractive this dangerous lunatic was. My words were a whisper when I said, "Why do you hate me so much? To my knowledge, I've never done anything to you."

I caught a flicker in his green eyes, which were the darkest shade of forest I'd ever seen. "It's not what you've done now— it's what you're going to do. You're trouble, Evelyn. The others might want to play happy family and pretend you're not our downfall, but I know fucking better."

I opened and closed my mouth, but I couldn't actually find the words to reply. He'd stunned me. There was only one real reason I'd ever be a threat to them, and that was if they knew about the shooting and thought I might...I don't know, bring the same situation down on his friends?

A super illogical sort of thought. It wasn't like I'd asked to be attacked and almost murdered. I'd never asked for any of the shit in my life.

"If you stay out of my way, I'll stay out of yours," I rasped, emotions pressing down on me until it felt like my chest cracked. "We only have to make it through this term."

"Deal," Connor snapped. "Clean up after you finish your sandwich."

He was gone before I could formulate a scathing response, but let it be known, in my head, I tore him to pieces.

My appetite was gone, but not wanting to waste food, I finished fixing my lunch and grabbed a bottle of water to wash it down. It annoyed me to follow his orders, but I did clean up after myself and left the kitchen in what was fairly pristine condition compared to how it had been when we moved in.

Not wanting to stay in the house when Connor was still upstairs, I trekked back to school, heading for the cafeteria. By the end of this punishment, I'd be almost as fit as I'd been before the shooting.

Stepping in the crowded room, I looked around for Nina, but it was Brodie who I noticed first.

"Evie babe," he called, waving me toward the table he was at with two other guys.

Deciding I could use a break from the darker side of life, I headed straight for him, and it was only when I dropped into the chair that I realized who the two guys with him were.

"Dexter Jays," Brodie said, pointing to the Calvin freaking Klein model on his left. Dexter Jays was tall, with a soccer-player physique. Muscled but not heavily so. His skin and hair were dark, but his eyes were olive green, adding to his striking looks. Brodie motioned to his other friend. "And Hewie Macintyre." Hewie—with his purple-streaked blond hair, multiple tatts, eyebrow and nose ring—was a rock star.

Yep. World famous, multiplatinum-selling rock star.

Of course Brodie Keller would have equally famous friends.

"This is my girl Eve," Brodie continued, slinging his arm around me. "You two can look but don't even fucking think about touching. I'll destroy you without remorse."

My elbow swung back to slam into Brodie's ribs, and just

like with Connor, I was fairly certain it hurt me more than him. The asshole basically laughed.

Dexter and Hewie stared at me, their expressions open and curious. "Ignore the idiot," I said drily. "He's punishment dished out by the dean. I'm here under duress."

Brodie brought out his saddest face again, and to my annoyance, it still worked on me. "Evie babe, you are horrendous on a man's ego. You've smashed me to pieces."

Hewie chuckled, flashing two rows of perfect teeth and a tongue piercing, and I tried not to notice how good-looking he was. He wasn't really my type, but a girl would have to be dead to not at least notice. "I think you've finally met your match, Brodes."

Holy fuck. Okay, now I knew how he'd managed to become the lead singer of the hottest band to grace the world in five years. The deep rasp of his voice was enough to send goose bumps across my skin.

"I didn't realize you were in college," I said to Hewie. "Weren't you touring a few months ago?"

Brodie groaned. "No fucking fair winning her over with the rock-star thing. I won an Academy Award and an Emmy last year. Doesn't that count for something?"

I had no idea how this was my life, flirting with famous people, when only a few months ago I'd been in hospitals and rehab, trying to recover from the attack.

Dexter patted Brodie's arm. "It counts to your mom, bro."

Brodie dropped his head back. "Well, fuck. She wasn't even that proud of me. Guess I'm on my own then."

Hewie ignored them both and leaned toward me. "I've been making music since I was a kid, and as much as I love it and couldn't live without the buzz, I also wanted to experience a normal life. At least for a while. Brodes convinced me to give college a try, and the dean is cool for me to pop in and out as needed, so I haven't even had to give up touring. Just cut back a bit."

All three of them were rich, famous boys playing at normal life. It shouldn't be amusing, and yet I found myself enjoying my time with them during lunch.

Who knew they'd be so likable? Connor could really take a page out of their books.

Maybe I'd suggest it the next time we crossed paths, because no matter the deal we'd struck today, we lived in the same fucking house—it was the literal definition of forced proximity.

There was no way to avoid him forever.

18

EVELYN

As ahead as I was with my assignments—largely thanks to my inability to sleep properly—I really didn't have much to fill my time with when I wasn't in classes. At least, that was my excuse when Brodie asked if I'd spend Friday afternoon with him running lines for his callback on the audition he'd attended over the weekend.

Initially we were sitting in the living room to read the script, but about an hour after we started, Connor and Haze came in and turned on the Xbox to play *Call of Duty* with some guys online, on the other side of the world. After relocating to Brodie's room, I couldn't stop myself from snooping through his things a bit.

"Evie babe, what happened to running lines with me?" Brodie teased, lying across his bed like a big old snack.

I tried not to look directly at him because I kept getting stupid little butterflies when he met my eyes. Damn actors and their ability to make you feel things that weren't necessarily true.

"When's your callback?" I asked, flicking through one of the many, many highlighted and annotated scripts on his desk—after having already gained his permission, of course.

Brodie sighed. "Next Friday. Which is not ideal because I have a work thing the following night out in LA but...whatever." He seemed out of sorts about it, though. Like he didn't really think he'd be getting the part.

I frowned, putting the script back down to give him my attention. "Who else are they considering for the role? If you can tell me."

"It's between me, Travis Peters, Braxton Crumpet, and Seven Harrison." He pouted, and it was way too fucking endearing.

"That seems like an odd mix. Those actors are like ten or fifteen plus years older than you, and the character is meant to be your age, isn't he?" I moved back over to perch on the edge of his bed, picking up the script once more.

Brodie sighed again, the dramatic beast. "Yeah, they're thinking about maybe aging the characters up for the sake of the movie. I dunno...I'm not getting my hopes up. The casting director mentioned my role in *Bloodstone* at least ten times, so I feel like he's having a hard time seeing me as anything else."

"That casting director sounds like a fucking moron," I informed him with a nod. "You'd be incredible in this role, and they'd be stupid to try and age up a bunch of snowboarding badasses to their late thirties. Wouldn't that put them at risk of knee injuries and shit?"

He barked a laugh at that. "You're probably right. And this isn't the be-all and end-all... I just really love the script and think it'd be an exciting change of pace, you know?"

I nodded, leaning back on one of the pillows to read the script again. "Where did you want to start from?"

Brodie cleared his throat, shifting his position somewhat so he faced me. "Can I ask you a question, Evie?"

"Sure, ask away. We're all locked into our house of secrets, remember?"

"True," he murmured, thoughtful. "So...what's going on with you and Ethan?"

Oh. That was *not* what I thought he was going to ask. Then again, he'd walked in on us making out in the middle of the Economics of Crime classroom just this morning, so it was a fair question.

"I mean, is it just casual, or are you guys dating or..."

"No," I quickly replied, shaking my head. "No, we're not dating. It's just... I don't know. Chemistry. We aren't—" I cut myself off, blowing out a long breath as I tried to come up with the right answer. "He's my teacher. So we aren't anything." Right? That was what I was supposed to say, I was sure of it.

Brodie narrowed his eyes, clearly not believing me. And really, why the fuck would he after what he'd seen going on between us after class?

"Uh-huh," he said skeptically. "So hypothetically speaking, if someone *else* were interested..."

Holy hell, is it hot in here? I feel hot.

"Someone else?" I repeated, unable to actually form a smooth comeback to what was more than likely just flirty banter or teasing from Brodie. We were besties, right? He'd friend-zoned me, and I wasn't stupid enough to think that Brodie freaking Keller—the sexiest man in Hollywood—would ever be interested in me. Evelyn fake-last-name with the mysterious past and truckloads of trauma.

With all of that running through my head, I was totally stunned when he cupped my face, leaned in, and brushed his lips over mine ever so softly.

What the fuck is happening?

"Sorry," Brodie murmured, shifting back just an inch or two. "That was... I should have asked first. Maybe I misread the vibes between us?"

Shit. Snap out of it, Evelyn!

Blinking, I shook my head. "You didn't misread anything."

A slow, sexy smile curved his lips. "So, can I kiss you, Evie babe?"

Holy shit, was this a dream?

I nodded, and he quickly closed the gap between us, but this time his kiss was more confident and eager, melting me into a puddle of goo. If it was a dream, it was one I badly didn't want to wake up from.

"Brodie! Have you seen Eve?"

Ethan's voice calling up the stairs made me jump so hard I fell off Brodie's bed entirely, crashing to the floor in a seriously inelegant pile of limbs.

"Holy shit," Brodie spluttered, peering over the side of his bed with a grin plastered across his sexy face. "Are you okay?"

"Ow," I moaned, rubbing my hip where I'd hit the wooden floor.

"Eve?" Ethan said, appearing in the doorway with a puzzled look on his face. "Are you okay? I heard a crash…" His gaze tracked from me on the floor, to Brodie sprawled out on his bed, then back to me with a small frown.

My hip hurt, as did my elbow, but nothing quite compared to the bruise on my dignity. "I'm fine," I muttered, scrambling up from my tangled position. "No harm done."

"What are you guys doing up here?" Ethan asked, his eyes narrowing as he looked to Brodie for answers.

"Running lines," I said.

At the same time, Brodie replied, "Making out."

My face flamed, and I quickly grabbed the highlighted script from where it'd fallen to the floor. Then used it to smack Brodie over the head…gently.

"I'm helping Brodie rehearse for his callback next Friday," I elaborated, giving the smug-as-fuck actor a hard glare. He seemed to be far too fucking amused by my awkwardness.

Luckily, Ethan seemed suitably distracted by the news of Brodie's callback. "No way! That's great news, Brodes. Come down to the kitchen while I cook dinner and tell me all about it." He glanced at me with a sly grin as Brodie sighed and got up from his bed. "Coming, Eve?"

I tried really hard not to pout as I muttered under my breath, "Apparently not." Then covered it by replying, "Sure. What are you cooking?"

"*We* are cooking lasagna," Ethan informed me. "Someone ate the chicken I'd intended to use for chicken parmesan."

Brodie jogged down the stairs two at a time, but Ethan grabbed my waist before I could follow, spinning me to face him and pinning me against the wall.

"You're blushing, Lilith," he whispered in a husky voice, doing all kinds of unspeakable things to my insides. "Was Brodie flirting?"

I swallowed hard, my brain not fully functioning with how my hormones were raging and my pulse raced. Rather than lie, I just nodded. Technically, he had been flirting.

Ethan hummed a thoughtful sound, his gaze dipping to my mouth as his fingers caressed my jaw, tilting my head back against the wall. "I haven't stopped thinking about you all day, fantasizing about what could have happened if Brodie didn't interrupt us after class..."

Oh my God. A somewhat obscene whimper escaped me, and Ethan's gaze heated. His head dipped lower, his lips meeting mine for just the briefest moment.

"Eth! You get lost or something?" Brodie yelled up the stairs, and I groaned.

"Asshole," Ethan grumbled, then kissed me again, quick and hard, before releasing me entirely. "We still need to talk, Lilith. After dinner?"

I blew out a heavy sigh, leaning my head back on the wall.

"I suppose so. I'll be down in a minute." I gestured for him to head downstairs while I quickly went to my room.

Once inside, I closed the door and very firmly turned the key in the paint-splattered lock, testing the door to check it was *definitely* locked. Confident no one would come bursting in, I dove onto my bed and reached into my bedside table for my vibrator.

Between Brodie, Ethan, and the fear of getting caught hanging over my head—plus my trusty rechargeable vibrator— I got myself off in less than a minute. Then needed to lay there on the bed gasping and buzzing for another five before I could force myself to head back downstairs.

Wandering into the kitchen, I could safely say I was a shit-load calmer and in control of my dumb hormones once more. Not to mention I was a *lot* more relaxed.

"Evie babe," Brodie purred from where he sat at the kitchen table. "Come sit with me." He patted his lap, and I rolled my eyes, grinning.

"Rein it in, Brodes," Ethan scolded. "Eve, can you dice those tomatoes for me, please?"

I nodded, trying to ignore the way Brodie watched me move through the kitchen with pure lust in his eyes. I'd made the right move, taking a minute for myself upstairs. If I'd come down here with all that sexual tension still sky high...well, I'd soon be finding out how Ethan and Brodie felt about three-ways.

A few minutes later, my libido cooled as Connor joined us in the kitchen and made a snide remark about how I was dicing tomatoes wrong—as if there was even a wrong way to dice a fucking tomato.

Ethan seemed to be cooking without a recipe, so I simply followed his instructions about what was needed, and two hours later, we were serving up the most delicious lasagna I'd ever tasted.

Surprisingly, Andrew and Haze joined us right as we plated up, and everyone sat down to eat together.

"Did someone clean in here?" Andrew asked, pausing halfway through his dinner and squinting at the kitchen. "Like, deep clean, I mean."

I glanced over at Connor, but he just stared back at me, his expression unreadable.

"I think campus staff were here today," Ethan commented, casual and confident. "They must have done it."

Andrew frowned. "Huh. Well, they did a good job."

I quirked a brow at Connor, but his response was just to hold my gaze steadily while he scratched his stubble-dusted cheek...with his middle finger. Fucking immature asshole.

19

EVELYN

I was running. Running and screaming. Running harder than I'd ever run before, but nothing moved around me, as if I were stuck in the same spot.

"Come out, come out, Evelyn. Your time in this world is done."

He hit me from behind, and my skin burst in flames as gunfire filled the air.

A crash had me shooting up in my bed, my heart pounding so hard that it hurt my chest. At first I thought the crash was part of the dream, until there was another bang, and the windows shook in my room.

A storm had rolled in while I slept in fear, and now I had a waking fear to deal with. I yanked the blanket over my head, having hated the sound of thunder since the day my world was destroyed.

It reminded me of his footsteps crashing around the class-room, each bang bringing another surge of fear. My limbs trembled, and my head felt light as I fought the debilitating terror, fought through the air frozen in my lungs, while black spots danced before my eyes.

Fuck! Fucking fuck. I had to get out of here before I lost my mind and started to scream at the top of my lungs. Connor would love to see me fall apart like that, and honestly, I'd rather die than give him the pleasure.

Stumbling from the bed, I mindlessly moved, struggling to get the lock on my door open. This ancient relic might be solid, providing a false sense of security against the men in this house, but it wasn't easy to maneuver when one was in a rush.

"Come on," I sobbed, wiggling and jiggling, relieved to hear the heavy click as it finally released.

Falling through the door, I caught myself on the handle, and there was no real thought of where to go until I reached *his* door. I couldn't ride this storm out alone, not without losing my shit completely, and I had no more drugs left to dull the pain.

No more painkillers. No more sleeping tablets.

Which was fine most of the time, but I'd have given anything for a pill tonight.

At first, I thought his door was locked, and in my panic, I let out a low sob. Trying again, I was relieved to hear the low click of it opening; these old handles needed an extra shove to get them moving.

It was pitch-black inside, with only the occasional bolt of lightning illuminating his room.

Thank Jesus fucking Christ that it was set out in a similar style to my room, so I headed straight for his bed, too panicked to second-guess my actions. My breaths wheezed in and out so loudly that I woke him up with a start. "Eve," he mumbled, shooting up in bed as I shuffled closer. A flash of light showcased his concerned expression. "What's wrong?"

"Storm," I choked out, another rumble of thunder shaking me as hard as it shook the house. "I can't handle storms after the attack."

Without hesitation, Ethan was out of bed, arms wrapping around me as he lifted me from the floor and into his body. He felt all warm and rumpled from sleep. "Come on, baby," he whispered against my cheek. "I'll keep you safe."

A fraction of my panic eased as I let Ethan encase me, dragging us under his blankets, until we were cocooned together. He held me close, his hands rubbing up and down my spine in a soothing manner, and I felt myself relaxing against his hard body.

As we melded together, I felt his muscled chest, bare and firm under my touch. I couldn't see anything in the dark, but his hard length was pressed against my side as he held me close, and now all I could think about was sex.

Sex with Ethan.

Damn. It wasn't that I'd run into his room looking to bang my professor, but the attraction between us was like wildfire, intense and hard to control.

"Brodie and I kissed."

The words spilled from me in a rush, making it very clear that I'd been harboring a little bit of guilt over what happened. Ethan's hands stilled for a moment before he resumed his gentle, soothing rub along my spine.

"I'm sorry that I didn't tell you straightaway," I continued, my mouth running away from me once more. "I know we've been skirting around this intense attraction between us, and the kisses are amazing, but there's something with Brodie too... I'm sorry I'm such a hot mess, but I really don't know what the hell is happening."

Ethan let out a long sigh, his warm breath feathering over my skin. "I wish I could say I'm surprised, but he's Brodie."

Confused, I shifted to face him, trying to make out his expression in the darkness. "I don't... What does that mean? Are you angry?"

He groaned, one hand leaving my body to rake through his hair. "Furious," he admitted, "but not at you, beautiful Lilith."

"At Brodie?" I asked in a small voice. That idea filled me

with a sick feeling. I respected the family connection between them all, and the last thing I wanted to do was cause fights.

Ethan gave a small laugh, then pressed a kiss to my throat. "No. That dickhead is too damn loveable for his own good." He kissed my throat again, scraping teeth over my skin and causing a sultry moan to escape me. "You don't owe me anything, Eve. I'm not just your teacher. I'm also eight years older than you and tragically mixed up in a criminal organization. I'm desperately thankful for the moments you give me, but I'm in no position to tie you down and demand exclusivity."

This bothered me more than I'd admit, because I didn't want Ethan hooking up with another woman. I wasn't nearly as open-minded about a casual relationship, and selfish or not, I wanted him to touch no one but me. The criminal comment was something I filed away for later.

"Do you have a girlfriend?" I asked him. "Or plans to get one who is someone else?"

"Nope." His reply was instant. "There's no one I'm interested in other than you, Eve. I want to explore whatever this is between us."

"But what about your job? And Brodie?" Because that kiss was still in my head, and I'd be lying if I said I didn't want to do it again.

His chest rumbled, and his fingers flexed against my skin. "Don't get me wrong, sweetheart. I intend to do everything possible to capture your *whole* focus, but I won't begrudge you exploring things with him if that's what you want to do."

I was so fucking confused. "You won't be jealous?"

Ethan laughed. "I will. I'm already intensely jealous of him sitting next to you while I present in your Economics of Crime class. Did you even notice he was playing with your hair during today's session?"

"What?" I squeaked. I hadn't noticed, because I'd been so

fucking focused on my sexy, enigmatic professor, no doubt. "But—"

"Jealousy isn't a bad thing, Lilith. It just makes things... spicy. Trust me to manage my own emotions, beautiful." He kissed my jaw, then nipped my earlobe between his teeth. "But if he hurts you, all bets are off. I'll fucking kill him."

Holy crap. Why was that dark edge to his threat so hot? Maybe because it wasn't a threat—it was a promise. The kind that made me go all fluttery and warm inside.

I'd all but forgotten about the storm during this somewhat awkward but necessary discussion, but as the loudest boom so far rocked the room, I was catapulted right back into my distress, a whimpering scream wheezing out of me.

Ethan wrapped his arms around me and yanked me into his chest as his lips crashed against mine. It felt like the storm infiltrated his room and erupted between us, energy crackling as I moaned into his mouth. This time, Ethan didn't ease up on the kiss, his tongue swiping against my lips, demanding entry. Apparently, he was making good on that intention to consume my focus in its entirety. There was no room between us now for thoughts of any other man, that was for sure.

As soon as I opened my mouth, he devoured me as if he'd been desperately waiting for a chance to taste me again. "Fuck, Eve," he groaned, gentling a fraction as his hands traced down my spine. "Kissing you is destructive perfection."

I understood exactly what he meant. We shouldn't be doing this, and it was my fault for coming into his room in the first place, but of any of the men in Bluebell House, he was my safe harbor in the storm. A literal storm, in this case.

Using both hands, Ethan cupped my face and tilted my head back for better access. His kisses were slow and drugging, until my body throbbed so intensely that it actually hurt. "Ethan, please," I mumbled, half-delirious from the sensation of his hands and mouth on me.

"What do you want, baby?" he rumbled. "You need to tell me exactly. Nothing is going to happen until I hear the words from your pretty mouth."

Oh, God. He was giving me a chance to back out if this wasn't what I wanted. He was my professor, and I was the student, but tonight, I held the power.

"I need you to touch me," I said, no hesitation. This was going to happen, and I wanted it to be tonight, when I needed him the most. "Touch me wherever you want, Professor Sullivan. I'm already wet, and I need your mouth on my cunt and your cock inside me. I need you to make me come over and over until I can't breathe. Until there's no fear. Please. *Please.*"

I wasn't beyond begging—in fact, I was ready to get on my knees for Ethan if that was what he wanted.

A guttural, desperate sound erupted from his chest, and he flipped me over to my back so fast that I was dizzy from the sensation. "I've been dying to taste you," he murmured, his touch slow and firm as he traced over my breasts. "I'm going to take my time with you, Evelyn Lewis. I'm going to enjoy every fucking moment of this."

In one swift movement, he yanked my shirt up and over my tits, his mouth on my nipples, moving between them as he sucked the throbbing ends between his teeth. When he bit down, I cried out, and he slammed his big hand over my mouth to choke out the sound.

"Quiet, baby," he murmured against my skin. "If you bring the other guys, the fun stops."

His teeth pressed down harder, and I had to bite my lip so hard I tasted blood to halt from crying out. He slid his palm off my mouth, pressing it down to my stomach, as he kissed his way down, tasting every inch of my skin he could reach.

"Oh my God," I gasped as he hooked his thumbs under the elastic of my panties and tugged them down my legs, baring me entirely. If there was even a touch more light in the room, I might have been embarrassed—not to mention he'd glimpse the bullet scars on my back, which I'd rather not dwell on during sex—but in the semi-darkness, I eagerly spread my legs wide.

Ethan's breath fanned across my core as he kissed my inner thighs, his rough stubble tickling my flesh. I squirmed in need, and he responded by kissing me right where I needed him.

"*Ethan,*" I moaned, no longer giving a flying fuck who heard us. In return, his tongue flicked my clit, and his finger slid inside my aching pussy. I was already so hot, so wet... "More," I pleaded, bucking my hips against his face. "I need—"

He added another finger, curling them to tease my inner walls, and my pleas evaporated into a sultry whimper. One thing was for sure: Ethan Sullivan knew how to eat pussy. My responsiveness only spurred him on, making him double down on his efforts with one hand pinning my thigh so hard I knew he'd leave bruises. Knew it and loved it.

I came loudly, but by some small miracle the storm had ramped up and a thunder crack perfectly masked my cries of ecstasy. Ethan cleaned me up with his tongue like some kind of big cat, then prowled back up my body with smug satisfaction radiating from his every pore. A flash of lightning lit up the room briefly, betraying his pleased grin.

"Had enough, little Lilith?" he purred, cupping my breasts and tweaking my already hypersensitive nipples.

Moaning, gasping, boneless...I shook my head. "Not even close, *Professor.*"

Summoning what little strength I had left in my shaking legs, I flipped our positions and settled my weight across Ethan's hips. He'd been sleeping in just his boxers, which I clumsily stripped him out of without losing my dominant position.

Ethan, bless his socks, let me manhandle him with a dazed sort of smile flashing at me with the lightning strikes.

"You're so freaking sexy," I marveled, running my hands over his well-toned chest. A dark shadow covered one side of his ribs, curling up over his shoulder and bicep. "Is this ink?"

He hummed, hands on my hips as his hardness ground against my soaking core. "Yeah. Want me to turn on the light, so you can take a better look?" He was teasing, but I was tempted. If I didn't have more urgent plans I probably would have accepted.

"Maybe later," I murmured, reaching down to grasp his erection. He was solid, girthy, the kind of handful that was going to hurt in the morning...in the best kind of way. Unable to wait any longer, I rose up on my knees just enough to notch him at my entrance. Just the tip stretched me, and my eyes widened with anticipation.

Sucking a breath, I lowered myself in a smooth, aching motion right as Ethan hissed my name.

"Wait," he groaned, grasping my hips tight as our pelvises lined up, his entire thick length buried between my folds. "Shit. Eve...condom..."

Ah. Crap. That would definitely have been the responsible thing...and yet, there was something so intimate and raw about having his flesh against mine. "I've got an IUD," I whispered, already breathless and trembling with need.

"Thank *fuck*," he replied with a feral sort of growl, then flipped us and took *all* control back. He pounded into me hard enough to shake the bed, each thrust drawing a cry of delight from me as the headboard smacked the wall.

My pussy clenched and pulsed around his thickness, grasping tight each time he buried deep, and when Ethan snaked a hand between us, I couldn't hold back any longer. His long fingers tweaked my clit, and I exploded.

This time, his hard, demanding kisses swallowed my screams, and just a moment later, his hips jerked, his rhythm faltering as he also found climax deep inside my body.

He rode it out, thrusts slowing as my pussy quaked and spasmed around him, then he kissed me over and over, collapsing in an exhausted heap half-on, half-off my equally jellified body. For a long time, we just lay there, legs intertwined and breathing heavy while the storm continued to rage outside.

"I changed my mind," I finally said, my voice rough and husky.

Ethan lifted his head slightly, his body tensing. "Oh?"

I grinned into the darkness. "Mm-hmm. I decided storms are actually pretty great after all."

Tension flowed out of him in an instant, and he buried his face into the side of my neck. "Cheeky girl," he muttered. "But I agree. Storms are my new favorite weather event. I hope it storms every night forever."

Every night. Forever.

20

EVELYN

The storm was long gone by the time I woke the next morning, a heavy arm draped over me, keeping me close to his chest. Ethan's scent was everywhere, leaving me with memories of the many times he woke me through the night, his mouth on my body and that impressive cock inside me.

Professor Sullivan was fucking insatiable, and as predicted, there was a delicious ache inside as I languidly stretched.

"Morning, baby," he murmured against my throat, his nose brushing across my skin as if he was breathing me in.

"Morning," I squeaked back, feeling both aroused and a touch freaked out. I'd never done the morning-after thing before, and with no idea of the protocol, I wondered what I should say.

Ethan's low chuckle dragged across my skin, and just like that, I was less interested in escaping and more wondering if I was too sore for round six. "Remember," he rasped and pressed slow kisses to my skin, "there are no expectations. Our lives are both complicated, sure, but I also decided long ago not to waste days. You never know how many you have. Don't expect me to walk away from you, Lilith."

The very thought had my insides clenching and my body tense. "I don't want you to walk away. And I promise to always be honest with you about what's happening in this house with the guys."

His rumble wasn't angry—if anything, he sounded like he was about to snuggle me back to sleep.

It was Saturday, so neither of us had any classes to be at, which meant we could nap and fuck the day away. I'd honestly never felt more excited about staying home.

As my eyes closed, drifting to sleep, the door to Ethan's room slammed open so hard that I almost flew off the bed. It was only Ethan's strong arm around me that kept me from falling as he yanked us into sitting position, situating himself in front of me so quickly, it felt impossible that he reacted so fast.

"Bro, Eve's missing!" Connor's shout rang out through the room, and it took me seconds to get my heartrate to retreat from coronary levels. "Oh, for fuck's sake, Eth!"

Trying to peer around the broad shoulders blocking me, I caught sight of Ethan slipping a handgun back into his bedside table. How in the—when had he grabbed that?

Weirdly, for the first time since the shooting, the sight of a gun calmed me. He'd been prepared for Connor's intrusion, and if it had been an enemy, he would have protected me.

It was comforting.

"Are you actually kidding me?" Connor snarled, sounding more pissed off than I'd ever heard from him. "I should report you to the dean, you perverted fuck."

I straightened and leaned even farther to the side to glare him down. "Listen here, you fucking spoiled-ass bitch. I chose to come to Ethan's room, and I'm twenty years old. Not a child. We've done nothing wrong."

He opened his mouth to shout at me again, and I rose to my

knees, completely forgetting I was naked. The sight shut Connor up temporarily, and he was no gentleman as his gaze dragged slowly down my tits.

"If you mention this to the dean and get Ethan into trouble, I will take your gun and shoot you in the leg. Don't fucking try me."

For a beat, his lips twitched, and I thought he was going to smile. Though his expression remained dark and framed in fury. "Don't threaten me, Evelyn. I've killed more people than you fucking know, and I have no issue adding you to the list. Remember that." His gaze flicked to his brother again. "Your gutter-trash side is starting to show, brother."

"Get the fuck out," Ethan drawled, but there was no missing the danger in his tone. He wrapped the blanket over me and yanked me back down, looking annoyed. I had no idea if it was just at Connor or at Connor seeing me naked, but whatever— they were just boobs and a waxed vagina.

If he'd killed more people than I knew, there was zero doubt he'd fucked more people than Ethan and I knew combined. He had *gorgeous, dangerous asshole* written all over him, and there was nothing like a bad boy to get girls to drop their panties.

Connor scoffed as he left the room, and I heard what suspiciously sounded like *whore* and *magic pussy* before he was gone, leaving me alone with Ethan once more. Unfortunately, that was the end of the day of lounging around, though, the mood iced out thanks to that prick.

"I should get up and shower," I mumbled, feeling disappointed and put out. "Thanks for last night."

My cheeks heated when I realized that he might not understand I was thanking him for the comfort and not the sex. Not that I wasn't also thankful for that.

He appeared to understand. "My door is always open," he said, gently capturing my chin in his hand, keeping my gaze locked on his piercing green eyes. "You don't have to fight the dreams and trauma alone, Eve. Promise me you won't let Connor stop you from taking what you need."

"Promise," I whispered, knowing that I couldn't stay away from Ethan even if I wanted to.

Which I absolutely didn't.

It took me a few seconds to find my clothes, and when I slipped them on, I forced myself not to look back to the bed, where I'd left Ethan sprawled. *No, Evelyn. No more professor for today.*

My therapist would have a lot to say if he got me in his chair, and no doubt, I was desperately in need of advice. I was well aware that I had exchanged pills, anxiety, and bad dreams for lusting after my professor and obsessing over the comfort he offered me.

None of these coping mechanisms were healthy, but I knew for sure which was more enjoyable.

As Ethan said, we had no idea how long we'd be on this gravity ball, and I, for one, was glad not to miss out on the sort of mind-blowing sex we'd had last night.

I made it back to my room without running into any of our housemates and grabbed clean clothes and underwear, escaping into the bathroom. My body ached in many places, but thankfully all the love bites and bruises from where he'd gripped me were hidden under my jeans and shirt.

Not that it'd be a secret to Connor, but best not to go flashing the evidence around.

I was hesitant as I wandered downstairs, but it was quieter than I expected, and it was almost a relief to wander into the kitchen and find it empty.

"Who are you really, new girl?"

I jumped a foot in the air, and fuck, if Connor had meant me harm, I'd have been dead before I even saw him standing in the doorway to the living area. Was this asshole a ninja? How did he keep sneaking up on me?

Shrugging despite my absolute lack of calm, I casually replied, "What do you mean? I'm Evelyn Lewis."

He moved closer, and I tried not to reveal my unease as he backed me into the side of the kitchen counter. Even as he dropped a hand on either side of me, completely caging me between his massive body and the island, I never lowered my gaze. He was the predator, but I refused to become his prey. "Where are you from, Evelyn? Who are your parents? Where did you live before you were here?"

Fuck. FUCK. Did he know? Did Ethan tell him? If I mentioned that I was from Tennessee, it wouldn't take him long to search news stories and find out what happened back there. The college had made the news for weeks. *I'd* made the news for weeks.

I'd been under the suspicion that the guys knew about the shooting, but I still refused to be the one to confirm the truth.

"I'm no one, Connor. You don't have to waste time and energy trying to unravel my very basic life. I lived with my guardians because my dad couldn't look after me any longer." For reasons I didn't even know. "My mom died when I was young. I've lived a very ordinary life."

Outside of that whole school-shooting incident. Which fucked every part of my regular existence to pieces.

He leaned in even closer, and I swear his body threw off heat like a hot water bottle. We didn't touch, but my exposed skin still felt flushed. "You have no fucking idea who you are, do you? Just a dumb, naive, uninteresting chick. Happy to float through life without a clue. Happy to let others take bullets for you."

I jerked like he'd slapped me, the rush of memories drowning out everything else, and I didn't even realize I was breathing heavily until Connor's touch landed against my chest.

He pressed against me firmly. "Breathe. Be stronger than

your demons, Eve. You can't keep falling apart. You don't have the luxury of it, and I wouldn't rely on Ethan to keep pulling you together."

We locked gazes for a protracted moment, and I was surprised to find that his touch did ground me. "Who are you?" I threw the question back to him. "It seems you all know my secrets, but I know fucking nothing about you. Including why you five manufactured a reason for us all to live in this house."

Abruptly, he released his hold on me and stepped back. I'd have thought I imagined his touch if my chest didn't burn right where he'd placed his hand. "I'm your worst fucking nightmare, new girl. Don't think you can bat those pretty blue eyes at me and I'll forget the danger you pose to us."

"Are you the dad of the group or something?" I said with a snort. "You keep coming in here, claiming I'm dangerous, as if you need to defend their honor. Last I checked, you were younger than Ethan. Pretty sure he can handle my pussy without losing himself."

There was a flicker of darkness in his green eyes, until his iris was close in color to his pupil. "Can he, though? I mean, don't get me wrong, it's a pretty pussy but—"

"Let me guess, don't bat my vagina at you either?"

His jaw twitched, and with a shake of his head, he turned and left me alone in the kitchen, and if I hadn't already been leaning against the counter, I'd have collapsed on the floor. Holy intensity, Batman. Connor was beyond intense, and I had no idea what information I could offer him to keep him from hating me for just existing.

Maybe it was time for me to try a little harder to fit into the house? A peace offering of sorts...

Deciding to briefly stop acting like being here was the worst thing to happen in my life, I got to work in the kitchen, preparing the breakfast of a lifetime.

An hour later, the old table was laden with my full breakfast repertoire, including homemade pancakes, fluffy scrambled eggs, crispy bacon, toast, and fresh orange juice that I'd had to hand-squeeze because there was no juicer here.

Brodie and Ethan had popped their heads in a few times while I was working, but I shooed them away, wanting to do this on my own.

"Breakfast!" I called, when I was satisfied everything had come out perfectly. My guardians had been huge foodies, and I'd learned how to cook at their side. This was a part of my life I was solidly confident in.

To my surprise, Andrew was the first through the door, perfectly pressed, of course. He eyed the table I'd set, and then his gaze came back to my face. For a brief moment, I remembered that second we'd locked eyes in the girl's bathroom, but there was no real awkwardness as he smiled. "This was a really nice thing to do, Eve."

I gestured for him to sit as Brodie and Ethan arrived, shoving to see who got through the door first. Ethan ended up just in front, and he brushed a hand across the sliver of skin between my jeans and shirt before he took a seat too.

Brodie dropped a kiss on my cheek. "Bestie, this looks amazing! Marry me?"

Rolling my eyes, I shoved him away. "You know it's illegal to have more than one wife, right? Sure you don't want to tie yourself down?"

"For you, I'd tie myself to anything. Mostly the bed, but also other things."

Ethan laughed, and I was relieved to find that he looked amused by the shit coming out of Brodie's mouth.

When the three of them were seated, I glanced toward the door, wondering if the other two were still in the house. With a sigh, I almost gave up and sat too, but then Haze appeared— silent, as always—and the relief I felt at seeing him was beyond just wanting him here for breakfast.

He occupied my thoughts far too often for a guy that was both a ghost and an enigma.

"I made breakfast," I said stupidly. *Fuck, Evelyn. Get it together.*

Haze's stoic expression wavered slightly as he nodded. "I know."

That had me wondering if he'd known before I called them into the room.

As he took a seat, Ethan shouted, "Connor!"

To my surprise, not even a second later, his brother strode into the room. He didn't acknowledge me, or anyone else really, just took a seat beside Andrew and immediately started to fill his plate.

Yep, he wasn't going to make it easy, but I was determined that by the time our punishment here was done, I'd win over everyone in this house.

I'd be the best fucking housemate they'd ever had in their lives, and they'd wonder how they ever lived without me.

21

EVELYN

My thighs clenched, my pussy throbbing as I shifted in my seat and wet my lips. I needed to concentrate, but it was our first class back since the night of the storm, and all I could focus on was what it felt like to have Ethan's head buried between my legs and—

"What are you thinking about?" Brodie asked in my ear, and I just about jumped out of my seat. He smirked knowingly. "Something dirty, I'll bet."

Brodie. Shit. Now I was thinking about his kiss and whether it was a one-off. What would he do if I leaned in right now and—

"Shut up," Andrew hissed from my other side. "Some of us don't have an automatic passing grade in this class."

My eyes widened, and I stared at him in shock. If I'd been under any illusions that Connor would keep my secrets, that dispelled them.

"Is there a problem, Ms. Lewis?" Ethan asked from the front of the class, his voice projecting with authority that made my face flush...and not with embarrassment.

I cleared my throat, willing my cheeks to stop burning. "No, sir. No problems here."

Ethan's lips pursed and he ran a hand over his shadowed jaw. "Hmm well, I'd like you to stay behind after class nonetheless."

Wait, was he serious?

Andrew muttered something that sounded suspiciously like an insult, but Ethan had already moved on with the class and I bit my lip in an attempt to concentrate.

Brodie seemed totally unfazed by the attention we'd drawn, placing his hand on my knee beneath the desktop and shooting me a lazy grin.

"How come you're so late?" I whispered when he held my gaze, curiosity burning within me.

Brodie shot a pointed glance toward Ethan, then withdrew his hand to flip open his notebook. He scribbled out a quick note, then pushed it in my direction to read.

Got caught on a call with my agent. Did you miss me?

I rolled my eyes but smiled as I replied on his notebook.

Yes.

Brodie's grin was brighter than the sun itself as he took the pencil back, our fingers brushing deliciously.

Do you have plans next weekend?

I arched a brow, scribbling my quick response.

Maybe re-grouting the bathroom tiles? Why?

Now it was Brodie's turn to roll his eyes.

Can I take you on a date?

Of all the things I thought he was going to write, I hadn't expected that. I stared at him for a moment, trying to guess if he was maybe messing with me or joking around or...had I maybe misunderstood the question?

A date?

Another mischievous smirk from him that made my heart go all melty.

Yes. Sort of. I have a work thing, and I'm allowed to bring a date.

I blinked slowly, rereading his neat handwriting several times while trying to decipher some sort of hidden meaning.

And you want to take me? Why?

It was a dumb question, considering he'd basically told me he was interested in me and then kissed me, but if it was a "work thing," then it was a celebrity thing, and Brodie must have had his pick of hundreds of gorgeous actresses and models he could take.

Brodie gave a soft laugh as he wrote his reply.

Because Drew looks shitty in a dress, and I like you, Evie.

He dotted the *I* of *Evie* with a heart, and I just about died dead right there. RIP me. Until Andrew reached over and snatched the notebook from under my nose.

"No," he said firmly to Brodie, leaning forward to glare over me. "And I'd look fantastic in a dress. I look fantastic in everything."

His indignation was sincere enough that my shoulder shook with amusement, and Brodie grinned like the Cheshire Cat. But Andrew didn't give the notebook back, so we both reluctantly started paying attention to Ethan's lecture.

Or...I tried. Brodie's hand rested on my knee once more, and the little circles his thumb traced on my thigh had me all twisted up and practically panting by the time class finished. I'd have thought my needs were fully satiated by Ethan during the storm, but evidently, I'd been wrong.

"Ms. Lewis," Ethan called out as we packed up and the class emptied, reminding me that he'd asked me to stay behind.

I licked my lips, anticipation thrumming through me as I approached his desk at the front of the room. "Professor Sullivan," I replied, unable to keep the sultry purr out of my voice. We hadn't discussed where we stood with one another or what this would all mean for his job, but I was pretty sure he wanted more.

That made two of us.

His gaze flicked up from the notes he was skimming, heat blazing in his sexy face. Then his eyes shifted past me. "You can go, Brodie. I only need Ms. Lewis."

Brodie slung his arm around my shoulders in an almost possessive way. "I just bet you do."

Ethan's glare darkened and he straightened up to his full, imposing height. "Brodie, I didn't ask for—"

"Oh good, I'm just in time," Connor announced, strolling into the classroom with a smirk.

Ethan threw his hands up with a frustrated gesture. "What the fuck are you doing here? You don't even have classes today, Con."

His surly brother shrugged. "I heard our favorite professor wanted *alone time* with our sweet, innocent little housemate. Decided I should make sure there's nothing inappropriate going on." He jerked a short nod to Andrew, betraying who'd tipped him off. Traitor.

I shook my head, shrugging Brodie's arm off my shoulders. "Okay, I think that's my cue to leave. We can talk later, Ethan. I need to visit the library after lunch, anyway."

Before anyone could point out that my comment about the library was entirely irrelevant—we could talk at the house tonight—I scurried out of the classroom, almost colliding with Haze at the doorway.

Somehow, I managed to pull myself up right before I face-planted into his chest, and he extended a hand as if to help me balance. It didn't connect with my elbow, but the thought had been there before he'd flinched away.

"Haze," I gasped, craning my neck to look up at him. "What are you..." I glanced behind me to the class I'd just left, frowning. "Did you and Connor—actually, never mind. I'm heading to lunch. I'll see you later."

Ducking around him, I resumed my quick pace out of the

building, inhaling deeply once outdoors. Maybe I could track Nina down and tell her...what? I couldn't tell her *shit* thanks to the NDA, but maybe if I skirted the truth and swapped some key info? Maybe if I posed hypotheticals?

"Can I join you?" Haze asked from right beside me, and I jumped.

"How are you so sneaky when you're so *you*?" I waved a hand at his impressive size, shaking my head. "I need to get you a collar with a bell, just to save myself from the jump scares."

Haze gave me a thoughtful look, like he was debating the fashion statement a bell collar might make. Then he shrugged. "So can I?"

I blinked again, then connected the thoughts. "Oh. Sure, I guess."

He nodded, satisfied with my agreement, and didn't speak again until after we had loaded up our trays in the cafeteria. Even then, it was just a firm, muttered, *I'll pay*, before swiping his watch on the reader.

Nina and Sven found us only a few minutes after we sat down, and I relaxed when they joined us with their lunches.

"Haze, these are my friends," I introduced them, remembering my manners. "Nina and—"

"Sven," Haze rumbled, giving my friend a cold glare. "You're the one who walked Eve home last week."

Sven gave an uncomfortable chuckle in return. "What, do you have security cameras spying on us or something?"

He intended it as a joke, but Haze's expression didn't change. In fact, it gave me a weird sensation that he was about to admit that *yes*, he did have hidden cameras everywhere. But that'd be absurd...right?

"Okay, awkward," Nina muttered, spearing a piece of watermelon with her fork. "How are things over at the Haunted House? I'm guessing none of you have encountered any ghosts yet?"

She'd been teasing me about the "ghosts" since the day we'd moved in, and I shook my head with a grin. "Ha-ha, very funny. It's just a house, and actually a nice one if you can look past the decades of neglect and disrepair. Nothing that can't be fixed, right, Haze?"

My quiet companion quirked a brow like he hadn't expected me to continue including him in conversation. "Right," he murmured.

"If you say so," Nina continued, chomping on her fruit, "but I wanna hear more about Connor's budding career as a backup singer. Any more shower concerts?"

Haze's attention flicked back to me from his food, the faintest sparkle of amusement gleaming in his eyes. "What?"

I carefully schooled my expression, doubling down on my bullshit since I couldn't tell my friends anything real. "I told Nina about Connor's shower concerts," I informed him with a straight face, "and how impressive it is that he knows every lyric of Taylor's full set list. Not even I could nail all the eras like that."

Haze's lips twitched, but that was all the reaction he gave before wiping his mouth with a napkin. "Yes, well, he's been to at least ten of the concerts. You should see his friendship bracelet collection."

Nina gasped. "Shut up. Is it bad that makes him kinda hot?" Sven snickered, shaking his head, and Nina amended her question, "*More* hot, I mean. The man is straight fire. Eve, you'd know—"

"Oh!" I quickly exclaimed, cutting her off before she could bring up the whole Connor-Ethan kiss mix-up situation. "How'd your study date go on the weekend? You never texted me back!"

Easiest way to distract Nina: get her talking about herself. Specifically, her love life. I let out a small sigh of relief as she started in, about a guy she'd been talking with for weeks and finally met in person.

Haze watched me silently, but I just gave a tight smile back and busied myself with eating my lunch. To my surprise, he waited for me to finish, then offered to walk with me to the library as it was on the way to his chemistry lab.

That comment made Nina glower. "Now that you mention it, Haze, are you totally aware you nearly killed Eve with that explosion the other week? She was really hurt and—"

"I'm aware," he acknowledged. "I said sorry."

A laugh snorted out of me, and I couldn't hold back my grin. "Yeah. I'll catch you later, guys."

Nina and Sven both gave me cheek kisses and promised to text later as I headed out with Haze. For a few moments we walked in silence, and I got the weird feeling he was angry about something.

Right as I was about to ask, he turned to me with a bemused frown on his face. "Con loves to sing Taylor Swift, huh?"

I grinned. "I didn't hear you denying it. In fact, I heard you adding fuel to the fire. Besides, if I can't tell my friends anything true, why not make some shit up? It's harmless and less weird than being secretive."

Haze just grunted in response, and I got the distinct impression it was his version of approval.

22

EVELYN

What in all of the fucks are you doing, Eve?

As I crept along the bushes that lined the front of the college, I kept asking myself the same question, all the while urging myself to stop, and yet...I hadn't. I wouldn't. At least not until I figured out what he was up to.

It was late, nearing midnight, and not even twenty minutes ago, I'd woken from a bad dream, dragged myself out of bed, and glanced out the window to find Connor sneaking off into the darkness. No car. No friends. Dressed all in black.

Why I thought it was a brilliant idea to slip some sweats and runners on and dash after him, in the hopes of uncovering one of his many secrets, was so far beyond me. Yet here I was, tripping over my own feet because I'd forgotten to bring my phone in my rush to stalk my housemate.

Not that I could have used the light and given myself away. It was pure fucking luck I managed to catch up to him without alerting the asshole to my presence in the first place. Not that he was particularly sneaking along—he strolled quite casually toward the front gate.

I'd never seen Connor look worried or nervous in whatever

he did; his confidence and general capabilities were annoyingly attractive. Not that it made me hate him any less though.

Hate and curiosity warred within me every single time I was in this guy's presence.

It had been a week since he'd smashed into Ethan's room to find me naked and fucked to within an inch of my life, and since that morning, he'd steadfastly ignored me like I didn't exist.

Which sounded like heaven in theory but pissed me off, for some reason. I'd spent the week studying, cleaning, and cooking every fucking dinner, which Andrew made all of them be present for. Connor refused to look at me. He chatted and smiled at the others, he ate every dish I created like he enjoyed them all, and he laughed when they addressed him.

But if I spoke, he suddenly had selective hearing and never responded. Fuck, he never even looked my way, his gaze skating over whatever space I occupied like it was empty. I'd have been impressed by his ability to ignore an entire human if I wasn't so busy fuming over it.

Tripping over a rock I missed in the low light of the half-moon, I recovered just in time to glance up and notice that Connor's broad shoulders were no longer in view.

Motherfucker! How could he disappear that quickly?

Hurrying my steps, I headed for the last place I'd seen him and, to my surprise, found a small gap in the perimeter of the fence around Meadowridge. *Tightest security in the world, my ass.*

With a shake of my head, I leaned out through the gap and tried to spot him in the darkness. There was no sign of Connor at all, and when I was about to finally give up and go back to bed, I noticed a flash of red light quite a few yards away, and it took a few seconds for me to figure out it was the end of a lit cigarette, only visible because the moon had ducked behind the clouds, making it darker than ever.

The witching hour.

Dad had always told me midnight was the hour for the darkest and most depraved of individuals to be out and awake. He'd probably kick my ass if he knew I'd followed Connor on a midnight walk, but then again, he had no right to give a shit any longer, since he'd gone out for milk and never fucking returned.

Cliche that he was.

Okay, it wasn't exactly milk, but the sentiment remained the same. He'd said he'd be back for me and then never showed his face or called again. I was lucky that Mitchell and Karolyn hadn't just thrown me out on my ass and left me to a group home.

My anger pushed me forward from the gap in the fence, heading toward the spark of red that occasionally flashed far off in the darkness. I remained close to the fence line, among the fancy-ass trees and decorative hedges that the college had planted to rich up the front facade. I could duck in behind them if absolutely needed, especially if I was now chasing some rando psycho who wanted a smoke.

Rather than the psycho I shared a house with, whom I'd never seen smoke.

When I got closer, voices filtered through to me, and I crept even slower. There was more than one person out here, and I was fairly sure I recognized the deep rumble of Connor's derisiveness, since it was burned into my brain after the last time he insulted me.

"...think you fucking are, motherfucker?"

That voice wasn't familiar, with a deep accent that I couldn't place. Somewhere Eastern European, if I had to guess, but as I'd never traveled outside of America, it was a weak guess at best.

"My father is going to wipe you all from existence," Connor said, so casual despite the seriousness of his statement. He could have been talking about the damn weather or who won the Super Bowl last year.

The other voice grew a touch louder as he lobbed back a bunch of words, and this time they weren't in English, but it was clear they were just as uncomplimentary as the previous ones he'd used.

From my angle, I couldn't see them, and as stupid as it was to get any closer when I was able to hear from this position, I still pushed through the bushes. Leaves and sticks scratched at my skin, lodged in my hair, and dug into my back, but I'd come too far to turn back now.

I just had to hope the ranting guy kept the rustling of my approach from being noticed.

Connor cut him off after another long outburst in whatever language. "Look, I could have just walked out here and shot you all in the head."

There he was, that absolute charmer of a guy I knew.

"But I was nice enough to give you one fucking chance. Stop dealing on our territory. Stop attacking my father's guys on the streets. And stop coming any-fucking-where near Meadowridge. This is *my* territory, and I'm done letting your little gang in on our turf."

The other guy scoffed, and I shuffled around so I could finally see where the two of them were standing. The moon shifted from behind the clouds right at that moment, and it shone down on a wiry guy with dark olive skin and a shaved head. He was covered in tattoos, right up the sides of his face and over his entire skull. The cigarette hung from the side of his mouth as he paced and glared.

In the semi-darkness, his eyes looked squinty and dark as he kept shooting death glares across the trunk of his black car. Toward Connor, I could only assume, not that I could see him from where I was crouched in the bushes.

"Your confidence is going to be your downfall, Sullivan.

Your family might have controlled this town and half the East Coast for the past ten generations, but eventually, every empire crumbles."

Who the hell were the Sullivans?

Did that mean Ethan was part of this as well? Was that why he'd said he was involved with a criminal organization the other night?

I'd been too dick drunk to really delve into that statement during the storm, and then it had slipped my mind until this moment, but it was clear that there was more to these brothers than I'd initially thought.

Connor's scoff made his feelings more than apparent. "This empire was built on blood and sacrifice, and it will continue to flourish long after you're gone. Which will be in the next two minutes if you don't get the fuck out of here."

The tatted guy chuckled darkly. "You made a mistake coming out here tonight. We don't want to start a war...yet. But a little warning wouldn't go astray."

There was a scuffle, and I could only see the guy yank out his gun, but he was too slow, Connor's muzzle already pressed squarely to the side of his head. "If you move, even to breathe, I'm going to blow your brains out."

I've killed more people than you fucking know.

Apparently, that hadn't been an exaggeration to scare me.

I'd been sleeping under the same roof as a legit murderer who hated me, with just an old skeleton key lock to keep me from being killed in my bed. Still, he'd never actually done anything to harm me or anyone else in the house, so maybe we were actually *safer* with Connor under the same roof.

The way I reacted to violence and danger was different now. I enjoyed being around the people who were dangerous in general and not to me, because in situations like this, they knew how to take care of themselves. My therapist had names and titles for everything, but I called it survival.

I was well-versed in what it took to survive these days.

Shifting in the bushes, I could finally see Connor, his face darkened by shadows to match his full black outfit. A glint of silver caught my attention next, and before I could run through the repercussions of what I was about to do, I shouted out a warning.

"Connor, behind you!"

He spun just in time to miss the silenced shot that had been aimed right at his torso, shoving the tatted guy into the path of whomever else was out there.

He dove behind the car to give himself cover and, without missing a beat, added a silencer to the end of his gun. I was half-frozen in the bushes still but saw him laser a glare at me while he returned fire in the general direction the other guys had gone.

Unfortunately, those two weren't the only ones, and I froze at the feeling of a firm nudge in my back. "Hands out beside you," a low, heavily accented voice hissed at me. "One sudden move and you'll never walk again."

The scar in my back chose that second to ache, as if in remembrance of the last time I almost didn't walk from being shot. Or more accurately, almost didn't live.

Despite the rising panic, I kept my eyes locked on Connor, who was still firing back at his enemies. It allowed me to lift my hands to the side and obey the order, and then I was jabbed hard in the spine. "Walk."

If I looked away from Connor, I found I couldn't move, but keeping my eyes locked on him helped me step through the bushes, adding a few extra cuts and scratches to my body, until I was out in the open.

Connor swung his weapon around and trained it on whomever was behind me. Meanwhile, I just kept moving my feet, even as my head spun and I was seconds from screaming hysterically.

"One move and she's dead," my captor snarled.

Connor scoffed and didn't bother to lower his weapon. "I have no fucking idea who she is. Some rich bitch from Meadowridge who snuck out to meet her boyfriend or buy drugs. Why would you think I'd give a single fuck about her?"

Another jab in my back, and I took another step forward, my eyes locked on Connor's too gorgeous face, even as he scowled at us both. Connor denying any knowledge of my existence would probably bother me normally, but tonight, I was beyond the ability to care about such a rejection.

I was about to get shot again, and I had the feeling that there wasn't another chance waiting for me in the wings.

EVELYN

Even with the rising panic, in my peripherals I saw the approach of the tatted guy, another man who looked eerily similar to him, and a giant blond man who carried a machine gun and could have given Haze a run for his money in sheer size.

"Told you your confidence would be your downfall, Sullivan," Tatted Guy said. "Now, as I also said, we're not here to start a war *yet*. I don't need the sort of heat your father would bring down on the Crusades, but I also think a nice lesson is in order."

Connor's angry expression morphed into one of boredom halfway through the speech. "What do you want?"

"You and your girlfriend here, who just saved you a bullet in the side—painful injury to recover from, trust me—need to go for a little drive. I need you out of Meadowridge for a few days while I take care of some business."

He turned his gaze on me and ran his eyes up and down my body. "You're a pretty little thing, aren't you? What's your name?"

I wasn't sure my voice would work, but I managed to stutter

out Nina's name, instinct—or maybe Connor's brief shake of his head—telling me not to give my own away.

"Well, Nina. I need you to get in the trunk and shut the fuck up. If you do that, I won't shoot your guy here in the knee before I dump him in there, giving you both the best chance of surviving."

He hit a button in his hand, and with a beep, the back of his black car opened revealing a fairly tight trunk space.

"You're making a huge mistake," Connor growled. "I don't care about Nina. And you're not taking me anywhere, Elijah."

Tatted Guy aka Elijah just shrugged. "Well, if you don't care about her, you won't mind if we take her for a little ride on her own then."

My heart, already slamming in my chest, picked up pace to the next dimension. No one would have to worry about me in a second because I'd have a heart attack and die right here in front of the school.

I heard the roughly muttered *fuck* from Connor, and then I was shoved into the trunk, tumbling down hard and crying out as my arm slammed against the metal edge, before a boot on my stomach shoved me back even farther.

"So, what's it to be, Sullivan?"

There was a snarl from Connor, but to my relief, he moved toward the car. I could see that his gun remained trained on them as he crossed closer and slid into the remaining space in front of me. The edge of my panic attack had me unable to breathe easily, but as his size filled the trunk and the scent of spice and cinnamon surrounded me, it got worse.

The others kept their guns pointed on us, and I wondered if this had all been a ruse to kill us once we were inside, making the disposal of bodies and evidence slightly more convenient. They looked wary though, all the way until the lid was slammed down, shrouding us in darkness.

A few seconds later, the car started, and I couldn't contain my sobs any longer, pressing my hand over my mouth to try and choke down the panicked squeaks that wanted to escape.

I had no idea if Connor heard me or not, as he spent many minutes maneuvering his giant frame to kick out one of the taillights. He managed eventually, and then he hit the other with his fist before he stilled.

"The broken lights might lead them to getting pulled over by a highway patrol, but I wouldn't bank on it," he muttered, as if it annoyed him to have to explain his actions. "They disabled the release lever already, so we're most likely stuck in here until they get to wherever they're going."

I'd have loved to reply, maybe ask a few questions of my own, but I was too busy hyperventilating. Connor started to move again, right as the breaths heaved in and out of my lungs, and my brain started to go foggy. He turned over to face me, and I have no idea how he managed it in the tight space.

"We're absolutely going to fight about what happened here tonight, Evelyn," he growled roughly, and our faces were so close that his breath washed over me with the slightest minty scent. "You're a nosy, annoying brat, and I will figure out how to punish you for this. But that won't work if you pass out and die right now. So I need you to calm the fuck down. Now."

My eyes were locked on where his face would be, but I couldn't see him in the darkness, and that had been the only thing before that kept me from panicking. Those green eyes, so like Ethan's, and the face of a Greek god, all wrapped up in one asshole bundle.

Heavy hands gripped my face, and the pressure against my skin actually helped regulate my breathing. Especially when he started to breathe in sync with me. "That's it, brat," he murmured, lips so close, I swore I touched them as I inhaled deeply. "Breathe in and out."

"I saved your life," I choked out, my limbs trembling against him, our bodies touching everywhere in the confined space. "That's not brat behavior."

His lips curved, I could feel them against my cheek. "You followed me from the house, snuck around in the bushes, and got us kidnapped because you drew attention to the one weakness in my vicinity. Even if they'd shot me in the side, I'd have killed all four before I bled out. It wouldn't be my first bullet or my last, so this is your fault, *brat*."

What the fuck did I even say to that? There were no words.

"Oh," I squeaked, at a loss for anything more profound or snappy. I was too frazzled to be cool.

Connor scoffed something that sounded a little like a laugh. "Oh, indeed." He was silent for a moment before muttering, "Ethan's going to kill us both when we get back to the house."

"When?" I repeated, clinging on to the hope that one word offered. "Not if?"

He shifted his position again. Considering his size, there was no way he'd be able to get comfortable, but he seemed determined not to squish me for some reason. "When. They're not going to kill us, brat. The Crusades can't afford to start a war like that; they're just messing with us to pretend they're stronger than they are."

"Oh," I said again, feeling somewhat silly for interfering. Then again, the bullets they'd fired had been real, and if I hadn't warned Connor... "Has Ethan killed people?"

Connor didn't reply for what felt like forever, then he sighed, and his warm breath fanned across my neck. "Ask him, maybe he'll tell you."

I stifled a gasp. "What does that mean?"

"It means," Connor grumbled, his eyeroll evident in his voice, "that although we're related by blood, we aren't brothers. Not like—" He cut himself off, swallowing the words he'd been about to say.

I frowned, rubbing my sore elbow in the darkness. "Like you and Andrew?" Silence. It was confirmation enough, though. "Brodie and Haze, too? You guys are all...weirdly tight, considering."

Connor just grunted, and I suspected that was all I'd get out of him on this topic. It made me crazy curious, though. How did they all meet? What did they even have in common? And why the fuck go to such lengths to hide their friendship from the rest of the school?

"Are you thinking or panicking?" he asked after several moments of silence.

"Thinking."

"Good. Because I'm not kissing you just to snap you out of a panic attack. Even I can recognize an abuse of power when I see it."

Outraged, I gave him a little shove. "Excuse *you*. For one thing, it wasn't an abuse of power. *I* kissed *him* the first time because I had no idea that he was a teacher."

"Uh-huh," Connor replied in a drawl. "But the second time, *he* kissed *you* when you were in a vulnerable state *and* he knew you were his student. So many red flags you may as well be a bull." He paused, then clearly decided I had no comeback to that statement. "What was the other thing?"

I frowned, despite the fact he couldn't see my expressions. "Other thing?"

"You said 'for one thing,' so what was the other?"

"Oh, for *another* thing, I wouldn't let you kiss me even if I were about to pass out from hyperventilation." I said it confidently and with a generous helping of indignation that he'd even suggest such a thing. What I didn't anticipate was his response.

He fucking *laughed*.

"What's so funny?" I muttered, not seeing the humor in our situation.

"You," he chuckled, but didn't elaborate any further.

Sulking, I pursed my lips and decided I didn't want to chat after all. Instead, I turned my thoughts inward, to where the hell they might be taking us and how the fuck we'd get back to Meadowridge.

After what felt like hours, I must have drifted off to sleep because the next thing I knew, I was waking up to Connor's hand on my waist, squeezing me gently.

"Brat, wake up," he whispered. "We're here."

My neck hurt. So did my back. Fucking hell, everything hurt, but then again, what did I expect after taking a nap in the trunk of a car with a six-foot-whatever dude jammed in beside me?

"Here? Where?" I was still half-asleep. How the fuck I managed to sleep *and* avoid nightmares while stuffed in a trunk, I had no clue.

"Beats me," he muttered back as a car door slammed and boots crunched on gravel.

Connor wriggled away, turning onto his back so that as the trunk started to open—*Wham!* His boot hit the lid, slamming it into the gang guy's face and sending him flying. Connor followed the movement through, springing out of the car and landing on his feet with a fluid grace that should not have looked so natural on such a big guy.

"W-wait!" the guy stammered as I scrambled to climb out of the trunk myself, my legs weak and wobbly as the blood started to flow again.

The guy was on the ground, blood pouring from his busted nose and his hands held out in front.

Connor bent, scooping up the guy's gun from where he must have dropped it.

"Evelyn, shut your eyes and cover your ears," he ordered, his voice like ice.

I blinked rapidly, sweat pouring down my spine and my

lungs tight as I looked from the gun to the bleeding man and back. "What? Connor, you—"

"Do it, brat!" he barked, and I instantly obeyed.

Even so, there was no mistaking the near-deafening sound of a gunshot a split second later as it echoed through the trees.

24

EVELYN

This was my opportunity to run. If he doubled back to the classroom to search again, he'd find me for sure. If I wanted any chance, I had to run. Now.

"Evelyn...come out, come out wherever you are!" the masked gunman sang through the empty halls, and I covered my own mouth to stifle my sobs as I made a break for it.

Sunlight hit my face as I burst through the doors, freedom so close I could taste it and then...

Bang!

The sound of the shot registered in my head before the pain, but then the pain was everything.

I'd been shot. He'd shot me.

Warm hands shook my shoulders, making me moan in pain. Didn't they realize I'd been shot?

"Come on, snap out of it!" a deep, gruff voice ordered.

My eyelids fluttered in confusion. Green eyes framed with dark lashes met mine and my reality blurred. "Ethan?" His eyes widened, and my whole body quaked in relief. "Holy shit, Ethan—" Then my lips were on his. My lifeline, pulling me from the depths of my trauma yet again.

He seemed startled but quickly wrapped his arms around me, pulling me close as he dominated my mouth with his own, stitching our very souls together with each stroke of his tongue. Rather than just pulling me from the darkness of my own mind, he kissed me like he was drowning, and I was his only hope for survival.

A low moan rolled through me as I reached for his waistband, desperate for more, but he broke away with a curse.

"*Brat*," he growled. "Stop."

Those two words were the equivalent of being struck by lightning, and I jerked away so violently I smacked my head on the back of the car. The car we'd just spent hours traveling in the trunk of. The car that'd been driven by the man now lying dead in a pool of blood a few twelve feet away.

"Oh my God," I gasped, clapping a hand over my mouth. Then, in horror, I realized who I'd just been mouth-fucking like he was the last scoop of ice cream while I was PMSing. "No..."

My gaze snapped back to the dead man, and at the perfect circle between his eyebrows, and at the dark puddle slowly spreading... Nausea ripped through me like a freight train, and I scrambled on hands and knees to the nearest bush to vomit.

"That's a first," Connor muttered, then gently held my hair back as I upended the full contents of my stomach. The last thing I'd eaten were the Swedish meatballs I'd made for dinner, and I could safely say they were not as good the second time. "You okay?"

I groaned, wiping my mouth with the back of my hand. "No." I was so far from okay it was almost laughable.

"Okay, well we need to get the fuck out of here," he replied, casual as anything like he didn't just execute an unarmed man minutes ago. "Come on. I need to get back in cell range to call this in."

He offered his hand, and I took it without even thinking about what I was doing, allowing him to pull me to my feet. My knees wobbled dangerously, though, as I took a few steps toward the car.

"Call it in?" I repeated, shivering. "To the police?"

Connor didn't reply as he opened the passenger side door and gently pushed me into the seat. The car was all black leather and smelled like cigarette smoke. Disgusting. My teeth chattered as Connor buckled my seat belt for me like I was a helpless child, then firmly closed my door.

He circled around to the driver's side and slid inside.

"Evelyn?" he said after a moment of silence. I hugged myself tighter, trying to control my shivers as I stared out into the woods. Connor gave a frustrated sigh. "Brat, snap out of it. You're in shock."

I swallowed hard. Shock? No shit. He'd just killed a guy in cold blood.

"I know," I whispered, keeping the snark inside my head simply because I lacked the energy to unleash.

Connor grumbled something under his breath, then jerked off his black hoodie and tossed it over to me. "Use this as a blanket. You'll be fine once we get some distance." He didn't wait for me to do what I was told, just started the car up and sped away from the crime scene with dust flying from the tires.

Numb and sluggish, I snuggled into the warm fabric of his sweatshirt as he tapped the climate control to turn up the heating. It took maybe ten minutes, but eventually my trembles did subside, just like he'd said.

But in the absence of shock, logic crept its way back in.

"You murdered that man," I said out loud, turning my face to stare at Connor in disbelief. "You shot him. In the head. He was unarmed and—"

"And he deserved it," Connor replied, utterly unrepentant. "Don't cry over spilled milk. He's done worse to plenty of better people."

I had nothing to say to that. Absolutely nothing. I just

huddled lower in the seat of the stolen car and stared out the window blankly. Trees passed the window, none of it looking familiar in the least. Or all of it. We could be in the next state or just down the road for all I knew of the area.

"Didn't you need to call the police?" I reminded him after some time driving.

Connor glanced over at me, his gaze dark before flicking his eyes back to the road. "No. But I do need to make *a* call. Can you keep your mouth shut, or do I need to wait until we're back at school?"

My lips parted in outrage. "I'm not a child, Connor. How far are we from Meadowridge anyway?"

He lifted one shoulder in a shrug, checking the time on his watch. "Five or so hours." He seemed to debate his options for a moment, then sighed for what felt like the thousandth time. "Just stay quiet, all right? No talking, no noises, nothing. Am I clear?"

I scowled and folded my arms beneath his hoodie. "Crystal."

"Fine," he growled, then brought up the Bluetooth phone display on the car's dash. Using the steering wheel controls, he cycled through to the most recent phone number and clicked redial. It rang for just a few moments before it was answered.

"You get it done?" The voice was vaguely familiar, and it only took me a moment to place it as the tatted guy in the woods. Elijah. I stifled a small gasp, realizing that Connor wasn't calling for *help*; he was calling to gloat.

His sharp glare told me even that was too much noise, and I covered my mouth with my own hand to prevent it happening again.

"You could say that," Connor replied with a dark chuckle. "Sorry about your man, Elijah. He seemed dispensable, though, or you wouldn't have sent him alone."

A short silence filled the phone line, then a muttered curse. "You motherfucker. He wasn't going to kill you, just—"

"I know," Connor cut him off. "Doesn't change how dead he is now, though, does it? I've warned you once before, Elijah, you're getting too big for your boots. It's time you remember your place in the pecking order. One. Dead. Man. At a time."

Holy *shit*, he sounded like an actual honest-to-God psychopath.

"Listen...Connor...we fucked up, all right? I can see that now. Between you and me, we got hired for a job at your fancy school and just needed you out of the way for a couple of days. It was harmless, right? Just drop you off across state lines and leave you to walk home. You didn't need to go killing anyone." Elijah sounded like he was on the ground, rolled over to expose his belly to the alpha wolf. Submissive and whining.

Connor's hands flexed on the steering wheel, his knuckles white as he strangled the leather. *"What job?"*

"Nothing to do with you, Connor, I swear. It's just a little harmless kidnap-ransom shit. Some chick. We just didn't want you messing up the payday, you know? It's just business." More whining. Fucking hell, this was the guy who'd stuffed us in a trunk at gunpoint?

Connor's jaw clenched so hard, I could hear his teeth grinding, and I reached out to touch his arm without really thinking about what I was doing. The touch startled him, and his death grip on the steering wheel instantly loosened as he shot me a confused glance.

I withdrew my hand like I'd been burned, unsure why I'd done that in the first place, but Elijah was babbling again on the phone.

"...no need to involve your father, right?" he was saying in a slightly panicked voice. "You killed my guy; the score is settled. Let's just leave it at that."

Connor flicked another puzzled look my way, then shook

his head like he was trying to rearrange his head. "Make sure your guys are gone from Meadowridge before I get back, Elijah. Anyone I see wearing a Crusades tag will get executed on sight, no questions asked. Am I clear?"

"Absolutely, understood, you won't see them near the school again," the wannabe gangster gushed. "And your father?"

Connor rolled his eyes and mouthed a silent *for fuck's sake* before glancing at me again, thoughtfully. "I don't see why he needs to know," he finally decided. "Unless you try to shoot me again, of course."

"Of course," Elijah quickly agreed.

Connor ended the call, then gusted out a heavy breath. Silence filled the car with a heaviness that physically hurt, but I refused to be the one to break it. What could I even say when he'd just so thoroughly fried my brain with revelations?

He seemed in no rush to explain *anything* so we just drove in tension for a while.

Then he glanced my way with a thoughtful squint.

"Do you want to talk about what happened back there?" he asked, shocking the hell out of me.

Eyes wide, I shook my head. "Absolutely the fuck not. Nothing happened, Connor. Nothing. I never ever want to talk about it, and so help me if you tell Andrew—or Ethan—that we kissed, I will cut your dick off and make you swallow it."

His lips twitched, then curved into a full-blown grin. "Vicious brat. I meant your panic attack. You've got some real trauma with guns, huh?"

Oh.

"I don't want to talk about that, either," I muttered, my face utterly *flaming* with embarrassment.

He nodded and seemed content to let sleeping dogs lie as he drove. An hour later, he slowed and pulled into a gas station that looked like it hadn't been operational in a hundred years.

"What are we doing?" I asked, fear sparking in my chest. Was he going to kick me out and leave me there as some sort of punishment? He said he'd punish me for being stupid, didn't he?

Connor shifted the car into park and turned off the engine, then unclicked his belt. "Waiting for your ride," he informed me, then climbed out of the car.

Confused, I followed and pulled his hoodie on properly to keep the warmth. "My ride? I don't—"

My question was cut short with the roar of a motorbike approaching, then a blacked-out sleek machine sped into the gas station where we waited. The rider was completely covered in leathers, not a single inch of skin showing, and I stiffened with anxiety as I noted the enormous gun strapped to the side of the bike.

Panicked, I shifted until Connor was positioned as a human shield in front of me.

"Cute," he muttered with a scoff. "You know bullets would go straight through me and still kill you at this range?"

My throat tightened. "I'm well aware."

The biker chose that moment to flip his visor open, and I instantly recognized the warm brown eyes creased in concern.

"Haze," I breathed in relief. "What are *you* doing here?"

"He's taking you back to school," Connor informed me, checking his watch *again*. It was one of those fancy military-style ones, and I was just now suspecting he had some sort of tracking and or communication installed in it. "I need to take a trip home."

"To speak with your scary overlord father? I thought you said you wouldn't tell him?"

Connor shrugged. "I lied. Go on, Haze will see you safely back to the house. I won't be long."

I took a couple of steps toward Haze before hesitating. "I can't. Haze, you..." I flapped my hand, trying to explain the whole *don't touch Haze or he will get violent* warning that Brodie had given me without actually having to say it.

"It's fine," he rumbled from within the helmet, then reached to the far side of the bike and produced a second helmet, which he extended my way.

"His issue is skin contact," Connor said quietly, his lips brushing my hair as he leaned close. "Leathers should dull things. You'll be okay, brat, get on the bike."

Swallowing hard, I put my faith in both of them and took the helmet from Haze's gloved hand. Connor helped me secure it on my head, then steadied me with a hand as I carefully positioned myself on the pillion seat of Haze's bike.

"Hold on to him," Connor ordered, taking my hand and placing it on the thick leather of Haze's jacket. "Gravel rash is no joke." Then he fist-bumped Haze's leather-clad knuckles and returned to his stolen car.

It wasn't until the bike engine roared and we rocketed out of the parking lot that I fully processed Connor's choice of words. Leathers *should* dull things. Great. Apparently I was guinea-pigging the extent of Haze's touch aversion while sitting on the back of a high-speed motorcycle.

25

EVELYN

The sun was high in the sky by the time Haze's powerful bike slid to a halt in front of Bluebell House. At this stage, I'd half worked myself into a tizzy deciding what I'd say to him. Having my arms wrapped around his powerful frame for the hour plus it took to make it back to the school was an interesting experience.

He smelled good.

He felt good.

But the tension in his muscles was a constant reminder that he hated to be touched and I was forcing it on him. As he turned off the bike and dropped the kickstand, I opened my mouth to apologize once more, but he was gone.

Like, if we'd been in a cartoon, all that would be left behind was the dusty outline of his giant frame and me with my jaw hanging down to my belly button.

Fuck.

Swinging my leg off the bike, I took a second to let my wobbly legs adjust, breathing deeply as I tried to mentally work through everything that had happened since I stupidly decided to follow Connor into the night. What a fucking shit show.

Though, truth be told, it had almost been worth it to build a tiny bridge with Connor. I would never say that we were friends, but maybe we weren't quite enemies anymore either.

Sure, he was a raging psychopath who murdered people without thought, but as I'd reasoned earlier, as long as that murderous rage wasn't directed my way, it was almost a relief to know he existed under the same roof as me. Connor could take out any asshole who broke in.

With a sigh, I started to work the strap of the helmet to get it off when rough hands wrapped around mine, halting me in my tracks. My head jerked up to find Ethan's concerned face peering in through my clear visor.

"Lilith," he breathed, and there was no hiding the fine lines framing his tired face. "Fuck, sweetheart. I've been worried out of my mind about you."

In two hurried movements, he had the strap free, and then the helmet was gently removed before his hands cupped my face as he kissed me soundly.

Out here. In the fucking open where anyone could see. *And after I'd vomited.*

I gasped against his lips, about to protest, but his tongue dove between my parted mouth and I was lost. It wasn't until Brodie's soft laughter startled us both from the kiss that he pulled away, and I sucked in air embarrassingly loud.

"My turn," Brodie said, and despite his laughter from before, his expression was uncharacteristically somber as he took me in. I had no idea what I looked like but no doubt I was a disaster, my hair everywhere, and covered in dirt from being shoved into a trunk.

Brodie didn't appear to care as he moved Ethan out of the way, who to my surprise didn't protest, and wrapped his arms around me, lifting me full-bodily off the ground. His kiss was gentler but no less demanding, as he too slid his tongue against mine, devouring my lips as he continued to hold my weight like it was nothing.

By the time I was back on my own feet, the two guys pressed in on either side of me, and I felt dizzy and breathless. "Maybe I should get kidnapped more often."

The joke fell absolutely flat as they narrowed their eyes on me, but thankfully they didn't move away. I still wore Connor's hoodie, but the events of the last twelve plus hours had taken its toll, leaving me chilled to the bone. .

"Connor gave us sparse details," Brodie said, taking my hand to lace his fingers with mine, sending a wave of butterflies through my stomach. "But we want to hear from you, Evie babe. Tell us everything."

"Yes, *Evelyn!*" This was a snap from behind me, and I turned to find Andrew on the steps of Bluebell House, his face creased and thunderous as he crossed his arms and glared down at me. "Time to explain why you would act so stupidly and irrationally when we're doing everything in our goddamn power to keep you—"

He abruptly cut himself off, and the low-level headache that had been hovering at the back of my head since I was kidnapped roared to life at his harsh tones. "Keep me from what?" I snapped back, pushing between Ethan and Brodie, my hand pulling free as I gave into my need to rage at this demanding asshole. "What have you ever done for me, Andrew Knightsbridge? Tell me? I'm not your goddamn responsibility, and if I want to sneak out at midnight and follow Connor to his creepy gang meetings, then I will sneak out and go to them!"

I was well aware that my argument and rebuttal were weak at best, but fuck this guy. I'd had a really bad night, and the absolute last thing I needed was Andrew jumping in and acting like my dad, reprimanding me for my stupid actions.

He wasn't my father. I didn't even have a real one of those these days.

"Everyone in this house is my responsibility," Andrew replied stiffly, staring down at me like I was an annoying puppy who'd peed on his shoes. "And from now on, there are rules—rules you will follow."

"Or what?" I shot back. "Going to spank me? You wouldn't have the balls."

His eyes darkened, but strangely, he didn't appear angrier at my rebuttal. Frustrated, I stormed up the steps, annoyed that I had to push past him to make it inside. I was almost through the door when his hand shot out to wrap around my arm. Of course, he managed to land on the elbow I'd slammed on the edge of the car, and my gasp of pain had him releasing me just as quickly.

His gaze turned weirdly frantic as he ran his gaze over my torso and down my legs. "Connor said you were uninjured. What's wrong? Do you need a doctor?"

Shaking my head with a huff, I forced the part of me, which had warmed at his obvious concern, down under my annoyance. Rules. He'd said he had rules for me.

Not a chance, *Dad*.

I continued into the house, and this time no one stopped me. In my room, I took advantage of that heavy old lock and twisted it closed, leaning back against the door.

My body hummed, as if adrenaline scorched through me, even though I'd done nothing more than kiss two guys and fight with a third. Oh, and get kidnapped with a fourth and ride on a motorbike with a fifth.

Honestly, it was almost starting to feel normal living in a house with these five larger-than-life men, all of whom drove me crazy in different ways.

I felt sort of bad that I'd stormed away from Ethan and Brodie, who'd given me the greeting I hoped for after being kidnapped, but it was better for me to take a nap and clear my head before I had to relay the story. Possibly by that time

Connor would be back too, and if he'd already filled them in, then it would save me going into details.

Avoiding reliving trauma was a specialty of mine, according to Dr. Graystone anyway.

Eh, look at me go with my own internal therapy. Barely even needed professional help these days. If all the fucked-up stuff in my life continued, pretty soon the trauma would just merge as one, and eventually I'd be remade in the strongest version of myself.

Or completely shattered. Time would tell.

In the midst of my musing, I fell into a restless sleep. I had no idea how long I slept, but when I woke, it was dark outside again, and the house was strangely quiet. Rolling over, I grabbed my phone to see it was nine p.m. My stomach and bladder both chose that moment to rage at me, reminding me that I hadn't eaten or used the restroom for far too long. Not to mention I also still hadn't brushed my teeth or showered, and at this stage, I was too gross to keep existing in my own filth.

I'd made my point with Andrew by giving him exactly what he wanted and locking myself safely in the room. Whatever. He'd never had a chance to tell me the new rules, and that had been my main reason for the rapid and fury-filled exit.

It took a concerted effort to turn the lock on the door, and when it clicked over, the noise echoed loudly. I pulled it open and stepped out, gasping as I ground to a halt, locked in a pair of bright blue eyes.

Brodie was slouched against the wall, his face drawn as he stared up at me. He got to his feet quickly, and I found myself hurrying closer to him. "What are you doing out here?"

He flinched, his forehead bunching. "You locked your door." His voice was soft, and there was an emotion brimming under the neutral tone that I couldn't quite get a read on.

"Sorry," I found myself saying, even though the last thing I wanted to do was apologize for taking what I needed. "I routinely run from trauma, and the last twenty-four hours were a lot. Andrew pushed me over the edge."

Brodie stepped closer to me, and with his features all shadowy, he was less superhero and more villain. I wasn't sure which version of him I liked better. Maybe both. "You were having a nightmare, Eve. I've been sitting outside your door for hours listening to you cry and scream, and I couldn't get in to help you. You're lucky I didn't break the door down. It was only Haze telling me that could make it worse that held me back."

I swallowed roughly. "Haze was here too?"

Brodie nodded, rougher than his usual smooth movements. "Yep, he kept me company for a while. He just went to make you some food because you haven't eaten or drank anything, according to Connor."

I straightened and grabbed Brodie's forearm. "Connor's back? Is he okay?"

My question took Brodie by surprise, if his widening eyes were any indication, but he didn't push me for a reason. "He's not back yet, but he called in."

It bothered me that he was out there in the middle of a gang war. Or maybe it bothered me that he was out there without me. In my mind, I'd still saved his life, and I wondered if anyone else would have his back in the same way. Surely his dad wouldn't let anything happen to his heir? Or was Ethan the heir?

No doubt that family was far more complicated than I could understand from my brief interactions, but I knew I'd feel better once Connor was back home.

My new trauma-bonded bestie.

I almost snorted at the thought, and that was when I knew it was time to eat before I passed out from delirium. "I'm sorry that I screamed the house down," I told Brodie, feeling my shoulders sag at the realization that I was getting worse, not better. "I was doing so much better with the nightmares when I first started school"—minus first day panic attacks—"but anything with guns triggers me right back to my past. I won't lock my door again at night or maybe we can get you a key cut."

Pressing up on my tiptoes, I kissed him right on the lips. "Thank you for sitting out here waiting for me. I don't know what I did to deserve you, Brodie Keller, but I'm fucking grateful."

The blue of his eyes darkened until they were almost violet in their intensity. "I'm the one who is grateful. You're the first real thing to walk into my life since these four assholes found me at youth camp. Don't think I'm ever letting you go now." He pressed his lips to mine once more and then pulled away. Finally, his smile reappeared, and it warmed me all the way to my frozen core. "Now that you're back out here with us, I feel it's my duty to tell you that you smell kinda ripe, Evie babe." He slapped my ass gently and nudged me toward the bathroom. "Why don't you shower and get changed, and I'll make sure Haze has the food ready to go for all of us. I can't skip meals when I need to bulk up for my next role."

I pretended to sniff my armpits, which did in fact smell quite ripe, with the resulting gag not faked at all. "Yep, definitely in need of a shower."

Brodie laughed as I ducked back to my room to grab a change of clothes, all the while wondering if I could sneakily keep Connor's comfy hoodie.

Just for a little while longer.

HAZE

What the *fuck* had I been thinking, taking my bike when Connor pressed the emergency-alert tracker? Clearly, I hadn't been. I hadn't thought things through because I'd just realized that *Eve was missing* and then Connor pressed his SOS... Logic hadn't factored in.

The worst part about driving the hours back to campus with her small hands clutching my jacket and her thighs pressed against mine? I wanted to enjoy it. I *liked* being around her, but even with the barrier of leather between our skin, it took all my willpower to keep myself under control and not crash.

By the time we got back, I was both dripping sweat and shivering as pure, undiluted trauma coated every inch of my skin beneath the bike leathers. I was utterly disgusted with myself.

I heard Eve's small protest as I smoke-bombed myself out of her vicinity, and it gutted me.

Why was I such a fucking mess? Oh yeah. Trauma. It was amazing how fucked up a guy could be after enduring torture in a Serbian prison camp as a young teen.

After showering and taking a Valium, I was calm enough to try to apologize to the mysterious, violet-haired temptress living down the hall. Trouble was, Andrew had apparently pissed her off and she'd locked herself in her room.

"You don't have a lot of experience with people, do you?" I asked him when I found him ironing his dress shirts in his room.

His head jerked up from the perfect pleat he was pressing. "And you do?"

I folded my arms, leaning against the doorframe. "Never said I did. But even a social outcast like me knows not to pick a fight with a woman who just survived a kidnapping. Did it occur to you that she might be fragile right now?"

Andrew glared daggers, placing his iron carefully on the holder so not to burn anything. His glares had no effect on me, and he damn well knew it. I didn't give a fuck who his mommy was.

"Did it occur to *you* that you're on a dozen government watch lists and any number of those organizations would have wet their pants to snatch you up the moment you left Meadowridge grounds?" He folded his own arms, mirroring my defensive stance. "You could have told Brodie or Ethan to retrieve them, rather than risk your own incarceration."

"I was the only one home when the alarm activated," I murmured, knowing full well that wasn't a good enough reason. I shouldn't leave Meadowridge. Not for anything. "Considering she's your debt, Drew, I'd think you'd be saying thank you right now."

Andrew blew out a heavy sigh, running a hand through his perfect hair and messing it up which was a clear sign that he wasn't okay. "Yeah. Right. Thanks, bro. I never anticipated that keeping an eye on some chick would be so stressful."

That amused me enough to crack a smile. "She's not some

normal chick, that's why. Even if she doesn't know it, she's still Abraham's daughter."

Andrew grimaced, nodding. "You're right. I just don't know how long he's expecting me to keep this up. The girl is a danger magnet." She was, but I kind of liked that about her. She was a little bit spicy and intrigued the shit out of me. "Did you hear there was an attempted break in at the south gate while you were gone? Some dickheads from the Crusades trying to get onto school grounds."

I hadn't. I'd been too occupied with having Eve's hands on my jacket for the whole drive back, I simply hadn't checked my messages. "I take it they were stopped?"

Andrew scoffed, rolling his shirtsleeves in a clear sign of his anxiety. "Of course they were. The Meadowridge security is better than my mother's own Secret Service. It is uncomfortable timing, though. Abraham asked me to keep Evelyn safe for a reason...he must think she's in danger."

I quirked a brow. "More than getting shot in the back at her last school? I'd think that was reason enough to be worried."

"True," he agreed with a scowl. "I dunno. She just gets under my skin."

Now that was a feeling I could identify with. She also got under mine, though I was confident it was in an entirely different way.

A muffled scream from upstairs echoed through the house, and before I could even comprehend what I was doing, I'd taken the stairs three at a time. Brodie beat me there and held up a hand to tell me to calm the fuck down.

"She's asleep," he said in a hoarse voice. "Nightmares. What happened out there with Connor?"

I shrugged. "Fuck if I know. Call him and ask." Another muffled scream came through the door, and I jerked forward, reaching for the handle.

"It's locked," Brodie informed me—unnecessarily, since it

didn't turn more than a couple of millimeters. "She always locks it when she's pissed off."

Scowling, I refrained from telling him that I had a spare key that I *could* use if I wanted to. But if I did, I'd lose that safety net. Instead, I knocked gently on Eve's door. "Eve? It's Haze. Can we talk?"

No response.

Brodie gave a heavy sigh, sliding his back down the wall until his butt met the floor. "She's asleep, bro. Though I'm tempted to kick the door down, because I'm not sure how much longer I can listen to her sobs without losing my mind."

To reiterate his words, sobs echoed through the door, and now I was the one considering whether I was willing to kick it down. "It'll make it worse," I told him, aware that startling her awake in the middle of a terror could do further psychological damage. "She's already afraid of being attacked, and us breaking her door down is quite violent."

"If she wanted company, she wouldn't have locked the door," Andrew called in a hard voice, glaring at the both of us. "Haze, call Con and get more info about what the fuck went down out there. We can't do shit if we don't know what happened to her."

He had a good point. I flipped him my middle finger but left Brodie sitting guard outside Eve's room as I returned to my own. Connor had been heading to his family estate to visit his father, so I wasn't going to risk calling him. Instead, I sent an encrypted message to his smartwatch, telling him to call when it was safe.

I didn't wait long before my phone lit up, and I accepted the unknown caller.

"All good?" I asked carefully.

"Yeah, I'm on my way back to the house," he replied in a tired voice. "Is she okay?"

There was no need to ask which *she* he was asking about,

but I was surprised to hear his concern. He'd shown nothing but irritation and distrust for pretty little Eve and, for the past week, had practically ignored her existence entirely. And yet, there was undeniable vulnerability in that simple question.

"She's alive," I replied carefully. "You gonna give me the whole story?"

Connor gave a huffing groan. "Not that much to tell, Haze. I went out to warn Elijah and his dipshit thugs to stay the fuck out of Meadowridge. She fucking followed me like some sort of obsessed stalker, then screamed when one of the Crusades were about to put a bullet through my side. Fucking idiot." He was gruff, but there was no heat in his words. *What the hell had actually happened out there between them?*

"So she saved you from getting shot. How'd you end up across state lines in the middle of a fucking forest?" Because Connor wasn't the type to willingly get kidnapped. Ever. He'd have rather been shot.

"Fucking reckless brat was about to be taken at gunpoint, so I volunteered to go along for the ride. Then dealt with the driver when he stopped to dump us in the forest. Then she freaked right the fuck out about one tiny little gunshot and went into shock, so that's when I hit the alert to link up with you." Connor sounded cagey, like he was leaving out some of the finer details. Not that it really mattered. "Otherwise, I would have just brought her home myself and not bothered you."

I drummed my fingers on the edge of my desk, cycling through our security cameras and locating the timestamp for when he'd left the house, then found the frame showing Eve following. Sneaky little panther. She blended beautifully with the shadows. Maybe she'd be good for espionage one day.

"Crusades," I said, clicking through more cameras at dizzying speed. I wanted to see the attempt on the South gate that Andrew mentioned. "Anything to do with a failed break-in here at school?"

Connor grunted. "Yeah. They had a kidnap-ransom job that they must have been paid big bucks for."

I found the footage in question and watched it through, silent, inspecting every inch of the scene, then swapped to a different camera angle to do the same. Connor waited, not breaking my train of thought, until I was satisfied.

"They will be hurting after today. Between you and the gate security, they lost a few bodies." I closed the campus video feeds and switched to our house account—to one camera feed in particular.

Eve's bedroom.

She tossed and turned in her bed, sheets tangling her legs, but didn't appear to be screaming and crying anymore. That was comforting. If it'd gone on much longer, I would have had to distract Brodie long enough to use my key and...

And then what? I couldn't exactly comfort her like Ethan had last week, though the fantasy of it played out in technicolor within my mind.

"I should be back in a couple of hours," Connor said, breaking through my suddenly pornographic thoughts. "Maybe tell Evelyn to book a session with the school psychiatrist or something. She can't keep falling to pieces at the sight of guns, not in our or her father's world, anyway."

Shit, he was right about that. "Will do," I muttered. "Anything else?"

"Yeah, make sure she eats something. She must be starving, and she vomited up what she'd eaten for dinner last night." Connor—of all fucking people, *Connor Sullivan*—actually sounded like he cared. Then I grinned.

"She vomited? Eth and Brodes both kissed her when we got back." I said it like I wouldn't have if I were in their shoes. I would've.

A heavy silence filled the phone line for a minute, then Connor made a strangled noise. "Excuse me? Brodie did *what*?"

I rolled my eyes. "As if you're shocked. I'll go sort out some dinner in case Eve wakes up."

Another grunt from Connor. "She likes pasta."

My brows shot up. "I'm aware." I just didn't realize he'd been paying attention to *anything* Eve liked. I ended the call without offering any further conversation. I'd already reached my max capacity for small talk and gossip, and, frankly, my head hurt.

I sat there for a few minutes, watching Eve sleeping on my huge computer monitor. If she ever found out I'd placed a camera in her room...if *anyone* found out...I'd be toast. Worse if they found out about the one in the shower. That feed was my favorite, for totally perverse reasons.

The way I figured, I could never actually touch her. My trauma wouldn't let me. So where was the harm in looking?

Deciding she was still fast asleep, if still in the grips of a nightmare, I closed my browsers and headed downstairs to cook. Maybe she'd wake up if she smelled dinner on the stove, since she'd cooked every night of the past week.

At no point did I stop and ask myself why I cared. It was simple: she intrigued me, and she *fit*. With the house, with my found family, and oh so perfectly on the back of my bike. Andrew might think this was a short-term assignment, but I knew better. She was ours now. For good.

27

EVELYN

Returning to my normal life after being kidnapped and taken across state lines should have been weird and surreal. But I'd had more than enough experience adapting back to a normal life after a traumatic experience, so I just breezed into the lecture hall on Monday morning and took my normal seat between Andrew and Brodie.

"Evie babe, you said you'd wait for me this morning, but you were gone when I got up."

Brodie leaned over and nuzzled into the side of my cheek before he pressed a heated kiss to my skin, and I had to squeeze my thighs tightly against the sudden ache in my center. My body was fully on board with the sexy movie star, while also being into the sexy professor. It was a lot of stimulation and not a lot of sex to go along with it, and I was suffering the consequences.

"I had to head for the library first. I was meeting Nina for a quick study session before class."

Andrew scoffed, and I swung around on him. We hadn't spoken since the blow up, and I had no interest in starting now, but that derisive noise immediately pissed me off. "Something to say, Mr. Knightsbridge?"

He smirked, and the only response I got was a shrug. Right. Still being an asshole apparently.

Thankfully, Ethan was at the front of the room, ready to roll, and I was able to spend the next hour focused on the sexiest teacher I'd ever seen, while Brodie rubbed his thumb up and down my thigh, my dual distractions for the day.

I barely managed to take notes, and when I laughingly knocked Brodie's hand away near the end of the lecture, I knew we'd drawn Ethan's attention, as he paused and glanced up to our spot. For once, though, he didn't call me out and request I stay behind. Maybe he was realizing how suspicious it looked for me to be constantly singled out when I wasn't the only one who ever disrupted his class.

When class was over, Brodie linked our arms and flashed a smug smile at Ethan as we passed. I thought I saw a flash of annoyance on the handsome professor's face, but he got his expression under control so quickly, I might have been wrong. We were supposed to meet up at the library later today, so I'd ask him if everything was okay then.

Brodie and Andrew left me at the door of my next class, which was a makeup class from a subject I usually had on Thursday, and I was surprised when I walked in to find Connor sprawled in the middle row, in the seat I usually occupied. It was the first time I'd seen him since he dumped me onto the back of Haze's bike, our paths not crossing for the rest of the weekend.

"Hey," I said softly, feeling weirdly shy. As he lifted his face from his phone, green eyes locked on me, and I was reminded of our time together squished in that car. The kiss which brought me out of my panic. The way he'd been so capable as he'd shot that asshole in the head to protect us.

"Hey," he replied casually, his gaze running over me like he was checking for injuries.

With a shake of my head, I dropped into the seat beside him, on the aisle. "Have I just missed you in this class for the past few weeks? Or did you skip the first quarter of the subject?"

Connor shrugged, letting his phone fall to the desk, but not before I caught a glimpse of a message from what looked like a pretty, dark-haired girl. "Maybe it was a bit of both."

As weird as the response was, I let it go, afraid of disrupting this fraction of peace between us. The professor strolled in ten minutes later, and the room was only half-filled with students, since most of them didn't care about a catch-up class.

As I pulled out my laptop to take notes, Connor just relaxed in his chair, his long legs extended and spread until our thighs almost touched. I'd been in a trunk pressed against his guy, and there hadn't been as much tension flowing between us as I felt right this second, with plenty of space separating us.

It took me a few minutes of regulating my breathing to realize I was nervous being near Connor and not because he was an infuriating asshole most of the time. Nope. I had these warm, fluttery feelings for him, that felt a lot like...hero worship.

Oh, fuck.

That wasn't good, and I needed to stop immediately before he figured it out and used it to make my life miserable. I was under no misgivings that his feelings toward me had changed, outside of slightly tolerating me now. But if I upset the temporary truce, I'd no doubt feel the full force of his annoyance and hatred once more.

The thought of going back to that bothered me. A lot.

By the time class was over, I'd taken two lines of notes and had literally no idea what the fuck we'd just learned. Not that it mattered as I hurried from my chair in the hopes of putting distance between Connor and me.

He gave me no chance though, his long strides catching him up to me before I was even out the door, and he fell into step at my side all the way to the cafeteria. "Are you having lunch with me?" I asked, hoping he thought the heat in my cheeks was from a sunburn.

As if I didn't have enough shit to deal with—and men in my life, for that matter—that I had to nurse another freaking crush on a guy who was both dangerous and out of my league.

"I mean, we shared a near-death experience," Connor said with a shrug, staring out across the busy grounds. "I don't see why we can't share lunch as well."

Don't say it. Don't say it. "Are you trauma-bonding with me?" *Fuck, I said it.*

I would have taken another immediate kidnapping to escape my stupid mouth if I could. Connor halted briefly and squinted down at me like I was a slug he'd accidentally stepped on. "Sorry, what? What the fuck is a trauma bond?"

Figures this asshole would deal so well with trauma that the thought of sharing a connection over almost dying never even occurred to him.

"Never mind," I mumbled before I all but ran to the dining hall, that smirking psychopath right behind me the entire way. Even after I grabbed a tray and randomly pointed at food, before I chose an empty table near the back, he stayed on my ass like we were connected via a physical hold.

Forcing myself to breathe deeply until I could act normal, I was scouring my brain for a neutral topic when Connor dropped his arm over the back of my chair. He'd gotten a serving of the shepherd's pie and two salads, but he touched neither as he curled his fingers into my jacket. "I think we need to talk, brat. About what happened on the weekend. Sorry I wasn't around much, but my father and I needed to deal with those assholes and ensure that the Crusades know their place, once and for all."

Swallowing roughly, I tried to focus on his words and not the heat of his fingers as he toyed with the material of my denim jacket. "You don't have to apologize," I said, forcing myself to pick up my chicken parmesan sandwich. I didn't taste anything as I took a bite, but at least it kept my hands and mouth busy.

Connor watched me as I ate, never touching his own food or removing his hand from the back of my chair, as if he anchored me to the spot. It wasn't until Brodie appeared, Andrew and Haze behind him, that I found myself a few inches farther away from Connor, who was now plowing into his food, as if he'd been starving all along.

My stomach swirled at the sensation of being watched, especially when the other guys took the empty seats across from us and I was the center of attention in a way that threatened to drag me down into the depths of both desire and embarrassment.

I had no idea how this was my life, but I was thankful I didn't die that day in my last college. It would have been a real shame to miss out on knowing these five guys.

"Is it okay for you to all sit here?" I asked as they settled in with their lunches.

Andrew nodded, his expression cold. "Yes. We've spread the word that this is part of our punishment. No one will question it."

Oh, right. The big old secret had to be maintained. I still hadn't figured out the whys of that, and it was probably about time I did.

Before I could ask, though, Brodie reached out and grasped my hand. "You okay, Evie? You seem kind of..."

"Spaced out," Haze added.

Connor let out a low laugh that I wasn't sure the other guys heard. "She thinks we've trauma bonded. Which one of you wannabe therapists put that notion in her head?"

"Not me," Andrew said, his only reaction as he proceeded to eat his usual lunch of boiled eggs, five-hundred-seed bread—with extra fiber—and plain chicken breast. If there was ever a guy who needed a little seasoning in his life, it was this one. Though, he had been eating my dinners lately without complaint, which I'd taken as a huge compliment, because he didn't vary his routine much outside of that.

"She *needs* a therapist," Haze said in his usual blunt way. "To help with the gun trauma."

I blinked, a sliver of hurt erupting at his harsh reference to my brokenness. As if I hadn't already been aware. Just when I'd felt like I was gaining ground with all of them, suddenly I was once again a freak who was the cause of a mass shooting in my last school and still needed therapy.

It was fairly obvious they all knew what happened to me. Just because they hadn't spoken directly to me, didn't mean they weren't aware. Maybe it was time for me to drop the act as well and just get that shit out there. My former therapist would agree with this plan of action.

"I was in therapy for months before I came here," I said shortly, dropping the last half of my sandwich on the plate. I couldn't stomach anything else. "After I got out of the hospital, I went to therapy five times a week. Three for my mind and two for my body. I've done the therapy."

"Doesn't mean you don't still need it," Andrew added, and when no one asked me what I'd been in hospital for, it confirmed that they'd all know about the shooting—probably since before we'd moved into the damn house together.

Connor nudged my tray toward me. "You need to eat, brat. You've been picking at your food lately like a fucking bird." A fraction of my hurt eased at the thought that he'd noticed my eating habits and cared enough to comment. *Stupid trauma bond.*

Brodie let out a loud laugh. "Maybe they are trauma bonded. Otherwise, Con has been snatched up and replaced by a new model. Model A for asshole is gone, so this must be model B."

Feeling the telltale signs of embarrassment creeping up my throat, I was about to jerk to my feet and rush out of here when Connor released a low rumble. "Ignore the moron at the table, Evelyn. You are not leaving until you eat!"

A rush of anger helped to keep the other, softer emotions at bay. "Look, I'll tell you the same shit I told Andrew. I don't need more father figures in my life. I'll eat when I'm hungry. I'll leave the grounds if I want to. And I will not have you four interfering in my life just because we live together."

"And occasionally kiss and fuck," Connor drawled, back to model-A again apparently. "Better tell Ethan about your new rules because he's a bossy prick who likes to control."

I choked on a gasp, which set Brodie off into the loudest laughter I'd ever heard, shutting up only when I glared him into oblivion. "I could fuck all five of you on a regular, rotating schedule," I shot back, as their eyes widened and jaws slackened, "and that still wouldn't give you the right to dictate my life. Not now. Or ever."

"Excuse me!" The nasally voice came from the side of the table, and I turned to find a familiar, annoying face standing there: Laura Sandiconte.

"You're excused," I shot back, jumping to my feet and hefting my tray like I was about to throw it at her. Andrew looked mildly concerned, which was a huge step up from his previous apathy, while Brodie and Haze only looked amused. Connor just looked disgusted as he ran his gaze over her.

"I thought we decided that this was a no-whore zone," he drawled, lacing his fingers together over his flat stomach.

"Shouldn't you be off on your knees somewhere, making Andrew some money?"

Laura's face turned to a shade of red that I had no idea a human could attain. "You lowlife thug. Just because all of you share a house now doesn't mean you're anything but scum." She swung toward her boyfriend, voice lowering into a whine. "Andrew, I don't understand why you're sitting here with *them*. Are you sure the dean would enforce this punishment? Have you spoken to your mother? They're your enemies, for fucks sake."

If only you knew, bitch. These boys had never been enemies, and she was clearly not important to Andrew if she didn't know the basic facts of who his best friends were. These four and Ethan were the ones that appeared to have a lifelong trauma bond.

Now I just had to get them to admit the whys and hows of their odd friendship—and soon.

They already knew too much about me; it was time to even the scales.

28

EVELYN

The next week was shockingly *normal*, if I could consider the shift in dynamics with the guys normal by any standard. We ate together at lunch every day even though the tension was *thick*—not between us but from everyone else in the room. The guys' respective friends were confused at best—irate in some cases—to discover the new arrangements, but Andrew smoothed it all out by blaming the dean.

And that was the weirdest part: I knew he was just *blaming* the dean, and that made me question the whole suspicious forced-proximity situation that saw the six of us living together in the first place.

Friday afternoon I made my way to the library to pull some research books for my Applied Economics assignment. For a change, none of the guys were shadowing me. I'd just had a class with Haze—which I had quietly been looking forward to —then he'd been called aside by his chemistry professor. Brodie and Connor were at home, according to Brodie's texts, and Andrew... Well, I didn't give a flying fuck where Andrew was. Probably getting his dick sucked in the girl's bathroom again.

Humming quietly along to the music in my earbuds, I gathered a selection of books and carried them upstairs to a dark, quiet corner, where a huge table sat blissfully vacant. Smiling to myself, I got set up with my laptop and the huge stack of books.

After an hour, the small of my back ached from the hard wooden chair, so I lifted myself up to stretch. I groaned at how tight it was and braced my hands on the bookshelves to get a better stretch. Would it kill the library to put a cushion on their chairs?

"Fancy meeting you here," a familiar voice commented just moments before warm hands clasped my waist. "Sore back?"

I moaned, leaning back into Ethan's touch. "Yes...those chairs aren't ergonomic in the least."

He shifted his grip until his strong thumbs rubbed my tight muscles, and my eyes basically rolled back in my head. I wanted his hands somewhere else...

"Ethan," I sighed as he grabbed the skirt of my dress, bunching it in his fist. I didn't even waste time turning around, just craned my neck and met his mouth in a harsh clash of desperate need.

We'd been carefully keeping our distance at home for a bunch of reasons. Connor's disdain was uncomfortably right up there as one of the biggest deterrents, even though I'd never admit it out loud. My conflicting feelings about Brodie—*and a little bit Haze*—had me too twisted up in guilt to spend every night in Ethan's bed.

That didn't mean I hadn't been thinking about it, though. When his tongue met mine, I nearly combusted with pent-up desire.

"This is dangerous," I murmured against his kisses, turning

in his arms as he boxed me in with the bookshelves. "What if—"

"Shhh," he cut me off, a sexy grin playing over his lips. "So long as you're quiet, no one will ever know." More dizzying kisses, then he hiked up my skirt. "Can we be quiet, Lilith?"

Holy shit. Was he seriously proposing more than just a few sneaky kisses in the campus library? I nodded, not wanting to stop kissing long enough to give a verbal reply. Instead, I tilted my hips into his touch, quivering as he stroked my throbbing core through my thin panties.

"Thank fuck," he uttered on an exhale. "I've been going out of my damn mind all week, watching Brodie's hands on you during class." In a quick motion, he tugged my panties clean off my ass and I stepped out of them as he cupped my pussy.

Anxiety about potentially getting caught tangled all up in arousal as I unbuttoned his jeans with shaking fingers and he found my clit. "Shit, Ethan..." I gasped at the intense sensations zapping through me from his touch.

"Shhh," he chuckled. "You're in a library, Lilith. You're meant to be quiet." Then he winked, and it was way too sexy for his own damn good, so in retaliation I wrapped my hand around his hard length and gave a squeeze.

A strangled moan escaped him and I grinned. "Shhh, Ethan, you're in a library."

His answering smile was *everything*. We both quieted one another by kissing again, and when he lifted me, I wrapped my legs around his waist without hesitation. It was a tight squeeze as his dick slid into me, pinning me to the shelves at my back, but he was kind enough to swallow my gasps and moans with more of those addictive, drugging kisses of his.

"Holy hell," he whispered, breathless as he moved his kisses to my jaw. His hips rocked, thrusting that thick cock of his deep inside me. "Eve...*Lilith*..."

Teasing, I clamped my hand over his mouth, grinning

cheekily despite the fact that I was about to orgasm faster than I'd ever managed during penetration alone. My head tipped back against the books, my eyelids fluttering as he fucked me harder.

Thank the damn stars this shelf was secured against a wall or the whole thing would have come down and caused a domino effect. As it was, we knocked countless books to the floor and cared nothing for potential damages as Ethan removed my hand from his mouth and pinned my wrists above my head.

"I so badly want to make you scream right now," he confessed in a dark whisper. "But we can't get caught, so be a good girl and bite your lip while you come, okay?"

I nodded frantically, already gasping and sweating as my pussy tightened around his length. He thrust hard another couple of times and then I broke. My vision darkened and my ears rang as fireworks exploded in my core, and I only remembered at the last moment to clamp my lips shut and not scream Ethan's name in euphoria for all the library to hear.

He whispered a few choice curses, burying his face in the crook of my neck as his hips jerked. He came at the same time, filling me up and sealing us together with hips flush to mine.

"Fuck," he breathed, lips against my earlobe as we both gasped for air. "If you can believe it, I didn't actually come here to do that."

I chuckled quietly, sweat dripping down my spine as he gently lowered me back to the floor. "No? Why not? It's part of the reason I chose this corner to study in."

Ethan took a step back, shooting me a sexy glance as he fixed his jeans. "I wondered." He bent down to swipe my panties from where I'd kicked them, then knelt to help me step into them. It was obscenely intimate, him slowly drawing the lace up my legs and over my ass. Then the way he teased a finger over the crotch, where it was already growing wet with his cum...positively filthy. I nearly orgasmed again right then.

"You look...so fucking delicious right now, Lilith," he murmured, reluctantly rising back to his feet and cupping my face in his hands. "Your lips are flushed and pink, your pupils are all blown out with arousal...I could get hard again just looking at you."

"Don't." The snapped response didn't come from me, and I jerked my gaze past Ethan to where Andrew stood with arms folded and an expression like ice. "Unless you want to get fired and kicked off campus grounds, in which case, by all means, don't let me stop you."

My jaw dropped. "How long have you been standing there, you creep? Did you watch us?"

Andrew's eyes narrowed and his jaw ticked. "Fair's fair, Evelyn."

"Jesus Christ, you're a pervert!" I exclaimed, brushing my hands down the front of my dress to make sure I hadn't slipped a tit out or something. My face was positively flaming as I hurried to gather up my laptop and study notes from the table.

"Takes one to know one," he snarked back, utterly shameless. "Besides, you two were far from subtle. Anyone with half a brain could tell someone was fucking back here, you're just lucky it was me and not some do-gooder willing to go screaming about Professor Sullivan taking advantage of a student."

My hands shook as I stuffed my shit back into my bag and slung it over my shoulder. "Go to hell, Andrew. Stop threatening Ethan's job." I made to storm out, but he blocked my exit with his hand braced against the shelf.

"Or what?" he taunted. "I could get him fired like *that*." He snapped his fingers in my face, making me jump. "And you couldn't do a damn thing about it. In case you forgot, the NDA only extends to the house, not the library."

Anger bubbled up in my chest, and my eyes narrowed. It irritated the hell out of me that I needed to tilt my head back to meet his gaze, because he clearly thought that gave him some sort of intimidation advantage.

"Eve, ignore him," Ethan said softly, his hand on the small of my back. "He's full of shit."

I wasn't so sure, but short of threatening him right back—and I had nothing of substance to use—I could only resort to name-calling. "You're just salty because Laura won't let you rail her in the library," I accused, refusing to let him have the last word. "Maybe if you weren't so worried about creasing your pants, you'd actually get off more often."

His eye twitched, and I suspected I'd hit a nerve. That was good enough, so I shoved past him and hurried out of the library before our little argument could turn into a whole scene. The moment I stepped out into the late-afternoon sun, guilt rippled through me at the mess I'd just left in the library. Books everywhere, all over the floor *and* table. Hopefully Ethan would pick them up?

I pulled out my phone to text him, just in case, and breathed a sigh of relief when he assured me he had it handled. Leave it to me to worry more about making a mess in the library than living with a houseful of criminally adjacent men.

Connor and Brodie were on the sofa when I got home, battling it out on the Xbox with some first-person shooter that immediately got ditched when I called out a quick hello. My plan had been to head straight up to the bathroom and rinse away the evidence of my little study session, but Brodie was quick to call me into the living room to chat.

"Uh, I just need to...um...get changed. Give me five minutes?" I evaded, taking a step closer to the stairs.

Brodie instantly vaulted over the back of the couch and closed in on me with a suspicious look on his handsome face, his eyes raking over me. "Where have you been, Evie babe? And with *who*?"

My eyes widened. Was it that obvious? "I was just studying at the library."

His eyes rolled. "Ah. I see. Ethan."

Crap. I guess it was that obvious. Before I could escape to shower, Brodie grabbed my wrist, hauling me back to him and kissing me so thoroughly my knees turned to jelly.

"Don't forget our date tomorrow night, Evie babe. I wanna be the one that puts that look on your face." He nipped my lip between his teeth, then released me with a wink.

What was I doing again? Oh right. Showering. Because of the cum slick in my panties, courtesy of my sexy professor. Right.

29

EVELYN

Brodie told me we needed to leave early in the afternoon for our date and had helpfully let himself into my room to browse my closet in order to choose a dress. The one he pulled out was short and silky, pale blue with a flirty skirt. An easy access kind of dress. He didn't *say* that, but I definitely thought it.

I took my time getting ready, putting on makeup and curling my dark-purple-toned hair with butterflies wreaking mayhem inside my belly. I had no idea where he was taking me, only that it was a "work thing" in the closest bigger city, about an hour-and-a-half drive from Meadowridge.

When I was ready, with glittery heels on and a coat draped over my shoulders, I left my room. Two steps down the hall, I heard the raised voices from downstairs. Most notably, Ethan's raised voice.

"She is *not* going with you, Brodie, and that is *final*!" he bellowed with so much authority, I nearly scurried back to my room to change before remembering that I was a fucking grown-ass woman and Ethan did not control me or my actions. With that in mind, I threw my head back and strutted my primped ass right down the stairs and into the middle of their fight.

A fight that was cut off midsentence by my appearance, as both guys watched me like they'd never seen a dress or a pair of tits pushed up in said dress before.

Ethan's eyes darkened, and Brodie's went all dreamy as he took a step toward me. "Evie babe," he breathed. "You look like a fucking dream." He leaned down, his lips brushing my cheek. "A wet dream."

That set Ethan off as he tore his gaze from me and rounded on Brodie. "You cannot take her out to one of your bullshit Hollywood parties looking like that. You're asking for trouble, and Eve can find that all on her own."

Wait... "Are you referring to my little kidnapping incident? Because that could have happened to anyone."

He stared at me, shaking his head. "So why does it always happen to you? You've been here for a few weeks and already nearly got blown up and kidnapped. For fuck's sake, Eve." He took a step closer as well, until I was nearly sandwiched between them. When he turned the full force of his gaze on me, I had to shore up my resolve again or I was about to blindly obey his command. Dominant Ethan did things to me that were downright depraved, and I lost every ounce of feminism in my body.

"I'm going to this event with Brodie." A firm statement, and I would not waver, despite my own misgivings about it. "I need to know I can venture out into the real world and not lose my shit. My therapist was constantly encouraging me to get back to *living,* as he called it, and until now, I've been hiding."

And I could have died in the trunk of a car without truly experiencing life; I'd been wasting time. Well, no fucking more.

"You can't stop her, Eth," Brodie reminded him quietly. "That's not how this is going to work while we all live in Bluebell House. Here, Evie belongs to all of us, and you have to learn to share."

Jesus. Fucking. Christ.

"Evie belongs to Evie." My statement and tone were weak, because his claiming only added to my current drought of feminism. The thought of belonging to them all—*minus Andrew*—just about sent me to my knees.

"Right, babe," Brodie confirmed. "You get a claim as well, but that doesn't take away from my claim. And I have you tonight."

With that, he threaded his arm through mine and started to lead me away. My legs were a little wobbly after that claiming, but I managed not to fall.

Last second, Ethan reached out and grabbed me, dragging us both to a halt. "I'm the professor in charge here, and I'm saying that you can't go, Eve."

There was a sudden pain in my chest, like he'd stabbed me with his harsh command.

How dare he?

"You weren't a *professor* when you were banging me into the library shelves," I hissed at him, my temper rising with each word. "You don't get to pick and choose, Professor Sullivan. And you don't own or control me. If this is what happens when we spend time together, then you know what? Count me the fuck out. We're done."

I yanked my arm from his hold, and now I was the one hurrying through the house toward the front door. Before Ethan could respond and before I could analyze the slash of hurt I'd seen on his face.

"You okay?" Brodie asked as I dragged him down the stairs, suddenly able to run in heels when I could barely walk in them before. "Because I can go back in there and beat the fuck out of him if you'd like."

"Nah," I said, far more casually than I felt. "He's not worth it. I want to go to this event with you and enjoy myself. It's been too long since I've done anything for fun." And *forever* since I went on a date.

Not like it was easy to date when you'd been the cause of a school shooting because a guy had grown a little too obsessed with you. Made it hard to venture into the dating world again, though I'd certainly been giving it a red-hot try here.

Speaking of... "Ethan isn't going to do anything stupid, right? He doesn't strike me as unstable, but his attitude right now felt a little extreme for the situation."

Brodie looked uncomfortable as he led me over to his waiting Bugatti, the black car shiny in the early evening light. "He's just worried about you, Eve. I'm not sure he knows how to express that, and the fact that he can't just go out on dates with you probably bothers him as well. But I promise, he would never harm you; you are perfectly safe with all of us."

As if to prove his point, as he opened the door for me, a large black SUV pulled in directly behind us. He leaned closer, his handsome face creasing into a grin. "I've got extra security for the night."

Right. Of course he did. Because he was a freaking movie star, which I was finding harder and harder to remember.

As I settled into the leather seat, he closed my door and strolled around to his side. I glanced out the window to see Ethan and Connor were on the steps, arguing away, though neither followed the path down to the car. It bothered me to see Ethan upset like that, even if it was all, as Brodie said, over his concern for me.

When you were concerned, you discussed those concerns with the other person. Demanding I stay without even listening or talking to me about it was a whole other red flag. Maybe I had been crazy to think I could have more than one relationship within the house, even though we were all just casual and no promises had been made.

It was naïve of me to hope that there wouldn't be jealousy and other issues. Ethan had proved that tonight, and for once, I wanted to be away from him and the house.

"So...what *is* the event we're going to?" I asked once we'd passed the front gate security and pulled onto the main road. "You haven't told me anything except that it's a 'work thing' and Ethan mentioned a Hollywood party?"

Brodie chuckled, shaking his head. "Don't worry, Evie babe. We're not flying to Hollywood. Eth was being way too dramatic. We're just going to Arrowville...there's a small film festival on this weekend and they'll be showing a first cut of *Bloodstone Sentinel: The Resurrection*. I thought maybe you'd like to see it with me? Or... Jesus, now I'm second-guessing that. Do you think I'm a narcissist for taking you to see *me* on screen for two hours?"

My jaw had dropped right to the floor. "Brodie Keller, are you kidding? I'd love to see it with you! Is this the first time you'll see it, too?"

He nodded, seeming sheepish all of a sudden. "Yeah. They had some delays in post-production, so I haven't had a chance to get over to LA for a screening."

"Well, shit. I'm honored. But aren't these things a big deal? Like with, um, photographers and stuff?" I smoothed my hands over the silky skirt I wore. It was pretty, yes, but it was hardly a designer gown for walking the red carpet.

Brodie reached out and laced his fingers through mine, squeezing reassuringly. "Yes, and you look amazing. You don't need custom couture to look breathtaking. Everyone will be asking who my gorgeous girlfriend is. I can't wait."

My mouth went dry. "Oh wow. Um, that's a lot to unpack, Brodes. I don't... Okay, I really don't want to sound like I'm not crazy flattered, but I don't think it'd be a good idea for me to be photographed with you. Is that... Would you be offended if I skipped that part and met you inside?" Because for all my big talk to Ethan about reclaiming my independence and not being scared to leave campus grounds, I wasn't ready to see TMZ plastering my face—and my Target dress—all over the internet. Brodie was so famous that they'd have my entire life history detailed for the world to see in no time.

He glanced over at me, concern etched across his handsome face. "Yeah, of course. I mean, no, you can't *meet me inside,* but we can totally skip the red-carpet shit. Done. I'll contact the organizers and make sure we can enter through the back of the venue. Sorry, I should have—"

"It's not that I don't *want* to be seen with you," I quickly added, realizing how my reluctance might have come off. Drawing a deep breath, I decided to take a little leap of faith. "It's a safety thing. Um, about six months ago, there was a shooting at my old college. Twenty-three people died and more were injured, but he wasn't there for a random act of terror. He wanted to kill *me.*"

Cold sweat rolled down my spine as I gave Brodie the very abridged version of events. His fingers tightened around mine, and the strangest expression crossed his face, but then it was gone, and he was completely focused, showing only concern.

Making me think I'd imagined that slightly guilt-ridden expression. I was probably projecting my own trauma onto him.

"I would fucking love to be Brodie Keller's girlfriend," I continued, "but the guy was never caught, and the idea that I might be putting a target on your back actually makes me feel sick." I pursed my lips, uncomfortable as fuck. "Also...we should probably address the whole *girlfriend* label before Ethan has a nervous breakdown. Not that he's particularly in my good books right now."

Brodie said nothing for a moment, then flicked his indicator and pulled over onto the shoulder to stop the car.

"What are you—" I started to ask, but he cut me off by grabbing my face and kissing me hard.

"I'm sorry you went through that, babe, but I'm so happy you trusted me with your secrets. I want to say that you're the bravest, kindest, prettiest woman I've ever known." His voice was husky as our kiss eased. "You're the most real thing in my life, and I never ever want to put you in an uncomfortable situation. We can skip the movie and just go to dinner, if you want?"

Brodie always had all the right words, and it was still hard for me to believe that this famous, gorgeous movie star took one look at me and decided I was the one he wanted. But that was how it had seemed to happen. From that first moment in class, when he'd ground to a halt when he saw me.

A feeling that was absolutely mutual.

I shook my head firmly, smacking another kiss on his lips. "No. Definitely not. I wanna see you as Bloodstone Sentinel, dammit! And if I can sneak in the back door, I'm cool with that. But you should still do the famous-guy shit without me."

"Not a chance," he growled. "It's our first date, Evie babe. I'm not letting you out of my sight for even a second." He kissed me again, making me moan before shifting the car back into drive.

As he pulled out into the road once more, he linked our fingers back together, then kissed my knuckles. It was the sweetest gesture that said *everything*. I was safe with Brodie and more than just physically.

I was starting to believe that maybe even my heart was safe.

30

EVELYN

After a few phone calls from Brodie's manager and the cinema venue where the movie was being shown, we parked in a secluded alleyway around the backside of the building. Two uniformed staff met us at the fire escape beside the dumpsters, and Brodie's bodyguards shadowed us after getting out of their SUV just moments after we parked.

One of the staff chattered nervously as we were escorted through the staff areas of the cinema and popped out right beside the theater, where guests were already drifting in to find their seats. I recognized several big stars from the film and became totally tongue-tied when Brodie introduced me to the woman who played his love interest in the film.

She was stunning, and I reminded myself mentally that she was an actress. They were *acting*. It definitely helped that she was attending with her husband, who she smiled at like he hung the very stars in the night sky.

With just a few minutes to spare, Brodie snagged us some popcorn and drinks, and we found our seats. It was one of those fancy upper-class theaters with recliner chairs, but Brodie frowned when he saw the fixed armrest between us.

"Hey," he stage-whispered to the couple sitting beside me. "Can we switch?"

The older guy shrugged and nodded, grabbing his own popcorn to move seats along with his date. Brodie gestured for me to take one of their places, and when we sat down, he grinned and lifted the armrest.

"Now we can snuggle," he whispered, snaking an arm around my waist. "No funny business though, babe. This is a work event, after all."

I snickered because if either of us was planning on any *funny business,* it was him.

When the opening credits rolled, I felt an absolute blast of pride to see Brodie's name not just under his acting credit but also as an executive producer. "Executive producer?" I breathed near his ear, shaking my head at the many dimensions of Brodie Keller.

He shrugged. "It's more of a token title than anything, but I like to add my own flair to the character and storyline after so many years. They indulge me."

He was underplaying his talents once again, and I marveled at how humble he was with so much success to his name. It was hard to believe, and yet I'd had the evidence presented to me time and time again.

"How are you so down-to-earth?" I whispered, not sure if I wanted him to hear or not.

He did, though, his expression serious as he stared into my eyes. "I wasn't always this way, Evie babe. Something happened to me that changed my entire perspective on life, and I'm a better man for it."

I almost asked him what happened, but the movie was kicking off, and the last thing I wanted to do was talk through his movie premiere. There'd be plenty of time to learn everything about each other in the future.

The opening scene was Brodie in the middle of a warzone,

facing off against his archnemesis, and I recognized this as the final scenes of the last movie. This was where he'd been attacked with a special weapon developed in an alternate Earth and containing the crystal of Tartarus—the only stone that could pierce through the bloodstone's power.

I'd forgotten until this moment that he'd been shot and presumed dead, and as I watched Brodie get blasted to the ground by Sycophant Demonaide, a dark entity from alternate Earth, my heart clenched in my chest. When the light died in Bloodstone's eyes, heat burned behind my own eyes, and I barely managed not to cry.

Pressing closer to Brodie, I slipped my hand up to his chest, the solid beat of his heart an assurance that he was alive and well. Brodie reached out and wrapped his big palm over mine, the heat of his skin pressing into me, while his other hand flicked away a tear that had escaped.

The scene abruptly changed as his love interest in the movie shot up in her bed, sobbing and screaming, as it had all been a dream about when her love was torn from her.

Fuck, this was so much harder with Brodie's familiar face reflecting in the photo she grasped and cried against, and now I was actually crying, my damn makeup that I'd taken an hour to apply running down my face.

Brodie chuckled under his breath, and I gasp-sobbed as he half lifted me out of my seat and into his lap. This startled me from my empathizing with the beautiful actress on the screen, who was mourning her love.

My love. Okay, that was a little far, but he was certainly *my like* at the moment, and seeing his death on a massive screen was too much.

Brodie turned me toward him and rubbed my back soothingly. "I'm right here, Evie babe. I'm not going anywhere." He whispered it over and over, and no doubt we were drawing attention from those around us, but I was so busy burying my face against his suit to care. Eventually I calmed down and went to get off his lap, but he kept me solidly pressed against him, his arms wrapped around me, one hand caressing up and down my thigh. Getting far too close to my lace underwear for how near our neighbors were.

Under my ass, his hard length remained for the entire two hours, all the while he stroked my bare thigh. By the time the final credits rolled around, I was a desperate, dripping, needy woman.

"Not fair," I growled, as the lights came on and noise erupted as everyone cheered and gave a standing ovation for the movie. "Teasing me through the whole—"

Brodie stood with me in his arms, and I had no idea how he'd managed it, but it did shut me up.

As he set me on my feet, he spun me to face him, leaning down to press his lips to mine, mouth opening as he devoured me. "Longest and best two hours of my life," he murmured against my lips. "You're driving me crazy, babe."

Okay, so the teasing hadn't just been one-sided, which I'd already been aware of. But I liked him pointing it out.

Pressing up on my toes, I wrapped my arms around his neck. "You were so amazing. That's my favorite one of the franchise so far, minus the part where you were dead for twenty minutes."

Hopefully no one watching the movie was breaking the rules and taking photos of us right now, or we'd be all over the tabloids tomorrow.

Brodie's smirk kicked in hard. "You have to admit, I looked good for a dead guy, though."

He'd get no argument from me, even if I would have to fast-forward through those opening scenes whenever I rewatched this movie. Which would be a lot.

"Come on, let's get out of here before they all demand my

time and attention," Brodie said, linking our fingers together and leading me down the aisle and to the stairs.

Part of me knew I should protest, because he was surely here to socialize with the other famous people, but a larger part was remembering the hard length of his cock under my ass for two hours, and it was going to be the winner here tonight.

Sorry, famous people. Brodie Keller and I had to get back to Bluebell House and finish what he'd started when he stroked my thigh all night.

We ended up using the same entrance way as before, but unfortunately, this time the way wasn't exactly clear. Brodie cursed as flashes blinded us when we stepped out, and he lifted his hand to shield my face the best he could as his security rushed to ensure that no one touched or stopped us as we headed for the car.

"Evelyn! What are you doing here with Brodie? How do you two know each other?"

Questions shot out from multiple places, and I was too freaked out to do more than squeak, keep my head down, and put one heeled foot in front of the other.

"Does Mr. Keller know about the shooting?"

I stumbled, but Brodie had me, getting me into the back of the SUV security had been in before. I would guess that it wasn't safe for him to drive himself from here, now that the paparazzi had found us.

"What the fuck?" Brodie snarled, ripping off his jacket as soon as we were inside and moving. "How'd they find out?"

On the inside, I was freaking out because they'd mentioned the shooting. *They had mentioned the shooting.* Which meant my cover was blown. But I couldn't lose it until I was alone; security didn't need to see my freak out.

"Theatre tipped them off," the driver said. There was another man in the passenger seat, who turned to face us. He was huge, with closely cropped black hair, dark brown eyes, and a no-nonsense expression on his face. He had to be a decade or two older than us, and as he leaned in, I could see a gun under his coat.

Tendrils of unease filtered into me, but I forced myself to look away, because there was no time for a panic attack. "And we might have another issue, sir."

Brodie just sighed and ran a hand through his hair. "Why am I not surprised? This is fucking Ethan's fault. He's been sending bad vibes to ruin our date, I'm sure of it."

That almost got a laugh out of my internally freaking-out self.

"We received word of a massive pileup on the motorway. It'll be hours before they clear it. We can head there and wait, but with all the extra traffic, it might be a better idea to grab a couple of rooms for the night and leave again in the morning."

"What do you want to do, Evie?" Brodie turned his whole body toward me, gaze resting on my face as he took in my every expression.

I liked that he wanted my opinion, even if I was more consumed by whether my entire life as I knew it was over. "A room for the night is good with me," I whispered. "I don't particularly want to sit in traffic for hours."

"I'll make some calls," the dangerous-looking guy in the passenger seat said, pulling out his phone.

Brodie threaded his fingers through mine, raising my hand and kissing my knuckles. "I'm so sorry, Evie babe. I should have known this might happen."

So should I, come to think of it. Brodie wasn't some D-list wannabe celeb—he was the real deal. Tabloids went mental to get pics of him, especially since he was rarely seen out partying anymore. Which, I now realized, was because he was at college with me in Meadowridge.

"It's not your fault," I told him with a weak smile. "Someone tipped them off, but it's more than that. Someone asked about the shooting...which means they know who I am." I shivered, and Brodie reached out to turn the heat up.

"You're still safe with us at Meadowridge," Brodie murmured. "Even without the anonymity of a fake last name, no one can touch you there. It's why Andrew's mom is okay with him living on campus and why Haze never leaves. It's the safest place in the country right now, largely thanks to the Sullivans."

I swallowed hard, digesting that information. He was right, though. If it was safe enough for the president's son, it was safe enough for me. Tonight was another matter, though.

"Sir," the guy in the front said, interrupting my melancholy thoughts. "All the big hotels in Arrowville are at full capacity due to the film festival and accident, but my contacts have two rooms available at a motel in Cessnock. I'm inclined to say it's a good option, since no one will be looking for a movie star in a drive-through town off the highway."

Brodie tipped his head to me, giving me the power to decide.

Wetting my lips, I nodded. "Yes, good thinking. They'd be waiting for you at the Covington or Palazzo right now. And Cessnock is on the way back to Meadowridge anyway, right?"

"Yes, ma'am, it is," the guy agreed. "Once they clear the accident, we're only an hour away from Meadowridge."

I nodded more firmly. "Then let's do that."

The guy returned his phone to his ear while typing the address into the GPS for our driver. Meanwhile Brodie shot me a sly smile and stroked his thumb over my wrist teasingly.

"Fuck, I hope our room only has one bed," he whispered, almost too quiet for me to even hear. "I can't wait to get you alone."

Heat flushed through me and I squirmed in my seat, remembering how worked up he'd gotten me during the movie. I, too, quietly hoped we'd be faced with only one bed.

31

EVELYN

"Room six," the bodyguard dude announced, unlocking the door in question and opening it. He gave the key to Brodie, then ducked inside to check the room was safe before returning to us with a nod. "Delany and I will be next door, in room seven."

Brodie gestured for me to enter ahead of him, and I failed to stifle my small groan of disappointment.

"Two beds," he said aloud, scowling at the offending furniture in question. It wasn't the *worst* motel in the world, but it was definitely not a *hotel* by any stretch of the imagination. It was clean, basic, and somewhat dated.

I bit back a grin and sat on the end of one bed to slide my high heels off. "You don't snore, do you? Maybe I should swap rooms with Delany."

Brodie chuckled, shaking his head. "Coming from Little Miss Screaming Nightmares?" He poked around at the TV unit, checking in the drawers and cupboards. "Oh yay, a mini-bar." He pulled out a can of grape soda and cracked the top of it.

Returning to the beds, he sat on the other one and gestured

for me to put my feet up in his lap, across the gap. I did so, and almost melted when he took one in his strong hand, rubbing the arch in a long stroke.

"*Fuuuuck…*" I moaned, collapsing backward as my foot spasmed. I'd fallen out of the habit of wearing heels, so I hadn't realized how much my feet were cramping until now.

"Whoops," Brodie exclaimed, his hand pausing. "Uh, I spilled my drink."

I sat up to see what he was talking about and eyed the puddle of purple soda on the bedspread near him. "Oh no. What a shame," I said with deadpan expression. "You can't sleep there now. I guess we will have to share."

The grin that lit up his face was brighter than the sun itself. "Thank fuck!" Then he launched across the gap, tackling me flat onto the floral comforter and slamming his lips to mine.

Laughter sparkled between our kisses as he rolled us over and I straddled his waist, grinding against his already-hard length. Suddenly we weren't joking around anymore, and there was no one interrupting us.

"Shit," Brodie groaned between kisses. "I've waited so fucking long for this, but I don't have protection."

Surprise saw me sitting up straighter, which allowed him to reach for the zipper of my dress and tug it down. "Seriously?" I asked, bemused. "You spent two hours of that movie getting me worked up to a horny mess, but you didn't bring any condoms?"

He rolled his eyes at my teasing. "I did, actually. They're in *my* car, though."

I bit my lip, anticipation fluttering through me like the most diabolical butterflies. "I don't even know how to say this without sounding…whatever. I've got an IUD, so if you—"

"I'm clean, so that's good enough for me," he enthused, basically tearing my dress as he whipped it over my head, then inhaled sharply. "Holy shit, Evie. You're gorgeous." His hands cupped my breasts through the sheer bra I'd worn, teasing my nipples into hardened points. His teeth indented his lower lip as he played, his gaze heavy. Wanting more of that reaction from him, I reached behind and unclipped my bra clasp, letting the fabric loosen in his grip.

He swallowed visibly, and my breath caught when he tossed the garment aside.

"Perfection," he breathed. Then he grabbed my waist and flipped our positions once more, pinning me to the bed as his mouth found my left nipple.

My cry was louder than I intended as I threaded my fingers through his soft hair, throwing my head back against the sensation of his mouth laving the hard peak of my nipple.

He moved to the other side, giving it just as much attention, and I was dying with how good it felt. I'd never realized how much stimulation could come from my nipples, but already my body was heated, with a heavy pressure settling low between my legs.

"Brodie," I gasped, moving against him as desperation fueled me. "Please."

Brodie chuckled, his mouth hot against my skin. "Please what, Evie babe? You're going to need to use your words with me."

Oh fuck. Words were hard. "I need to come. I need you to make me come right the fuck now."

Okay, maybe not that hard at all.

Brodie's eyes darkened as he stared up from my chest, taking in my expression. "Holy shit, you're hot, Evie. So freaking hot. I'm going to fucking devour you, babe."

He wasted no time kissing his way down my stomach, ripping my panties off so he could settle between my naked thighs. On instinct, I spread them farther to accommodate him, and he immediately shifted positions to throw them over his shoulders as he nudged in closer, his face right against my core.

"I've waited a long time for this," he murmured, giving me a searing look before he licked from my ass to my clit in one movement. The groan that escaped him was almost as erotic as the motion of his tongue as he flattened it against my cunt and lapped at me.

"Fuck." He pressed harder, licking and sucking, as the pleasure slammed into me with so much force that my ass almost lifted from the bed. Brodie's strong hold around my thighs kept me down, and even when I fought to move, he didn't let go.

"Oh God. Brodie. Fuck, I'm going to come."

I arched my top half off the bed, my fingers tightening in his hair as I came so hard that darkness danced on the edge of my vision. Brodie didn't stop his delicious assault on my pussy, swiping through my release as he devoured me. When he reached my clit, he gave it the same attention my nipples had gotten, and I was already panting and well on my way to a second orgasm.

My body was so sensitive that when he slid one and then a second finger inside me, curling them up to press against my G-spot, I shattered against him once more.

"So fucking responsive," he groaned, the sounds obscene as he growled and lapped against me. "You're better than anything I could have dreamed up, if I knew to dream of perfection."

"Brodie Keller," I panted, writhing against his hold. "You're—fuck."

"I am fuck," he confirmed. "As in, I'm about to fuck you."

He slid his fingers free, leaving me achingly empty as his tongue swiped two more times from my ass to my clit, as if he couldn't stand to leave one drop of my release behind. "You're delicious," he said as he rose up and settled between my thighs. "You want to taste?"

He didn't give me a chance to answer as he slid the two fingers that had been inside me into my mouth. "Taste yourself, babe. Taste how fucking delicious you are."

I sucked those digits deeper, rolling my tongue over the lengths, groaning at the sensation of tasting myself and Brodie together. "Good, right?" he said, watching me closely, his pupils dilating as I sucked harder.

"More," I huffed. "I need more."

His wicked grin was the only warning I got before he slammed his full, thick length inside me.

A long rasp of air released from me, and normally I'd have needed a few seconds to adjust to his size, but Brodie didn't give me any time at all as he pulled all the way out and thrust deeply again, over and over, his mouth meeting mine as he kissed me with the same fervor that he'd eaten my pussy.

"I've been waiting so long for this," he repeated between kisses. "I'm not going to last long. For the first time."

An orgasm was racing up my spine as he spoke, so it wasn't going to be any issue for me.

"What?" I gasped. "First time?"

He moved harder and faster, his movement less smooth as he lost control. "Oh yeah, baby girl. This is only the beginning. I hope you weren't expecting to sleep."

He swallowed my scream in a kiss as my entire body shook, and I found my third release since we'd entered the room. *Hot damn.* Brodie Keller could fuck like no one's business, and as he left me gasping and sated, I couldn't even find it in myself to care where all his experience came from.

His cock thickened inside me as he groaned. "Evie babe." He jerked harder inside me before slowing each thrust, drawing out both of our pleasure as the final tremors rocked through me.

My breaths were ragged as he collapsed against me, only his forearms on either side of me keeping his full weight from crushing me. Not that I'd have cared in my current sated state. I wasn't sure I'd ever feel my legs again after coming that hard three times in a row.

Brodie's harsh breaths joined with mine, until eventually he lifted his head and stared right into my soul. "I think I'm falling in love with you, Evelyn. Like...almost fucking certain."

Oh, shit. Before I could process those words and somehow form a response, he leaned down and kissed me again. This time it was slower, our bodies still locked together, as his tongue gently caressed mine.

Flutters in my core started to emerge as he moved against me, and I wondered if he'd just remained hard even after he came. Brodie fucked me much slower the second time, and when I orgasmed, it was deeper than it had been before. Stronger. Filled with more emotions that I had no idea what to do with.

It wasn't that I had no feelings for him. I had many, *many* feelings for this guy, but it was also complicated. "You don't have to overthink it," he whispered to me after we both shattered again. "There are no rules or timeframe for this. We just do what feels right for as long as it feels right."

Staring up into the intensity of his gaze, I decided that I'd take his advice and, for once, not overthink it. Brodie hadn't asked me to marry him or for a monogamous relationship. He knew about Ethan and that complicated situation, and he was cool to keep exploring our attraction. Which worked for me. "Okay, let's just take it day by day," I whispered, and then desperate for more of him, I placed one of my knees flat and used the other to nudge him over so I was on top. "My turn to fuck you now, movie star."

He threw his arms back and smiled the biggest shit-eating grin. "You say the sweetest stuff, Evie babe." Whatever else he was about to say was jumbled into groans as I sank down onto his once-again hard length, and I forgot everything, including my name, as I started to ride him.

The rest of our time in the hotel was spent fucking in every position we could find. At one point, after I collapsed in exhaustion on Brodie's chest, he started to trace the still-red and angry scar on my back, and I didn't feel an urge to move away. I was done hiding my scars, trauma, and secrets from those I cared about. This was who I was now, and Brodie seemed to be okay with it.

"I almost lost you that day," he whispered, and in my fatigued state, I couldn't quite figure out what he meant.

"I'm right here," I murmured sleepily, reassuring him as he'd done for me in the theatre. "Always here with you." He pressed kisses to my skin until we were once again busy.

When his security knocked to let us know the accident had cleared and we were good to go, we grabbed a quick shower together, too spent to do more than prop ourselves against the wall while attempting to use the cheap hotel soap bars to wash off our hours of screwing. "I think I need a drip to replenish my bodily fluids," Brodie groaned. "If it wasn't for me eating your puss–"

I slapped his chest, snorting out laughter. "Stop it. You're perfectly fine. You only came six times."

I had to add another ten to mine, which was an absolute record that I hoped we'd beat the next time we had this opportunity.

When we were dressed in our clothes from last night, Brodie led me toward the SUV. "What are you going to do about Ethan?" he asked as we got into the back. "He rang a dozen times last night."

I hadn't even checked my phone, and when I pulled it from my little clutch, it was completely dead. Shit. He wasn't going to be happy.

"Did you tell him what happened with the accident?"

Brodie nodded, settling back in with his arm over my shoulders so I could rest against his chest. "Yep, but he's still pissed off. I just want to prepare you for what you might walk in on."

Burying my face against his chest, I debated suggesting we just head back to our crappy little motel for a few more days. "Andrew too?" I guessed.

There was a snort of laughter that told me everything. Our bubble was burst, and I was about to walk into the line of fire.

32

EVELYN

As predicted, Andrew lost his shit. Like, actually seemed like he was about to blow a gasket or something. Ethan had started to lecture about how irresponsible it was—mostly aimed at Brodie rather than me—but a sharp elbow from Connor shut him up. Which was weird.

Andrew had no such restrictions. He went on and on and on about how dangerous Brodie's career was because of the constant spotlight on him. He ranted about the harassment Brodie endured from paparazzi and then waxed poetic about some truly hair-raising stalker-fan incidents he'd had over the years.

I knew, deep down, his intent had been to warn us that we'd acted foolishly. In reality, all he achieved was making me want to deliberately leave campus against his orders. That, and he made me fall ten times harder for Brodie "Orgasm King" Keller. Considering all he'd gone through already in his life, it was beyond belief how shockingly normal he was.

Throughout it all, Ethan glared absolute daggers at Brodie. Somehow, I suspected his sour mood had less to do with the potential danger and more to do with the embarrassingly obvious hickey on my neck.

Eventually I cracked, screamed in Andrew's face that he didn't own me and to shove his rules straight up his ass, then stormed upstairs to my room. I made a point of locking my door, because as much as I'd love to spend more time in bed with Brodie, things were tense. Real tense. And I had assignments that needed doing.

Brodie checked on me, sweetheart that he was, but I assured him I was fine and he left me to sort out my classwork.

To my surprise, it was Haze who knocked on my door around lunchtime, asking if I was hungry. Curious, I let him in and was touched to see he'd made me a sandwich and fresh juice.

"How's your Economics of Crime assignment going?" he asked, glancing around my sparsely decorated space. It was a huge room, but the only furniture I had was my bed and a chest of drawers. I'd been studying on the floor in a patch of sunlight, and Haze frowned deeply at my scatter of notes and textbooks.

I hummed thoughtfully, sitting on the window seat to eat the sandwich he'd brought. "Not too bad, actually. I'm almost finished. What's everyone else doing?" It was Sunday but the guys rarely all hung around the house doing nothing.

Haze shrugged. "Don't know, don't care. I was thinking about fixing those tiles in the spare bathroom."

It was a project I'd been planning on doing myself, but hadn't got around to it yet. I was surprised Haze was interested. "I'll help," I said, taking another huge bite of my sandwich. "I should have my assignment finished in like twenty minutes or so."

He nodded, expressionless. "Okay." Then he left my room. Strange man.

Amused, I finished eating, then tied up the remainder of

the assignment. I frowned, wondering how Haze had known what I was working on without me telling him. Maybe he'd guessed based on the books I had laid out? That seemed plausible.

For the rest of the afternoon, we worked together in near silence. It wasn't uncomfortable, though, until I slipped with a grouting knife and somehow managed to slice my hand open.

"Ow, *fuck!*" I hissed, dropping the knife with a clatter and grabbing my palm.

"What happened?" Haze barked, returning to the bathroom workspace with an armful of tiles to replace the cracked ones. He set down the pile so hard, I was sure I heard some break, but then he was all up in my personal space and all logical thought fled my brain as he grasped my wrist with his huge hand.

He. Touched. Me. Skin to skin, fingers wrapped around my wrist as he tugged me gently to the sink and turned the tap on with his free hand.

"You need to wash it," he growled, guiding my cut hand under the water.

I yelped as fresh pain bloomed, and my blood painted the sink bright red, but still Haze didn't release me. His eyes remained locked on my wound, making sure all the little flakes of grout were cleaned out before turning off the water.

"Hold still," Haze murmured when I flinched as he prodded the edge of the cut. "I don't think you need stitches. Wait here." Then he released my wrist as abruptly as he'd grasped it, disappearing from the bathroom in a puff of imaginary smoke. He could move *fast* when he tried.

Frowning at my bleeding hand, I tried to flex my fingers, which only made me hiss with pain as more blood dripped out. "That was dumb," I muttered to myself, gritting my teeth.

Haze came clattering back up the stairs a moment later, first-aid kit in hand. He gestured for me to sit on the edge of the bathtub, which I did. Then he dropped to his knees in front of me and opened up the kit with confident determination.

Neither one of us spoke as he disinfected my cut, then bandaged it up with gentle touches, and it felt like I held my breath the whole time.

"Thanks, Haze," I whispered when he was done.

He concentrated on packing up the first-aid kit, not meeting my eyes. "You're welcome, Eve. I'll tidy up in here." The dismissal was crystal-clear, and I wasn't dumb enough to push the issue. So I nodded and slipped out of the half-finished bathroom once more.

Anxious and confused about the whole interaction with Haze, I opted to go downstairs rather than be alone with my thoughts. Andrew was seated at the dining table, his laptop open as he worked on something. He glared at me when I entered, but I ignored his presence and made a beeline for Ethan, who was standing by the stove, instead.

"Need help?" I asked in a small voice, offering a metaphorical olive branch.

His response was to drop the wooden spoon he'd been using and grab me in a tight hug. The pure tension radiating through his body as he held me close left me speechless, and I just looped my arms around his waist to hug him back.

"I'm sorry," he murmured after the longest time. His face was buried in my hair, his words muffled.

I drew a deep breath, inhaling his spicy scent as I felt myself relax right into him. Our fight had been bothering me, even as I'd ignored it in favor of focusing on my time away with Brodie.

A sense of rightness returned in this moment of reconnection, but I knew it wasn't enough to completely wipe the slate clear. "We need to talk," I whispered against his chest, and his response was to tighten his hold further until he released a sigh.

"I know. I fucked up, Eve, and I owe you more than a two-word apology, but I couldn't go any longer without saying that. It's been killing me."

It had felt wrong to fight with Ethan. "Sorry I ignored all your messages while I was away."

I hadn't done it deliberately, but at the same time I'd been totally unable to deal with more fighting and anger, so I wasn't mad about it. But it wasn't fair, when he'd only been trying to care about me. In his somewhat overprotective, dominant way.

He released me to stare into my face. "You had every right. I overstepped, and I was an asshole about it. It's just...worrying about you makes me a bit crazy. It's no real excuse, but the feral part of my brain kicks in when it comes to you."

Popping up on my toes, I pressed a kiss to his cheek. "I like the feral part, Eth."

The green of his irises darkened as he stared at me, and it was only the hissing bubble of whatever he'd been stirring that broke through his focus. "Shit, the stew is about to burn."

He grabbed the spoon again to stir, and I crossed around the other side of the bench, my soul lighter than it had been as I started to slice the crusty bread sitting on the cutting board.

We worked in silence for a few minutes, and when he called everyone into the dining room, I found it odd that of all the guys I shared a house with, Andrew was the only one I wasn't a huge fan of. Not enough that I wished he'd fall off a cliff or anything, but I couldn't imagine a scenario where I'd actively search out his company.

However attractive I found him at times, it didn't make up for his annoying personality.

"What happened?"

I jerked, realizing I'd been glaring at Andrew, who hadn't even bothered to notice me as he focused on stirring an already-stirred bowl of stew. Turning to Connor, who stared at the bandage on my hand, I said, "Cut myself tiling. It's nothing big."

"She didn't need stitches," Haze added, "but it was close."

Connor's hard stare remained on the injury for a few extra seconds, but he didn't say anything else.

Brodie got the conversation going as we all started to eat, and I almost missed his question as I devoured the delicious dish. *Holy crap, Ethan can cook.*

"Anyone up for a game tonight?"

Haze answered Brodie first. "Yeah, count me in."

I hadn't partaken in any of their Xbox battles so far, but tonight felt like a great night to start. "Sure, I'll play."

Everyone stopped and stared like I'd just flopped my tits out on the table, and it amused me that this was what had shocked them. "What? How hard can it be to run around and shoot people?"

I almost died when Andrew laughed. Like, he actually relaxed the stick up his ass and, looking like a typical hot, rich boy, threw his head back and laughed. "The girl who's afraid of guns wants to play a game where you shoot people?"

Oh, right. I hadn't actually picked up any first-person shooters since my attack, but surely I could handle a non-real-life situation that involved weapons. "You all think I need therapy to help get over my trauma, maybe this is a way to help. A slight desensitization."

Andrew no longer looked amused, and weirdly, there was a flash of concern on his face before his features returned to impassiveness. "You might be right."

The rest of dinner passed quickly, and soon I found myself on the couch, controller in hand, with a smirking Brodie on my right side. "You're my girl, you know that, right?" he said.

It was impossible not to love this guy. "Hmmm, do I though?"

Brodie nudged me gently, before he pressed a kiss to the side of my neck, sending shivers to pool in my gut. "You're my girl, Evie babe. And I need you to remember that."

My head was fuzzy as he pulled away. "Why?"

His grin was wicked. "Because I'm about to kick your ass like you're not."

That statement should not have been as attractive as it was. "We'll see, babe," I shot back, hoping my skills weren't rusty after all this time. "We'll see."

The others filed into the room one by one, Haze with scotch in hand, while Connor and Ethan had beers. They'd brought a can for Brodie, too, but he was too busy gearing up his character in the hopes of blasting me to pieces.

Game on.

As I scrolled through the options to outfit myself, I found myself settling back into the familiar game like it had been hours and not almost a year since I'd last played. Brodie chose the map for us to head into, and while we waited for it to load, I brushed my fingers over the buttons to help with dexterity.

When we spawned, I took off toward my favorite spot to camp and quickly switched guns to my close-range shotgun. The sight on the screen didn't trigger me in any way, and it was so nice to feel like my old self that I almost missed Brodie sneaking up behind me.

The bastard had a knife, like he thought me such a noob that I wouldn't be able to stop him from stabbing me in the side. Swinging around the corner, I shot him point-blank in the chest, and he suffered enough damage that he was dead with one shot.

"Fuck," he exclaimed. "Baby, you didn't tell me you'd played before."

"You didn't ask," I replied with a laugh as I took off into the map, ready to kill everyone else.

The guys watched, wide-eyed, as I took down half the field, before a sniper got in a well-placed headshot and ended my run.

Still, not bad for a first go on rusty skills. "My turn next!" Haze rumbled, holding out his hand. "I want to go against Evie."

Oh, yeah, this was going to be fun.

245

33

EVELYN

After hours of gaming, I went to bed utterly exhausted, only to wake up barely ninety minutes later and lie there wide-awake and staring at the ceiling for God only knew how long. When my mind started whirling into conspiracy theories about the Sullivan family, and the Crusades seeking revenge for the dead man in the woods, I decided to get up.

The house was silent, and the creak of my footsteps felt painfully loud as I made my way down the hall past Brodie's and Haze's rooms.

I descended the stairs carefully, avoiding the steps that I knew had the worst squeaky patches, and the faint sounds of the TV trickled through from the living room as I drew closer.

Instinct told me it was likely Haze, watching more true crime shows, maybe *Unsolved Mysteries*, and I smiled with happy anticipation. It had been nice watching with him last time, but things were different now. We were closer, right? He touched me, without freaking out. That had to count for something. Maybe in the dark of the night we could talk about it?

I bypassed the living room and went to the kitchen to make

myself a chamomile tea, attempting to calm my busy mind, then wandered back through to join him on the sofa.

Except it wasn't Haze watching TV with the volume so low it was almost muted.

"Oh. I thought you were…" I stood there, awkwardly staring with confusion. "Never mind. Sorry. I'll just—"

"Sit down, brat," Connor growled, moving the cushion from the seat beside him in clear invitation.

Unable to make my brain do the braining thing, I just did as I was told and sat my ass down on the sofa beside Connor. I shifted around a little to get comfy, then took a sip of my tea while trying to work out what he was watching.

"Is this—"

"Yes," he snapped, cutting me off with a sharp side-scowl.

I quirked a brow, tilting my head to the side as I watched the old-school slasher flick playing on the huge TV with subtitles running. "Okay, no judgments here. This is a classic."

He cast another sideways look my way, then sighed. "Couldn't sleep?"

"What gave it away, Sherlock?" The snark slipped out without thought, and I pursed my lips after the fact. "Sorry. I'm getting somewhat irritated about the sleep situation. I might call my therapist tomorrow and get a new prescription for Trazadone."

Connor just grunted, like he didn't think it was a great idea but also didn't want to argue about it. Instead, he turned the TV volume up a couple of clicks and we both returned our attention to the movie.

I'd be the first to admit, I fell for *every* damn jump scare in *every* scary movie and found it hard to keep my sarcastic comments to myself when the characters did particularly stupid things. Connor didn't seem too bothered by my commentary, but I kept it mumbled, nonetheless.

When the Ghost Face killer appeared out of nowhere—for

probably the fiftieth time—I flinched and gave a little squeal, nearly spilling the last of my tea all over Connor.

"I thought you said you'd seen this," he remarked, taking the mug from my hand and setting it aside before I could make more mess. Our fingers brushed with the motion, and I tried really hard not to read too much into it. He'd saved my life, and I was inappropriately hero worshiping. Connor did *not* reciprocate that feeling, and I needed to remember it.

I cleared my throat. "I have. Lots of times. It's still scary, though. That's kind of the point, isn't it?"

His answer was just a firm roll of his eyes, like I was being stupid. He didn't change the movie, though, nor did he ask me to fuck off. So that was something.

I yawned heavily some minutes later, settling down deeper into the sofa as I mumbled another sarcastic comment about the female main character running *up*stairs to escape a killer. Connor snorted some sort of laugh at that, then tugged a blanket from the back of the sofa to drape over me.

"Lie down, brat. You're making me uncomfortable all squashed up like that." He grabbed a spare cushion and placed it down beside his thigh, indicating I could use it.

I smirked, shuffling down until I was horizontal. "Aw, you're being nice because we trauma bonded."

Another eye roll. "We absolutely did not. I'm being nice because it's two in the morning and I don't have the energy to be an asshole."

"Uh-huh, sure thing, trauma bestie."

A frustrated sigh escaped him. "Brat, trauma bonds require both parties to have experienced trauma together. We did not. *You* experienced trauma, but for me it was just Saturday night. Now shush, they're about to reveal the killer."

I bit my lip, keeping my thoughts to myself. The fact that being kidnapped at gunpoint and then literally executing a guy was just...*normal* for him? Blew my mind. I couldn't even begin to comprehend the kind of childhood Connor had survived, and it sort of made me understand why he was a surly grump all the time.

But then it led me into wondering whether Ethan had suffered the same upbringing. Had he also murdered gangsters and called it *just a Saturday night*?

The movie finished, and Connor didn't ask before starting the next one, which I was quietly glad for. I didn't want to go back to bed when I was so comfy right where I was.

So comfy.

My eyelids drooped, and my blinks became longer even before the title credits started rolling.

"Are you falling asleep, brat?" Connor asked in a low whisper.

"Mmhmm," I confirmed, letting my eyes close for another extended blink. I thought for sure he'd tell me to go back to bed if I was going to sleep, but he didn't. He just pulled the blanket up higher over my shoulders and clicked the volume down lower on the TV.

GLORIOUS SLEEP HAD ELUDED me for so long that when I opened my eyes the next morning to find the sun shining brightly into the house, I was so disoriented that I didn't realize for at least five minutes that I was still on the couch.

More than that. I was in Connor fucking Sullivan's lap.

Holy shit. Holy forking shit.

Trying not to breathe too heavily, I stared up into his sleeping face. He remained in a sitting position, his head back on the cushions behind, and his arms were wrapped around my shoulders because I'd somehow shifted into his lap. Not on the edge of his thigh—nope, right smack bang on his dick.

Thankfully with a cushion under my head still.

What time is it? The sun was bright and strong, and I felt better rested than I had in almost a year. No nightmares had plagued me with Connor, and as I stared into the handsome lines of his face, which was relaxed in a way it never was when awake, I felt those tendrils of our trauma bond cement just a little stronger.

"Stop staring at me, brat," he mumbled without opening his eyes, and I would have jumped, except I was too damn comfortable.

"You let me sleep on you, trauma bestie."

Connor's chest rumbled, but I swear the smallest of smiles tilted up the corner of his lips as he finally graced me with the gorgeous green of his eyes. "You're an absolute pain in my ass, but even I hate seeing the literal suitcases you've got under your eyes. I wasn't going to risk waking you, not even to get more comfortable."

Fuck. That was actually super sweet, and if I hadn't heard it from the man himself, I'd never have believed it. "I'm not sure you understand what literal means, gangster, but I appreciate the sentiment all the same."

Realizing it was weird to still be lying in his lap—why the heck was I so comfortable with this scary guy?—I jerked myself up and shook off any niggling aches from sleeping on a couch... and a person.

Connor stretched and reached out to grab his phone, cursing as he turned it on. "What?" I said in a panic. With his life, there was no way to guess what would upset him. But it would definitely be bad.

"You're late for class."

Not what I expected, but worthy of panic all the same. "Fuck! Why didn't Ethan wake us before he left?"

I lurched to my feet, flapping my hands as I grabbed for my phone as well to confirm the time. Ethan's class was half-over, and there was no way I'd make it.

Connor reached out and grasped my hand, slowing the rapid movements. "It's going to be okay, sweetheart. I know the professor, and I'm fairly sure we can work out an arrangement to get you caught up."

Shaking my head at him, I couldn't find my usually snappy reply, because for once he hadn't made a snarky remark about me banging my teacher. It had almost been a cute jest about me banging my teacher, and that was *huge* progress.

"I'm going to run upstairs and get ready," I said, knowing I still had a study session and a possible makeup class. I needed to check my online schedule.

Connor nodded. "I'm faster than you, usually, so I'll make you a sandwich to get you through until lunch. No one wants to see you hangry again."

With a snort, I flipped him off, and he just flashed his perfect teeth in a smartass smile.

As I raced up the stairs, I realized that I didn't want to leave Connor or that couch today. I could have quite happily remained in our little slasher-flick moment, vegging out with all the snacky snacks and ignoring the rest of the world.

Unfortunately, my professors wouldn't feel the same way, and I already dreaded having to explain my absence to Ethan. Not that he should be surprised unless he completely missed his two sleeping roommates on the couch when he left this morning.

There was no time for a shower, so I just scrubbed my face, brushed my teeth, and slapped on minimal makeup. Not that I fucking needed it. This girl was glowing with her full night's sleep, and when I had more time to break down my night with Connor, I'd analyze the reasons why he kept my dreams away. Just like Ethan. And Brodie.

Yeah, maybe that was the key. Always sleep with a gorgeous, somewhat dangerous man.

In my room, I changed into jeans and a tank, grabbing up

Connor's hoodie, before pausing to wonder if that was a little too far. He already thought I was an obsessed, trauma-bonded loser. And I wasn't going to deny it, but best to leave the hoodie for secretly sleeping in.

Snatching up my bag and denim jacket instead, I hurried back down to find Connor in new clothes, looking far too gorgeous and refreshed for what had to have been a pretty shitty night of sleep. "Here's your sandwich, brat," he said, thrusting a chicken and mayo roll at me. "Now move your ass, because I have a class in ten minutes, and I need to walk you into the main courtyard."

Clutching the sandwich, and then the bottle of water he also handed over, I shook my head. "You don't have to wait for me. I know I'm only going to slow you down. I don't have anything for an hour or so; it's okay to run ahead."

He looked at me like I'd just suggested he crawl on his stomach to class while wearing a onesie. "Not a fucking chance. I'm getting you there safely, just make sure you move your ass."

I almost saluted him. "Yes, sir."

He paused in the process of slipping his laptop bag over his shoulder, and I swallowed roughly at the heat in his eyes. "I knew I'd tame the brat into a good girl." He stepped closer, towering over me as I drowned in his intensity. "You want to be a good girl for me, Evelyn?"

Oh, fuck. *What was the question again?*

Connor's laughter released me, and I found myself hurrying for the door as he nudged me along. "Eat," he ordered, and I glanced down to find my now-crushed sandwich still clutched in one hand, the water in my other.

The fresh air cleared my head as we left the house, and starving, I bit into the delicious fresh bread. Connor had already finished his, but it felt like he kept an eye on me the entire way to campus, making sure I ate all of mine.

"A good night's sleep did you very well," he said suddenly,

when the courtyard came into view. "I've never seen you look quite so..."

He trailed off, gaze lifting as he stared above my head, and I swore he'd just seen a ghost. Turning as I twisted the lid off my bottle, it took me a minute to figure out what had drawn his attention.

A gorgeous brunette was hurrying across the grass, a large duffel over her shoulder as she waved. "Connie," she shouted. "Oh my God."

When she reached us, she all but shoved me to the side as she leaped at Connor, and he reached out and caught her by instinct, still looking shell-shocked.

"Oh, Con," she cried, wrapping her arms around his neck. "I missed you so much."

Then she kissed him right on the lips, and even as I hoped he was about to push her away, the shock finally wore off his face and he threaded one of his hands through the back of her shiny, golden hair and...kissed her back.

34

EVELYN

It felt like a whole damn eternity that I stood there like a creeper, watching Connor kiss some random girl, but eventually they came up for air before the seasons changed. Okay, to be fair, it was probably only a few seconds, but it *felt* like longer. My damn hero worship was in full force after our slasher-and-sleeping-together session.

"Oh my God, where are my manners?" the admittedly stunning girl gushed as she released Connor and swung her dazzling gaze to me. "I'm Lacey. You must be Evelyn? I've heard so much about you, it feels like we've already met."

She stuck her hand out for me to shake, her nails perfectly polished and her tasteful rings all worth probably more than a year's tuition at Meadowridge. Dumbstruck, I shook her hand with a floppy wrist.

"Um, yeah. Eve. You're...Lacey?" Was it rude to admit that no one had mentioned her to me *at all* so I couldn't return the sentiment?

The blonde just laughed and rolled her eyes. "Lemme guess, Connie and the boys failed to tell you about me? Out of sight, out of mind, huh?" That question was aimed at Connor, who ran a frustrated hand through his dark hair.

"It's not like that, Lay, you know it. We're late for class, though, so maybe we can catch up later?" He brushed a quick kiss over her cheek, then gestured for me to continue walking toward the courtyard.

The gorgeous woman—Lacey—just sighed. "Yeah, later. It was nice to meet you finally, Eve! I hope we can hang out now that I'm back."

Confused and thrown off-balance, I just nodded and mumbled a vague, "yeah, you too," that made not a lot of sense before following after Connor.

"Um..." I said when we were out of earshot of Lacey. "Who was that?"

Connor threw me a scathing look, like I was an idiot. "Lacey. She introduced herself. I heard it."

Ass. "And who is Lacey, *Connie*?"

He flinched and stopped walking. "Don't call me that." Then started again, striding across campus like he was being chased. "Lacey is my girlfriend."

Well, *fuck*. I hadn't seen that one coming, even with the way she greeted his tonsils just moments ago. I thought maybe she was a fuck buddy or...something. But...

"You have a girlfriend?" I squeaked in horror. Oh man, I needed to get the hero-worship thing under control. Immediately.

Connor released a frustrated sound. "Yes. You just met her. Lacey. Oh look, here's your makeup class, and there's Haze waiting for you. Catch you later, brat."

With that, he gave me a push in Haze's direction and legged it away like his ass was on fire. Apparently he *really* didn't want to chat about his girlfriend, but I felt like maybe Haze could tell me more. Then again, of all the guys, he wasn't exactly the chattiest. Where the fuck was Brodie when I needed him?

"Everything okay?" Haze asked, scowling after Connor, then holding out his hand. "How's your wound?"

Not even thinking about my actions, I placed my bandaged hand in his. "I ran out of time to change the dressing, but it doesn't hurt today."

He froze, and I realized what I'd just done. With a sharp inhale, I tried to snatch my hand back, but his fingers wrapped around my wrist, holding me tight as he swallowed.

"It should be all right for now," he murmured with a husky voice. "But we need to change it tonight, okay?"

I nodded, speechless. Haze frowned at my hand a moment longer, like he was confused about why the fuck he was touching me, then ever so slowly released my wrist.

"Um, are you taking this extra class with me today or just happened to be in the area?" Because last I checked, he wasn't in this class. None of the guys were.

Haze just nodded, falling into step with me as I headed toward the classroom. "Yes."

That wasn't an answer, but I sensed that was all I'd get. With a sigh, I let it go and found a seat in the middle of the room. Haze slid into the seat beside me but made no move to pull out any notes or his laptop.

There was still a solid ten minutes until the class started, and we were the only ones seated, so I figured it was a good time to chat a little. "Haze, can I ask you something?"

"Depends," he replied, slouching out in his seat like only huge dudes could do.

I rolled my eyes. "Okay. What's the deal with Connor and Lacey?"

His eyes widened in surprise. "He told you about Lacey? How'd that come up?"

"No...I just met her. Like five minutes ago, when she had her tongue halfway down Connor's throat. He said she's his girlfriend?" I sounded jealous even when really trying not to.

Haze nodded slowly. "She is...but I didn't think she was getting back to Meadowridge until next semester. I wonder what happened."

I chewed my lip, marinating on that information for a moment. "So you do know her? And she really is Connor's girlfriend?"

"You sound annoyed. Why is that?"

Fuck. I did. Why was that? Because he saved my life, then showed me the tiniest scrap of compassion, which was more than likely just stemmed from pity about how fucking damaged I was?

I wet my lips and shook my head. "No, I'm not. Just confused. None of you have ever mentioned her before, and I think that's strange. That's all."

Haze observed me for far longer than was comfortable, and I wasn't sure I should be revealing all my fucked-up, broken pieces to him. "She's Connor's girlfriend to talk about," he finally said, shrugging as if it made perfect sense.

But like... "She knew all about me, and yet I had no idea she even existed. Come on, H. That doesn't feel weird to you? What game is Connor Sullivan fucking playing?"

Haze was saved having to answer by the professor rushing into the room, a sheaf of papers under her arm as she dumped her bag on the desk. There weren't many of us in class again, but she wasn't fazed, dropping what had to be last week's assignments in the collection folder.

Pulling out my laptop, I retrieved my last lot of notes and started to add any pertinent information that came up in the lecture. All the while, my mind whirled and my stomach threatened to relieve me of the chicken sandwich.

It felt like a long time ago I'd worried about Ethan's stunner of a girlfriend after I kissed him, but it turned out to be Connor who had one. That sneaky bastard had a beautiful—and apparently lovely—girlfriend hidden in the background.

This was nothing like Laura, who was such a horrible bitch that you knew Andrew was only with her for the connections. Nope. Lacey appeared to be the full package, not showing one ounce of jealousy over the chick who'd been sharing a house with her man for weeks.

Haze nudged me when class was over, and I packed my shit up and filed down to grab my assignment. The high grade scribbled across the side didn't give me the same thrill it would have on a normal day, but at least one part of my life remained stable.

I shouldn't care about Connor's girlfriend, considering I was in a relationship slash situationship with two other men. While crushing a little on another.

There wasn't a single fucking leg for me to stand on here in my confusion and hurt feelings.

And yet, hurt I was.

Haze stayed with me as I left the lecture hall, and I found myself heading for the room where Ethan's class was held. The one I'd missed this morning. I knew he taught another class in here straight after mine.

Students were still filing out of the doorway, so I waited a few seconds and poked my head in to find him inside, packing up his desk.

"I'll leave you two to talk," Haze said softly. "I'll grab you a tray for lunch."

I was hit with a shot of warmth and caring for the big guy, because apparently I was just going to crush, at one point or another, on every guy I shared a house with. "Thanks, H. You're the best."

He swallowed roughly, and I could have sworn the slightest pink tinged his cheeks as he turned and hurried off. By this stage, Ethan had noticed me there, and I was relieved to see his warm smile. "Hey, baby." He stepped closer and brushed my hair behind my ear. "You look well rested."

Resisting the urge to press my head to his chest—this was not the time or the place—I forced a smile in return. "I'm sorry I missed your class this morning. I honestly don't know how I slept so deeply that I missed you all leaving, but I must have been tired."

He settled back against his desk, and there was no sign of darkness of jealousy in his gaze. "You were snuggled into Connor, and for once, both of you slept. There isn't a class in the world more important than sleep, so we left you be."

"Lacey's back!" I blurted it out, because apparently I was a psychopath with an obsessive mind.

Ethan straightened, that lightheartedness fading. "Lacey's back? Connor never said she was expected back this year."

Everyone knew about her except me. Every-fucking-one.

"Where has she been?" If he thought my tight voice was odd, he gave no indication of it.

"She went to help build orphanages somewhere in Africa, I think. It was supposed to be a gap year, but she's not even halfway through it."

Build orphanages in Africa... Was he fucking kidding me? A saint with a sinner like Connor. It made no sense, and yet I couldn't deny how nice she'd appeared at first meeting. Definitely the sort who'd take on an altruistic role during her gap year.

"No wonder Connor looked shocked as shit to see her racing across campus. Maybe she's just back for a visit." Like that was any better; Connor still had a girlfriend, whether she lived here or not. "More importantly, why didn't he tell me about her?"

Surely Ethan would know his brother better than anyone, even if they did have a strained relationship. His gaze was as sharp and observant as Haze's had been, and it was that factor that had me realizing I needed to reel myself back in.

I'd been letting the little fantasy world I'd built in my head with Connor cloud my judgment, and with the veil of illusion abruptly torn from me this morning, I was having trouble dealing with reality. "You know what? It doesn't even matter. Connor and I are barely friends, let alone more, so the fact he has a girlfriend changes nothing."

Except our movie sleepovers. Last night would have to be the one and only time.

"You and Connor went through a traumatic experience," Ethan said gently, and I hated the sympathy in his eyes. "It's understandable that you'd bond over it."

"We are *former* trauma-bond besties," I muttered, which resulted in a wider smile from Ethan.

"Right. And just because Lace is back, doesn't mean you lose that bond. It doesn't have to change."

That was where he was wrong, but I couldn't argue about it any longer. "I should get to lunch. I just wanted to check in about my missed class this morning and see if there were any notes I needed. Did you end up having a pop quiz today?"

Ethan's lips twitched. "Funnily enough, the mic wasn't working very well today, so I just let the class spend some time working on their projects. No new material got covered, and the pop quiz is Friday now."

My heart swelled, and it was enough to douse a fraction of my disappointment over Connor. I already had amazing guys in my life, and it was just greedy to want more. "You're the best, Eth," I whispered, getting all emotional. "I don't tell you enough."

He leaned in to kiss me, but chatter outside halted his actions. "Tonight," he promised. "You can make it up to me tonight."

Anticipation had me pressing my thighs together. "Leave your door open," I whispered.

"It's always open for you, Lilith. Always."

Connor Sullivan was a poor substitute for his brother, and the sooner I remembered that I couldn't have them all, the easier my life would be.

35

EVELYN

The mouthwatering scents of rich Italian tomato sauce hit my nose before I even opened the front door to Bluebell House that evening, and I groaned with hunger. I'd been too worked up about the Connor-Lacey thing at lunch to really eat, but now I was *starving*.

"That smells amazing," I commented, kicking off my shoes in the foyer before excitedly hurrying through to the kitchen. My mood instantly soured when I realized who was cooking.

"Thanks, brat," Connor replied, standing at the stove with a wooden spoon in hand. "How come you're home so late?"

I pinched my lips together, trying not to let my feelings show all over my face. "I was catching up with Nina. She just got back last night from visiting her aunt in Vietnam."

Connor looked like he was about to say something else, but I had come to a few harsh realities today, the biggest being that, despite his softened demeanor, he did *not* like me as anything more than his housemate. Everything else I'd imagined between us was just that: imagined. It was a bitter pill to swallow, and to be totally frank, it was embarrassing. So I'd made a pact with myself to just gain a little distance. Let the hero worship die down.

Rather than hang around to chat, I abruptly left the kitchen and went upstairs to drop my books and charge my laptop up.

"Evie babe," Brodie sang out, appearing in my doorway as I dropped my things on my bed. "I feel like I haven't seen you in forever. Wanna have a sleepover in my room?"

My cunt blushed. "Forever? Brodie baby, we spent all Saturday night fucking in a dirty motel. I'm *still* sore."

He gave an exaggerated pout, coming into my room and closing the door with his heel. "So...does that mean no sleepover? Or yes, sleepover so long as I promise to be gentle?"

I wet my lips, watching him prowl closer. God *damn* he was one handsome human being. I felt the need to pinch myself because surely it wasn't real that Brodie Keller—*the* Brodie Keller—was currently looking at me like his favorite dessert.

"You can be gentle? I don't believe you," I taunted, tipping my head back to maintain eye contact when he came toe to toe with me. "Prove it."

I was waving a red flag in front of a bull, but I couldn't help myself. Brodie smiled, his hand cupping the back of my neck ever so softly as he lowered his lips to mine. The kiss he offered was *painfully* gentle, slow and tender as he took his sweet fucking time exploring my lips with feather-soft caresses. I tried to lure him into a more passionate embrace but he held me firm, setting the pace and proving his fucking point.

"I don't think I like you being gentle," I grumbled.

Brodie smirked. Evil bastard. "I dunno, Evie babe, I could get used to this. Look how worked up you just got from a kiss. I bet those panties are soaked right now, aren't they?"

They absolutely were. Totally saturated, to the point where I'd need to change before heading down to dinner for fear of sliding off my seat. And yet, I couldn't seem to make myself put a foot on the brake.

I licked my lips. "Want to find out?"

Brodie's eyes blew wide, his pulse thumping in his throat at my eye level. "Fuck yes, I do."

Except apparently, fate had other ideas and a knock on my bedroom door made us pause. The boys of this house weren't big on knocking *politely*. They usually knocked once, then yelled whatever they came to say through the door.

"Who is it?" I called out, frowning. If it was Andrew coming to play dad again, I'd probably kick him in the nuts. He was getting right on my last freaking nerve.

"It's Lacey," the surprising answer came, making me stiffen up like a board. "Connie invited me over for dinner, but I thought we could hang out while he's cooking?"

I stifled a groan, and Brodie gave me a puzzled look. "Lacey?" he asked softly. "As in Connor's Lacey?"

Apparently, he also didn't know she was returning to Meadowridge, but he definitely knew all about Lacey herself. When I nodded, his smile lit up and he quickly threw open my bedroom door to greet the perfect specimen of a woman standing there.

"Lace-face! You're back!" he exclaimed, wrapping her in a huge hug and really sending a sharp pain through my chest. Did everyone love her? Christ, what the fuck was she doing dating a moody grump like Connor?

"Brodester! Holy shit, I missed you!" She laughed as she hugged him back, and a sick sensation of pure jealousy swelled in my gut. "Did you get bigger? Damn, they were working you hard onset for *Resurrection*, huh?" She squeezed his bicep, and I nearly choked on my own tongue.

Brodie laughed at that and released her, gesturing for me. "So you already met Evie? When'd that happen? Aren't you supposed to be in Haiti for another six months?"

Lacey rolled her eyes and shot me a smile as if to say, *this guy!* "I was in Malawi this time. Haiti was last year, doofus."

Shifting her attention to me, she shrugged. "I work with a volunteer organization that provides schools and housing to poverty-stricken communities."

I nodded, trying really freaking hard not to be a bitch to the literal reincarnation of Princess Diana, but damn, it was tough when her perfectly manicured hand was on Brodie's arm.

Snap out of it, Eve. She's not a fucking threat, you cavewoman.

"That's...very admirable," I muttered, brushing past Brodie. "We were just heading downstairs to play *Call of Duty*."

Brodie gave me a squinty look. "We were? I thought we were about to—"

"Play COD," I cut him off sharply. "Yes, we are. I promised Haze a rematch before dinner."

Total bullshit, I'd done nothing of the sort. But Lacey's arrival at our house had really turned the cold taps on that heated moment with Brodie so *that* wasn't going to continue. Maybe I could sneak away for dinner tonight or something.

Leaving her standing there with Brodie, I raced downstairs to find the house abuzz with conversation. Our other roommates had returned, and everyone stood in the kitchen catching up. I found myself pausing just outside the door, enjoying the banter between Andrew and Connor, Haze even piped up every now and then with his dry humor that I secretly loved, and for once, Ethan and Connor weren't in the middle of a sibling rivalry which should have died out when they were kids.

"You have the worst luck with students," Connor said, laughing like the asshole he was. "How do you manage to find them naked in your office at least once a week?"

Okay, now they really had my attention.

Brodie appeared behind me as I leaned in to listen, but he didn't push me to enter the room, choosing to wrap his hands around my hips and hold me against his hard length. *Fuck.* I almost groaned and gave our position away.

"Trust me, I kick their asses out so fast, their tits flap in the fucking breeze. It's annoying as hell, but rich bitches think the world owes them everything, and they can't seem to take no for an answer. If any of them cost me Eve with this bullshit, I will murder them."

Well, well... who knew the threat of murder could be so romantic?

My fists still clenched at the thought of those thirsty bitches, the cut on my palm smarting at me, and Brodie chuckled lightly. "Easy there, Evie babe. You heard Ethan. He hasn't got eyes for any other student in the college."

I was distracted when Andrew asked, "Why didn't you do the same with Eve? I find it odd that after two years as a professor, turning down students left, right, and center, you suddenly found yourself dick deep in the one we need to keep safe."

Need to keep safe? What the fuck was he talk—

"What's happening?" Lacey asked, having finally joined us downstairs. I had no idea what she'd been doing since I raced out of my room, but hopefully it wasn't planting cameras in there to spy on me. No one could be as altruistic as she appeared; there had to be a dark side.

Clearing my throat, I stepped into the kitchen like I hadn't been creepily hovering outside the door. Brodie remained close, and when I crossed to press my lips against Ethan's, I found myself sandwiched between the two.

When my gaze met Haze's neutral expression, I remembered my excuse for rushing down here. "We need to have our rematch of *Call of Duty*," I said, hoping he'd play along.

I did my best not to glance over to where Connor and Andrew stood, though my curiosity over what he'd meant by *keeping me safe* was filling my brain to capacity.

There'd been so many little oddities I'd ignored since meeting Andrew Knightsbridge, starting with his actual interest in me in the first place, followed by the weird fight in the dining hall and the punishment that followed.

Now that I knew them all better, absolutely none of this situation made an ounce of fucking sense. In my stupid grief, trauma, and sleep deprivation, I'd just been ignoring all the warning signs and red flags in my life, but my spark of clarity today—and maybe that full night's sleep—was opening my eyes in a whole new way. Andrew was up to something, and it involved me.

"That's right. I'll get it loading," Haze said, striding toward the door like he'd known this was the plan all along.

Lacey squealed, and I wondered why she stood so close to me and my guys and hadn't raced around to hang off her massive boyfriend, who stirred his stupid pasta on the other side of the island. "I don't know how to game," she said, "but I love to watch. It's so cool that you can hold your own with the boys. I knew there was a reason I liked you."

Liked me? She'd known me for about eight seconds of life, and I was the chick who had all but taken her place in this group, crushing on every guy in this house, including her boyfriend. Not that she knew that part of the equation, but still, this was weird.

"I'm really not that good," I mumbled before shooting her what had to be the most awkward smile in existence. I felt like a fucking alien wearing a skin suit, with no idea how humans actually acted.

Sure enough, the other guys were all looking at me weirdly, which I ignored as I made my legs move into the living room. Haze already had the system set up, and I crashed on the couch a few feet from him, wondering if the horror of my awkwardness was still written all over my face.

"I need to change your bandage," he said, glancing at the space between us. Lacey was temporarily wiped from my mind when he adjusted his seat, moving us much closer together, until I could feel the heat from his arm near mine.

"Yeah, thanks. I don't want it to get infected."

There wasn't a lot of pain, just tenderness when I clenched my hand, so I figured it was healing fairly well.

Haze made quick work of rebandaging my hand, but our fingers brushed on multiple occasions which earned a wide-eyed stare of confusion from Brodie when he entered the room.

My back straightened when the others joined us, Lacey chatting animatedly to Andrew, who was actually smiling and chatting back. She had them all completely charmed, and all I could think was how hard it had been for me to win even the smallest step of trust and friendship with half the guys in Blue-bell House. Lacey, on the other hand, was their favorite darling, knowing everything about their lives and showing genuine caring in her questions and conversation.

Monster.

"Boom!" Brodie shouted. "Evie, headshot again. Babe, what's happening? You're letting Haze own you."

He dropped down on my free side, and Ethan slid in between my legs on the floor, the pair offering me comfort, though I doubted they knew how badly I needed it. Even Haze being so close felt nice, and for the first time since I'd run into Lacey this morning, I was finally able to relax.

Until Connor opened his big fucking mouth. "Maybe last night was just a fluke. You oversold your skills, brat."

Focusing on the game for the first time, I grunted in response, not bothering to give him more of my time than that. The focus at least allowed me to get my head back into the game, even as I swore I felt a green-eyed gaze boring into the side of my face.

I managed to kill a few more of the bots we played against and got Haze more than once, and all the time Connor kept niggling at me. "Pouting doesn't suit you, Evelyn," he grumbled at one point, and I swung around like I hadn't even known he was there.

"Oh, Sullivan. I thought you were on kitchen duty today. Shouldn't you be checking on the pasta?"

He smirked, and the temptation to smack it off his face was strong. "It's well in hand. You'll find that there's very little outside of my control. Ever."

Was that fucking right? Well, he was about to learn a hard lesson then. "You know what?" I said brightly, before I reached out and wrapped my hands around Ethan and Brodie's shoulders. "I'm not really feeling pasta. I think a nice dinner out is exactly what we need tonight. A few drinks, food that's edible, and a chance to relax. What do you think, boys?"

Brodie was on his feet before I even finished speaking, and while Ethan turned his shrewd gaze on me, obviously sensing I remained out of sorts. Thankfully he didn't call me out in front of everyone. He just tilted his head and pressed his lips to my hand on his shoulder. "That sounds perfect, and I know just the place."

He got up first and pulled me to my feet, all but lifting me into his arms.

"Don't wait up for us," Brodie called, bouncing on his toes. "It's fucking date night."

Date night with two guys. Well, that was one way to take my mind off the other shit in my life.

36

EVELYN

I genuinely didn't give a shit where we went for dinner, so long as I could get out of the house and away from Lacey. Okay, fuck, *Lacey* wasn't the problem—she actually seemed lovely and I could see why the boys all thought the sun shone out of her backside. Connor was the problem. Or more specifically, my uncontrollable embarrassment over how deluded I'd been.

My plan to give him the cold shoulder wasn't working either. I'd tried, but then he'd been all snarky and teasing and the urge to snap back was all too much.

Embarrassing. No other word for it. I was acting like some kind of obsessive, controlling psycho who'd written *mine* on every man in Bluebell House, whether I liked them or not. Didn't matter. All *mine*.

"You okay?" Ethan asked, squeezing my hand as we entered the rundown country-western bar on the far side of town.

I nodded, shoving all thoughts of Connor, Lacey, and my underlying urge to piss all over my territory aside. "Yeah." Then I tipped my head to Brodie, who'd put on a black baseball cap in what had to be the lamest attempt at celebrity disguise ever. "Is it safe for him to be here? The fans…"

"He's fine here," Ethan assured me as Brodie swaggered over to the bar. "The staff are discreet, thanks to the nature of Meadowridge College itself. And as you can see, not many customers to worry about."

He was right. There were only a handful of patrons in the bar, which made sense considering it was a Monday night in a college town. In fact, I recognized the group of middle-aged guys playing pool as security guards from campus.

Brodie strode over to our booth with a jug of something and three tumblers in hand, not to mention a wide grin on his face as he plonked it down on the table.

"I hope you like spicy margaritas, Evie babe, because it's my favorite." He gestured for me to slide over in the semi-circular booth seat and sat down, trapping me in the middle.

I cautiously accepted the tumbler he poured for me and took a sniff. "I don't know, I've never tried it before."

Ethan groaned, then laughed, shaking his head. "Fucking hell, you're not legal to drink yet, are you?"

"Nope," I replied, taking a little sip. At first I thought it was just citrusy sour, but then the spice hit the back of my tongue and I gasped. "Holy shit."

Ethan rolled his eyes at Brodie's laughter, then ducked back to the bar to grab us some waters as well. "Here." He handed me one. "Brodie *really* should have asked before ordering."

My in-disguise celebrity lover just smirked and tossed back a much bigger gulp of the spicy cocktail. "Sorry, babe. Child actors lose all concept of legal drinking age before we even hit puberty. Try again. It'll grow on you."

Ethan started to protest, but I did as Brodie suggested, and now that I was prepared for the kick, it wasn't so bad.

"See?" Brodie smirked.

"Did you order food while you were up there, Sentinel? Or

just booze to corrupt our innocent Eve?" Ethan narrowed his eyes across the table, but there was a relaxed air about him, betraying the fact he wasn't actually pissed off.

Brodie pushed the third margarita tumbler across the table. "Of course, what do you take me for? I ordered the taco platter, a plate of mixed nachos, the mega enchilada, and the chips with queso."

"Holy shit," I chuckled, sipping more of my drink, "Thank fuck I'm not lactose intolerant, that's all I can say about that."

Ethan eyed the drink in my hand with a small frown. "You don't have to drink that if you don't want to. I can get you something else."

"I like it now," I informed him, drinking some more. "It just took me by surprise, despite the fact Brodie did call it a *spicy* margarita. Unless you're implying that I should be drinking soda?" I arched a brow at him, challenging.

Brodie snickered, clearly enjoying the awkward position Ethan was in—not only as the only one of legal drinking age between us but also as an authority figure within the university. "Yeah, Eth. Is that what you're implying? Because if alcohol is where you draw the line, you *probably* shouldn't be okay with fucking a student in the library during school hours. Just saying."

My jaw dropped, then I groaned. "Fucking Andrew is *such* a gossip. What happened to that iron-clad NDA, huh? Was that all for show?"

"It doesn't apply *within* the house, babe," Brodie said with a grin. "And he really is a gossip. Worse than your friend Nina, I reckon. He's just sneakier about it."

Our food arrived then, absolute truckloads of it, requiring two servers with enormous trays to deliver it all. Not a single gap remained on the table, but with how eagerly Brodie and Ethan dove in, I suspected they wouldn't leave much waste.

As we ate, we flip-flopped between casual banter and deep, meaningful conversations. Each time the mood shifted too serious, somehow Brodie reeled it back in with a sexy quip or teasing joke, and it worked. The jug of spicy margarita was refilled sometime during our meal, and by the time our servers cleared everything away, I was both full to bursting and more than a little drunk.

"Holy shit, Eve," Ethan chuckled when I tried to put my elbow on the table and missed. "I didn't realize you were a lightweight."

Neither did I, but then again, I'd never really been a big drinker, even at my last college. Couple of frat parties here and there, but it was all watery beer that made me bloated long before I got drunk.

"I'm not *that* drunk," I replied, frowning. "Just a little tipsy. Same as Brodes." I tipped my head toward Brodie, who took advantage of the movement to kiss me.

Taken slightly off guard—because we'd all been on our best behavior so far—I gasped, then kissed him back eagerly with a little moan.

"Fuck..." Ethan growled, pulling my attention once more. He'd shifted in his seat, swiping a hand over his hair with agitation. He was by no means *sober*; he was just holding his liquor slightly better than Brodie and I. Barely.

"You got something to say, Professor?" Brodie drawled, casually cupping my breast as if no one could see us. Apparently tequila made Brodie forget he was a celebrity, and it was a little bit adorable.

Ethan glowered, but it was a heated, horny glare. "Yeah, I do. You're gonna end up on TMZ if you keep that shit up." He pulled out his wallet and tossed some cash on the table, despite the fact Brodie had already settled our bill. "Call for your driver, Brodes." To me, he offered his hand in helping me out of the booth.

It was a good thing, too, because I wobbled a little on standing up and his strong grip saved me embarrassing myself.

"Lightweight," he muttered, chuckling as he pulled me close and wrapped his arm around my waist. "Lean on me if you want."

"I'm fine," I assured him. "Just a little wobbly."

He still kept his arm around me as we exited the bar into the parking lot, though, and I shivered when the cool night air reached my arms. Snuggling into Ethan's warm body was better than any blanket, though, and I shifted in his embrace until we were chest to chest with my arms looped around his neck.

"Thanks for taking me out tonight, Eth," I murmured, and ran my tongue over my lower lip. I could still taste Brodie's kiss there, and I suddenly wanted a whole lot more.

He smiled, his hand slipping between my shirt and pants to stroke my lower back. "You keep looking at me like that, Lilith, and we're not making it back to Bluebell House before I..." He trailed off, visibly biting his own lip as his gaze dipped to my mouth.

"Before you what?" I prompted in a whisper, rising up on my toes to bring us closer to kissing. "Before you bend me over the hood of a random car and take turns fucking me with Brodie?"

"Whoa," Brodie exclaimed, having just exited the bar himself. "We're doing what now? Fuck it, no explanations needed. I'm in. Which car, Evie babe? Your pick."

Ethan gave a pained groan, then kissed me so savagely I thought he might bruise my lips—not that I was complaining. I kissed him back just as hard, threading my fingers into the back of his hair as I strained my neck to meet his height.

"So fucking tempting," he whispered with frustration. "How far away is your driver, Brodes?"

"Uh, like five minutes, but I'm really not keen for him to watch, you know? He's a bit—"

"Dude, not what I meant," Ethan said, cutting him off with exasperation. "Eve, beautiful, just how drunk are you actually? Because as much as I'd love to do *exactly* what you just suggested, I really don't want you to have any regrets tomorrow."

It was a fair concern, considering how badly I'd wobbled when I stood up before. And it was so incredibly *Ethan* to voice that concern. But taking our three-way date night into the bedroom was not something I'd *ever* regret, drunk or not. So I told him as much.

"Same," Brodie added, kissing my neck even as I stood there, all twisted up in Ethan's embrace. "Unless you're not okay sharing, Eth, in which case, just say so. Me and Evie babe can take it to my room."

Ethan's brow dipped, like he was really wondering whether he was *this* okay with sharing. It was one thing to know about me and Brodie in theory; it was another entirely for him to watch me choking on another guy's cock and moaning for more.

"Car's here," Brodie announced, smacking my ass. "Continue your moral dilemma on the way, Professor. I, for one, am not ending tonight without the taste of Evie's pussy juice all over my tongue."

His matter-of-fact bluntness shouldn't have shocked me, but it did. Somehow he'd rendered me speechless as we clambered into the back of the chauffeur-driven SUV.

"You have this car on standby?" I asked the first thing that popped into my head as I settled into my seat. "Why?"

Brodie shrugged. "I don't always wanna drive myself. Besides, it comes with cool features like this." He pressed a button on the ceiling and a blacked-out privacy screen slid into place between the front and back seats. "It's soundproof," he added, then faster than I could blink, he was on his knees, unbuttoning my jeans and tugging them down over my hips.

"Brodie!" Ethan exclaimed, seeming shocked but, at the same time, intrigued enough to shift positions to sit opposite, giving him a better view.

My head spun, but there was no part of me that wanted to stop Brodie's hands as they explored along each sliver of skin he exposed down my thighs. With my eyes locked on Ethan across from us, I threw my head back as Brodie kissed and caressed me through my panties, before they too were torn from my body, leaving me bare and wanting.

"Fuck," Ethan groaned. "This is so wrong, but hell if it doesn't feel completely right."

Brodie's chuckle had me arching against him. "Wait until you taste her, bro. Fucking delicious."

Thank God for soundproofing as he flattened his tongue and ran it up my slit, lapping all my arousal right up. *Thank fucking God.*

37

EVELYN

As Brodie settled in to eat me like I was his last meal on earth, he pushed my legs wider, giving Ethan a very nice view. I gestured for the professor to come a little closer, while crying out as my clit was sucked and swirled around a very talented mouth. Brodie's tongue had skills that I never knew tongues possessed, but I sure as fuck wasn't complaining.

Ethan hesitated at first, but the desire was so plainly written on his face that I wasn't surprised when he caved and moved to sit beside me within seconds. Our lips met as Brodie groaned and buried his face deeper in my cunt, licking and sucking until I was mewling into Ethan's mouth, my lower half lifting off the seat as an orgasm exploded through me.

"You're so fucking beautiful when you come," Ethan said, brushing my hair from my face as I huffed and groaned, Brodie not giving an inch as he kept the pleasure rolling through me.

"Oh, fuck. God. Fuck." I threw my hand out for an anchor and found it landing on Ethan, sliding down the firm muscles of his chest until I cupped his cock through his jeans. His hips thrust against my palm, seeking friction, and I huffed out, "Cock. Get your fucking cock out, Professor."

Brodie laughingly groaned, already building me to another orgasm. "I love when she gets all demanding and horny. Fuck. If I could bottle you, Evie babe, I'd make a fucking fortune."

"No bottling," Ethan snarled. "She's ours and ours alone."

"Bluebell House's," Brodie confirmed with a rasp, though I wasn't sure that was exactly what Ethan had meant.

He didn't get a chance to clarify, though, as he'd complied with my demand, and when his hard cock sprang free from his pants, I wrapped my hand around the length and leaned down to run my tongue along the slit already seeping precum.

Ethan tasted good. Clean and salty, with just the hint of musk. As I adjusted myself to suck his cock deeper, Brodie adjusted with me, getting to his knees and ripping his jeans down as well. "I'm going to fuck you now, baby girl. You have five seconds to object."

"Now!" I demanded when my mouth popped off Ethan's cock, causing them both to groan. "Don't tease me, Brodie Keller, or the movie industry will be down one superhero."

"Yes, ma'am," he rumbled, and I caught a glimpse of his eyes darkening before he slammed his thick length into my cunt.

My scream faded into a moan as he thrust again, and I turned back to Ethan, hollowing my cheeks as I sucked him as deep as I could. He was too large to be easy to swallow, and as I tried to relax my jaw, he ran his thumb over my face, coaxing me along. "That's it, baby. Just like you were made for us, filthy little Lillith."

The low rumbles of his praise had my body tightening, and I came screaming around his cock, my cunt tightening on Brodie as I milked his length through many seconds of pleasure. It was overwhelming enough, especially teamed with my semi-drunken state, that dark spots danced on the edge of my vision.

Ethan eased up briefly, and I sucked in a few lungfuls of air before he thrust his length down my throat once more, and I found myself determined to make him come too.

Brodie adjusted my position again, so I was on all fours with him pounding behind me, his movements jerkier as he started to lose control, and I focused on the cock in front of me, using my hand and mouth to work Ethan's length.

"Oh, shit. Just like that, Evie. Just like that, baby." Ethan buried his hands in the back of my hair and fucked my face with enough force that tears streamed down my cheeks, and I only got a few fragments of air into my lungs.

I fucking loved it. When he tensed under me, it was at the same time Brodie jerked behind me, and both guys came together like they'd fucking choreographed it beforehand.

Swallowing as Ethan's cum spilled down my throat, my lower half tightened, and to my fucking astonishment another orgasm barreled through me as Brodie painted my insides with his release. Ethan's hold on my hair gentled as he thrust a few more times, and I took everything, enjoying tasting him in this way.

When the last tremors of my release rocked through me, I collapsed between them, and barely felt it as the guys rearranged me in the car, cleaning me up the best they could and dressing me again as I ended up cuddled between them.

"You're a fucking dream, Evie babe," Brodie murmured, holding me close.

Ethan didn't move away on the other side, even though Brodie was half cuddling him as well. The three of us were in a delicious, satisfied ball, and when the car pulled up to Bluebell House, we remained tangled around each other as we stumbled through the front door and headed for Ethan's room.

He had the biggest bed, after all.

We tried to remain quiet as we crept past the common spaces, but no one was around, and I sighed as Ethan closed and locked his door, encasing us in darkness. Brodie hit the light for a lamp, and as I fell back onto the soft bed, both guys prowled closer as I eagerly wriggled out of my clothes entirely, tossing them aside and parting my legs to offer myself up.

"Look at you, Ms. Lewis," Ethan rumbled. "Spread out there for our pleasure. You want us to take you again, baby? You want me to fuck you this time while you choke on Brodie's cock?"

Brodie threw his head back and groaned. "Fuck, I could come just thinking about it." He palmed his hard cock through his jeans, his eyes fluttering at the sensation. "Though, I have another idea that you might like...if you're brave enough."

Ethan shot him a smirk, as if he knew exactly what Brodie was talking about. "I'm not sure our sweet, innocent Eve is up for that."

Propping myself up on my elbows, I narrowed my eyes on them, looking between the pair. "What are you talking about? I'm not innocent, assholes."

I'd just had my first threesome. Look at me go.

Brodie placed his hands on the bed, and my throat went dry as he crawled up and toward me. "Not innocent, eh? So you'd be down for me to fuck that delicious ass of yours, while Ethan slams into your perfect pussy? That sounds like something our *not* innocent girl would be into, right, Eth?"

My sight had been firmly on Brodie, but now I jerked my gaze up to where Ethan watched us, his expression feral with need. His jeans were unbuttoned, his hard cock grasped in his fist. "What do you say, sweetheart? Think you can take both of us at the same time?"

Honestly, my immediate answer was *no fucking way*. Both guys were far above average in the cock department, and I only had so much space in my lower half, but seeing that darkly captivating, almost *possessed* desire in Ethan's gaze had me responding with, "I'm willing to try."

Brodie, who'd reached me now, his body above mine as he used his arms to keep his weight off me, leaned down and pressed a kiss to my lips. "That's our good girl. We're going to need lube though." He lifted back up and twisted his head toward Ethan. "You have any?"

Ethan nodded. "Of course."

He crossed to the drawer on his bedside and pulled out a new bottle of lube, the plastic still sealed over the lid. "Fuck, I love organized professor in the bedroom," Brodie said, his pupils dilating as he stared down at me—with lust or alcohol or a combination of the two. I wasn't the only one who'd been slugging back spicy margs. "And you're about to get fucked in a way that'll change you forever, Evie babe."

Reaching up, I grasped at his shirt, pulling him down so his weight rested on me. My thighs parted to make room for him, and as we started to kiss, I felt Ethan's weight dip on the side of the bed as he joined us.

Plastic crinkled and Ethan muttered some curses as he wrestled the wrapping from the lube but eventually popped the cap with a satisfied sound while Brodie tongue fucked my mouth so hard I grew dizzy with need.

With a nudge from Ethan, Brodie flipped us over until I straddled him, my wet heat grinding against his jeans and probably leaving a hell of a damp patch. Cold wet lube drizzled down my ass crack, and I gasped, stiffening right the hell up with shock.

Was I seriously going through with this? I'd never even had *a* dick in my ass before let alone one in my pussy at the same time. This seemed like an advanced level three-way, and surely I was only just at beginner status? Maybe intermediate at best.

Then again, the way Brodie's mouth latched on to my breast and Ethan's strong hand stroked down my spine...it couldn't hurt to try, right?

"Shhh, Lilith, just relax," Ethan purred, his fingers sliding through the lube and teasing at my tight asshole. "We'll loosen things up a bit first, don't worry."

Oh, I was worried. But the tequila pumping through my veins told me it would all be okay—people got ass-fucked all the time and loved it.

His fingertip applied pressure, and I squeaked at the unfamiliar sensation. Before I could panic, though, Brodie pinched my nipple and sucked hard on the other, totally distracting me from what Ethan was doing until—

"Oh! Wow, um..." The sudden penetration of his lubed-up finger made me startle.

"Was that a good wow or a bad one?" Ethan asked in a husky, needy voice as he pushed a little deeper.

I wet my lips, my breathing harsh and ragged. "I don't know. Good?"

Meanwhile, Brodie was frantically trying to wiggle out of his jeans beneath me, and I instinctively grabbed a handful of his cock when it sprang free, stroking down his length. He moaned, hips bucking up from the bed, and Ethan took that as his cue to continue fingering my ass.

"Shit, Evie," Brodie exclaimed, grasping both my tits in his hands as Ethan worked his finger in and out, teasing the opening each time. "Can I fuck your tits while he does that? I've been dreaming about these."

Unable to form words, I nodded feverishly, my head swirling. Again, ticking another thing off my list of firsts as Brodie slithered up the bed enough that his cock perfectly aligned between my breasts.

"That's it, Lilith, just relax," Ethan murmured, grabbing the bottle of lube again and squirting more onto my ass. "We'll make you feel so good." Then he shoved what felt like his whole cock right into my slippery but still-clenched hole.

I cried out, even as Brodie gripped my tits around his cock, and Ethan whispered soothing words of encouragement for me to relax my muscles.

"I don't know if I can take you both," I moaned a minute

later. I'd finally unclenched my jaw, and it didn't *hurt,* but it was uncomfortable as hell, and he felt massive in my ass. I definitely couldn't take anything in my pussy at the same time. "You're so fucking big, Ethan."

He paused. Then laughed. "Oh, baby girl. That's still just my fingers, see?" He moved them in a scissor motion, stretching me in the strangest of ways. "My cock is bigger than that."

What?

Brodie laughed as well, thrusting between my tits until the tip of his cock smacked my chin. "Can you suck the tip, Evie?" I did as he asked, his precum coating my tongue as Ethan moved his fingers a little more, and I rocked back against him.

"Want me to stop?" Ethan asked even as he delved deeper. "If it's too much—"

"No!" I exclaimed as Brodie's tip slipped out of my mouth. "No, keep going. I want to try."

That was definitely the margaritas talking. Brodie gasped, then grabbed his own dick to stop himself titty-fucking me. "Sounds like you need a better distraction," he murmured. "Something to help you enjoy the process."

Before I could ask what he was thinking, the two of them had maneuvered us into a new position with my legs straddling Brodie's face and my hands clutching the headboard for dear life as he ate my pussy again.

"So much better," Ethan groaned with approval, working his fingers faster. "Fuck, I'm about to come in my pants I'm so horny right now. Eve, can I try—?"

"Yes!" I gasped, already halfway delirious with what Brodie was doing between my legs. "Yes, fuck me..." I moaned, lost to the euphoria until something a whole hell of a lot bigger than two fingers pressed against my back door.

"Fuck, Lilith, you're tense." Ethan sounded somewhat frustrated.

I shook my head frantically. "It won't fit, Ethan. It just won't—"

He cursed, then looped an arm around my waist, lifting me clean off Brodie and slamming me into the mattress. A split second later saw him buried balls deep in my pussy and I screamed with my instant orgasm.

"Holy shit," he moaned, pumping hard and fast, sweat dripping down his chest as he chased his own release. "Fucking hell, you get me so horny, Eve. Christ, you're gorgeous. This pussy is like fucking heaven."

"Greedy," Brodie protested, giving Ethan a shove. "Let me try."

Ethan held me tight, rolling us even as my orgasm waned. I knew I was good for another one. These two had proven that already, so I was more than happy to keep going. In fact, that climax had loosened up all my muscles in a way that, when Brodie grabbed a handful of lube and slicked it down his shaft, I didn't freak out. Hell, I just wiggled my ass with invitation.

"Shit, yeah." He smirked, then positioned himself behind me. "Ass up, Evie babe."

I moaned, my pussy stuffed full of Ethan's dick already. "Yes, Brodie, I want you to—" He started to push into my asshole, and I yelped. "Nope! No. Too big. Too much. This isn't going to work. Not both together. There's no space."

Ethan threaded his fingers into my hair, pulling my face down to kiss for the longest moment while Brodie swapped his huge cock for a finger instead. Finger, I could handle.

"You're perfect, Eve," Ethan whispered as his hips started to rock more forcefully, fucking me from below. "We'll work up to it. Lots of practice." Then he moaned as he came with a hard jerk, filling my cunt with his cum, triggering another mini-orgasm for me.

"I like the sound of practice," Brodie agreed while my limbs trembled. "How's this?" He added a second finger, fucking my ass with his hand like Ethan had just done.

I swallowed hard, my mouth dry and my head swimming with the aftershocks of climaxing. "It's okay. I mean...it's good. I'm good with this now."

"Practice," Ethan said again, kissing my shoulder as he slipped out of my pussy. "Try now, Brodes."

Fingers swapped for cock once more, and this time I tried really hard not to tense up. The three orgasms since dinner, plus all the tequila, it wasn't hard to stay loose as he worked the broad tip of his dick inside my ass.

"Good girl," Ethan praised, watching over my shoulder as I gasped and whimpered. "You're doing so good, Lilith. You can take more, can't you?"

Unable to form words, I jerked a frantic nod. Brodie grunted, his fingertips digging into my hips as he pushed deeper. The feeling was so full, so incredibly stretched and stuffed, I couldn't fathom what it'd be like to still have Ethan in my pussy right now.

"Holy shit, I'm going to bust any second," Brodie admitted. "You're so fucking tight, and it feels incredible."

"That's okay," Ethan replied, his hand cupping my face and his thumb stroking over my lower lip. "Practice makes perfect, right, Lilith? We might have to fuck this ass every day for a week, but eventually you'll be begging for more."

Holy shit. His words alone were going to make me come again. And now that I was growing more accustomed to the stretch, I was actually enjoying myself.

"Bro..." Brodie groaned.

"Where do you want Brodie to cum, Lilith? On your back? In your ass? Your choice, Ms. Lewis." His voice had taken on a smoky, sex-drenched quality that I could easily get high on.

I wet my lips again, my tongue brushing over Ethan's thumb, and I gasped for breath. "In my ass," I decided.

Those words alone seemed to trigger Brodie, and his carefully controlled movements snapped, his hips surging forward and a whole lot more cock jamming into me as he came. My insides tensed and quivered, the whispers of another orgasm teasing me as hot jets of cum shot into me where no cum had ever been before. Somehow Ethan was in tune with my body, because he reached down and gave my clit a firm pinch, sending me spiraling.

"That's my girl," he purred, kissing my hair.

"Our girl," Brodie corrected, his voice already thick with sleep. "I'm calling big spoon tonight."

"Who the fuck said you could sleep over?" Ethan grumbled even as he rearranged us all into the bed with heads on pillows and limbs intertwined together.

Brodie laughed, kissing my sweaty shoulder. "Evie babe did. Shh, Professor, go to sleep. You have classes to teach in the morning."

Thank fuck I don't have early classes. Neither does Brodie. Maybe we can work on that practice thing...

38

EVELYN

"Well, don't you look rested and refreshed."

I spun around to find Nina with her hands on her low-rider jeans, staring me up and down. "I swear, this is the first time I've seen you without designer bags under your eyes. It's a nice freaking look on you, girl."

With a shake of my head, I had to laugh. "I know there's a compliment in there somewhere."

She waved me off. "You know you're hot. You just always have that burning the candle at both ends vibe going on. And you pull it the hell off, which only makes me hate you a little." Her expression softened. "But it is nice to see you so well rested."

If only she knew that all it had taken was ten orgasms, a cock in my ass, and spooning between two hot-as-sin men all night. As per previous nights with my guys, I'd slept between Brodie and Ethan without a single nightmare. One of them was a sprawler, the other was a cuddler, and yet somehow, it had been the most comfortable sleep I'd had in years.

"Wanna grab some lunch?" I asked, my stomach rumbling as a reminder that we'd raced out the house without breakfast this morning. I might have slept well, but I'd also slept late. Again.

Nina groaned and glanced quickly at her phone. "Look, I've got twenty minutes. Let's rush."

Holding my bag against my side, we moved fast across the courtyard, dodging around the groups of students catching up and already eating lunch. We were almost at the cafeteria doors when a familiar, lanky bitch stepped into our path, and I had to grind to a halt.

Laura eyed me up and down, and I noticed she was dressed to impress today in a rich-bitch suit, including a short pink skirt, white blouse, and matching pink tartan jacket. Her knee-high black boots finished the ensemble.

"We need to talk, whore," she said casually, and it was delivered in such a refined manner that it took me a second to register the insult.

"Did you want me to arrange another nose job?" I shot back just as casually. "Because I could probably fit you in."

Nina laughed before coughing to cover it up. She might have been the one who'd actually arranged the first one, but I was okay with taking the credit for it now.

Laura's face darkened. "You have no idea who you're fucking with, but I'm here to educate you. My father is the vice president. Second-in-fucking-command. Andrew and I were destined to be married before we were born, and I will not have some whore with loose morals, who's fucking her way through Bluebell House, ruin my future. I'll kill you first."

As if they'd been waiting for this line, three of her blonde, ass-kissing friends stepped out from the cafeteria doors and joined Laura in a line of pastel suits.

Nina leaned over to me and whispered, "On Wednesdays, we wear hideous suits."

My laughter couldn't be contained, because this was absolutely giving me *Mean Girls* vibes. These bitches were fucking stereotypes of real humans.

"I honestly have no idea what you're talking about," I finally said, too hungry to deal with this shit any longer. "I haven't touched Andrew. In fact, Andrew and I are star-crossed enemies, and it'd have to be the apocalypse before we'd be desperate enough to consider each other a romantic partner."

It wasn't the *whole* truth. I was attracted to Andrew, physically at least. His personality was a whole other issue.

"You should write romance novels," Nina offered as a friendly suggestion. "I could get behind the whole star-crossed enemies-to-lovers trope."

"Not helping," I replied quietly.

She didn't appear to care, crossing her arms as she leveled a glare on Laura and her mean girl army. "Are we fucking done here?"

Laura stepped into me, and I flinched as she jabbed her pink-tipped nail right into my chest, shoving me back an inch. "I don't fucking believe there's nothing going on between you two."

I was so damn confused. "Why? It's the goddamn truth."

"He called your name during sex."

Laura and I both swung around to face blonde number one, who had just blurted that out. The dark pink in Laura's cheeks told me she was considering the ramifications of killing off her sycophants.

Nina's laughter broke through the awkward tension as she doubled over and slapped a hand on her jean-covered knee. "Oh, that is absolute gold. Like, I had scenarios running through my head of how this was going to go, and it's even better than I thought."

Laura lost her shit then, the fury and embarrassment clearly too much as she lunged toward me, all of her claws out this time. Bracing myself for the strike, I gasped when a small chick darted in front and slammed her fist right into Laura Sandiconte's face.

It took me a second to recognize Lacey, and I blinked as she squared up again. "How dare you touch my friend?" she snarled, her pretty features somehow prettier when she was furious. "Eve is the nicest person ever, and she wouldn't touch Andrew with a ten-foot pole. She respects other people's relationships."

Ah, right. *Awkward.* I mean, in general, she was absolutely correct, and there really hadn't been anything with Connor outside of a brief, confused kiss and some trauma bonding. Which was absolutely his fucking fault. He'd never told me he had a damn girlfriend.

Laura looked between Lacey and me. "What are you even doing back here?" she asked, her chest heaving as she clenched her fists. "Thought you were off being a patron saint or some shit."

Lacey crossed her arms and stared her down, even though Laura was taller. "It's none of your business. Just because you're in an archaic arranged marriage with Drew doesn't mean you get to know anything about his friends." She leaned in. "Which includes Eve. Don't freaking forget that or you'll find that the arrangement"—she flicked her fingers in front of Laura's face—"can go bye-bye that fast."

Turning her back on the basic bitches, she stepped forward and linked her arm through mine, waving Nina over to join me on the other side. "Come on, girls. Let's get some lunch."

Inside, Lacey and I grabbed trays and food, and with Nina having to run to her class straightaway, I found myself staring at Lacey from where she sat across the table. "Thanks for that out there," I said, meaning it. She'd stepped up and defended me when I'd done little except run away from her at every opportunity. I'd put my stupid embarrassment before finding a possible new friend, and that wasn't who I was.

"Never liked Laura," she said, wrinkling her little nose. "She's only ever been interested in what she can get from a person. Chasing those with more power, money, or status than her, while belittling anyone beneath her. It's the worst of the worst kind of chicks, and I could never stand by while one of my friends was being bullied."

To my surprise, I reached out and briefly grasped her hand, giving it a comforting squeeze. "If you ever need my help, I'm there for you. And...I'm happy that Connor and the guys have you in their lives as well. They all need someone in their corner."

She waved me off while also looking a little teary. "Those five have been blood-brothers since they were in middle-school —and Ethan was in high school, obviously. They've never really needed anyone else in their lives." She leaned closer. "Chicks have come and gone, with only a few of us sticking around, but we're still always on the outside, if that makes sense. At the end of the day, I know that if Connie had to choose between me or one of his brothers, I wouldn't like the end result."

I pondered on her words for a moment, trying to figure out why it hadn't felt that way for me. Maybe I just didn't know these guys well enough, but I'd never gotten the impression that I was an outsider, not even with Andrew, and we all knew how that asshole felt about me.

He called your name during sex. I mean, first, ew. Andrew and Bitch-face having sex turned my stomach, but second...why would he do that?

Lacey must have been watching the cascade of internal thoughts and emotions flitter across my face, as she patted my hand. "You make them different, Eve. I wanted to tell you the other night when I watched them with you. The way they all kind of orientate themselves around you, I don't think you're just an annoyance like the rest of us."

Swallowing hard, I couldn't let myself believe her words. I'd already lost a lot in my life, and if I let myself fall into that fairy tale, I'd only set myself up for more hurt. "Why are they such good friends? Did they all go to school together?"

She shook her head, taking a bite of her pasta. "Nope, they met at summer camp. Would you believe it? Apparently they didn't even grow up in the same state, but their parents all had the means to send them to one of those survival-style summer camps when they were around ten and eleven. Ethan was coincidentally there as an older camper, too, even though he and Connie were estranged."

I wanted to ask why they were estranged. I wanted to ask every fucking question. But the whole point of this friendship with Lacey wasn't to grill her about the guys. They should be telling me their stories, and if they *orientated* themselves around me like Lacey appeared to think, they would have.

"The guys are weird with me," I said, playing with my salad. "There's been a lot of things they've done that haven't made any sense, and I admit, I didn't ask the right questions at the time. But...can I truly trust them? Their motivations? They made me sign an NDA, for fuck's sake, which means I can't even tell you the shit that's been happening."

For the first time, the open expression that I was coming to associate with Lacey shuttered. "I trust them with my life, but as I said, they're not very welcoming to outsiders. The fact that they moved you into Bluebell House with them...they would have had a reason, of that I have no doubt. But I don't think it'd be the same reason they'd keep you there now. Does that make sense?"

It didn't really, because I didn't have enough answers to believe what she said. "Connor never told you?"

She shook her head. "Yeah, he doesn't tell me that much. We grew up together, you know. Our families run in the same circles, sort of not dissimilar to Drew and Sandy-cunt. It's a comfortable relationship, but..." She cleared her throat. "Anyways, I was actually looking for you in the courtyard earlier to ask if you'd like to come dress shopping with me on Friday. I've got this huge event with my parents coming up, and I have nothing to wear after months overseas."

"I'd love to," I said, trying not to overthink what she'd almost said about her relationship with Connor. Now that I'd met Lacey, I had to stop thinking of him as anything to me other than an annoying housemate.

He wasn't mine. He belonged to this kind, generous, caring woman, and I would never betray her trust by trying to steal her boyfriend.

Lacey's face lit up as she bounced in her chair. "Oh, that's so exciting. I don't always love shopping, but if it's with a great friend, then it changes the whole vibe." She held out her phone to me. "What's your number? I'll figure out a time and let you know."

I input my number quickly, and she shot me a message almost instantly so I had hers.

"And if you have any issue with Laura again," Lacey said when we got to our feet, trays in hand, "let me know. I may not look scary, but trust me, she doesn't want to mess with me. I will destroy that vapid bitch."

I laughed. "I'm really happy you returned from Malawi."

Weirdly, I meant every word of it.

39

EVELYN

My lungs burned, my legs ached, and I thought for sure my head was about to explode simply from how hard my blood was pounding through my brain. Surely this wasn't survivable. Something must be wrong. Maybe I was dying?

"Come on, brat, you've barely done two miles," Connor drawled, catching up to where I was currently bent double and wheezing like a pack-a-day smoker.

I gasped a few times before summoning the breath to respond. "Fuck you, *Connie*."

Lacey snickered, not even slightly out of breath as she waited for me to catch my wind. I was sweating so freaking much, and my face was hotter than the surface of the sun. Was running always this awful? When Lacey asked if I wanted to go "jogging," I had pictured a nice casual outing barely any faster than a brisk walk where we could chat and enjoy ourselves. Not this military-level marathon-training *bullshit* with Connor tailing us the whole way.

A sharp smack on my rear end made me yelp and straighten up with shock. "What the fuck?" I exclaimed in a strangled voice, glaring at Connor. Did he seriously just smack my ass in front of his girlfriend?

He shrugged. "Told you not to call me that. Come on, we're not even halfway, get moving."

My eyes narrowed in a glare. "Why are you even here? No one invited you."

"And yet, the last time you went wandering the grounds surrounding Meadowridge, you got kidnapped. So consider me your safety blanket, trauma bestie." He folded his thickly muscled arms over his chest, and I tried really hard not to check them out. His arms *or* his chest *or* those ridiculous amount of abs. Why wasn't he wearing a shirt, for fuck's sake?

Lacey sighed and handed me a water bottle from the little backpack she'd worn. Apparently *she* knew what sort of endurance we were getting into and had failed to inform me. "Here, drink some water. We can take it slower from here, okay? I just got a bit caught up in the zone."

"Fuck that," Connor disagreed. "It's about time Evelyn learned how to run as though her life depends on it. Someday, maybe it will." His hard look my way made me shiver, reminding me I'd recently been kidnapped.

"Maybe," I mumbled, dropping my gaze to my feet with embarrassment. "It wouldn't hurt to lose a few pounds anyway. Let's keep going, Lacey."

She frowned, glancing between me and Connor for a moment, then nodded and put the water bottles away. "Okay, just let me know when you want a break."

She set off once more, but Connor grabbed my wrist before I could follow her. "To be perfectly fucking clear, brat, you do *not* need to lose any weight. You just need better survivability. That's all. If anything, you should eat more."

Scowling and a little off-balance, I jerked my wrist free of his grip. "What the fuck is that supposed to mean?"

His lips twisted in a smirk, and his gaze turned borderline

seductive. "It means—" He cut himself off with a headshake. "Nothing. Just...let's catch up to Lacey."

With *that* confusing interaction, he gestured for me to run ahead and followed from the rear, just like he had for the last two miles. As if he thought something was going to snatch me right off the path. Or Lacey, for that matter. Maybe since her family was in a similar business as Connor's, she could also be in permanent danger from creeps like Elijah?

Somehow, I survived another two miles trailing a long way behind Lacey's perfect, activewear-clad ass before I tripped on a rock and fell face-first into the dirt. Instinctively I put my hands out to try and catch my fall, but that just resulted in a jarring pain through my wrist and multiple lacerations on my palms and knees.

"Ow," I moaned, lying still for a moment to mentally curse my own clumsy feet. Also, my whole damn body hurt from that tumble.

Connor caught up in a flash, skidding to a stop and dropping to his knees beside where I lay. "What the hell happened?" he demanded, seeming...angry?

"What the fuck do you think happened, Connie?" I snapped back, angry simply for the fact that he was angry. Fuck him and his attitude—I was the one bleeding. "Clearly I decided I was so done with running and figured I'd deliberately trip over a rock to break my own ankle."

His eyes widened with visible concern. "Is it broken? Let me see."

"No, it's not broken, you asshole," I growled, swatting him away as I sat up to inspect the damage. "I just tripped. Not a big fucking deal. People trip all the time."

He scowled back at me. "Why are you snapping at me like this was my fault? You really are a brat, you know that?"

My jaw dropped. "Me? You're the one who came at me all

growly when I'd just hurt myself. Where's the compassion, Connie? You'd be the worst nurse in the history of nurses."

Barking at him helped me ignore the pain in my palms and knees. I'd somehow managed to graze myself in multiple locations, and the blood was oozing down my legs while the stinging pain burned right through me. Grazes fucking sucked, but they weren't exactly life-threatening.

Connor sighed heavily. "Brat, you know me well enough by now: compassion isn't in my nature." And yet, he scooped a gentle arm around my back and lifted me to stand. "Can you walk?"

I gave an irritated sound. "Of course I can fucking walk." Sort of. Okay, it was more of a limp, but when Connor tried to carry me, I pushed him away so hard I nearly fell on my ass all over again.

Lacey, thank goodness, had been far enough ahead when I fell that she probably assumed I'd stopped for another breather break. One person to witness my clumsy shit was more than enough, it was just a shame it had to be Connor.

When I took another limping step forward, the wince appeared on my lips before I could prevent it, and Connor cursed as he wrapped his hands around my waist. This time, when I batted his hands away, he completely ignored me, leaning down to scoop me up against his chest.

"You can't carry me all the way back," I snarled, trying not to think about how easily he held me and how good it felt to be in his arms. This trauma bond was really the *fucking worst.*

Connor shook his head. "Your sense of direction is as solid as your ability to run without injuring yourself. We're almost back to Bluebell. Look—" I gasped as he lifted my entire body to the right, as a way to indicate direction. "There's the edge of the garden and tree off to the side."

Sure enough, we'd been going in a loop, and I'd been too busy trying not to die to notice. With a huff, I crossed my arms and settled back with the full intention of ignoring Connor completely.

"I was going to tell you about Lacey," he said after a minute of silent walking. "It's just...complicated. Not to mention, we haven't been trauma besties for that long, and I know fuck-all about your life, so I don't think it's as big a deal as you're making it."

Men really were the stupidest creatures on this planet. "Not knowing that I hate olives and have a fear of continuous rolling waves isn't the same as not knowing I'm in a fucking relationship, Connor. Yeah, we weren't dating or fooling around or anything, and I get that the one time we kissed I thought you were your brother, but having a girlfriend is a big deal. I would have treated you differently. I'd have looked at you differently. We should never have gotten to *this* place."

Oh, God. Shut the fuck up, Eve.

Sharing my deeper emotions with Connor was a huge mistake. He couldn't be trusted, and I'd just been figuring out how to distance myself from whatever bond had been building between us before Lacey returned. Finding myself in his arms now was highly inconvenient. Especially when it caused my mouth to run away with me.

Connor stopped walking, his gaze blazing as he stared down at me. "What place are you talking about?"

Nope. Not a fucking chance. "Put me down. The house is right there, and I can walk the rest of the way."

With a shake of his head, he ignored me once more and strode up the stairs and straight inside. He called out when we entered, and I could have smacked him up the side of the head. I did not need the others here witnessing my shame as well. It'd be bad enough when Connor told them what happened.

Footsteps sounded from behind us, and we turned to find Lacey racing into the house after finally realizing I wasn't just taking a break. "Holy shit, Evie. What happened?"

Her expression was threaded with concern and not the slightest annoyance that her boyfriend carried me like a damsel in distress. "She tripped and hurt herself," Connor said shortly, turning away from Lacey to head for the living area. "Can you grab a first-aid kit from under the kitchen sink? I think Haze stashed one there. I need to get her cleaned up."

Haze had put the kit back there after rebandaging my hand last night, but that didn't mean I needed Connor's help as well.

"I can clean myself up," I called in a rush. "In fact, I'm feeling much better overall. Think it was just a shock."

"Nice try, brat," Connor said with a snort of laughter. "But you're quite possibly the worst liar I've ever met in my life. Everything you feel is displayed clear as day on your face for the world to enjoy."

I really, *really* hoped he was kidding about that, because I couldn't be out here with feelings for multiple men clear on my face. That'd be highly inconvenient.

Lacey patted my arm. "Let Connie help you, Evie. He's really good at this shit. He's been patching up members of his family for years."

Connor made a rumbling sound of annoyance. "Enough with story time. Go get the fucking kit."

Lacey just laughed lightly, not at all fazed by his cranky ass as she raced off. Meanwhile, I again wanted to smack him upside of the head, but my palm was too injured, so I settled on a jab from my elbow. "That was rude, Connor," I told him coolly. "She's a good person and doesn't deserve you talking to her like she's unimportant and annoying. Don't fucking do it."

He blinked at me, our gazes clashing for many long seconds as if he couldn't quite process that I'd admonished his behavior. "You think she can do better than me?" he finally said, moving toward the couch and taking a seat.

I tried to wiggle out his arms at this point, but he just tightened his hold, keeping me in his lap.

"I think *you* can do better than treating her like that," I shot back. "Your girlfriend should come first, you know. And that includes her emotions. You might think you're covering all bases by protecting her from other people, but what about from you? Don't be the guy she needs protecting from. If you can't be better, then don't be surprised if she finds better."

He still stared at me with that unreadable and unwavering expression. Thankfully, before it got *way* more awkward, Lacey raced back in with a red bag in her hands. "Found it. It was hidden behind some cleaning supplies. Andrew has really gone all out on the full cleaning kit."

My lips twitched because, in this case, it was actually Connor, trying to add ease to his best friend's life. I'd seen how well he could show love and knew he was capable of being an amazing boyfriend. I just couldn't figure out why he didn't do it for Lacey, when she was so deserving of an epic, forever love.

40

CONNOR

Evelyn was all about picking at infected wounds these days. Metaphorically, not literally. She would never do something *that* stupid in real life. But mentally and emotionally, she was creating scars. I didn't want to sound like an asshole, but also didn't want to lie when she asked me why I wasn't *better* to Lacey.

It wasn't like I was bad with her. We didn't fight, ever, and I'd rather sit on a barbed-wire dildo than hurt her. I loved Lacey, but I wasn't *in love* with her. She felt the same, I was sure of it. We'd been together for almost five years, and in that time barely spent more than a couple of months together at a time. We were friends. We occasionally hooked up. And we both knew what was expected of us.

That was the crux of it. Our relationship was never born out of *love*—it was business. Our families had been forcing us together for so long that Lacey only had two options for her future: me or Ethan.

"Wanna get your ass kicked?" Haze asked, tossing me an Xbox controller as I entered the living room. Eve had been fully patched up from her grazes, and Lacey had taken her over to the campus medical center to get her ankle and wrist checked out. I'd tried to tag along, but Eve had firmly declined. Fucking brat was starting to think she actually called the shots around here. That needed to change soon.

I sighed, flopping down onto the couch. "Sure. What are we playing?"

"*Street Fighter*," he replied with a toothy grin. Haze almost never smiled, so clearly something had him in a good mood. It made me suspicious as hell.

I squinted his way as the game booted up and old-school title credits rolled. "Why are you so cheerful? Blow up another building or something?"

He huffed. "That was an accident, and I already apologized to Eve."

"Okay, but you're still in an unusually good mood. You kill someone?" It wouldn't be the first time. There was a reason Haze Michaels was a wanted man, and not just because of who his parents were.

"Shut up and play the game, Sullivan," he growled. "If I wanted to talk about my feelings, I'd have called my therapist."

I snickered, selecting my character, E. Honda, on the screen. "You don't have a therapist, dickhead."

"Exactly," he muttered. "So shut the fuck up."

Chatting about our feelings wasn't exactly my vibe either, so I focused on the game for a while and whooped my victory as I took down Haze's character over and over with E. Honda's Hundred Hand Slap move.

"Eat shit, Zangief," I snarked, delivering the final smack-down of the match. "What was that about getting my ass handed to me, Haze?"

The big guy just rolled his eyes and clicked rematch. "Whatever. Best out of three."

My phone buzzed, and I pulled it out to check the message. It was from Lacey, letting me know that Eve was fine.

"All okay?" Haze asked, watching me a little too intensely.

I quirked a brow. "I thought you didn't wanna chat with me." He just stared. Blank expression, staring, no blinking. Creepy as fuck, honestly. "It's just Lacey."

More staring. He was fully prepared to wait me out, apparently.

I sighed. "She said Eve is fine. She's just bruised, not sprained. They're heading back now with Brodie."

Twenty minutes later, the front door opened, and as hard as it was, I didn't glance at the trio as they walked in, more focused on destroying Haze once more, though he'd learned a few moves from my last annihilation and was holding his own much better. The fucking genius learned at a rate that was impossible to keep up with.

Eve ended up being a distraction for our resident mercenary, though, as he gave up trying. "You okay?" he asked her, and I swear I felt her fucking presence tracing down my spine. Annoying brat. Here to drive me crazy in every which way.

"Yes, just a few bumps and bruises," Eve said, her smooth voice warming up as she hovered behind the couch. "Lace and Brodie all but carried me home, and now I'm all dosed up on painkillers. I need to rest, apparently."

"I'll help you upstairs, babe," Brodie said, which fucking annoyed me for reasons I wasn't about to delve into.

Forcing myself to keep playing the game, I knocked Haze's character out again, and he threw his controller down, apparently too distracted to give a fuck. "I feel absolutely terrible about what happened," Lacey said, her perfume growing stronger as she moved in behind me and rested her hand on my shoulder. I glanced up into her familiar, comforting features while she stared at Eve—who I still refused to acknowledge, since she'd insisted on heading out without me to begin with. "Keep me updated with how you're feeling. I think I'll head into town to grab some groceries for you guys and maybe look around the shops."

Haze glanced my way like he thought I would object, but I just shrugged. "Yeah, sounds good. Let me know when you're back on campus."

Lacey leaned down and pressed a warm kiss to my cheek, and I breathed her in, wishing that there'd be even the smallest stirring inside for my oldest friend. I couldn't lose her, but I also didn't want to marry her like was expected. We needed to have that chat soon.

"I'll call you later, Connie."

Hated the name, but from her, I tolerated it. "Okay, Lace. Stay safe out there."

Her laugh was light and sweet. "You know I can take care of myself."

Turning back to the game, I heard Eve shuffle away and head for the stairs with Brodie. It took every fucking ounce of control not to follow her and make sure she wasn't more injured than she'd let on, but she'd already told me to fuck off once.

When Haze settled back into the chair beside me, I felt his probing gaze once more. "What?" I snapped with a huff. "You've clearly got something on your mind."

He ran his hand over his mouth, brows furrowing. "You seriously don't mind if Lacey heads into town on her own?"

Was he for real? "Why would I mind? She's a grown fucking woman. I don't control her."

I didn't even want to control her. Our relationship worked because we didn't live in each other's pockets. She'd just gotten back from all the dangers of Africa, and I never cared.

Haze was silent for a few seconds, and I decided it was time to switch up the game. I was done with this old-school shit. As I leaned over to grab my controller, he finally said, "I wouldn't let my girlfriend out in the world without me. We know what's out there, Con."

I shrugged. "Lace can handle herself. Now, are you ready to play? Or are we booking that therapy session?"

Thankfully the pitbull motherfucker finally gave up on questioning me to within an inch of my life, and we got back to trying to destroy each other via a video game. A few hours later, when my bladder screamed at me, I took a piss and leaned against the stair railing, wondering if anyone had checked on Eve. Maybe she needed a snack or a drink?

It was just being a good roommate to make sure she hadn't died from her injuries, and as I placed my foot on the first step, Haze careened around the corner of the house, his phone in his hand. "Bro, get the fuck up there and make sure Eve's in her room."

Knowing his stalking ways had picked up on an issue, I tore up the stairs three at a time, slamming my shoulder against Eve's door, but it was one of those old, reinforced frames, and I bounced right off. "Brat!" I shouted as I banged my hand against the door. "Why is your door locked? Are you okay in there?"

Haze hadn't followed me, but he appeared a few seconds later with a key in hand. When it slipped right into Eve's lock, I side-eyed the crazy bastard. "You've had a key to her room the entire time?"

Brodie popped his head out of his room a few seconds later, looking ruffled like he'd been taking a nap. "Eve with you?" I barked, and he immediately shook his head, concern marring his pretty-boy features.

"No, she said she wanted to rest. Is she not in her room?"

Haze clicked the lock over, and we all pushed inside to find it completely empty. Bed nicely made. "What did you notice?" I snarled, getting right in Haze's face. "Why did you think we needed to check on her?"

He flipped his phone up, and there was a red dot beeping in the middle of the screen. A screen which was showing up in the middle of downtown Meadowridge. "I put a tracker on her phone ages ago, but I don't fucking check it every second, especially not when she's supposed to be sleeping in her room. I thought it had malfunctioned or something."

Utter rage darkened my vision, and I reached out and grasped his shirt. There was no way I could throw around Haze easily, but he didn't appear to be thinking clearly as he let me jerk him close. "Are you telling me Eve is in fucking town? Without one of us?"

Haze's eyes narrowed as he slapped my hands away. "You didn't care when it was Lacey."

Fuck. Fucking, fuck, FUCK. "This is Eve. It's completely different. Or have you forgotten that someone shot and killed over twenty people at her last school while aiming for her?"

He looked like he was gearing up to probe into my psyche, and I'd have to shoot him if that happened, so I turned to Brodie. "We need a car, Brodes, and we need it now."

With a nod, Brodie took off down the stairs, his face wreathed in panic. I'd never seen him look so pale, and it was clear that what he felt for our Eve was much more than just infatuation. Her fucking witchy ways were taking all of us out.

Haze was trying to call Eve, so I quickly dialed Lacey. She didn't answer on the first call, but I immediately hit her number again. "She knows she's not supposed to be out without us," I snapped. "Which makes it likely that both of them will avoid our calls until they're ready to come home."

Lacey, because she didn't know about the danger, and Eve because she was my little brat and needed a firm hand on her ass.

"Why the fuck did she go out without us?" Haze rumbled, and I was surprised by the tinge of true worry in his voice. It took a fucking lot to rattle him, and I did not like that he was. "It's not like her to be so risky."

That was true, but she also didn't understand the full risks. We hadn't told her everything with her dad and Andrew being coerced-slash-blackmailed into keeping her safe.

She had no fucking idea what waited out there for her.

As we raced down the stairs, we almost crashed right into Andrew and Ethan, who were heading through the hallway into the kitchen, probably to start dinner. A dinner that was never going to be made tonight.

"Eve's in town," I barked. "She must have snuck out and joined Lacey, for some fucking reason."

Ethan was the first to react, and I had to give it to my half-brother, he also seemed to care for Eve in a way I'd never seen with any other woman who'd passed through his life. "What? Are you sure? There's no way Eve would take off without telling any of us. Why would she?"

The color drained from Andrew's face at those words, and I knew my best friend well enough to recognize the expression he now wore. I'd have fucking killed and died for this guy in a heartbeat, but as red-tinted my vision, I slammed him into the wall, my hand around his throat as our gazes clashed. "What the fuck did you do?" I demanded, pulling him off the wall only to slam him against it again.

Ethan and Haze got to me in a second, tearing me off our friend, but they didn't let Andrew skulk off into the shadows like he was prone to do. "Drew?" Ethan said with soft menace. He was almost as dangerous as me, just with stronger morals.

Andrew let out a frustrated sigh and shoved me away. "We had another fight. She got into it today with Laura, and then she was all banged up. I'm sick of finding her fucking hurt under our watch. We're supposed to be keeping her safe."

The rumble from my chest surprised even me; I'd never lost it like this with Drew before. "You drove her out into danger, asshole," I said calmly, even as the rage burned. "You better start fucking praying she's okay."

A horn from outside broke through our tension, and after checking my gun was secured in my jeans, I headed out the door and threw myself into the passenger side. The other three were right behind me, with Haze's phone our only means of finding Eve.

"We'll get her home safe," Brodie said, his voice wavering as he stared blankly through the front windshield. "She'll be fine. I mean, no one even knows she's out there."

Andrew remained silent as he slid into the back seat, and I threw a dark stare back at him. She'd better be fine, or we'd all have a huge fucking problem.

41

EVELYN

Fuck Andrew. Fuck him and all his arrogant, entitled bullshit. Especially, more than anything, fuck his bitchy, nasty girlfriend for being such a goddamn pain in my ass. The way he'd come at me while I was lying on my bed reading had been totally uncalled for. Not only had he not knocked—rude-ass motherfucker—but then he'd repeatedly refused to leave when I told him I was done with our conversation.

Lesson learned: always lock my damn door.

"You're thinking about murdering Drew again, aren't you?" Lacey asked, nudging me with her elbow. We'd been in town for a few hours, trying on dresses that I could never afford. Lacey needed an outfit for some fancy party her family expected her to attend now that she was back in America and insisted it was just more fun if I tried on dresses too.

She was right; it was fun. Except when I started dwelling on the fight with Andrew.

I was extra pissed off because he'd been so careful not to *yell* at me the whole time, therefore not drawing the attention of anyone else. In hindsight, I should have just raised my voice back at him and I'd have had Brodie and Ethan there in a flash, but no, silly me, too stunned at his audacity to do anything more than hold back my tears and ask him to leave.

That, in itself, had me more annoyed than the argument itself. I'd been so drained from my fall and shocked at his aggression that I hadn't stood up for myself. Andrew had a way of getting under my skin that stirred the parts of me that had felt abandoned for most of my life.

He poked at old wounds. It was too much to take.

Sneaking out my window hadn't been a particularly mature response, but I knew the guys wouldn't let me go out alone. Not without one of them tailing me—for some unknown reason, because Elijah was no longer a threat—and I badly just needed time away from all the testosterone.

I sighed, then licked up the melting frozen yogurt around my cone. "Yep, sure was. Grizzly death, of course, nothing discrete like poison."

Lacey snickered. "Aw, that's a shame. Haze could have helped you with the perfect poisons."

Wait, what? "Excuse me? Haze could do what?"

"Poisons," Lacey repeated with a shrug. "He was super into them a few years back, and his dad is a big-shot scientist working for the KGB."

My jaw hit the floor. "What?" I was starting to sound like a broken record, but shock would do that to a girl. I blinked stupidly at her. "I had no clue. That's..." *Kinda hot.*

Lacey smirked like she could read my mind. "I know, right?" Her phone beeped in her pocket, and she pulled it out with a groan. "Looks like we've been found out." She showed me the screen, displaying Connor's photo and contact as the incoming call. It was a hot picture of him, too. Smiling.

I groaned and reached out to hit the "reject call" button for her. "Maybe he's just calling to talk to you. You guys *are* dating, so…maybe he wants a booty call or something?"

Lacey shook her head and pulled down the notifications tab, showing six missed calls all within the last couple of minutes. "Yeah, no. Connie is never this desperate for my company."

"Damn it. I thought we would get longer for sure. I left my door locked so they'd think I was asleep." Suddenly sick with anxiety, I dumped the remains of my frozen yogurt in a trash can and wiped off my sticky fingers with a napkin. "Wait, how the fuck does he know I'm gone? My door is *locked*."

My new friend gave me a pitying look and sighed. "Oh, Evie, honey. You're too innocent for your own damn good sometimes, I swear. I can almost guarantee that someone in that house has a key for your room or a security camera inside. Or both."

Floored. I was dead-set fucking floored. "No. You're joking. They wouldn't do that." Because all of a sudden, I remembered the number of times I'd used my vibrator in that room. Or walked around naked. "You're joking. *Right?*"

Lacey wrinkled her nose. "Maybe a little bit? But also kinda not. Anyway, irrelevant. I can't dodge Connie's calls forever. Do you wanna keep shopping and make them sweat it out or head back?"

It was a valid question. Sure, they knew I wasn't at Bluebell House in my room fast asleep, but that didn't mean they knew where we were, just that it was a good chance I'd gone to meet Lacey or Nina, and Nina was out hiking with Sven right now.

"Fuck them," I decided. "We still haven't found you the perfect dress and then you obviously need shoes to go with it, and I was thinking I could really go for a mani-pedi, how about you?"

Lacey tossed her head back laughing and put her phone on

silent. "I think that sounds like a fantastic plan. There's a great nail salon over on Lemontree Lane, about twenty minutes walking or like five by car." Then she gave a pointed look at my various bandages and bruises. "Let's drive."

"Excellent choice," I agreed, because although I had a medical all clear, I was still aching from my dumbass fall in the woods. After I'd climbed out my window at Bluebell House, Lacey had picked me up in her Chevy, and we'd parked right outside the frozen yogurt shop.

Hopping into her car once more, we cranked the air and the radio. "Oh, I love this song!" Lacey crowed as the latest hit single by Bellerose came on, so I turned the volume up more. I also happened to love that song—Lacey had great taste in music.

She grinned at me, pure sunshine, as she pulled out of her parking spot and started down the street. For the duration of the song, we sang together, and I could safely say I understood why the guys all loved Lacey so much. I could also say, without a doubt, she deserved better than Connor.

"So!" she said after the song finished. "You're hooking up with Brodie *and* Ethan? How'd that all come about?"

I flushed bright red instantly. Of course she'd noticed me and Ethan were together. We really needed to be more careful, or he was likely to lose his job.

"Uh...yeah. I dunno how it happened. It just did, and I'm not mad about it," I admitted sheepishly.

Lacey offered no judgment, though, as she smiled. "I think it's cute. They're both so totally infatuated with you. Have you guys...you know...?"

I had a feeling I did know but decided to play dumb in the hope that she'd let it go. "Have we what?"

She rolled her eyes, slowing to a stop at a yellow light. Lacey, I'd noticed, was a very cautious driver. "Have you all fucked? Together? Like a three-way?"

Oh man. I thought my face was red before, but it was positively *lava* now.

Lacey gave a squealing laugh. "Oh my god, you have! What was it like? I need details so I can live vicariously though you, *please!*"

Panic rendered me speechless for a moment, then I turned the line of questioning back on her. "You've been dating Connor since high school, right? Is he the only guy you've ever slept with?"

It was Lacey's turn to blush, and her gaze shifted back to the intersection we were stopped at. "Um, yeah, we've been dating since we were fifteen. Technically my mom tried to set me up with Ethan first. Can you believe it? He was like twenty-three then and was totally horrified. Understandably, given I was still a child. But then Connie and I got together and..." She shrugged. "It all worked out in the end."

There was something sad in her voice, though. Like she wasn't really as happy with how it all turned out as she pretended.

"Lacey...you and Connor—" I started to ask as our light turned green and Lacey put her foot back on the accelerator. Before I could get the rest of my question out, my gaze shifted past her to where a blacked-out F-truck was speeding down the cross street at a million miles an hour.

I gasped, realizing that there was no way he was going to stop at the intersection. "Lacey! Watch out!"

She turned to look, then screamed and slammed her foot down on the gas, but it was too late. The truck smashed into us a split second later, punching us and our car across the intersection and sending us into an out-of-control spin.

Somehow, I managed to grab on to my door handle, gripping it for dear life as the car rotated over and over, then hit something and flipped. I screamed, terrified as we went weightless for a moment, then crashed back to earth like a ton of bricks.

Then, silence.

My seat belt held me suspended upside down, agonizingly cutting into my shoulder and chest. I fumbled for the buckle to release myself.

"Lacey?" I groaned after collapsing into a heap once the seat belt unclicked. The airbags had all deployed, and all I could make out of her behind the white fabric was blood. Holy shit, was she even still alive? "Lacey!" I cried out, trembling in terror that my new friend was now dead. The truck had hit our tail end, I was pretty sure, that was why we'd spun so hard.

I needed to get out of the wreckage and get help. My window was already smashed entirely, so I awkwardly turtle crawled out through the opening while wincing at the bite of gravel and glass. It didn't matter, though. Lacey needed help, which meant I needed to get—

Pain lanced through my head as someone grabbed a handful of my hair and pulled.

I yelped, thrashing and clawing in an attempt to remove the person's hand, but they didn't let go. Instead, they started dragging me across the tarmac and away from the wreckage of the car.

"Let me go!" I howled, fighting to free myself. Fuck, if I needed to lose a chunk of my scalp, then so be it.

To my shock, the grip on my hair released, and I tumbled back to the pavement. Frantic, I rolled over onto my butt, ready to fight whoever had just dragged me by my hair away from my possibly dying friend...then I nearly died of pure terror.

"Y-you!" I exclaimed, blinking against the bright sunlight. Surely I was imagining things.

"Hello again, Evelyn Cromwell. You're a hard woman to kill, you know that? This time, I'll make sure to stick around to make sure the job is complete." The man from my nightmares smiled a sick grin, then aimed his gun directly at my face. "Be a good girl and die this time."

Click.

Bang.

315

READ the epic finale of Eve's story in...
TRAUMA BONDED
Bluebell House Duet #2

ALSO BY TATE JAMES

Devil's Backbone

#1 DEAR READER

#2 WATCH YOUR BACK

#3 YOU'RE NEXT

Madison Kate

#1 HATE

#2 LIAR

#3 FAKE

#4 KATE

#4.5 VAULT (to be read after Hades series)

Hades

#1 7th Circle

#2 Anarchy

#3 Club 22

#4 Timber

The Guild

#1 Honey Trap

#2 Dead Drop

#3 Kill Order

Valenshek Legacy

#1 Heist

#2 Forgery

#3 Restoration

Boys of Bellerose

#1 Poison Roses

#2 Dirty Truths

#3 Shattered Dreams

#4 Beautiful Thorns

The Royal Trials

#1 Imposter

#2 Seeker

#3 Heir

Kit Davenport

#1 The Vixen's Lead

#2 The Dragon's Wing

#3 The Tiger's Ambush

#4 The Viper's Nest

#5 The Crow's Murder

#6 The Alpha's Pack

Novella: The Hellhound's Legion

Box Set: Kit Davenport: The Complete Series

Dark Legacy

#1 Broken Wings

#2 Broken Trust

#3 Broken Legacy

#4 Dylan (standalone)

Royals of Arbon Academy

#1 Princess Ballot

#2 Playboy Princes

#3 Poison Throne

Hijinx Harem

#1 Elements of Mischief

#2 Elements of Ruin

#3 Elements of Desire

The Wild Hunt Motorcycle Club

#1 Dark Glitter

#2 Cruel Glamour (TBC)

#3 Torn Gossamer (TBC)

Foxfire Burning

#1 The Nine

#2 The Tail Game (TBC)

#3 TBC (TBC)

Undercover Sinners

#1 Altered by Fire

#2 Altered by Lead

#3 Altered by Pain (TBC)

ALSO BY JAYMIN EVE

Shifter City Fated Mates (Shifter Romance 18+)

Book One: A Curse of Fate

Book Two: A Twist of Luck

Book Three: A Claim of Fortune (TBC)

Book Four: A Bond of Trust (TBC)

Fallen Fae Gods (Dark Romantasy dragon shifter/fae 18+) (complete)

Book One: Gilded Wings

Book Two: Crimson Skies

Shadow Beast Shifters (Dark and Sexy wolf shifter/god Romantasy 18+) (complete)

Book One: Rejected

Book Two: Reclaimed

Book Three: Reborn

Book Four: Deserted

Book Five: Compelled

Book Six: Glamoured

Boys of Bellerose (Dark, RH rock star romance 18+)(complete)

Book One: Poison Roses

Book Two: Dirty Truths

Book Three: Shattered Dreams

Book Four: Beautiful Thorns

Demon Pack (PNR/Urban Fantasy 18+) (Complete)

Book One: Demon Pack

Book Two: Demon Pack Elimination

Book Three: Demon Pack Eternal

Supernatural Prison Trilogy (Complete UF series 17+)

Book One: Dragon Marked

Book Two: Dragon Mystics

Book Three: Dragon Mated

Book Four: Broken Compass

Book Five: Magical Compass

Book Six: Louis

Book Seven: Elemental Compass

Supernatural Academy (Complete Urban Fantasy/PNR 18+)

Year One

Year Two

Year Three

Royals of Arbon Academy (Dark, complete Contemporary Romance 18+)

Book One: Princess Ballot

Book Two: Playboy Princes

Book Three: Poison Throne

Titan's Saga (PNR/UF. Sexy and humorous 18+)

Book One: Releasing the Gods

Book Two: Wrath of the Gods

Book Three: Revenge of the Gods

Dark Legacy (Complete Dark Contemporary high school romance 18+)

Book One: Broken Wings

Book Two: Broken Trust

Book Three: Broken Legacy

Secret Keepers Series (Complete PNR/Urban Fantasy)

Book One: House of Darken

Book Two: House of Imperial

Book Three: House of Leights

Book Four: House of Royale

Storm Princess Saga (Complete High Fantasy 18+)

Book One: The Princess Must Die

Book Two: The Princess Must Strike

Book Three: The Princess Must Reign

Curse of the Gods Series (Complete Reverse Harem Fantasy 18+)

Book One: Trickery

Book Two: Persuasion

Book Three: Seduction

Book Four: Strength

Novella: Neutral

Book Five: Pain

NYC Mecca Series (Complete - UF series)

Book One: Queen Heir

Book Two: Queen Alpha

Book Three: Queen Fae

Book Four: Queen Mecca

A Walker Saga (Complete - YA Fantasy)

Book One: First World

Book Two: Spurn

Book Three: Crais

Book Four: Regali

Book Five: Nephilius

Book Six: Dronish

Book Seven: Earth

Hive Trilogy (Complete UF/PNR series)

Book One: Ash

Book Two: Anarchy

Book Three: Annihilate

Sinclair Stories (Standalone Contemporary Romance 18+)

Songbird